THE
BLUE

GABRIELLE NEWTON

To my Grandmas, thank you for being a part of *my* story.
And to the souls that yearn for more.

Yurdau

OAKSTEAD

PALMERIA

Cerdic

Iyuoca

Crossroads

Oyencra

WESTERN
WASTES

her

A

Pagos

REN

RN

Freina

CONTENTS

CHAPTER ONE

—·—

ALTHEA NOVA

Althea landed hard on her back, the air tearing from her lungs in a violent whoosh as the ax swung down aiming straight for her head. She rolled quickly to the side, narrowly missing the blade. It struck the ground, so close she could smell the metallic zing from the freshly shined steel.

She twisted onto her stomach, leaning her weight on her right side and swung out with her left leg kicking the leather boots out from under her opponent. The ax slipped out of his grip and fell just out of reach of both of them.

Althea scrambled to stand, just as her opponent tucked his knees into his chest and jumped to his feet, using the momentum to rock forward and bring both of them down. He knelt over her, his legs pinning her arms to the ground and held the cold blade of his dagger to her throat.

Dust and dirt clouded around them and made it so Althea could not see his face clearly, but she knew he was smiling. She could see the glint of his teeth, the angle of his mouth set in a smug smile.

The blare of the mock war horn shattered the silence, "Mark Niklas! All Square," shouted the announcer.

The crowd that had gathered around the long oval arena to watch the matches broke out in a cacophony of cheers.

"You're going to have to do better than that, Little Althea," Niklas said pitifully, like he was talking to a dog trying to bury a bone in rock instead of his equal, and patted her cheek.

As he stood, he raked a hand through his chestnut hair, shaking the dust purposefully over Althea's face. She coughed and sputtered as the grit fell into her mouth and eyes. He sheathed his dagger back into his boot and stooped to grab the ax, going to replace it on the weapons table.

Althea helped herself to her feet and straightened her sparring jacket, brushing back the hair that had fallen out of her braid as she walked to stand beside Niklas and looked down at the table, bowed in the middle, its surface covered a great deal with the armaments.

She glanced out of the corner of her eye to the accessors seated on the raised dais at the north side of the arena. Their heads were bent close to each other, discussing the tallies and marks of her match.

"You really can't let me do anything without your interference can you," Althea muttered grudgingly, picking up an arming sword and ran a sweaty hand, shaking from adrenaline, along its dulled edge.

The weapons would not do any lasting harm if hit by one, but they still hurt just the same and would leave nasty bruises. It taught them to not get comfortable with just sparring, it put a real threat behind each match, and made them wish to never meet the metal. It prepared them for the real thing.

"Come on, you know as well I do that today would have been utterly boring had I not come to show our guests what a *real* match should look like." He garnered his usual egotistical air about him, and set down the particularly unholy looking wooden club that he had been examining. The sound of another match echoed around them.

Niklas had ascended the season before, but had volunteered to spar in the assessment matches, knowing that Althea would have no trouble passing with her preassigned opponents.

She had two more matches to fight. Out of the five matches in the assessments, she needed to clear three of them to attain the fifteen marks to pass. She had already completed two of her previous fights without impediment, earning ten out of the fifteen marks. In order to ascend she would have to win at least one of the next two matches or she would have to wait six months for the assessors to come back from the City of Valor for the next set of tests.

Each team was allowed a ten minute break between their matches to switch out weapons, discuss tactics with other guards and drink water out of the large barrel next to the weapons table, served by a servant girl who was the same age as Althea, with wild, bouncy curls the color of the sweetest champagne. Almost like she had read her thoughts, the girl brought over two wooden cups of water for them.

"Thank you, Annavey." Althea graciously took the cup and drained it, washing away the sticky thirst from her mouth. Annavey didn't respond to her thanks, she only turned to Niklas and blushed fiercely. Althea took a step back, holding her hands up in mock surrender behind the girl's back.

Niklas took the cup without averting his eyes from the match, twirling a needle thin dagger around the fingers of his right hand.

"You fought really well, sir. I was wonder–" Annavey was cut off by a burly man demanding a drink, she ducked her head, hair spilling across her red face and rushed over to serve him.

Both of the men had long swords, they parried and struck with quick precise movements. Althea didn't have to be an assessor to see that the match between the volunteer and the student had been choreographed.

The student – Barty – shifted his weight from his right leg to his left and swung his sword down in a high arc just as his opponent rushed him. Both evidently forgetting which move had been next in their little play. Their heads slammed together, the sound of the collision as loud as a gong ringing out across the arena. Gasps erupted from the onlookers, as the two men staggered, and fell flat onto their backs in perfect synchronization.

"No contest!" The announcer called out the draw with a wince. The student would not be moving on. Two guards came to move the limp bodies into the infirmary tent followed by the sounds of the crowd cringing and hissing in sympathy.

"I'll call that bet in now." Niklas leaned over to whisper in her ear. "Make them spotless."

Althea groaned inwardly and rolled her eyes at Niklas's back as he walked back into the center of the ring, twisting a scimitar in a circle with the slight flick of his wrist.

Niklas had been suspicious of Barty trying to fix his matches, but Althea had protested that Barty wasn't that desperate, and they made a bet that if Niklas was right she would spit shine his hunting boots, which were so caked in mud, and the leather worn so dull, that no one would be able to tell that they were boots unless they were on his feet.

And if she had been right, he would have to wash her clothes that were soiled from mucking the barracks horse stalls and mend her cloak. It was his fault that she had been given the chore anyway.

Althea grabbed the arming sword again and stalked into the white chalked circle of the fighting ring.

Even though Althea barely came up to Niklas's chin, she was stronger than anyone gave her credit for. She had speed and agility and could easily dodge the long reaches of almost all the men she had to spar with.

Niklas was on the lower end of tall, neither thin nor large, but somewhere right in the middle. The muscles of his arms were visible beneath his leathers, but he was still lithe and moved as graceful as a cat, something Althea had always been envious of. He was one of the very few men that actually gave her a challenge.

The announcer stood between Althea and Niklas, raised his hand and brought it down with the call, "Fight!" before rushing to exit the circle.

Althea locked her thoughts in the back room of her mind, built over her many seasons of training specifically for these moments, drowning out the sound of the crowds' anticipation, her eyes honing in until she could see only Niklas. How he shifted his weight onto his back foot, his hands forming around the leather grip of his scimitar. It was like it had been made specifically for him.

She took one long breath in through her nose and let it out through her mouth, the leather grip of the sword creaking as she adjusted her grip and began to circle Niklas. He followed her, turning in time with her every step. They appraised each other, waiting for the perfect moment when the other gave the slightest opening.

There.

Niklas shifted his elbow out from where he held it close to his body, ready to make the first strike. Althea moved, feinting right, and when he went to block, she made a swipe for his ribs on his exposed left.

Just before her sword could make contact, Niklas twirled and lowered into a side lunge, her sword flew over his head.

Using the momentum, she swung the sword in an upward arch from right to left. He crab walked backward a few feet, coming dangerously close to the boundary line. If she could just get him to cross the chalk it would be the fastest match she had ever had with him.

Wishful thinking.

He swiftly got his feet under him and shouldered her in the stomach, pushing her two steps back, giving him a precious foot of space. He moved fast with the scimitar, thrusting it on angles, left and right, left and right. She parried each one until they were back in the center.

Althea took a miniscule, quick step toward Niklas forcing him to pull his blade back to block her jab. Even though it was barely an inch, it was all she needed to twist her sword in a circle around his, drawing all her strength into her arms and shove with all her might, sending his weapon flying out of the ring toward a small group of people that were hanging on the fence. They scrambled away, shrieking with excitement, to avoid the blade. Its tip dug into the ground, hilt pointing towards heaven.

Before she could square herself, Niklas spun in a circle on one leg, kicking her sword out of her hand; the blade struck his own across the line with a ring. The clamor of the crowd hit Althea like a brick, her focus frayed like a piece of twine pulled too tight, and then snapped altogether when Niklas's fist collided with her jaw. The sharp taste of iron filled her mouth. She started to fall and reached out, grabbing onto the front of Niklas's jacket. They went down together, both landing hard on their sides.

"Out of bounds, concurrent, draw!" Althea could barely hear the announcer over the ringing in her ear.

"Let go of me, you dolt," Niklas grunted. She didn't realize that she was still clutching at his jacket until he was prying her hands away.

Althea unsteadily pushed herself to her feet, shaking off the hit and made her way to where her father was standing at the fence, under the shade of a red dogwood tree. Her sight was blurry in her left eye, and she could already feel the tight swell of the skin on her cheek.

"One more round, Goose, that's all that's left," her father said, taking his dark gray handkerchief from his pocket and dabbed at her lip. It came away stained with her blood. "Remember. With the jaws of lions," Althea's father quoted the motto on their family crest.

Confused as to why he would say that now, Althea just assumed she didn't hear him right, her ears that still rang disoriented her and threw off her balance.

The ten minutes were over in what felt like seconds and Althea and Niklas were called back after another match had finished, for her fifth and final fight.

Win or lose, it was now or never for Althea.

She chose to stick with the arming sword, as it was what she fought with best. Niklas had switched out the scimitar for a flail that had the spikes removed.

Immediately after Althea entered the circle she forgot all about the ache that had started to spread over her body from the long day of events, her mind going straight to that back room that it knew and loved so well.

Two people, one purpose. Win.

He was no longer Niklas, and she was no longer Althea.

"Fight!"

Chapter Two

Niklas Stallard

It was the final match of the assessments, and they had been fighting for nearly ten minutes.

Althea was giving everything she had. Somehow she was faster and stronger despite the exhaustion he could see setting in by the dark purple under her eyes. Sweat beaded along her temples before falling, leaving streaks down her dirty, swollen cheek.

Niklas had cast his jacket off onto the servant girl by the barrel of water, and was glad he did, his movements were less restricted in his simple, white tunic.

He swung low, aiming to wrap the chain of his flail around Althea's ankle. She jumped back and flipped over onto her hands before landing back on her feet. He followed, keeping the distance between them short. He spotted an opening on her left shoulder while she was still crouched from her landing and raised his arm, preparing to let the iron ball meet its target. But before he could blink, Althea was gone, making to jump through the space between his legs.

He grappled for her before a razor-sharp pain seared through his leg. Howling, Niklas leapt forward, shooting a quick glance at his ankle. A tiny sliver of skin between his leather boot and where his pant leg had ridden up was a red line of... teeth marks!?

Astonished, rage rose in his chest. But before he could act, the frosty edge of a sword pressed against the hollow of his throat. Althea stood before him, panting heavily, a wickedly joyful gleam in her eyes that sparkled in the reflection of the blade.

"Mark Althea, complete!"

Just when he thought the crowd could not cheer any louder, the screeching that came from the stands shook the very air around them, the earth rumbled with stomping feet.

A reedy man – Niklas recalled his name to be Aezel – climbed over the arena fence and ran toward them, scooping Althea up into a hug. He spun her around with her feet several inches off the ground, both whooping in laughter. Niklas jumped back before he was hit by her sword as she held on.

He hated to admit that he more or less respected her skill and sheer willpower in a fight, but really, to bite him? He was sure that was a new experience for both of them.

Taking Aezel entering the ring as a signal, a wave of people rushed in from all sides, pushing Niklas out of the chalk circle. The crowd swallowed the air with shouts of cheer and delight as was customary to do after the final match. Niklas used the excitement to slip away and wash up, to bring his mind out of its fighting calm before the celebratory dinner in the mess grounds.

"Excuse me, Sir Stallard." A soft voice came from behind him on the path to the bath house. He turned his head and slowed, but didn't stop walking when he saw it was only the servant girl from the arena shuffling toward him.

"Sir, I am very sorry to interrupt you on your way, but you forgot your jacket. The night is called to be cold and I didn't want you to catch ill. I hope you don't mind, but I wiped the dust from it and applied oil so you wouldn't have to." She spoke so quietly and kept her head down, angled away from him. He wouldn't have been able to understand her if it wasn't for the path being as deserted as it was.

"Thank you," was all Niklas said as he gathered the freshly softened bundle of leather into his arms.

"Sir Stallard, if I am not overstepping my place, I would like to ask you something."

"Just Niklas please. By all means, ask away." His tone seemed to ease some of her anxiousness, her hands stilled from the wringing they had undertaken. The tips of her fingers were stained a strange color of blue. He furrowed his brows. It looked like the color of *ketabome*. But that couldn't be right, maybe it was from dyeing clothes.

"Well, my Master Archibald has given me leave from my duties tonight. Since the matches did not produce any severe injuries the infirmary is as empty as a barrel of rum on the harbor and he gave me permission to attend the dinner. I was wondering ... if you would like to join me tonight?"

Niklas sometimes forgot that she had come from Llyr – a small port city in Marella – until she used idioms that she had no doubt picked up from the old freebooters as they made port to deliver their goods.

"Miss – Um –" Niklas started.

"Annavey. Annavey Alouette," she smiled sheepishly.

It was no surprise to Niklas that she would ask this of him. They had grown up in the same small east quarter of Taris, and always seemed to have been fond of him. It wasn't that Niklas disliked

Annavey, she had an endearing countenance, and never complained about the hardships she had had to face being one of the orphans in servitude like many others did. But his only focus had always been on upholding his place in the Guard and taking care of his father.

He never once noticed the swooning women he passed on his morning runs, or when he was sparring. That was until his friend Attilio made fun of him for it and expressed his jealousy. Now he saw them everywhere.

"Miss Annavey. I'm sorry, but I can't this time. I had already agreed to go with Attilio and Magnus." He kept his voice in an even tenor, almost like he was trying not to spook an animal. Her smile fell, disappointment pursing her lips.

"Silly me, I shouldn't have assumed that you wouldn't already have company prearranged. Forgive me, Sir – Uh – Niklas, perhaps I will remember to ask in advance next time. Enjoy your evening." Annavey curtsied and Niklas nodded his head in a shallow bow.

"You as well, Miss Alouette."

She turned and strode away with her shoulders tense.

Niklas exited the bathhouse, clean at last from the dust and sweat that had caked his skin, feeling like the grit had been absorbed into his muscles. Donning his clean leather jacket, the Guard issued wool cloak in the darkest emerald green, and a freshly bandaged ankle, he started on the path to the mess grounds.

Making his way through the darkening woods he could already smell the roasted venison, slathered with garlic and a variety of herbs, the freshly baked bread and sweet wine. It all made his mouth flood in anticipation and with the prediction of eating. His stomach made an embarrassingly loud protest. He had not eaten since morning, and thankfully he was the only one on the trail that evening. None of his fellow guards were filthy people per say, but they had never been the type to wait long. Where food was a concern, bathing could wait.

Niklas found that he enjoyed the moments of solitude he got on occasions like this. He didn't necessarily like being alone, but the constant companionship that entailed from being in the Guard made him appreciate the fresh air he could get. If only for a minute to not smell a hundred sweaty men in the barracks.

The silence was stirred by the distant sound of hooves beating a steady rhythm somewhere in the leaf strewn forest. He paused at the well trodden fork in the path. To the right was the road that led in and out of town, to the left was the guest stables and inn, planted directly in the center of the market square. And straight ahead went toward the mess grounds, where Niklas was headed. The vibration of the horses grew stronger and was coming from the right. There were no mentions of any guests that were to attend tonight's graduations.

Maybe just someone who has ill time management and wanted to get a room in the inn before night fell, Niklas hypothesized when suddenly, three, massive black horses burst through the gates, their riders cloaked in the darkest black. He jumped back, narrowly missing the steeds and slipped in the mud on the side of the trail. When he regained his balance, the men were already past him, heading for the stables.

He froze, his boots sinking in the mud. Were those the queen's guards?

CHAPTER THREE

—◦—

ALTHEA

The crowd began to disperse at the call of the dinner bell and the excitement from the day's events was starting to catch up with Althea. She was certain that she would sleep the entire next day. She already required more food than the average lady her age, but on top of that, the extra training that led up to that day and the exertion she had put herself through with the matches made her ravenously hungry. Her stomach had been bellowing out a haughty protest for the last hour and Aezel laughed at her, gesturing in the direction of the mess grounds.

"Walk with me?" He asked, a smile tugging at his lips, creasing the corners of his eyes.

"Please, I don't think I can make it on my own."

Their feet fell into a rhythm, arms occasionally bumping into each other as they blended into the flow of the others who were streaming to the mess grounds for the feast. They would be eating the biggest and freshest catch of venison that had been roasting since dawn, all the different types of cheeses that she could dream of, and thick slices of the softest, buttered bread.

"Hey, you're limping." Aezel's brow was furrowed, eyes cast down to where Althea favored her left leg. She only felt a little stiff as of now, but it was probably due to the lasting effects of the adrenaline.

"I'm alright, it twisted a little when I fell. Nothing more than a full stomach and a nice long, hot bath won't heal," Althea assured him.

"Right, because the way to a woman's heart is through her stomach, I forgot," Aezel teased her, but she couldn't exactly deny it either and shoved his arm playfully, laughing with him.

"Still, let me have a look at it after dinner. Can't have one of our best guards go lame now can we?" She nodded her head, obliging him and his nurturing tone.

They were nearing the mess grounds when someone roughly shouldered past her. She tripped, and Aezel caught her with a grunt of surprise before she could fall. Althea rightened herself to see who her assailant was, just as they turned, walking backwards.

"I wouldn't say she's one of the *best*."

"*Niklas*," she snarled.

He put two fingers to his brow in a mocking salute. "The one and only." He smirked down at her before twirling to walk ahead in one fluid motion that made his cloak flare out behind him as if it was a dance, one that – knowing Niklas – he was leading. Aezel still had a hand gripping her arm, his green eyes, dark as the towering evergreens that surrounded them, drilled into the back of Niklas's head.

"I'm okay." Althea knew Aezel couldn't stand Niklas – goodness – she despised his guts too, but he had too good of a soul to waste on the foolishness of the likes of him. "He just caught me off guard." She gently took his hand and held it, swinging their arms between them with each step.

15

"Are you sure you're okay? It's not like you to be 'caught off guard'. Maybe I should be looking at your head instead of your ankle?" Aezel pursed his lips, bringing a hand to her head and pushed aside her hair, looking for a bump. She brushed his hand away with a chuckle.

The mess grounds always reminded Althea of an ant hill. Everyone and everything knew just where they were supposed to be. People stood in trailing lines alongside the long tables to the left that held the feast. Cooks and servants piled food on the waiting trays, the eyes of the people glinting with desire.

Taking a place in line with Aezel, Althea grabbed a tray from the stack next to the dish of steaming potatoes – which she accepted a generous scoop of – as well as a little bit of everything else until her tray was dangerously close to warping. Except for the grilled fish, Althea *hated* fish, but managed to hide her scowl as she politely refused.

She made her way down the line, half of her mind scanning the faces of the people milling around, at the families that sat together, heads bowed in prayer. A little boy in his fathers lap plunging a fist into a chocolate cream cake, licking the sweetness from his stubby fingers, all the while a wicked grin plastered on his plump face.

"Althea! Over here." She looked around until she saw the waving hand, her fathers face beaming over the heads of those around him. Her face split into a matching smile.

"Come on, Aezel." She grabbed his arm and pulled him away from the barrel of wine, almost making him drop the drinks that he was balancing on his tray.

"Woah, Althea. Go on ahead, I'm right behind you." He chuckled, righting the cups on his tray.

Althea picked her way through the tables, giving quick smiles and thanks to whoever patted her on the back and gave her their congratulations.

When she was finally able to set down her tray, Althea leapt into her fathers open arms, fingers just barely meeting around his middle, his familiar woodsy scent filled her nose.

"I'm so proud of you Goose, I knew you would understand what I meant by our motto." He took a step back, his large hands grasping her shoulders and looked at her with pride in his eyes. The only physical trait that they shared were their wide, gray green eyes. Otherwise – her father told her – she looked just like her mother.

Her mother had passed away due to a sickness when she was four. She only remembered snippets about her, mostly the sound of her mother humming while she worked in the kitchen. The only way she knew what she looked like was from the small portrait of her father and mother that hung in the gathering room of their small cottage. Her mother's belly was swollen, the portrait having been painted months before Althea was born.

She guessed she could see the resemblance if she squinted in the dark and tilted her head slightly to the side. Her mother was soft, feminine, lips permanently curved into a perfect smile while Althea's was crooked.

Although she had her mothers slight curves, she had already had her fathers hard muscles by the time she was ten, and had always preferred to play rough in the arena with the other boys instead of learning to cook and make clothes like other girls.

"I don't think I would have ever done that if ascending didn't mean as much as it does to me." Althea sat down and pondered on her choices of food. What did she want to start and end with?

"Well, what else do you think gave inspiration for our motto?" Her father said in his husky chuckle.

"Wait a minute, *that's* how you came up with 'the jaws of lions'!?" Althea's eyes widened, wincing at her bruised jaw and rubbed it gingerly.

"Sure is." Her father nodded a greeting to Aezel when he took the seat across from them. Aezel returned the gesture.

Althea began to shove food into her mouth after a quick prayer of thanks, holding back from making a sound at how good everything tasted.

A couple of young servants bustled around the raised dais in the back of the mess grounds, lighting the torches that surrounded the platform. A signal that Captain Delmar was ready to make announcements.

Her Captain entered to the sound of applause, and walked up the few steps to the center of the dais, his booming voice was able to be heard over the ruckus.

"Attention people of Taris, Kingdom of Valarie." A thick, anticipating silence swelled among the tables. "Today, God has blessed us with five, wonderful new additions to our Guard. And even though it is not official until the ascension ceremony tomorrow morning, these five young men and women are already a part of my army – and consequently – a part of my own family. So I would like to raise a toast." He raised a glass goblet, the wine inside a deep red mahogany. "A toast to the sons and daughters of Taris who have trusted me with the sacrifice of their blood, sweat, and tears. To the service of the Kingdom of Valarie, and most importantly, to the Kingdom of God. I am more than honored to serve alongside you, my new brothers and sisters. Awo awo!" He howled into the night.

Althea stood with Aezel and her father. Alongside every last man, woman and child. She lifted her cup into the blue streaked, starry night sky and let loose a shout, "Awo awo!"

CHAPTER FOUR

NIKLAS

A guard rushed onto the dais before Captain Delmar could even lower his glass.

Sweat soaked through the guards' fatigue, his face held a sickly green pallor. He was breathing heavily, small puffs of white clouded around his head as he bowed in respect. Delmar leaned in close to the guard, whispers were shared between them, his face became more tense with every word.

Eventually the Captain nodded, excusing the guard who had been off duty before running there, and turned back to address the crowd, clearing his throat, his brows furrowed ever so slightly.

Niklas could not remember a time that Captain Delmar was ever anything other than reserved and confident. But now, sweat was beading on his temples, making his raven black hair stick to his forehead. His eyes swinging to the left, uncertainty bunching up his shoulders.

"People of Taris, I am well aware of the rumors you have heard concerning the tensions between Palmeria, and the Kingdom of Valarie."

Niklas had heard the rumors. Palmeria was vastly desert, and the southern area where the land was habitable had been in dire drought throughout the last two seasons, with snowless winters and rainless springs, making their crop production fall to a halt, and any quarry scarce. The animals had begun migrating north to the mountains of Oakstead where water flowed in great falls and fresh springs ran throughout every forest, all in great measures. Valarie had been giving very little of its abundant resources to Palmeria. Niklas and most every citizen of Valarie could not understand the queen's callous reluctance to help.

" 'If we give deliverance from one hardship, all the kingdoms will come tearing at our walls begging like mangy strays.' " His father would quote the queen from his time serving in the palace before Niklas was born.

He had overheard Miss Florence, the mayor's wife – a raging gossip – in the market once, saying that if Queen Azora, the ruler of the four corners of Laisren, did not decree help from Marella and Valarie, that it would receive help from someone who would give it. The rebellion.

"It appears we have an unforeseen visitor. A very respectable man from the Queen's Guard has come to quell any misinformation and to give word of the sanctions to be imposed."

Gasps filled the lines of tables, and whispers of who it could be.

"Chancellor Mael?"

"Ambassador Kindrel?"

Names were tossed to and fro, melding into a wispy hum. It was not often for someone of high importance to brave the two week journey from the palace that was poised beyond the high mountain in the center of the land, next to the City of Valor, through the muddy and creature infested forests that separated them from the city of Taris.

Captain Delmar cleared his throat, earning the crowd's attention again.

"May we give Sir Admiral Erling of the Queen's Guard of the Kingdom of Valarie, City of Valor, the established welcome of Taris."

Niklas stood alongside his fellow guards with his back straight, his booted feet together, and brought his right hand, closed into a fist to his right shoulder, and punched his fist straight up, stepping out with his left foot with the salute of Taris, "For God and Kingdom!"

"Be at ease." Delmar released them from their salute, but no one relaxed, the anticipation stole everyone's attention to the man on the dais.

If the Queen's Guard is here, something really is *wrong.* Niklas thought to himself. He could not make out the face of the man who stood next to Delmar. The sun had set over an hour ago, but he recognized the black armor from the riders earlier. The man did not remove the hood of his cloak, the lanterns not quite breaking through the shadows that the hood cast.

"Thank you, citizens of Taris. I know that today is the day of the ascension evaluations that all of you look forward to as you become of age to serve." The man's voice was ruff from long days of travel. It looked like he had just stepped off his horse before coming straight there.

"But unfortunately, this day will be one that holds both joy and sorrow for many of you." The mirth that the mess grounds had been filled with was gone. Niklas had never felt it hold such a feeling of trepidation. The silence felt so thick that Niklas could cut it with the dull butter knife next to his dirty, empty plate.

"Despite having had peace between all the four corners for nearly a century, Palmeria, during its most desolate time in history, has made a declaration of war against Valarie, demanding a transition of power."

Shouts of disbelief and dismay rose among the crowd.

The kingdom of Valarie had been the center of power in Laisren ever since King Brioc came to the crown of Valarie during the four nation war, and had presented an entente that all could agree upon and quelled the tensions between the lands who were at both political and physical odds. His only request was that his bloodline would remain in succession to the throne, so long as the sanctions remained intact and peace reigned. All the rulers wanted one thing, peace, and King Brioc presented them with that option. The Brioc line continued to rule the four corners to this day.

No one really knew the exact concordance that was made. There had been a fire in the palace by a band of rebels that opposed the partitions, and the documents had been too damaged to read, let alone taught. That rebellion was still alive.

But, despite the rebels' attempts, the stories never died out about how great King Brioc had been, and how his bloodline was blessed. A bunch of swooning men and women no doubt threw in little en-hancements along the way, though no one could doubt the peace that followed in the lands. So something must have held strong, until now, that is.

The earth seemed to dip and upheave around Niklas as he waited for the man to continue once the crowd quieted, but the next words from the queen's guard rent his world in two.

"All who have succeeded the trials and passed graduation, even those from today when they are ascended, shall take up arms to defend the rightful heir and ruler of Laisren, Queen Azora of Valarie. Only men, women and children outside of the Guard, the ungraduated, and those older than forty-five complete seasons will not be accounted for the march. Preparations are to begin at first light. We set out in a week's time." The man dismissed himself with a customary bow and walked down the dais's stairs and out of sight. His words hung over the frozen crowd like a noose.

At one moment, the world seemed to have frozen like a lake in the winter, and in the next, people rushed in every direction. Some to their houses, others to the church. But the older men and women of the Guard moved as normal, they were indeed, trained for this.

Niklas felt the strong sensation that someone was staring at him, the hair on his neck raised. He looked behind him and searched along the benches, finding the pair he knew well from the endless bouts of fighting between him and the owners.

Althea's eyes were as round as the lemon slices that hung around the perimeter that kept most of the late summer bugs from the gatherings, her mouth hung open in a shocked stupor. Her ascension would be completed in the morning. She would march with Valarie.

Niklas turned away when he saw her stand and started to walk home.

CHAPTER FIVE

— · —

ALTHEA

War. War. War.

The word bounced around Althea's head, echoing over and over. She could see it painted on every face she passed on the way to her home, heard it in every crackle of the torch her father carried.

She supposed that she shouldn't really be surprised that it had come down to that. The queen wasn't one to like being told what to do.

Althea still couldn't figure out why the queen even kept her court. At that point the money they were taxed was going to the group of counselors who got paid to enjoy the luxuries that normal people, like Althea, were providing and protecting. The queen never listened to their advice anyway, or maybe they were the ones telling her to do these things.

Althea kept a hand clutched to her fathers fur lined vest as they shouldered and maneuvered their way through the packed passes that led out of the main square, to their small cottage on the outskirts of the forest. Aezel followed behind her with a hand on her back, helping her keep pace with their long strides. He lived alone at the barracks and often spent his time at her home.

Once they had made it into their cottage, Althea took what felt like her first breath in hours, sucking the air down into her stomach the way her Poppa taught her. It always helped soothe the feelings of anxiousness she felt before a match.

It also helps when you are called to fight in a war.

"What do we need to do Poppa?" Althea asked. Her father closed his eyes and ran a hand down his face with a sigh. "Aezel?" She turned to where her friend was still standing in the doorway.

He didn't look at her. "I will begin preparing at first light. Head down to Archibald's and get medicine and bandages, then over to the butcher to get jerky. There won't be enough to go around so we might have to rely on foraging for most of the trip. I heard that half of us are to march to Caedmon through the Cerridwen, and the other half will go around to join the extra armies from Valor. It will be a long journey," he sighed, rubbing the back of his neck. When he finally looked up at her, his eyes were filled, glinting in the light of the fireplace.

Althea hadn't even seen her father move to light the fire, only now feeling the chill that had settled in the cottage while they had been out enjoying the evening. A violent shiver ran through her as the weight of the last few hours started to settle onto her.

It would take nearly two and a half weeks to make it to Caedmon if they took the standard route around the Cerridwen forest. But Althea knew they would have to go straight through the dense woodland in order to get there within the month if they were to leave a week from then.

Growing up, Althea remembered hearing the stories about how the forest seemed to move in the night, confusing soldiers and sending them in the wrong directions. Or blocking out the sun completely, even at high noon, and anyone who went into the Cerridwen only made it out with scraps of their minds left.

She knew they were only tall tales to keep children from playing in the depths and getting lost or hurt. But there were still very real predators, and plenty of poisonous plants that only someone who was trained could tell the difference between.

Aezel gently removed the heavy cloak from her tired shoulders, tossing it over the bench by the door and guided her by an elbow into the small gathering room.

His calloused hands were proof of his diligence to the work of the Guard. Many seasons of training with a sword, archery, and down right grub work from when they were children when he would not let Althea execute her punishments alone after she and Niklas would get in trouble for their tussles. And only recently, the harsh cleaning involved in working in the infirmary where he was apprenticing the head physician Archibald.

Althea settled into the big leather chair closest to the fire, wrapping her arms around her middle and watched silently as Aezel grabbed the iron kettle from a hook on the mantle and fetched water from the pump in the kitchen. Bringing it to a boil over the fire he mixed in chamomile and mint leaves from her stash of garden herbs she had dried throughout the summer.

His steady movements helped calm her racing mind, bringing it back to a more logical side of thinking.

She suddenly thought of something so blatantly obvious she did not know how she hadn't remembered earlier and gasped, moving to kneel in front of her father where he sat across from her.

"Poppa, how could I forget? You just became forty-six seasons this month, you will be spared from the march."

"You must not think very highly of me if you believe for one second that I will not be coming with you," her father said with a sad smile.

"No, Poppa, you can't, who will watch over the garden and make new weapons for the armory. What about Raphael?" Althea scoured her mind for all the reasons she could think of that might keep her father there. Their measly crops that fed them dutifully. Niklas's father, her fathers best friend who was more like a brother to him. Anything to spare her from the thought of her father marching into battle... or worse.

"I will ask Narie if she would stay in the house while we are gone. She already knows how to take care of everything, and I am not the only smith in this town." Narie was the maid he had hired when Althea was little and wasn't old enough to be left alone while her father worked.

"But Poppa, your leg, you won't be able to travel through the forest, let alone fight afterwards." Althea was on the verge of desperation, she would not let him march, she would find a way to make him stay there. She couldn't lose him, she *would not* lose him, he was all she had.

"I can't just sit here and let my daughter walk five hundred miles through the forest to fight a war that she has no business being involved in. You're too young Althea, war doesn't just hurt your body, it hurts your soul. It destroys what makes you, *you*." Her father grasped her hands on his knee.

"Poppa, I am eighteen seasons old, I know what war entails. I am not as fragile as you think I am. If the assessors say I meet the standards to ascend, then I am strong enough to fight both in mind and body. I may be your daughter, but you don't get to decide what I am and am not capable of," Althea huffed, pulling her hands away and started to undo her braid. "I'm going to bathe."

She stomped outside, breathing furiously. She knew her father would not take her anger personally, she was always known to have a short temper. But Althea hated when her frustrations got the better of her, it always left her chest feeling tight with guilt when she finally managed to calm down.

Moving carefully through the moonlit pass to the bathhouse, Althea prayed. Not a prayer of words, she wouldn't even know what to say. Determination swelled in her chest, warring with the strength of the grief threatening to suffocate her. It was an indescribable feeling.

With her God on her side, no war would destroy her. If she was sure of anything, it was that.

Chapter Six

Niklas

Niklas took the long way home.

Everything he tried to do to calm his racing mind seemed unable to quench the burning of his thoughts.

He was walking past the bathhouses again when he heard the snap of a branch from behind the building. He froze, holding his breath as he listened.

It was not uncommon for there to be a stray *brav* in the night, especially when they had such feasts in town. Guards were supposed to be on a rotation every hour, like they were every time there were celebrations. Animals were always hungrier than the men.

Niklas felt reckless, he wanted a distraction from the buzzing in his head, so he let his curiosity get the better of him. He vaguely remembered something his friend said about a cat dying? Besides, if there was a danger, it was his job as a guard to protect the city.

He slid a small dagger into his hand from the sheath on his waist, stepped off the path, light on his toes and pressed his back into the thick wood as he crouched to look around the corner.

He had expected to see a giant creature, but it was only a woman. It was too dark to know who it was. She sat with her back against the building, knees pulled up into her chest, head buried in her legs.

His leg started to cramp and he shifted his weight slightly, trying to ease the tightness in his thigh as quietly as he could, when suddenly a bullfrog jumped onto his leg, letting out an atrocious croak.

Before he could think or reason, Niklas let out an embarrassingly shrill yelp and leapt away from the building, slapping at the frog on his leg. It flew through the humid air and landed with a sickeningly wet slap in the mud.

"Oh yuck!" He swiped the slime off his hand onto the nearest tree.

"What are you doing?"

Niklas, during his melee with the batrachian, forgot he wasn't alone. The woman's voice startled him and he turned quickly to face her, his cloak tangling around his limbs. She was still too far away for him to make out her features, but she had stood, squaring her shoulders to him. Niklas cleared his throat and rightened his clothes, brushing an imaginary piece of grass from his shoulder.

"I was just walking past and heard something. I was checking it out, making sure a *brav* wasn't getting close to town. Are you okay, Miss?" He was flustered that the woman had seen him freak out so girlishly, but it was a horrendously large frog, and Niklas hated frogs, of any variety and size.

He heard her chuckle. "I'm fine, thank you for your concern, I just needed a moment alone. I'm sure you understand, with the announcement and everything. I was actually just about to head home."

31

"Oh, okay. It's dark, do you need someone to walk with you?" Niklas asked to be polite, he crossed his fingers behind his back, hoping that she would say no. He really wanted to be alone himself.

"No, but thank you, Sir. I'll make sure to watch out for any evil amphibians on my way." He heard, rather than saw her, smile.

"Very well, have a safe night," he said, tilting his head in a slight bow, and when he straightened, she was gone.

He raised a hand to his face, but stopped inches away, remembering the goo from the frog and switched hands, running it through his hair and down his face, smiling, sighing in relief and shook his head.

Niklas barely registered that he had made it home. Not even walking inside, or hanging his cloak up on the antlers that they used as hooks by the door. His father hobbled into the small foyer, waving a hand in front of his face. "Earth to Niklas, are you in there?"

He snapped out of his daze, thinking about the strange interaction between him and the woman behind the bathhouse. He hadn't even thought to ask her name, and in his confusion he couldn't place her voice either. He wasn't even sure it was anyone he had met before. It could have been anyone.

"Sorry father, I was just distracted. There is something I need to tell you." Niklas walked over to the lounge room and sat on the plush sofa across from his father, opened and closed his mouth a few times, trying to think of how to tell his father of the news that would change their world as they knew it. But his mouth refused to work.

He scrunched up his nose and sighed, cracking one knuckle on his hands at a time. His father was patient at first, but Niklas could see the worry beginning to deepen the lines on his forehead.

"Son, whatever it is, you can tell me. I may not be a spring gosling anymore, but I have had my fair share of heartbreak when I was in the guar-"

"There is going to be a war, father," Niklas interrupted. The words finally sprung from his mouth of their own compulsion. "All of us were conscripted. I leave in a week, there is much to be done before then."

They sat in silence for a few minutes, his father propping his chin in his hands, and Niklas didn't know how to feel.

"Do not worry about me son, there are plenty who are willing to help an old man out. I will be fine." And then after a moment. "I was waiting for your twentieth season, but I feel I must give it to you now." His father stood, walking over to grab a ladder from the corner, and propped it up onto the ledge of the loft.

Niklas stood and went to help him.

"I can't get it on my own. There is a chest on the far back wall, under the window. It has our family crest on it. Bring it please."

Niklas nodded and ascended the ladder easily, pushing aside dusty piles of old armor from when he was small, unveiling the chest.

It wasn't a chest exactly, more like a thin case. Flat and long. The Stallard family crest was engraved on the aged wood. A snake encircling a dove. Not violently, almost as if it was embracing it. It wasn't as heavy as he thought it would be, but it certainly wasn't light either.

His father had him lay it on the table before the warm fireplace. His aged hands unlatched the two clasps on the side and opened it facing Niklas.

Inside, resting on a rich burgundy velvet, was a sword. The hilt was the darkest onyx Niklas had ever seen, the blade a scintillating dark gray. It was a well worn sword, no doubt having been used in many battles, but it still held a perfect sharpness on its edge.

"This sword was mine, as it was my father's before me, and his father's before him. All Stallard men are given it at twenty seasons. But nineteen will have to do. As you know I never had any brothers or uncles. So this, my son, is yours." His father's voice became thick with emotion.

Niklas rounded the table, pulling his father in tight, gripping him like he was air and Niklas was drowning.

"It will be ok son, God has blessed our country in time past, we must hold strong in faith that he will do the same now. I will pray every minute you are gone. We *will* conquer."

34

CHAPTER SEVEN

ALTHEA

Althea made it back home, clean and smelling like the expensive vanilla and strawberry soap she had gotten herself at the spring market earlier in the season. Aezel wasn't there when she stepped into the dark house.

The moon was at its apex when Althea's body gave in to exhaustion, her eyes drifted close on their own. She barely made it to the chair before her mind gave way to the darkness.

The end of summer sun shone brightly through the window, directly into Althea's eyes. It disoriented her for a moment, before she remembered where she was. The colorful woven blanket fell off her shoulders when she sat up, yawning and mercilessly rubbed the sleep from her eyes.

Althea did not remember grabbing the blanket, it was usually folded inside the chest under the loft.

"Good, you're up. I made breakfast." Althea turned at the sound of her father's voice. Only then did she register the smell of freshly smoked bacon and the sweet butternut syrup they always ate with her father's famous pancakes.

She stood and stretched out the knot between her shoulder blades from sleeping curled up in a ball before taking a seat in front of the food. They ate silently, neither knowing what to say after the night before and both mentally agreeing that nothing would be the right thing to talk about.

Althea helped clean up the kitchen before going to her small wardrobe and picked out her best pair of pants, leather boots, and the red cloak she had been given when she first started training with the Guard.

It labeled her as a Red Jewel. An unascended member of the Guard of Valarie. Soon she would don the dark emerald green of the ascended.

For seasons, Althea had dreamed about this day with feelings of reverence and elation. Now she just felt a numbing hum in her chest.

She knew what would have to be done after today. And she was ready for it.

The town's main square was filled with a multitude of colorful ribbons that fluttered above the red cloaked group as they made their way down the path of cobblestone that had been painted in a sparkly gold, leading up to the announcement stage.

When Althea was young, she and Aezel would always watch the ascension ceremony from above, where they had snuck onto the thatched rooftop of Glady's store.

She remembered always thinking the group of graduates looked like drops of blood, trailing down the edge of the gold ceremonial sword as they walked down the glittering path to the stage.

She could see the symbolism now as her feet led her down that very same path. *Their* blood would be the ones shed for the kingdom. Countless drops dripping off its sharp edge. A life lost in exchange for a life spared. It was her turn now, as it was the generation before, and the one before them, and the ones to come.

Captain Delmar and Mayor Florence stood in the center of the stage, the former wearing his ceremonial armor, the gold sword a brilliant light in his dark hand. The latter wore a black vest, trousers and a long emerald green coat. The hem settled at his feet that were encased in the softest looking brown leather.

Althea and her fellow classmates arranged themselves in a line parallel to the stage, friends and families crowded behind them on either side of the painted path to watch.

"Ladies and gentleman, here stands before you the next generation of our warriors. These five young men and women are resilient, faithful, and wholeheartedly giving of themselves, in both blood and honor, to serve not only the throne of Valarie, but the throne of our God. But tonight it is *our* honor, brothers and sisters, that we are granted this opportunity of ascending these brave ones." Mayor Florence didn't move an inch as he spoke, only his eyes floated down to the faces standing before him.

"From here on, as this sword descends upon your shoulders, you will no longer be known as the Red Jewels, you will now be a part of the Chosen Emerald, the Guard of the Kingdom of Valarie. You will swear your oath of fealty to the throne, and who's seat it belongs, Queen Azora."

The crowd behind them rang out with hundreds of clapping hands, nothing like the excited clamor from the night before. Althea could feel the sadness in the echoing sound.

"When your name is presented, please come stand before your captain and receive your ascension." Mayor Florence finished his speech, pulled out a wrinkled piece of paper from his coat and called out the first to the stage. "Sir Eamon Kerdesc."

Althea only knew Eamon in passing, he was a half season older than her and had been under a different teacher during his training. He had always seemed very shy, but he held his shoulders back with confidence now and Althea felt pride for him as he knelt before Delmar.

"Sir Eamon, do you this day swear to defend and protect the throne of Valarie?"

"I swear on my honor," Eamon's voice rang out over the square, strong and sure, and he bowed his head.

"I hereby declare your ascension and dub thee in the service of the queen. Arise, and go forth in the name of God." Captain Delmar laid the sword upon Eamon's left shoulder lifting it over his head and laid it on the right. The crowd waited to cheer until the cloak on his broad shoulders was replaced from scarlet red to emerald green.

Althea was at the very end of the line, as she was the youngest out of the five. In the order of ascensions, they went by age instead of grade. If they had, she would have been first instead of last. But she didn't have any reason for pride, they would all be at the mercy of how well their enemies fought now.

The sun rose high as the line dwindled down and the speeches wore on, and soon Althea was the last one standing before the stage.

Mayor Florence's face grew confused as he studied his list. He turned to her Captain and motioned him over. They whispered back and forth for only a minute that felt like an eternity as Althea's heart started to pound. Something wasn't right, why were they taking so long?

"This hereby completes the ascensions, may God's grace be upon you all." The words spilled blunderingly out of the Mayor's mouth. He walked down the stairs hurriedly and came toward Althea. Murmuring rose around the square, quiet at first as he wrapped an arm around her shoulders and led her away from the rising questions as they grew more frantic.

Althea's mind went blank, she couldn't even bring her own questions to the front of her mind let alone fathom the notion that this meant she didn't ascend.

Althea was led into the Mayor's stately home by the servants entrance and was set down in his study by a servant, trailed quickly by Mrs. Florence, who was in a flurry about someone being in her home on such short notice.

Mr. Florence, seeing his wife flitting about, straightening things, asked his wife to have tea brought up and for a servant to fetch Althea's father. All the while, Althea sat, withdrawn completely within her mind.

It hadn't even been three minutes before her father sat next to her on the richest of blues sofa, a cup of warm tea in her hand she didn't remember being given. She couldn't get herself to drink it and she felt the tea grow cold as she listened to the mayor's explanation that there had to have been a mistake on the assessors report.

He said that the judges had left the night before as soon as they found out about the declaration and were afraid they wouldn't have been able to make the trip back to Valor before unrest rose in the capital. In their rush, Althea's passing status must have been lost in the quick decamping.

For a brief moment, all Althea could feel was relief, she *had* passed her exams, but the feeling was gone as soon as it had come. She sat silently, listening carefully as her father asked questions and was given answers to the best of Florence's ability. She hardly even blinked until his next words.

"So, Althea please do not fret, as you will be rewarded your ascension at the earliest it is possible." Florence looked relieved that he was able to give her what he thought was an equal outcome to the equation.

"Wait, what do you mean? You know it was a mistake, why can't we go back out there and finish this now? This is war, the sake of ceremony doesn't exactly apply here does it?" Althea asked, a headache beginning to form between her brows.

"I'm sorry, Althea, but the law of Valarie states that only the assessments that are stamped with the assessor's seal of approval are allowed to ascend. I wish I could do something, Miss Nova, I really do. But

I took an oath before the throne of Valarie to honor the laws of this land. This is not something I can change. Fair or unfair."

"I'll volunteer!" She quickly retorted, determined to not hide behind her town's walls while everyone else marched without her.

Her father rested a hand on her arm, squeezing tightly. She couldn't even feel it, but could see the fear on his face. "Now, Althea."

"Mr. Nova." Florence turned to address her father. "I think it best you take your daughter home; get some rest. Tomorrow we will need help with the preparations in any way you can. We only have five days left, and seven thousand guards to arm and feed for the long journey."

"I can't believe he would just shove us away like that!" Althea growled out her complaint while she paced the fourteen foot width of the lounge room in her home. "I mean, it wasn't *my* fault the assessors messed up the papers, why must I be withheld from fulfilling my duty alongside my men."

"I know it's unfair, but he took an oath, and he has to honor it just as you will have to honor yours when it is your time."

"It is *not* the same Poppa, and you can't know how unfair it is because you weren't held back from the war against Marella. You fought alongside your friends. You met amazing new people from new lands. You ate on the open waters. You *won*. How am I supposed to just sit here and do nothing while they go out there and die!"

Her fathers eyes trailed her movements, leaning his elbows on his knees. Althea's gaze drifted to his folded, scarred hands. He'd earned those scars fighting in the battle for the kingdom of Marella when it was attacked by Freina from across the southern sea. He had been on one of Marella's large war vessels, when an enemy among their ranks had broken open all the ale barrels and set the ships ablaze, marring her fathers hands and arms.

Only him and Raphael – Niklas's father – had made it off. Ever since then they had been closer than brothers.

Shortly after, when he had healed, he had been directing the citizens of Llyr in their retreat, and his leg had been broken by a frantic carriage driver who was fleeing with his family. It had not healed correctly and he was no longer able to fight in the long grueling days of battle. He was dismissed from service, but he did his physical treatments everyday without fail, and always anticipated letters from Raphael, who was still stationed, and gained enough strength back into his leg to pass the exams to become a palace guard.

Two seasons later, when the war ended and was won by the combined efforts of Laisren's kingdoms, Raphael came to stay with her fathers in his guards quarters in Valor until he could pass the exams to become a teacher in the palace. All before Althea was even a speck of dust in existence.

"You will be doing no such thing, there will be more work than ever in the forge, and I will need your help. The people of Taris will need your help," he tried to reason with her.

"Everyone I know and grew up beside has ascended and is marching together. What if I never get to see them again Poppa? What if this is it?"

"I have never seen such fine men and women of the Guard in my time. I have no doubt they will return, safe, and stronger than you can imagine."

"I can't fathom life without Aezel here." He was her best friend.

"I'm sorry, Althea, I am. But I'd be lying if I said I wasn't a bit relieved as well. I want you to be safe. And here in Taris, you will be safe, with me."

"You don't know that, I could get hurt from a falling tree branch, or I could be stuck with a pin at Glady's because I know she has been dying to get me into a proper dress." She knew she was being insufferable, but she felt she was betraying her friends.

There has to be a way. I will find it.

Captain Delmar's quarters were empty and so was his map room.

The small space was lit by the moon shining in from the single skylight in the center of the ceiling, illuminating the cluttered table covered in unopened scrolls and maps with the edges pinned down by square blocks of wood.

Althea turned to leave but stopped with a hand on the door. A tiny glint of light flickered on the floor by her foot. She stooped to pick it up, thinking that maybe it was one of her captain's trinkets that had fallen off his table in the haste of the testings. But when the cold, sharp metal pricked her finger, she realized it was an earring. A white stone set into a silver casing.

It looked familiar to Althea. She was sure she had seen it before. On one of the servants maybe? It was cheaply made, not something one of the higher generals would wear, and the Guard were prohibited to wear jewelry in the training grounds and barracks. Servants were not allowed in this room. Althea tucked the earring into the pocket of her pants and made a note to show Delmar when she found him. Which she did, just not where she expected.

He was standing in the empty hall of the barracks, the students opting to stay with their families for the last few days that they remained home. He looked like a shadow in the dark hall, unmoving and silent. If Althea didn't know the man, she would have thought him to be a ghost. But she was familiar with the way he held his shoulders, pulled back and down. Ready to strike. His head always tilted ever so slightly to the right, so small it was mostly unnoticeable.

"I am assuming you only made that noise so that I would know that you were there, and not because my teaching has failed you?"

"You always know me best, sir."

"What are you doing here so late?"

"I was looking for you. I found this in your mapping room, I didn't think it belonged."

Althea set the earring in Delmar's calloused hand. He lifted it up to his eye and turned it this way and that, analyzing.

"Huh, I will look into it." Now that she had his attention, she asked what she had really come there for.

"I want to – I need you to help me. I know I passed the ascension tests, and I feel like I should not be excluded from ascending based on a missing slip of paper. You can talk to Mayor Florence, convince him. Please. He is your brother, he will listen to you."

His shoulders dropped further – lower than Althea had ever seen the broad set go. He rubbed his eyes roughly, sighing, before he responded, "You want to serve your kingdom. And that is very honorable, Althea. More than you know. If you only knew how many have come to me today, begging me to make an exemption for them *not* to march. But Florence is not a man of negotiation, brother or not. What he says is final, that is the law of Taris.

"Besides, many will need to be protected here while we are gone. You will still be serving your kingdom. Just in a different way."

"Sir–"

"That is *enough*, Nova." His voice was not one of a friend anymore, but of her captain. He sounded weak. "It is final. Go get some rest, there is much to be done tomorrow."

CHAPTER EIGHT

ALTHEA

Althea didn't speak much the next day as she went about com-
pleting her daily chores. Horses did not stop needing to be fed
just because the world felt like it had shifted out from under her.

She only gave necessary hellos and good-byes as she went through
the market, not giving the shop owners time to ask the questions she
knew they were itching to have answered. Every single member of Taris
had been there yesterday and saw what had happened. She kept her
head down, handed over the proper amount of money and collected
her things.

The day should have been filled with joy and dancing around the
square to stringed instruments, but the streets held a forlorn atmos-
phere. The skies had turned to a dark, rainy gloom to match. Vastly
different from the bright blue morning that had graced the ascensions.
There were many merchant shops still open despite the dampness and
people ran from one stall to the next, hiding under the canopies to
escape the steady drizzle.

Althea scurried her way through the sodden streets, dodging small
children splashing in puddles, none the wiser to the coming change

brewing before them. The familiar smell of oil wafted to her from one of the blade shops.

She pulled her heavy, water laden cloak tighter around her shoulders and tugged the hood down until she could barely see out, but no one could see in, and kept walking.

She had almost forgotten about her deal with Niklas. The smell of the dubbin oil lingered, reminding her that she might not see him again for a very long time. She might not be able to make herself even with him.

The sharp scent followed her through the mass of people and rain, around the corner and down the first alley she came across. She started running, trying to escape from the scent that haunted. It hunted her.

She ran until the alley gave her no more room to run, then dropped to her knees, casting her bag aside and sucked the air in, trying to fill her belly like her Poppa taught her, but the air was so thick with moisture it wouldn't go farther than her throat.

Her vision fizzled around the edges. Digging her fingers into the cracks between the stones under her, she tried to hold onto the world while it spun.

She began to laugh hysterically, she was going to pass out. She had never had an attack from fear before, but she had seen it enough times in the Guard after the intense training they endured to understand that it was what was happening to her.

For the first time in her life, Althea was afraid.

Her laughter turned into a hacking cough, the warmth of tears burned behind her eyes, but she did not let them fall. The tight feeling in her throat was foreign as she dragged herself to lean back against the building beside her. Althea closed her eyes, lifting her face to the sky and let the rain wash away the sickening feeling, trying to steady her shaking breath.

Her eyes cracked open when she heard the sound of leather soles crunching against the stone. The rain fell heavier, meddling with the sounds of the market, and she was soaked through to her bones now. But the instinct that was drilled into her, calmed her and steadied her lungs, sharpening her focus once more.

The sound continued to echo down the alley.

Footsteps, one man, one hundred and eighty – no – one hundred ninety pounds, Althea calculated in the time it took her to blink, and let her eyes fall closed again.

She hated assuming the worst about every situation, but her father made her swear that she would at least *consider* that people could be dangerous, no matter how nice they looked or sounded, after she had been robbed by a drunk man two summers ago at the town festival.

She had tried to explain to her father that the man would have never gotten as close to her as he did if she hadn't felt sick from eating too much for breakfast. But, she made the promise after seeing the terror on his face when he saw the bruise on her arm and her money pouch gone.

After that, she'd trained an hour longer every day for months, and still did. She promised herself in the reflection of her water basin that night, that she would never let anyone think her weak again. Not if she could help it. She'd spent countless of her free hours in the rafters of the barracks, memorizing the gaits and sounds of her classmates and teachers as they walked, focusing on the smallest details, all the way down to the type of leather on the soles of their boot and the cloth of their clothes.

"Hello, Niklas." Althea said, but didn't stand. The sound of his steps halted before her, squelching in a puddle.

"Goodness, how do you do that?" Niklas shuddered. "It's freaky."

"What do you want?" She asked, ashamed at how defeated she sounded.

"I was getting oil for my blades and saw you run past." That explained why the smell seemed to have followed her, because it had been. But *why* he followed her, Althea did not know.

"What are you doing back here anyway?" He asked, unconcerned that she was crouched in a dark alley by herself.

"Why do you care?" She looked up at him, squinting against the rain.

"Because... I'm not supposed to say."

"Not supposed to say *what*?"

"It's probably best if I just leave, I have my answer anyway."

"Niklas!" Althea jumped away from the wall, tripping over her feet to where her bag lay, sodden with mud and slung it over her shoulder, jogging to catch up with his long strides. "What are you not telling me?"

"Oh you know, a little bit of this, a little bit of that. I don't have to tell you everything you know." He spun a wheat woven umbrella around his hand as deftly as he would a sword, spraying water off of its edges.

"Ugh!" Althea growled, grabbing his arm and pushed him against the wall. "Stop being cryptic you dolt, tell me right now or I will mess up your pretty hair," she threatened, scooping a handful of mud off her bag and gestured to his head.

"Aw, you think my hair is pretty? Thanks. I guess yours has been worse." Niklas brought a hand to his chest and pouted his bottom lip. Always one to turn an insult into a compliment.

Althea reared back and threw the mud. Niklas ducked, barely avoiding the thick sludge as it plastered the wall behind him. They stared at the splatter on the stone for a long second, both shocked she actually threw it.

He turned, not smiling anymore. "Now you've done it."

He grunted and reached for her, but she was already on the move. It couldn't really be called running, for her heavy cloak weighed her down, it was more of a scamper. The thrill of running from Niklas made her forget the sorrow that had choked her only moments before.

Althea let out a whoop of laughter when she broke out of the alley's entrance and back into the market. She turned left, racing toward the training grounds, pumping her arms and legs as fast as they could go, her breathing came easy at last.

She made it outside the market just as Niklas caught up to her. He wrapped an arm around her waist from behind, sending them both flying and skidding on the wet grass as they fumbled to gain an edge on each other.

The men, women and even the children of Taris knew well enough about Niklas and Althea's fights. They happened often enough and just about anywhere. No one stared for too long as they grappled with one another.

Althea briefly made it to her feet before Niklas grabbed her ankle and dragged her back down. He leaned over her, breathing heavily, his eyes slightly unfocused like they always were when he sparred or hunted. Before Althea could protest, he swiped a handful of mud down the side of her face, from her forehead to her chin.

Usually, she would have been furious at him, but she couldn't seem to garner the familiar anger that came from being around him.

She laughed.

She laughed until her side ached. She laughed at Niklas's look of confusion. Laughed at her pitiful self.

It didn't take long for Niklas to join her, he flicked the rest of the mud from his hand onto the sodden ground and flopped down beside her. She didn't know how long they stayed like that, lying on the wet earth as people passed by, giving weird looks at the two, muddy, frizzy haired guards.

Their errands forgotten, they watched the rain as it fell through the trees and splattered the earth. She turned her head and looked at him. *Really* looked at him. He laid still for a long time, rain gathering in the hollow of his throat.

"I'm sorry, Niklas, that I'm not going with you."

"Don't be. I can't afford to forget who the *real* enemy is and end up fighting you," he said with a chuckle and met her eyes for what felt like the first time.

"Yeah, wouldn't want you to go savage on me, would we?" She smiled.

"No, we wouldn't."

CHAPTER NINE

—•—

NIKLAS

They parted ways as the sun began to descend and the first of the lanterns were lit.

He had completed the last few errands he needed to do. Getting extra bread, jerky, oils and flour for not only him and his father, but took large overfilled burlap sacks of the stuff to the covered wagons in the stables to be used for the march. He didn't know what stopped him from telling Althea the truth. That her father had asked him to keep an eye on her.

"Why not have Aezel do it?" He had asked.

The burly man paused, contemplation playing on his features. "Aezel is her good friend, but he doesn't know Althea like you do. You know how she thinks, where she likes to hide. I'm worried about her. She is heartbroken. I have never seen her like this." Niklas had only accepted out of respect for the former member of the Guard and his father's friend.

Earlier, when he followed Althea, he had paused at the entrance of the alley, hearing her cry out. He had never heard a sound like that from anyone before, especially not from her. It made his mind go blank. Something inside him lurched when he saw her reddened face, staring up at him from the cold, wet ground.

Instead of going inside his home to the warm air and drying off, Niklas grabbed the ax leaning against it and lit a small lantern, making his way into the small woods.

Shucking off his wet cloak and shirt, Niklas swung the ax into a fallen tree limb, sending up a spray of wood shavings as he swung again and again. He kept moving, cutting every suitable kindling he could find into foot long wedges to dry out in time for winter. He would need to leave a lot of wood for his father as winter was only a few months away.

It was five hours before dawn when he felt like he could stop, wiping away the sweat on his brow and admired his work. The pile of lumber stacked up waist high and was as wide as he was tall. Satisfied, Niklas brushed his hands together and dusted the splinters from his hair and shoulders. His father had come out with water twice earlier in the night, each time Niklas had turned him away, assuring him that he was nearly done, but had continued for two more hours.

He eased the front door open, cringing at the whine that came from the old hinges, adding it to the list in his mind of things that needed to be done before the end of the week.

Niklas stretched his cramping back and flopped on his bed, not bothering to wash away the dirt and grime from the day, already asleep before his head hit the pillow.

The next day looked much the same. Rain came and went sporadically while he hunted, bringing in three bucks that he and his father spent the afternoon skinning and preserving the meat. He would sell the skins and antlers to a tailor in the market.

In town, people ducked in and out of buildings and homes, restlessly preparing in the short amount of time. The uncertainty that had clutched the city had begun to melt away, turning into steady streams of persevering work.

Women cooked for families where the father would be marching. Men too old to serve helped with loading wagons, and Niklas volunteered to help with extra training classes alongside Captain Delmar, where he taught his key moves to people he would normally use them against.

The Guard is mighty, I just hope we are mightier than the enemy.

Althea did not attend training. In fact Niklas had not seen her since they had ran after each other in the market the night before. Aezel asked Niklas if he had seen her as did a few others. He had no clue, he told them. It was unlike Althea to miss any opportunity to practice and teach her favorite techniques, she loved helping others in the art of the sword.

She wasn't the only one missing, Niklas noted. He had not seen Sir Erling or any other of the queen's guards since they announced the war at the feast. But their horses, with the shiniest, blackest coats he had ever seen, he saw everyday working alongside the duller coated horses volunteered by some farmers.

The crookback old men who had served in wars past were warriors of their own even then.

With two days left till the march, everything was nearly completed.

The cloth coverings on the wagons were close to bursting from the sheer amount of food needed to last the week-long journey, not to mention the wagons holding the weapons.

Those were hulking ones, the walls made of steel so thick that a *brav* wouldn't be able to get in. They had no windows and the wheels were wrapped in knobby chains. No amount of rough terrain would get it stuck. They were usually used for transporting prisoners that were to have a trial in the presence of the queen.

Niklas had been on a few of those trips when he was thirteen seasons and he knew that the prisoners were not treated well by the queens guards, most beaten too close to death to even plead their cause, and were in most cases, sent to be hanged for crimes as simple as stealing food to feed their families.

He had always tried to talk to the guards for the sake of the prisoners and ended up having his own hands whipped. He would later sit by a fire, holding a bandage to his hand and watch the prisoners, backs bleeding and raw, sharing his pain with them.

Eventually he had stopped going on processions as he rose in rank, his spot being taken by some other young guard that didn't talk back.

Niklas fisted his hand, running a thumb over the two, thick scars that crossed the back of his left hand in a protruding X. His reminder of who the queen really was. He had still sworn his oath to protect the throne, but not for her. He did it to protect the innocent people of his kingdom.

The last day, there was nothing left to do and was a day to rest, pray and spend precious time with loved ones before they all would leave at two hours past dawn.

Niklas and his father stayed up late, eating and packing what few unnecessary belongings he wanted to take. Some extra underclothes, a few of his favorite daggers and a palm sized sketch of him and his father in the palace gardens. It held no color other than the charcoal used by the artist. But Niklas's mind filled in the vibrant red of the rose bush behind his father holding him when he was an infant. The dark blue delphinium, and summer golden sun flowers soaring into the sky. And the wizened, piercing blue eyes of his father.

Niklas must have gotten his eyes, a mix of muddy brown and scarlet red from his mother, who had left days after he had been born, no explanation and leaving nothing of her behind for her son. That was what his father had told him.

The picture had been drawn after Niklas's father had retired from teaching in the palace and moved far away, claiming to want a simpler life from the hustle of the city. He had encountered a student one day, traveling through the kingdoms of Laisren, that he had taught from his beginning days in the palace and remembered she was an excellent artist. She drew the sketch using the descriptions from his fathers memory.

Niklas hoped to one day see those gardens in person and find out if it was anything as brilliant as what the paper showed. But for now he just needed to survive the next few months, the next few days, the next few hours.

CHAPTER TEN

—·—

ALTHEA

She could not believe what he had asked her to do.

Niklas's father had come to her home late, after she had already crawled into bed. She had been tossing and turning for at least an hour, her brain refusing to quiet. Her father always slept like a log and never woke up from the knocking.

Althea was surprised to see Raphael on the other side of the door. She had tried to invite him in from the cold but he had adamantly refused, saying he only needed a moment. She slipped outside, barefoot, but wrapped a cloak around her shoulders.

"Mr. Stallard, is everything alright? Is Niklas okay?" She didn't know what it was she felt, thinking that something had happened to him.

"Miss Althea, I am terribly sorry for waking you, but it is urgent." He looked behind her into her home to make sure no one was listening. "You *must* go with the march tomorrow, it is imperative that Niklas isn't hurt, or worse. I know you were probably relieved when you found out you wouldn't be going, but *he cannot die*." Raphael whispered the last words, fear filling the wrinkled lines on face.

"What do you mean? I can't march, it would be leaving my post. Believe me, I've been looking into everything. I cannot find a way around my pardon. Mayor Florence and Captain Delmar are not bending. I've even tried to contact the assessors themselves but all of the mail carriers are refusing to make rounds. I want to go more than anything." Althea expressed her lack of findings drearily.

"And why do you only mention Niklas when there are hundreds of sons and daughters leaving their homes?" She didn't mean for it to come out as harsh as it did, she knew the man well. He was like an uncle to her for how close he was to her father. But she didn't like that he was pleading for one soldier and not for her to help them all.

"I can't explain it to you now, but you need to know that Niklas must be protected at all costs. Please, Althea, for the sake of Laisren. For God and Kingdom."

Raphael pulled out a bag from behind him and pushed it into her frozen hands, bowed stiffly and turned to leave, quicker than she had ever seen a man his age move. She watched him walk away, fading into the night, dumbfounded.

Sighing, she looked into the bag, her breath clouding in front of her before she stopped breathing altogether.

She hurried back inside and climbed into her loft as quietly as she could, throwing the bag on her bed. She paced, shaking her head and rubbing at the goosebumps on her arms that had nothing to do with the cold. Then for an hour she sat on her bed, hugging the bag to her chest with the emerald green cloak rolled neatly inside.

The sun rose, and Althea had not slept. She had spent the night shining Niklas boots. It didn't help ease her mind, but it at least kept her in her loft and away from seeking answers.

After attempting to eat breakfast with her father, Althea quickly discovered that she could not stomach the food she normally loved. Not on a day like that one.

Rows of wagons stood in uniformed lines in front of the gates of Taris, wood creaking. Metal twinkled on the men's armor and horses were strapped into harnesses as they did a second check of their equipment.

The bag on Althea's back had weighed heavily on her already burdened shoulders ever since that morning before the sun rose, when she had carried it outside the main gates of Taris and hid it in a group of dried out bushes. Even though she had dropped the bag several hours ago, she felt the ghost of its weight as her gaze swept over the organized movements of the soldiers.

She paused when she saw Niklas, sitting atop a beautiful brown horse with a midnight tail. The bronze pauldron on his armor indicating him as an upper Lieutenant and a sword she had never seen before strapped to his side. He spoke with his father, placing a hand on the older man's shoulder, giving a comforting squeeze. His attention was pulled away by a young man, fourteen maybe, clearly only having been a farmer his whole life, and needed help with tying down a strap on one of the wagons.

Niklas' eyes skimmed over the crowd before he dismounted and handed his reins off to a nearby soldier. His gaze landed briefly on her, and gave an almost imperceptible nod before taking the ties in his hands. Althea returned the gesture and kept searching.

Aezel, who she had been looking for, finally caught her eyes, standing tall in his shining silver armor and leathers. He didn't stand out from the foliage in his green cloak, with his green eyes almost as dark. He almost blended into the crowd, but she could not miss his golden hair, the sun rising up behind him, casting a halo around his head as he came to stand in front of her, a crooked smile splayed on his lips.

"If you think this is how you get rid of me, think aga–" He didn't get a chance to finish. Althea threw her arms around him, not caring that his armor scratched the skin of her face.

"Hey. Al, it's okay." Aezel wrapped his warm arms around Althea, one hand on her back, the other keeping her head tucked close so no one could see her face hold the worry she felt.

Even in the midst of his own fears, Aezel still cared that Althea had a reputation, one she didn't want disputed. She took a deep, steadying breath and wiped the back of her hand across her cold nose, pulling back just enough to see his face.

"Aezel, I have to tell you something. You have to promise not to tell *anyo*–" A loud whistle swept through the fog, cutting her off. The confusion on Aezel's face from her frantic tone disappeared, replaced with suppressed sorrow. His mouth quirked playfully but it didn't reach his eyes.

"Don't forget what it is. You can tell me when this is all over, when I come back." He brushed away the stubborn section of her hair that she could never keep in her braid, tucking it behind her ear.

And with that, every guard that was called to march, lined up on either side of the train of horses and wagons. Soldiers held gold tipped spears, guarding the line of food and equipment. They all looked straight ahead to Captain Delmar sitting on his steed, flanked by the three queen's guards, looking past the gates and into the Cerridwen forest, awaiting the order.

"Today, we embark with seven thousand, may God return the same home. For God and Kingdom, for the Kingdom of Valarie, and for those we leave behind. MARCH!" Captain Delmar shouted and tapped the flanks of his dappled gray horse, setting off a chain reaction.

Mud flew into the air, and wheels dug deep tracks into the earth. Three thousand men went towards the forest, Niklas in front with the higher guards, the other half taking off down the beaten path.

Before long, they were out of sight, and families moved, holding tight to one another. Parents soothing crying children whose siblings may never return, and slowly, they departed to their lives.

Althea stayed for far too long, the sun crawling through the sky faster than she could fathom. She told her father, who stayed beside her the whole time, an arm wrapped around her shoulders, that it was okay for him to retire for the night. His leg was bothering him more than usual today. She told him that she wouldn't be far behind him, her heart nearly breaking in her chest at the lie.

She had avoided Niklas and his father on purpose, not wanting to slip up and reveal herself and what she was about to do.

Althea waited ten minutes after her father left, and as soon as the sun dipped behind the tip of Mount Absinth, she moved. She forced herself to push away all the thoughts and voices in her head telling her to stop, that she was making a huge mistake.

She untethered her horse, saddled and waiting just beyond the gates, tucked in a shadow with her bag and swung into the saddle. She unhooked her bow from where she had it strapped on the horse's side and slipped it over her head, taking one last look back at Taris. At her home. At the life that she was leaving behind.

"I'm so sorry, Poppa," she whispered around the dryness in her throat.

Clicking her tongue, Althea commanded her horse Bronte to run, letting her eat up the distance.

Despite the feeling of her heart shredding apart in her chest, Althea felt a sense of peace in the deepest part of her soul. She had prayed relentlessly through the night, asking her God what to do. And when it came down to it, Althea felt that this was right.

She could only hope that what she wrote in the note on her father's bed would keep him home, far away from Caedmon. And far away from the war.

CHAPTER ELEVEN

— • —

NIKLAS

The first day in the Cerridwen was brutally humid despite it being the beginning days of fall.

The guards that chose to sleep without pitching a tent become sticky in the night with tree sap that fell from the largest cedar trees that Niklas had ever seen.

Despite what most people thought, the forest was not so densely packed that they could not fit the wagons through, which made the journey deceivingly easy. Niklas knew better. There were so many men walking on foot. Some were bound to stumble upon a *bravs* nest, or a curious, hungry *khourge* might stumble upon them. Some would find themselves hungry and think that a bush of *ketabome* were just regular blueberries. Like the name suggests, their stomachs would balloon out and make it feel like they were about to explode.

Niklas learned that the hard way. If you were lucky, you would survive and the effects of the berry's would wear off. If you weren't...

When they made camp on the second night, forty miles further into the forest, the temperature evened out into a subtle chill. He could almost smell the change in the seasons, the air was crisp and just cold enough for a cloud of fog to surround the camp as men and women blew heat into their hands and started small fires.

Niklas shoved the last bite of venison in his mouth and skirted through a tangle of vines around the command tent, pushing the flap aside and stepped inside to join the nightly briefing with Delmar and the three men still cloaked in black.

Is it a fashion choice, or is it just the color of your personalities leaking out. Niklas rubbed a hand over his mouth to hide a smirk, the sharp stubble on his chin scratched at his palm. He would have to take care of that before too long, he hated the feeling of his facial hair tugging on his clothing when he turned his head.

All the Queen's Guards, besides Admiral Erling, have never spoken outside of their company, and Niklas could understand why. Their voices were rough, like they had eaten sand every day of their lives. He wondered what hardships these men had faced in their lives to earn the scars that riddled their faces, throats, and hands. They kept their bodies covered and never bathed around the other men. Niklas was certain that it was not due to modesty.

"Lieutenant Stallard. Perfect timing." Delmar waved him over. His thick, tanned hands splayed on the map covering the table in the middle of the tent.

Niklas had been given the title of First Lieutenant a month ago, and had only been tasked with helping his Captain in small meetings with Mayor Florence and the local Guard watch. They were mostly about petty thefts, someone blaming his neighbor over a loose goat that ate his crops and such.

The most concerning thing Niklas had ever had to deal with was a series of vandalisms. A stray group of rebels that had painted the symbol of the rebellion all over Taris. The silhouette of a man's head, dripping blood.

The rebels claimed that the queen wasn't the rightful heir to the throne. But no one believed it, the queen's father had only had two children, the first child, a son, and the second, her. She had been the only birth since the king passed away shortly after she was born. There was no other child like the rebels were claiming.

The rebellion's stories always changed every season or so. Last winter they claimed the queen's first child, a still born son, was still alive.

Now Niklas was helping lead a war, and was expected to give his opinion on what direction was best to approach from, what passes they would have to navigate through that would be the fastest and safest. What soldiers were to be on the front lines and who would be most useful as physicians. It was a big shift in responsibility, but Niklas didn't mind the planning, having his voice heard and being debated with.

"We were just discussing what we should do once we reach the Norvern river tomorrow." Erling pointed at the wide, blue swirling line on the map. "It might take an entire day to go around and even if we did it is mud land."

"We may be able to find a high shelf in the river and cross at low tide, but it would be near dark." Niklas crouched until he was eye level with the map. "There." He stood and pointed at a marking next to the river that looked like an arrow, but also kind of like the head of a lizard, that pointed to a line on the river that was a little darker blue than the rest. "You wouldn't be able to tell the difference in the wax used for this line if it wasn't for the angle of the candle," Niklas explained.

His father, having been a teacher in the palace, helped Niklas greatly; they had a map hidden in the locked drawer of his fathers study, that at different angles of light, revealed hidden passages and warnings, so that if it were ever stolen, it would help no one if they did not know what they were looking for.

His father had made him swear that he would never tell anyone he had it and Niklas had wanted to learn the map so badly that he forwent his dinner for a week just to spend his time getting the information in his head. It made sense that the Admiral would possess such a map.

Jekel, one of the queen's guards, came around the table. He stood taller than all of the men and had to duck his head under the tent supports. He tilted his head side to side, leaning in to see the mark.

"Hmph, looks like the squirrel knows his way around a parchment." Jekel's voice was so low and rough that if you didn't know it was coming from a man, you would think it was a boulder rolling down a mountainside.

They had only known each other for less than a week but the nickname 'squirrel' was given to Niklas by the *brav* of a man. He figured it was because of the nuts in the toffee he had in his bag.

Jekel clapped a large hand on Niklas's back, almost sending him sprawling onto the table. A cacophony of gravel filled laughs erupted.

"All in support?" Delmar asked, raising his right hand.

Niklas waited until he was outside of the tent to grin at all of the hands that were raised in favor. He fought to keep his smile at bay all the way through the closely packed tents, to a small creek south of the camp.

He rinsed out his mouth and rubbed a cloth over his face and under his arms. It had only been three days since they left and he already could not wait until he could take a steaming hot bath again.

He had always been a man who enjoyed a few of his luxuries, but he could live without those. What he would miss more was the fact that after everything they were going to have to face, nothing would ever feel the same again. Not the quiet Sunday's with his father, going to the common room in the barracks for a game of cards with his friends, or even Althea, making him angry to the point his chest felt ready to explode.

The memory of her laugh resounded in his head. It seemed to escape out through his ears and bounce between the surrounding trees before finding its way back to him. Shaking the sound out of his head, Niklas deemed he was clean and smelled half-way decent, and pulled his shirt back on, tying his leather vest over it.

He was ripped away from his thoughts by the sound of a branch breaking behind him. His head snapped toward the sound. He couldn't see anything. The sky had already darkened into a rich purple, the blue lights that streak across the night sky starting to make their appearance.

The time had slipped away from Niklas and when he looked back to camp, he saw how far he had gotten from it. He pulled out his favorite dagger and started a calm but hurried pace back to his tent.

He had let himself get distracted, a mistake he would not be making again. He refused to die because he got in the path of some hungry animal.

The camp had to be packed up before sunrise if they were to make it to the Norvern river in time for low tide. They paused only long enough at noon to give the guards a chance to relieve themselves and for their horses to drink from a thin stream.

The flanks of his steed were foamy from the long hours they rode, and Niklas could only hope the horses strapped to the wagons were as strong as the farmers promised they were.

It became harder and harder to tell how many hours it had been since they left that morning, the trees had somehow become even larger than the ones he had been astonished at in the first two days. The smallest limbs at their crowns were wider than his horse was at the middle, and the leaves blocked out nearly all visible light to the point of having to use torches to navigate day and night.

They reached the river at what Niklas guessed was five o'clock in the evening. One last look at the map showed that they were within a few hundred feet of the shelf, and he guessed low tide would be around eight. They would have to be quick.

At least the river banks were solid, flat stone and they would make fast progress without the thick layer of leaves pulling at their feet.

To Niklas's dismay, the sky began to spit at them. He prayed the gusts of cool wind were sending the storm away and not straight for them

There was no way to know exactly where they stood in relation to the shelf, no landmarks were drawn in the map except for the lizard head arrow.

Erling called out to the soldiers to hold their positions and ready themselves to move at his proclamation. One hour passed, then two. The misty rain turned steady, still not enough to affect the tides yet.

A grotesque slurping sound came from the water and everyone froze, holding their breath. Niklas leaned closer to listen.

And then the water began receding, one centimeter at a time.

Sir Erling and Keetie, only shadows in their black cloaks against the night, walked in separate directions alongside the water, gazing in, tossing pebbles, looking for a sign of the rocky, or sandy, shelf as the water receded back to its source.

The two men walked one hundred feet away from the group before Keetie raised a fist and let out a high whistle. The water had drawn back enough that Niklas could see the flat expanse of sandstone that jutted out from where Keetie stood. Its middle, still covered in the cold looking water.

The soldiers gave a collective sigh, faces breaking into smiles at the prospect of not having to waste a day going around and through the mud lands. Admiral Erling jogged back to them and gave the order to move.

Keetie took fifty men with him to start, telling them to dismount and walk next to their horses on the path to make sure it was going to be stable enough for the wagons to journey across. They made it a hundred feet over the nearly three hundred they needed to cross and signaled that it was safe for the rest to follow.

The wagons went next and Niklas and Erling stayed with the group of the last few hundred that would bring up the rear when a sharp twang came from behind them. There was a shout from within in the first group that Keetie was leading and Niklas craned his neck to see what made the guards halt.

He wished he hadn't.

Keetie clutched at the arrow protruding out of his chest. It was just light enough for Niklas to see the red that sprayed out of the man's mouth onto the stone beneath him before it was washed away by the last trickle of water.

A massive roar came from behind him, the tree limbs lining the bank were shaking and bowing underneath the weight of the men that spilled out from their cover, swords drawn.

More arrows followed.

Niklas dove off his horse and unsheathed his sword in one motion, ready to engage with the first of the men as they came onto the bank. The black arrows of Valarie flew overhead, mixing with the ones of blood red coming from the dense trees, blurring the night sky into a frenzy of color.

He threw his mind into his fighting calm when the first man touched foot onto the shore. Niklas parried a brutal downward swing that made the nerves in his arm sing, threw his weight into his sword and pushed the man back.

He was big, but Niklas was fast and before he could make another move, Niklas had slashed the edge of his sword across his opponent's stomach, ready to meet the swinging ax of the woman behind the man when he fell to the side.

Her neck was covered in puffy scars and inked paintings covered them in a failed attempt to hide the marks. She was fast, but not faster than Althea, who he was used to sparring with.

Niklas switched his tactic and used the body strewn, uneven ground to his advantage, jumping back from the dagger she threw. She lunged forward but tripped on a stone and fell onto the sword of the man he had killed before her.

"NO! KEEP GOING, GET ACROSS!" Erling's voice was unmistakable. Niklas took down three more men, and spared a quick glance when there was a break in the flood of battle.

The horses that weren't attached to the wagons reared back and bolted, sending a spray of water into the air. Niklas saw the soldiers on the shelf stumbling, trying to turn back to help, but the wagons blocked them in. One man slipped off the side and was whisked away by the current.

Wait, there is a current? Niklas turned his attention to the water and was horrified to see the tide was already rising back, faster than it had gone out.

"GO WITHOUT US!" Niklas called out. "THE TIDE!"

"FALL BACK! SCATTER, SWIM ACROSS IF YOU CAN!" Delmar screamed from his spot among the wagons, the water beginning to lap at their ankles and the wheels of the wagons.

Aezel knelt on top of one next to Delmar alongside two other soldiers with his bow in hand, shooting arrows fast, their arms a blur of motion. He had oozing cuts on his face and hands as he dodged arrows that were being fired back.

The attackers were wearing thick, fur cloaks, their faces covered in swirling red ink. *These are not Oaksteadian men, nor Palmerian.* He had never heard of savages living this far east before, certainly not in the Cerridwen.

Niklas swung again and again. Parried and ducked, his heart pounding in his chest. It became mayhem as his soldiers found breaks in the battle and jumped into the water, making a swim for the shelf. Niklas was pushed violently by one of his own as the soldier ran for the water, but was struck down by an enemy arrow. The water pulled him into its depths and he was gone.

A man, easily twice the size of Jekel, stood over him, grunting something in a sporadic language. Spit flew out of his mouth as he chanted and raised an ax over his head. Niklas did not close his eyes.

A spray of hot blood blanketed him, speckling across his face. He didn't feel any pain, the sound of battle still raged in his ears, his eyes still opened and closed as he blinked, the world slowing around him.

The monster's eyes, looking down on him, became confused, and then blank, before he slumped forward and fell beside Niklas, a dagger sticking out from his back.

He blinked the red out of his eyes and his breath caught in his throat when he saw a dappled gray horse, flanks covered in frothing red blood, the rain streaking it down its legs. It slid to a stop in front of him. His vision blurred in and out, reminding him to breathe. He gasped, a mouthful of iron tinged air filling his lungs, bringing his sight into sharper focus.

He must be seeing wrong. It must be a hallucination from something he ate, or the rain must be creating the image before him. Because there was no way what he was seeing should have been possible.

Sitting on the horse was a small woman, cloaked in green. Her brown hair braided back in a way he knew all too well.

Althea.

She extended her hand down, yelling something at him. Everything sounded muffled. An arrow landed in the dirt beside him, dusting him with a spray of soil and the world sped back up, the sharp sound of metal on metal, arrows whistling filled every inch of the shore. The shelf that had separated the river for them was gone.

Niklas pushed himself to his feet and grabbed onto Althea's hand, pulling himself onto the back of the horse behind her. She steered the mount away from the river and kicked the horse into as fast a gallop as it could manage, dodging blades and arrows that aimed for them.

Niklas swung his blade from the higher ground, taking down as many of the savage men as he could as they raced away from the battle.

There were no more of his men left on their side of the river. Besides him and Althea, there was only the enemy.

CHAPTER TWELVE

— · —

ALTHEA

What in God's green earth was I thinking? Althea shook her head.

She had nearly been seen last night. She had gotten way too close to the camp. Her hunger had begun to nag at her and the smell of the variety of foods had made her reasoning stumble.

For the last three days she had been surviving solely on the berries she brought and scavenged and the rock hard bread that she knew her father would not miss from home. If she had planned a little more carefully she would have brought tea and fresh jerky. But she guessed one could not plan very well at all when trying to hide their sudden departure.

She was certain that the man by the creek had not seen her, but it made her fall back farther than she liked. Afraid of being discovered, she had kept a mile between them. That was until she heard the screaming. It came from in front of her, behind, and... above?

Before Althea could blink, the trees grew limbs, arms and legs broke free from the cover of the foliage. Leaves, the smallest of which, were at least as big as her bed back home. Why had she not thought someone might use that to their advantage?

Althea drew her bow in her left hand and held three of her throwing knives in her right with an arrow between her fingers.

She murmured to Bronte, whose ears were flattened to her head, telling her to calm. Althea used her knees to give the signal to back up.

The men did not see her in the dying light, nor did they hear her horse shuffling in the leaves as they screamed and ran in the very direction she was headed.

Toward her army.

"No," she whispered.

Over the cries of men and clanks of steel she clearly heard the sound of orders being shouted. She could not make out what they said, but she knew the voices were Valarian.

Althea itched to race into the battle to help her men, but she knew that she would only end up face to face with death before she would be able to see even one green cloak.

She waited for the forest to settle, until the only sounds were now in front of her by the river. She squeezed Bronte's sides with her knees, sending the horse into a canter, eyes roving the trees, arrow nocked and ready.

She knew battle would not be pretty, but she had not been prepared for the scene that would meet her when she broke through the line of trees and flew onto the river bank.

The sound struck her first, it was disorienting. The flash of steel soaring through the air left streaks in her eyes. The strength of the iron in the air choked her before her thoughts slid into the back room. The adrenaline that fighting brought her back home was nothing compared to the way her heart was racing now. It was so, so much worse.

Althea's eyes darted quickly over the scene, not quite grasping the image, the fighting men and women all blurring into a muddy brown mist. All the wagons were on the other bank. Althea had no idea how; there was no bridge in sight. The dirt underneath her horse's hooves was covered in sharp rocks.

She saw a head of golden hair flash across the blue water and Althea felt herself take a breath, knowing that Aezel was out of range of the arrows that blurred the sky and no sign of attack was present on their side. She was brought back to herself when a spear came flying straight for her head.

Althea ducked backwards, a hot searing pain raced along her jaw and she shot an arrow when she identified who threw it before another spear could be sent her way.

Her heart dropped in the same moment as the man's body did. He fell face first into the bloody soil.

Oh God.

She sat frozen on her horse as arrows plunged into the earth around her, staring at the man's bare, tattooed back. Althea snapped out of her horrified state when a woman raised her sword, running toward her. Althea threw a dagger. And then another, and two more of her arrows found their homes in the flesh of the madmen.

She saw a flash of dark green in the corner of her eye as one of her men was pushed over into the path of who could only be called a giant.

The hulking figure, clothed in a patchwork of wolf skin, was so tall that if Althea were to ride up next to him, they'd meet face to face.

When the giant man reared his ax up, screaming something unintelligible, Althea threw her last dagger. Cutting through the furs on his back, burning deep until the hilt disappeared and the blade found its resting place.

Althea didn't have to look too closely to know that she and the man on the ground were the last two Valarian soldiers left on that side of the river. She rode over to him, ready to get both of them out of there.

"Get up." She commanded, reaching her hand down and tried not to show her surprise to find that the man was Niklas.

His eyes were wide and dazed.

"Pull yourself together, Niklas, and *get on*."

Niklas blinked once, his eyes refocusing and grasped her hand, pulling himself up behind her and they ran.

Althea wasn't sure how far they got. She had steered Bronte away from the river to lose the hoard that had chased them. Now the sun was beginning to rise upon the earth, chasing away the stars and filling the pale blue sky with streaks of orange and purple.

She was so tired. She leaned into the warmth that spread across her chest and legs. Her eyes threatened to close again. But at that thought, the memory of the last night and the rush of the fight woke her from her dreamless sleep. She had not remembered falling asleep. She was still moving, the jostling of her horse beneath her.

Althea raised an arm to rub the blur out of her eyes, gasping when a sharp pain went shooting from her left shoulder, down her arm and into her fingers. She let out a dry croak.

The warmth in front of her stiffened and shifted.

She raised her head, wincing at the pounding behind her eyes from the movement.

"Welcome back to the land of the living, darling," said the man she was pushed up against in the saddle. When she looked down, noticing that she was riding a brown horse instead of gray, a spike of fear sent a shockwave through her stomach.

"Don't worry. Bronte is behind us. She tripped and we took a tumble. You hit your head pretty hard." Now that she was more awake she recognized who the man was.

Niklas.

Blushing that she had been leaning so close to him, and had leaned into his warmth, Althea used her good arm and pushed against the saddle, putting as much space between them that the seat would allow. A quick glance behind her confirmed that Bronte was indeed following them, her reins tied to a metal ring on Niklas's saddle.

"How far-" Althea cleared her throat against the dryness. "How long have we been riding?" She felt along her leg and was relieved to feel that her water skin was still intact and took a small sip.

"Five hours since Maygo found us," Niklas said, scratching the sweaty horse underneath its mane. The horse snorted and leaned into his touch.

"Do you know where we are?" Althea asked him, rubbing at her sore shoulder, hoping that feeling would soon return to her fingers.

"A couple miles south of the Norvern river for sure. They stopped chasing us as soon as we got under the cover of the trees. It was like they just decided that was enough battle for the night and dispersed."

"That is weird," Althea agreed.

"Well, now, the troops will be running extra scouts ahead to make sure we don't meet any unexpected guests." Althea heard the accusation in his words without him having to say anything more.

"I couldn't stay behind. You can call me a coward, bu–" He cut her off, clearly not shaken enough from the ambush, or from her sudden arrival to lose his confidence.

"Doesn't matter, you saved some of our men, and you definitely can't go back now that we know these woods have an infestation problem." They rode in silence for a moment.

In a voice quieter than the autumn breeze that tousled the leaves, Althea spoke, "I've never killed before." Her voice broke on the word 'killed'.

She felt Niklas stiffen, but neither spoke again. There was nothing that could be said. She signed up for this when she left Taris, and she would have to learn how to deal with it. She wanted to serve her kingdom, and Althea had just found out what that really meant.

"We should stop, clean up a bit. There," Niklas spoke after a beat of silence and dropped down from his horse in front of a small cave opening. "I'll scout it out." He drew his sword and entered the cave cautiously.

Althea hopped off Maygo and clutched the hilt of her own sword, searching the trees and listening for any sign of danger. Human or animal.

"It's safe," his voice echoed out the entrance of the cave, making Althea jump. It was a tight fit for their horses, but once they had started a small fire and brought as much grass as they could find for the horses to eat, they were finally able to assess the damage to their bodies.

Niklas only had a small scratch on his forehead and a sore – but thankfully not broken – ankle. Althea hissed as Niklas pulled the needle and thread through the skin at her jaw.

"It doesn't get any easier," Niklas said, startling her out of her thoughts. "I killed a man when I was only thirteen seasons old." His voice was tender, and Althea was thankful for the distraction from the pain.

"When you went with the prisoners?" Althea guessed.

"Hmhm." He nodded his head, tying a knot in the stitch. "One had tried to escape. I meant for the arrow only to slow him down, but he tripped. The arrow I meant for his leg pierced his heart." Hearing Niklas talk about his past was strange, they never spoke about their private moments, and certainly not matters of the heart.

They had always kept each other at arms length despite their close upbringing. Their father's were closer than blood brothers, and they always joked about the bouts of bickering between the two, and how they sounded like an old married couple. They always teased about the two getting married one day. That shut them up from a fight any day.

"But that was an accident." Althea bit her lip against the pull on her skin as Niklas tied off the last piece of string.

"And I would consider stumbling upon an ambush in the middle of the night an accident too, wouldn't you?" He reasoned.

"I guess." Althea pressed a bandage to her jaw once Niklas had finished applying a slimy, stinging poultice to prevent infection. "Thank you."

One at a time, they took turns in the cave, washing themselves down with the freezing cold water from a fresh moon pool tucked in the darkness at the back of the cave, while the other went outside to give some privacy.

Althea made sure she was extra observant of her surroundings while she picked a rainbow assortment of berries she knew were safe to eat, skipping a bush full of *ketabome*.

It weighed heavily on her mind that she had not been able to sense the forest *full* of the savage men. She had been tired, hungry, and distracted. Her thoughts had been with her father, wondering what he was doing, if he was okay. She should have known they were there.

The forest was so quiet. Althea rapped a knuckle on a rock by the cave's entrance, just to make sure she hadn't gone deaf. A group of fireflies that had been buzzing around raced away from her before realizing that she was not a threat to them and continued on to cast their green glow onto the rocks.

"Almost done," Niklas called from inside.

Althea blushed, she hadn't been trying to hurry him. *What do you think knocking on the rock would have meant to him?* She bumped her fist into her forehead a few times, trying to shake the blush away.

"All clear."

Althea thanked God for being back in the cave. The dusk that fell over the forest brought with it a sticky fog and the sounds of howls from wolves and screeches of *khourges* had begun to replace the eerie quiet.

"Dinner is served. I have an excellent selection of berries to choose from. There is red, blue, purple, and green. Those would probably be best in a tea, but help yourself." Althea laid the bundle by the fire and lowered herself onto the hard ground with a groan. Niklas had added more wood to the fire while she had been out and the space was

81

blissfully warm and bright, a pot of water bubbling lightly over the flames.

He waddled on his knees around the fire, considering the pile of fruit, scratching at his scruffy jaw. Althea had never seen Niklas unshaven before. It was a sight so unfamiliar to her that she stared for a couple seconds longer, noticing that there was a small patch on his right cheek that didn't grow anything, giving a clear look at his one dimple.

She looked away, hoping he hadn't noticed her stare and stood to stretch, her hands brushing the low, stone ceiling. She took a deep breath in and fought to keep her mouth closed against a yawn so she would not break her fresh stitches.

As she began to spread out her bed roll, a sweet aroma filled the space, sending a painful lurch through her stomach, reminding her that she had not eaten since the night before. She turned around to see Niklas nibbling at what looked like a square vanilla cake with some mashed berries on top, his lips stained a deep red from the fruit.

A swell of annoyance flitted in her chest, but she forced it down, knowing that if they were going to have any chance of making it out of this forest alive, they were going to have to not kill each other first.

Althea rummaged around in her satchel for some of her stale bread and stiff jerky, but couldn't reach them without having to take out the pair of leather boots filling the small bag first. She set them aside, but paused when her fatigued mind caught up.

"Oh," Althea sighed.

"What? Did you say something?" Niklas looked at her over the fire, the red of his eyes absorbing the light.

"Yeah, I almost forgot. I never leave a deal at a dead end," she explained around a dry mouthful of bread, and handed over Niklas's favorite pair of hunting boots. The deal they had made that day at her ascension assessment seemed farther away than merely two weeks ago.

The day Niklas had found her in that alley, she had gone back to the stand that Niklas had bought dubbin oil from and had purchased some herself as well as a buffing brush. After his father had come to her, she had scrubbed at those boots all night and most of the next morning, until her fingernails had become stained black from the amount of muck that she sloughed off of them.

Niklas remained silent, his left eyebrow raised as he took the boots from Althea's outstretched hand. He twisted and turned them over, examining them in the orange of the firelight.

"Hmm," Niklas hummed, running his tongue over his red teeth. "They're not *that* clean. But, I will be gracious and give you a pass, *only*, until we get somewhere where you can try again." He set them aside and kicked off the Guard issued boots he had been wearing, wiggling his toes in thick wool socks, and leaned back against the cave's rock wall, sipping at a tin cup of tea.

"What do you *mean* they're not good enough? I spent hours on them," Althea sputtered, taken aback at his insufferableness.

"There are blemishes, Little Althea, that maybe if you had paid a little more attention, would have come right off," he spoke around a yawn.

"No. I think they are just so clean that you're seeing your reflection in them." Althea heard no response, and looked back over to Niklas. His head was tilted back, eyes closed, cloak draped across his chest.

"Niklas?" Althea whispered, and didn't breathe until she saw his chest rise and fall.

How can you fall asleep so fast? Althea scoffed at him in her head.

She poured the rest of his tea, that was cooling rapidly, into the empty cup next to him and drank it. The sweet tang of berries blotted out any bitterness that the tea had, and Althea had to fight back a groan at how her body responded to the sugar, giving her a well needed boost of energy, as it seemed she was going to be taking first watch.

Chapter Thirteen

— · —

Niklas

"Psst, Niklas. Wake up."

"Mmm, five more minutes father," he groaned, arching his back to stretch out his cramped muscles. He didn't know why his bed was so hard and lumpy this morning. He would have to bring out an extra blanket for his father now that autumn was here, the chill in the air would make him stiff.

"No. Now. They're out there. We need to go." The voice didn't belong to his father, but to a girl. He opened his eyes, mind still groggy with sleep as he remembered that he wasn't home. The cave smelt like smoke.

Althea snuffed the embers of the fire out with her boot and rolled up her bed roll.

"I think it's the men from the ambush again. I can't tell how many, but I smell fish cooking, they're close."

Niklas didn't hesitate, he jumped up and gathered his belongings as quickly and as quietly as he could, shoving them into his saddle bags.

It was dark without the fire, but they had both saddled their horses enough times to know how to do it even if they were blindfolded.

Once they had squeezed the horses out of the cave's narrow entrance, they spread some leaves over the tracks they had made at its entrance, hoping to hide their presence.

"I think we should scope out the area before we leave. I don't know about you, but I do not want to stumble into the middle of an ambush again," Althea whispered, peering into the trees.

"It seems we finally agree upon something," Niklas mused.

Althea dropped into a crouch, clutching a dagger in her fist, and Niklas dropped down next to her as they silently crawled toward the orange glow of a camp, not even two hundred feet from the cave where they had slept. The smell hit them first, body odor and old blood mixed with the smell of roasting fish.

Do these men seriously not have the slightest idea of hygiene? Niklas debated breathing through his mouth, but realized quickly that he would rather bear the smell of the rancid camp than to taste it and snapped his mouth closed.

From the position of the thin moon, Niklas saw that it was only an hour until dawn. He hadn't meant to fall asleep, his body had just given out on him. He did not do well with lack of sleep, and had been awake since dawn a day and a half ago.

Looking over at Althea, Niklas could see that she had been awake the whole night. Her usually bright skin looked dull, and dark crescents were set into the skin under her eyes.

They stopped twenty feet away, ducking behind the knotted roots of a fallen tree.

Niklas roughly estimated about fifty large men and women sitting in a circle around a dimming bonfire, ripping the flesh from roasted fish with their teeth, skin and all, grunting to one another in a clipped, sharp language that sounded like a southern dialect from Oakstead. He didn't know for sure, but he never wanted to hear it again.

They passed wineskins around, laughing and pushing each other playfully, almost like the ambush yesterday never even happened despite the blood that still coated their skin and clotted in their wolf skin cloaks.

Niklas scanned the rest of the space they took home in. He saw twenty, roughly pitched tents that were leaning precariously against the trees, dangerously close to collapsing. But other than that, there was no sign of any scouts or horses that he could see. How were they surviving out here?

Althea tapped him on the shoulder and pointed up into a tree that stood on the other side of clearing, and again to a tree ten feet to their left. Niklas followed her finger, but only saw green leaves and ... more green leaves. But a glint of light flashed between them. He squinted his eyes and it was so obvious. Once Niklas saw the men hiding in the treetops, idling lazily, with bows in their laps he didn't know how he had missed them at all.

Althea pointed a thumb over her shoulder, not risking saying anything. Niklas knew the sign, 'let's get the burning fireplace out of here'.

He turned around while Althea stayed facing the camp as she walked backwards, a technique they were taught during training. Majority of the time, guards who ended up getting caught while spying, was when they were retreating. Eyes in the front and back were key.

They had tied their horses behind a rock that jutted out from the side of the wall of rock beside the cave's entrance where no one would be able to see them.

As they neared and were out of sight, and sound, of the savage camp, they straightened and breathed in deep gulps of clean air when suddenly, a *brav* of a man pitched forward out of the cave, bringing with him the smell of rancid liquor. He locked his bulging eyes on Althea.

She gasped and stumbled, backing into Niklas's chest almost tripping on a thick tree root. The man smiled, showing that he had more empty spaces among his gums than he had actual teeth. He slurred something that Niklas was glad he couldn't understand.

He hadn't noticed Niklas yet. He backed away and slipped behind the man as he passed, but remained in Althea's sight as the savage advanced clumsily toward her, backing her into a tree. She cringed and turned her head as far she could as the man leaned over her, tugging on the end of her braid, and slowly reached for her dagger strapped to her leg.

Althea was strong, stronger and faster than a lot of men. But this man's size alone, even in his drunken state, would be too much for her to handle herself.

Niklas wiggled his fingers above his head to catch Althea's attention, and gestured for her to toss her blade to him. Her eyes were wide, but she did not so much as fumble or shake as she flipped the blade underhand, through the air, and right into his waiting palm.

The man continued to slur and grabbed Althea's chin, turning her face up to look at him. Her countenance became defiant and she spit in his face. He just laughed, wiping a hand across his cheek, but not for long.

At his signal, Althea lifted her knee, hitting the man in the groin. He only huffed, barely affected by her hit, but Niklas took advantage of his lowered height in that moment and jumped on his back, making a quick slice, and clasped his other hand over the man's mouth to muffle his shout of surprise as they both went down in a flurry of leaves and dirt.

Niklas did not wait to find out if the man was dead before reaching for Althea. He grabbed her hand, raced around the jagged rock and mounted their horses.

After the close call at the cave, they traveled a mile south and another mile east before turning slightly north to try and make it around the river in hopes to at least arrive at the base camp in Caedmon a day or two after the rest of the soldiers did.

They rode for a few hours, stopped for a quick afternoon meal and to relieve themselves. Let the horses drink water and rest for no more than thirty minutes, to which Althea expressed her sincere apology to the beasts, and were back on their way.

"I should have paid closer attention that day. I could have alerted Captain Delmar or Sir Erling of the ambush if I had just been there a few minutes earlier. Maybe we would not have lost so many." Althea kept her face turned away from him, but he heard the guilt in her voice.

"Are you kidding? Nearly three thousand men walked right under them. Not one suspected a thing, and can you imagine the outrage Delmar would have had if you showed up? '*Oh Captain Delmar Sir, I know that I have broken the rules of the kingdom, but hey, there is an ambush,*'" Niklas finished in a high pitched, mocking tone.

A bright flash and a loud boom rocked through the forest, startling all of them. And then the sky opened. Rain rushed down on them hard, blinding them from any sense of direction, soaking them through with its ice cold grasp, and that was the end of their short conversation.

Niklas's horse Maygo, let out a frustrated whinny and stomped his hoof.

"I know boy, I know."

He held out a hand to get Althea's attention and shouted over the rain. "Over there, that tree must have fallen recently, the roots should hang over enough to cover us and the horses."

"Thank God," Althea said weakly, but a smile spread across her face.

The roots were covered in a thick layer of moss and protected them well against the deluge. Niklas tried, and tried, and tried again to start a fire but nothing so much as smoldered from the soggy pile of wood. Althea attempted her hand at it and failed as well.

Lightning flashed, thunder roared, and rain washed the forest clean well into the night. The heat of day was long gone and Althea was shivering like mad, her teeth slammed together repeatedly. Niklas wondered if she would even have any teeth left by the morning.

Huffing a breath out, Niklas opened one side of his dry, wool blanket that had been sealed in his saddle bag. "Come here."

Althea's brow furrowed, a funny sight considering that the only part of her that wasn't covered by her cloak was her forehead. "What?" She asked.

"I *said,* come here, Little Althea. You are clearly freezing and don't have enough fat on your bones to give you any insulation."

"It would be inappropriate." Her voice was muffled by the fabric and a break in the clouds let the moonlight through long enough for Niklas to see a flush across the bridge of her nose.

"All right then, fine by me." Niklas covered himself back up. He would not admit that he was chilled himself, and that asking Althea to come over wasn't just for her benefit. After a couple of seconds, he smiled, knowing just what to do. "I am so glad my father made me pack this *thick*, *warm*, blanket. I don't know what I would do without him. He really kno–"

Niklas's teasing was cut off by the flurry of her movements. She all but leapt over to his side, ripping the blanket open enough for her to squeeze under it next to Niklas, her shoulder pressed into his ribs.

Niklas opened his mouth, but she interrupted. "Shut up, and no one finds out about this, do you understand?" He nodded his head with a smirk on his lips.

"Why didn't you wear proper armor anyway? You can't have expected to fight in just your leathers did you?"

"I thought there might have been a spare set when I caught up to you guys once we got to Caedmon. They wouldn't notice one extra soldier."

"You must not know Delmar as well as you think you do." The man would know if a single card was missing from a whole deck just by looking at it.

They stayed like that for the rest of the night, taking turns sleeping. Even the horses had given in to exhaustion, kneeling to lay down and huddled themselves together.

It was Niklas's second turn to take watch, and he was having a hard time keeping his eyes open, his tongue was glued to the roof of his mouth and his breathing kept evening out, the rhythmic lull of Althea's snore mixed with the patter of the rain was almost like a song, meant to drag someone into a dream. His head nodded forward once, twice. He still had another hour until it was Althea's watch and then they would be on their way with another long day of riding. He needed something sweet to wake him up.

Niklas stretched out his right arm, reaching for his satchel while trying not to move the shoulder that Althea pressed against. It was only one inch too far. He took a quick glance at Althea to make sure she wasn't stirring, and shifted slightly, reaching.

He let out a small breath of triumph when he was able to seize the bag. Althea made a noise. He froze, his heart stalling as he waited, not moving, not even to breathe. She settled, her snores returning. He reached over and turned her head in the other direction, tucking the blanket closer to her chin. The faint scent of vanilla filled his nose.

He waited for all of two seconds before digging in the small pocket at the back of the bag, and pulled out two wrapped toffee nut candies.

Niklas had always had a violent sweet tooth, so he had made sure that he would have a sufficient enough supply of sugar to last him at least a month. After that he would have to rely on fruit. He figured that it was the way of war, and Niklas was very adaptable, so he knew he would be fine.

The sugar coated the inside of his mouth and bits of the nuts got stuck in his teeth, but oh, did it taste so good. He almost felt a hint of guilt at the luxury, when all Althea had been eating was old bread and over cooked jerky, while he had been savoring his fresh bread and sweets.

Almost.

Chapter Fourteen

Althea

The next morning was miserable. Their clothes were damp. The ground had been transformed into a soggy mess from the storm that claimed the night as its own. The air was cold and wet, making every breath painful.

But the sky. It was worth the pain to see it. There was no one way to describe it.

In the clearing they were walking through, Althea could see the storm to their right, slowly fading as the winds drove it away. To the left, the sun was shining bright, with tall fluffy clouds that looked like cotton. Directly in front of them, the clouds looked like feathers from a massive bird. And behind them, in the direction they had come from, the half moon hung bright like an ornament.

The horses seemed to be in a pleasant mood now that they had been washed down from the blood that was crusted on their coats, and were given an hour to drink and munch on some dry grass. Even Althea felt a little better herself. She had prayed through the long hours of her watch as they waited out the storm. Relying on her true source of strength.

Neither of them talked much as they rode on and it was a surprisingly comfortable silence considering their history. There just wasn't anything to say until there was. Niklas had explained how there had been a shelf at low tide, and that was how the wagons got across the river. "If there is one, there has to be more." She hoped so.

They walked along the shore of the Norvern river for an hour and came across a section shallow enough for the horses to swim across with their humans clinging on for dear life.

They finally came across the tracks of their wagons by midday on the opposite shore. The footprints of the guards were vastly spread out, just like Niklas had said they would be as scouts scoured the surrounding areas.

"Should we follow the prints? Or go off to the side and just head in the same direction?" Althea asked, humbling herself. She wanted to believe that she knew what was the right choice to make, but she hadn't been to the point of training yet that Niklas had, that she would have learned after her ascension. She knew how to track and hunt game – she was good at it – but that never required her to assume an enemy was going to be involved.

"I'm beginning to think that the ambush wasn't a coincidence, but I may be wrong. Do you see anything in the trees?" He pulled his horse to a stop.

"I can't see anything from here. Give me a boost?" Althea hopped off Bronte and walked over to a tree, looking up into the leaves.

"Yeah." Niklas moved his horse to her side and gave Althea his hand.

She grabbed his hand with her good arm, the other still sore from her fall, and climbed onto Maygo's back, standing on his rump.

She took a small, steadying breath, and swung her arms back, bending at her knees, and launched herself up. Her chest slammed into the branch, fingers digging painfully into the rough bark as she fought for purchase. She was glad that she knew how to take a hit or else the wind would have been knocked out from her lungs. Using the knobby soles of her boots, she scrambled the rest of the way up, sending down a spray of loose bark until she sat, straddling the branch.

Out of habit she tapped the harness on her thigh and was comforted to feel that her dagger was strapped securely in the leather.

The weapon had belonged to her mother before she passed, the hilt jeweled in the deepest of blue sapphires. The blade, straight and as black as night.

It had been a gift from her father after Althea passed the entrance exams to train for the Guard at thirteen seasons and Althea carried it everywhere. She had felt off balance without the weight of it in her sheath yesterday, when she had tossed it to Niklas. But it was there now, and not a speck of blood was to be found on it. She didn't remember him giving it back to her, she would have to ask about it later.

"I'm gonna jump ahead. I'll signal to you if it's clear," she called down, waiting for him to nod before she walked to where her branch crossed with another from the tree next to hers and hopped over.

She crossed over the forest floor with more agility than she thought she could ever achieve. Maybe she had always had it in her, she just needed the right opportunity.

Althea made progress one tree at a time, moving parallel to the tracks of the soldiers, staying fifty feet in the air. Once it was clear for him to move forward, Althea rolled her tongue to give a sharp trill of a bird song that she knew only Niklas would recognize.

It was the sound of a bird in the lullaby their nursemaid used to sing to them on the days where both their father's were busy with work.

Their fathers could only afford one maid, so they grouped Niklas and Althea together most days before they were old enough to join the Guard and started earning extra money to help out.

The sound tickled Althea's tongue and she scratched it against her teeth.

They only made it a few hundred feet when she saw the scattered clouds of smoke. She whistled down a sharp burst of whistles, *down up*, *down up*, signaling Niklas to stop and wait.

Turning toward the smoke, she hopped across three trees in quick succession, looked at the branches above her and began testing her weight on them. When she deemed them stable enough to hold her, she gritted her teeth against the ache in her shoulder and pulled herself another ten feet higher.

Althea crossed her ankles underneath her and squeezed the thin branch with her knees, using the tops of her feet for balance as she shimmied to the end of the branch that was only as big around as her thigh.

The skin on her hands and forearms was puckered and red, burning with thousands of small cuts from being among the sharp needles and bark.

She ignored the urge to scratch relentlessly at her skin and peered over into a camp, littered with men buzzing around. Some pitched tents, others carried around baskets of bloody bandages and delivered platters of food to a tent not even twenty feet from the base of her tree.

They were all the same sandy color with faded sigils plastered on their sides. Althea squinted her eyes against the burn of smoke, and saw what the sigil was. Two crescent moons, the sharp ends meeting each other with the space between them empty. The word *Command* in the twirling letters of the Palmerian language was painted above the tent's open entrance.

Even from the height Althea was at, she could hear just fine with how loud they were speaking.

Palmerian was a strange language, all leaps and dives, it held no real order and sounded like a tumbling stone rolling through a river.

In Valarian, people talked low into their chest. Althea had been told by a foreigner long ago that it sounded like a sad song.

"– the damage." She caught the end of what a low baritone voice said.

"Sir Xade, the Valarian count is one thousand five hundred, and the remaining continue their march to Caedmon as planned." This voice was higher and belonged to a child, no more than fourteen seasons, Althea guessed with a sick twist in her stomach.

"What of our men?" A woman asked.

"Fifty, ma'am, men of Oakstead... and..."

"Annnd?" The first voice – Xade – prodded the young child like he was slow in the head.

His voice shook. "Two hundred of the brigands... and one-hundred sixty men of Palmeria."

"FOUR HUNDRED!?" Xade said in a whisper-shout. "Lill, you said those filthy men were the best fighters in your tournaments. Care to explain how the '*Valiant Valarian's*' managed to get away practically unscathed?"

"I specifically told you *to my knowledge*, that the mercenaries were of able body and were trained with the sword. I have already sent word out last night. But if I were to assume, the purveyor gave us duds and ran with the money," the woman – Lill – said.

Men for hire? Althea was shocked. She thought they had just stumbled upon a nest of savages even though they should have never been out there. Exiles were what they really were, people who served their time in prison but returned back to a life of violence and crime as soon as they were set free and were captured and sold by privateers who collected their bounties.

Niklas was right then, it wasn't territorial at all, they were commissioned. But for what? To weaken the Valarian forces so the Palmerians might have a slight advantage at winning?

A quick whistle shot through the clearing and Althea cringed. Niklas's signal was asking if it was okay to advance, but he may as well have just shouted her presence to the men below. But no one seemed to notice as they kept about their duties.

"This feat was a waste of time, money, and resources when we lost three times as much compared to them." Another voice, much deeper.

"Commander Falo, it wasn't all a waste, if anything, the ambush just sped things up, even if the Valarian guards cover more than fifty miles a day – which is not feasible with the supplies they carry – they would reach Caedmon a day after the blood moon ball and the queen will already be dead–" A loud smack echoed from inside the tent, earning a few turned heads of the men around it. Althea saw a shadow of boots moving from under the flap of the tent, a big pair pushing a smaller pair.

"You little piece of worthless horse dung, do *not* say those words aloud." A man peeked his head out of the tent and looked around. Xade, she guessed, looked to be in his mid thirties, tall and lanky, with long, dark blonde hair. He ducked back in and closed the split fabric.

"You should be glad that you are allowed the opportunity to be here, do not make me regret it. Now, go practice your archery and be quiet, or else I will do to you what I will be doing to that *queen*." The last word was growled menacingly, and the child ran out of the tent holding his reddened cheek, tears streaking down his face.

He paused, shoulders rising and falling fast and turned around, hatred burning in his eyes. The boy had clean, pale blond hair, grown out enough to curl around his ears, and he had the bluest of eyes Althea had ever seen with someone of his tanned skin.

She realized with a start that the boy had turned and was looking right at her.

He glanced around him at the busy camp, and when he saw no one watching, he gave a small, two fingered salute, and pushed his pinky finger against his lips like he was promising to say quite and ran off with a smile.

She could hear Lill begin to scold Xade, telling him he overreacted and that no one would find out about their plan.

Althea let out a breath, *someone just did*.

Shocked, she figured she had garnered enough information and shuffled herself back and raced across the trees toward Niklas. When she saw the familiar flash of chestnut hair she almost began weeping with relief.

She hopped down from the tree with reckless abandon, her feet sliding out from under her when she hit the slick leaves, landing heavily on her bottom. She did not pause as she sprang to her feet and vaulted onto Bronte's back, the dappled gray horse tossing her head at Althea's frantic movements.

"Wha– What?" Niklas stammered, startled by her rush.

"Camp, over a hundred men, change of plans, I will explain on the way. We need to reach the Blue before the blood moon ball." Her words came out broken from her labored breathing. She turned her horse's head toward their new destination.

She did not know if they would make it in time. Or if Niklas would even believe her about the threat on the queen's life, but her mission just shifted unexpectedly, and she was ready to follow.

CHAPTER FIFTEEN

—·—

NIKLAS

"What?" Niklas asked for the third time as he listened to Althea's rambling.

Her words came in short bursts, their horses jostling them as they walked – stumbled more like – down an uneven rocky pitch they had no choice but to go down.

If they had gone around to the right where the land was flat and even, they would have gotten to have a welcome party with the enemy's camp. That was not really on Niklas's agenda for the day.

They had tried to follow the path farther left, beaten down by thousands of boots and hooves to find a more level decline but had crossed paths with a very unfriendly group of *bravs* and had to make a quick retreat.

Niklas had taken the time to draw a crude map with a stick of charcoal, relying solely on memory to etch down the curves of the forest. The map was not perfect by any stretch of the imagination, but it helped them gauge, roughly, how far they had come and how far they had left to go. What the best path to take would be.

"The boy. He could not have been older than fifteen seasons. His uniform was lined in silver – real silver – so he must be of noble blood, they spoke of a plan to distract the Guard of Valarie by sending them to Caedmon so they could make a move on the queen's life during the blood moon ball. And then his commander, someone named Xade, cut him off before he could say more. He saw me."

"He saw you? Who? Were you followed?" His eyes widened, why didn't she tell him this first?

"No. No one else but the boy saw me, and I made sure no one followed. It was strange though, he smiled and gave a salute, not a formal one, but with just his first two fingers." Althea demonstrated the salute, placing her pointer and middle finger on her brow and flicked them down, like she was just brushing a piece of dust from her face.

"You say he looked like a noble. What color was his jacket?" Niklas asked.

"It was navy blue with silver buttons and trim. High neck, black breeches and black boots."

"Navy blue is the color of Palmeria. It makes sense that they would have a noble representative with them, but why only a boy," he thought out loud. The ground finally evened out beneath them and they were deposited beside a small, quick moving creek. Niklas was suddenly very thirsty.

"Why don't we go against the flow of the stream and find the source? We're headed in that direction anyway. Oh how I could use a good bath right about now." It had been three days since Niklas had bathed properly, and he did not call wiping a freezing wet rag across his body in the pitch of black, a bath. "And maybe if we are lucky it will open into a lake, so we can fish." The wince on Althea's face did not pass Niklas's notice.

"What's wrong?" He asked.

"What do you mean?" She countered quickly, scratching idly at her arms where she had rolled up the sleeves on her tunic.

"Do you have a better idea?"

"No, that sounds fine. I just... am not the biggest fan of fish," she finished with a soft humorless laugh.

"Well, well. I never thought I would see the day that Miss Nova had a weakness. Noted."

"Oh button up," she said with a chuckle, but she looked uncomfortable. "I think something might have bitten me when I was in the trees. It stings really bad," she confessed, and rubbed her hands on her pants.

An opossum startled at the sight of the horses, and pressed itself low into the ground, pretending to play dead until they passed.

"Let me see." Althea nudged her horse closer to his, her right knee bumping into his left, and shifted in her saddle. She swung her other leg around until she sat with both legs on one side like she was sitting in a chair, offering him her arms and somehow stayed sitting on the horse as they continued on.

He dropped Maygo's reins and grasped Althea's wrist. Her skin was red and beginning to blister, raised white lines marred her soft skin, evidence of her clawing at the rash.

"It looks like an allergy. My father has them. He can't use anything with lavender in it, or else his skin will blister just like this." He let her have her arms back and she righted herself in her saddle.

"I've never had an allergy to anything before, what do you think it could be?" She held up her arm inches from her face, inspecting it.

"The only thing I can think of that would be different than at home would be the pine trees. You were up there for a while."

Taris grew mostly evergreens, and oak trees that had started turning as red as fire before they left. Considering that Althea had never been outside of Taris, she would have never been exposed to pine before; it was a common allergy in the northern parts of Valarie where pine was more prevalent.

"Darn, I was starting to really like the smell of pine too." She took a deep breath in and Niklas found himself breathing in the sweet earthy scent as well.

They ran out of things to talk about as they walked along the bank, that had now deepened and flowed eagerly. Niklas glanced into the clear water, catching sight of a small group of fish swimming, fighting their way against the current. The sight gave his heart a little jump in anticipation, that meant there was food for the fish up ahead. The river steadily widened, forcing them to keep turning their horses until they were halfway turned back to the way they had come.

"Shouldn't we go back a bit? I don't like how far this is turning us around."

"If it doesn't change course in the next quarter mile we won't have a choice." Almost immediately after Niklas had answered her, the river bent at a sharp right angle, the shore ending at a wall of blackberry bushes.

He slipped down from his horse, stretching out his lower back and grabbed a handful of the fruit. His horse watched him, got the idea and nibbled on the bush next to his.

"Want some?" he asked around a mouthful, holding out a hand, fingers stained dark purple.

"Not right now. I'm not feeling too well. Must just be from the pine." She let go of Bronte's reins, allowing the horse to stain its elegant pink nose among the berries.

"Suit yourself." Niklas shrugged and ducked under a low tree branch, searching for more. His eyes went wide, the food in his hand forgotten.

"Get over here, you won't believe this," he swallowed his mouthful and began shrugging off the heavy metal layers of his armor, leaving a trail of steel as he ran to the body of water before him, the waterfall reflecting off of the late afternoon sun.

Niklas only stopped long enough to dip a toe in the water to test it, and when he felt how warm it was, he ran the rest of the way in, diving under the water fully clothed, sending up a splash of water in his wake. He raked the wet hair off of his forehead and let out a hoot of triumph when he resurfaced.

"Shh, Niklas, someone could hear yo-" Her reprimand was cut by a fit of coughing.

Great, just what we need, Niklas thought. She probably wasn't feeling well because she got a cold from the night in the storm. And on top of that her body fought against the allergen.

"There can't possibly be anyone this far out – well, maybe not anyone *else*. The water is sooo warm." He floated on his back and he let out a sigh as the heat worked out the knots in muscles he didn't even know he had.

He kept his eyes closed, but listened, trying not to laugh as Althea huffed her way across the pebbles, untying her thick leather jacket, kicking off her boots, and finally releasing a sigh as she eased herself into the water.

"It's good right?" He asked.

"Yeah, it's good." He cracked his eyes open a slit, watching her smile and the tension in her expression receded.

With the sun shining down on her and the water warming her cheeks into a blush, she almost looked pretty. He could not think of a single time being in her presence that she let herself look so relaxed. She looked so vulnerable at that moment, and Niklas felt a strange need to protect her, to make sure that nothing ever happened again like that first night after they left the cave.

He hadn't realized that was what he had felt that night, worry. Then the logical part of his mind caught up to him and he shook the feeling away. He must be *really* tired... and really hungry. Althea? Pretty? Never.

They treaded the water, basking in the warmth. Even the horses waded in up to their bellies, drinking their fill of the spring.

After a few quiet moments, Niklas bit his lip to hide a smile, turned and pushed his hand through the water, sending a wave careening straight in Althea's face.

She gasped, her mouth open, wet hair clinging to her head. She blinked at him in shock before she returned fire and soon a war of their own began. One full of laughter and water flying in all directions, forgetting all about someone hearing them. The horses threw their heads, annoyed at their humans, and went back to eat from the blackberry bushes.

The sun began its descent far too soon and Althea got a fire started while Niklas fashioned a spear out of a strong limb he found. He struggled out of his wet tunic, wringing it out as much as he could and draped it next to the fire to dry. If it wasn't for the heat wafting off of the water he probably would have had icicles hanging from his nose tonight. The temperature dropped lower each day.

He rolled the ends of his pants up to his knees and used the last two hours of daylight to catch dinner.

"I think that's enough, Niklas," Althea said after he had dropped two more fish on the pile beside the fire. She had cleaned and gutted the fish as he brought them in and they rested on a clean, flat rock, waiting to be roasted. He caught enough for a full dinner tonight, breakfast, lunch, and dinner for the next day.

He rummaged through his saddle bag for the ware to cook and mashed together a berry glaze to pour over the fish. It was a recipe he had learned when he visited a distant aunt in Marella. The thought of sweet fish had repulsed him at first, but when he tried it, he almost could not eat fish without it, and with the extra berries all around them, he knew he had to take advantage of it before snow fell and they withered away.

As he stirred the fragrant glaze over the fire, he noticed Althea was nursing her arms, lathering a thick layer of a poultice and wrapping them with strips of an extra tunic she must have brought. The only sign of discomfort she showed was a slight burrow between her eyebrows. He hadn't noticed before, but by the shadows the fire cast on the camp, he saw that her face was beginning to look swollen as well.

Niklas didn't say anything at first. She ate her share of fish with the berry glaze, and was shocked to find that she liked it.

"They don't call me a Cuisiner for nothing," Niklas boasted.

"When has anyone *ever* called you a Cuisiner before?"

"I did. Just now."

"Ok, since you made fish taste good to *me*. I will grudgingly call you Cuisiner."

They ate until all their plates were licked clean, and packed the rest around one of Althea's empty food wraps, tucking it far into his leather pouch. They made sure to hang it in a tree, outside the bounds of their camp in case a hungry *brav* or a *khourge* smelled the food.

It seemed that Niklas and Althea were both restless that night. She picked up a flat rock and chipped at its edges until she had produced a handful of little stone daggers, wrapping the ends in some dry stalks of grass and tested their weight by throwing them into a rotten log. Each one stuck within an inch of each other in a straight line.

She stood and went to retrieve the makeshift daggers, but halfway there, she froze and bent over at the waist. "Uhhhhh," she groaned, clutching at her stomach.

"Ha, ha, so funny. I know you didn't get sick from dinner, we ate from the same pot."

She unusually ignored his jibe, and fell to her knees, her hands digging into the pebbles that covered the sand. She groaned again and it turned into a whimper. He stood abruptly. "Ok, Althea. What's wrong?" He asked suspiciously, thinking to himself that she was really over doing it for a joke.

"Don't know. My stomach. Huurtsss."

He walked to stand in front of her at the same time she sat back on her heels, and looked up at him with a fearful pleading in her eyes, her skin pale and waxy.

"What did you eat earlier? For breakfast? That was the last time we ate separately."

"Some blueberries from home, they were in my kitchen and my father doesn't like them so I knew he wouldn't miss them," she responded in a raspy whisper, her forehead and upper lip beginning to bead with sweat.

Niklas went over to where Althea's bag rested, picked it up and turned it over, dumping the contents on the ground and began rummaging through the wrapped parcels, his nose wrinkling at the piece of clean women's cloth that he knew what was used for but did not want to touch.

There were only a couple pieces of burnt jerky and a single small loaf of bread.

"Ah ha." Niklas stood, holding a small cheese cloth with a few stray blueberries resting inside. He held one up to the light of the fire and squashed it between his thumb and pointer finger, the juice that rolled down his hand was tinged blue, not purple.

"Oh, burning fireplace."

Chapter Sixteen

Althea

"What is it," Althea ground out between clenched teeth.

"This is bad. This is really, really bad." Niklas dropped what was in his hand and ran to the water, sticking his hands in and used the gritty sand to wash the blue stain from his fingers.

Althea managed to crawl her way back to the fire, panting heavily and flopped onto her stomach in front of the strewn contents of her bag, the energy she had moments ago seeming to have vanished completely, misting into the fog that hovered outside the ring of light the fire cast and into the darkness beyond their camp. Niklas paced barefoot on the bank of the spring, running his wet hands through his hair, muttering to himself.

Althea picked up the cloth that had wrapped the blueberries. One came tumbling out, landing in her palm. It was squashed. And the innards were blue.

Ketabome.

"H – how?" Althea gasped. Niklas stopped his splashing, broken from his thoughts. "I don't understand. I brought these from home. They were in my kitchen, right on the table." Her throat tightened.

She felt the rise of her dinner, and she forced a bout of strength into her legs.

By sheer determination, she managed to run to the edge of the trees before she vomited. She hated throwing up, not just because of the acid taste that lingered after, but it was a waste of precious food, especially when she didn't know where her next meal would come from.

She heaved until there was nothing in her stomach and then heaved some more. Her abdomen felt tight, and sudden, searing spikes of pain jolted her. Althea did not know when Niklas had come up beside her and she hoped that the darkness concealed enough to hide her and that he had not seen all of this.

He did not seem to be phased by her sickness, but just extended her waterskin to her, which she drank greedily, and after only a breath, she vomited that up as well.

"Drink slowly, Little Althea."

She coughed into her arm and took a slow sip, focusing solely on keeping it down. Once she felt her nausea ease a bit, she wiped the back of her hand across her mouth and sat on her heels, gasping. Then the shivering began.

It was exactly like they had described it to be in training when she learned about which berries were edible and not. Niklas sat on his haunches and asked, "Do you think you can walk?" Althea shook her head, dizzy. Her vision started to shrink at the edges. She blinked once and was suddenly in front of the fire, two blankets and her cloak covered her, making her blissfully warm.

She sat up, no longer shivering and glanced across the fire. "How did I –" She cleared the grogginess from her throat. "How did I get over here?"

"You passed out, and I carried you. You know you are a *lot* heavier than you look."

She ignored his tone. "How long was I asleep?"

"I wouldn't exactly call what you were... sleeping, per se. You looked like you were having a dream where you were battling a rabid racoon over jerky on the hottest day of mid season. Yeah, let's call it that. Oh, and if you're curious, which I'm sure you are, I think the racoon almost won. It's been a full day."

"An entire day!? Why didn't you wake me up sooner?" Althea sighed, and tried to stand. Her legs still weak, she collapsed back into the pile of blankets.

"That's why."

"We don't have time to waste, Niklas. The queen's life is in danger, remember?"

"How could I forget?" Niklas stated deadpan. "How are you so sure that those people weren't talking about the Queen of Marella? Or maybe 'Queen' is a cipher for someone else?"

"They said it would happen around the time of the blood moon ball. The Queen of Marella doesn't attend those. And you know as well as I do that Queen Azora likes to make herself a pretty big spectacle wearing all those rare red diamonds."

"Sounds about right."

"I think the worst is past, we need to keep moving."

"No, not until you can eat something and keep it down. Or at least until you can stand on your own. I can't carry you everywhere. I need

112

to save my own strength," he countered and went to fill his pot with water, setting it over the fire to boil.

She hated that he was right. Althea still felt the lingering claw of nausea, and her eyelids felt like lead. She wouldn't admit it to him, but it felt like someone was carving her stomach from the inside out. Her thin, muscled abdomen was swollen, pushing painfully against her leather jacket.

When Niklas turned away to rummage through his bag, Althea tried quickly to tug at the strings binding the sides of the leather together, but just managed to fumble the strings into a knot and made the leather press even tighter into her skin. She looked up at the sound of a scoff.

Niklas watched her, shaking his head before standing and walking over. He slapped Althea's hand away when she tried to cover herself with her cloak, and began untangling the mess she made.

"Don't try and act tough. I know what *ketabome* feels like."

"You do?"

"I was ten seasons old, and I was playing hide and seek with Attilio, Magnus and some visitor's kid from Marella. Well, let's just say that I am very competitive, and was very good at hiding," he smiled at the memory. "It had gotten dark and I hadn't eaten for maybe five hours. There was no sign of anyone finding me soon, so I wandered a bit, found what I thought was a blueberry bush, bursting at the seams, get it? Bursting at the seams." He gave one last yank at the strings and the leather split with a creak. Althea ripped the vest off, sucking in full gulps of air at the release.

Niklas didn't move away, continuing his memory. "Anyway. I ate, and ate, until Attilio and my father crashed through the brush to find me curled into a ball, covered in my own vomit, and screaming. I made sure I memorized *exactly*, down to the last detail, what *ketabome* looked like, smelled like, and the differences in the bush it grew on, so that I would never make that mistake again.

"But that doesn't explain why it was in your house. Did you go and pick them yourself thinking they were blueberries? Or maybe your father?"

"No, he hates berries. I just thought that maybe someone like Glady or Narie dropped them off. They know I like them and they bring over stuff like that all the time."

"Well, we will have to put it away for now and focus on just getting through this forest alive. We can look into it when we make it back."

"Why do you sound like you care about me all of a sudden?" Althea asked incredulously.

"Who ever said I *didn't* care?"

Althea shrugged. "I don't know. We just never really got along like this before."

"Well, we weren't lost in the middle of the forest depending on each other for survival before were we? Besides, I like my beauty sleep, so having someone to take watch is good. And I might need someone to distract a *khourge* long enough for me to run to safety."

The pot of water over the fire began to boil and was spilling over the sides, hissing as it fell into the flames. Niklas jumped up and used the edge of his cloak to grab the pot, hissing as the heat burned through the fabric. He plopped the pot onto a rock, shaking out his hand with a hop like dance and blew onto his fingers to cool them.

The sight made Althea giggle, sending a spasm through her stomach, and she groaned, clutching her ribs. But the smile never left her face.

"You keep laughing and I will tie you to that tree." He pointed at a large pine tree. "And I will eat all of this by myself while you watch." He spread his arms out, gesturing to the ingredients that lay before him. Fish, but instead of the berry glaze he made the night before, there were the wild onions they had picked during breaks, and a lemon that looked like it had seen its better days.

Althea lifted her hands in mock surrender.

"Thank you," he said exasperatedly with a toss of his hands. She knew there was no real threat behind it and had to stifle the smirk rising on her face.

He rolled the sleeves of his tunic up to his elbows, the muscles in his hands and forearms flexing as he began preparing the meal, sending a delicious aroma her way.

By the end of this whole endeavor, if they made it – she shook that thought away, they would make it, she had to believe so – she might very well like fish as well as she did steak.

A glint of light flashed in her eye. It came from Niklas's belongings, where his sword was resting on his bed roll. Freshly cleaned and sharpened, the gray steel sparkled under the starlight.

"So, where did you get your new sword?" Althea asked, breaking the silence.

He sat back and looked over his shoulder. "My father. It was his, and from many generations before him, and for many to come." His face became somber for a moment, and Althea wondered what was going through his head, but the look was gone when he turned back to her.

"I didn't even know it existed until we found out about the war. I wasn't supposed to have it until I turned twenty."

"It's beautiful. I've never seen anything like it. And I can tell it's perfectly balanced just by looking at it." Althea had always been a bit of an enthusiast when it came to weaponry, and she assumed it came from her father being a smith. The work of separating metals from rock and shaping it into something lethal was an art in itself.

Suddenly, Althea was reminded of the weight on her leg and pulled out her dagger. The sapphires that studded the handle looked almost as black as the blade.

"This was my mother's. I don't think she was too keen on having a weapon, but she adored it because my father made it for her as a wedding gift." She cleared her throat and continued, "My Poppa gave it to me when I joined the Guard. It's the only thing I have of hers. Thank you. For not leaving it behind that night." He must have slipped it back into the sheath on her thigh when they had taken refuge from the storm.

He didn't need to say anything. Althea saw the understanding in his eyes, and they returned to a comfortable quiet. She looked up into the night sky, and by the position of the moon and the brightness of the blue streaks, saw that it was only a couple hours after the sun had set. An entire day she had been asleep.

While she waited, she pulled at the edge of the bandages she had wrapped her forearms in the night before, to look at her wounds. The skin beneath was not perfect, but it didn't burn as bad and the blisters looked better.

Niklas finished cooking and slopped a serving of fish stew into a mug and passed it over. She pulled it close to her, letting the warmth spread through her fingers. Now that her fever was broken she was freezing.

"*Thank you, God*," Althea whispered with her head tilted up to the darkness that spread above her and closed her eyes. "And thank you, Niklas. For everything."

He gave her a slight nod and began eating.

Once the cup in her hand had cooled some, she lifted it to her nose and sniffed before gingerly taking a sip. Once she deemed it palatable, she slurped her way through it, and had another serving. Her stomach had deflated some, closer to its normal size and now that the adrenaline and sickness wore off she fought a losing battle with her eyelids.

"Go ahead, I'll take first watch." Her eyes jerked open when he spoke.

She nodded and settled into the nest of blankets beneath her as he put another log into the fire. He stood and began to walk away, past the horses and into the dark forest. She shot up onto her knees.

"Wait, where are you going?" She called after him, scolding herself for sounding scared.

"To relieve myself. Why? Do you want to hold my hand?"

Althea was grateful that it was night, that the darkness hid the rush of blood in her face.

"Oh... No." Why would he say something like that? She was about to lay back down, but just the mere thought of having to use the latrine made her bladder ache after a full day of sleep.

She moved as fast as she could – her vision rocking back and forth – in the opposite direction that Niklas had gone. She was done and back in her spot tucked beside the fire before Niklas came back. She bid him goodnight and was asleep before she got the words all the way out.

Morning came during Althea's watch and she was very pleased to toe Niklas's snoring form in the ribs to wake him.

He gave her a death stare and grumbled unintelligibly under his breath, but got up, gathered his bedroll and washed the sleep from his face. She rolled her eyes at his seemingly careless attitude and called for her horse, "Bronte, come."

The horse walked over lazily, still saddled but with the girth loosened, allowing some comfort while making it easy for a fast escape if needed. Althea grabbed onto the leather of the saddle and pulled the straps tight and leaned heavily on her horse, winded from the simple task.

Bronte twisted her head around and held Althea close to her side with her muzzle. "Hey girl," Althea murmured, scratching the warm skin under Bronte's mane. "You ready to ride?" The horse tossed her head in a jerky nod and flapped her bottom lip making Althea laugh.

"Ready?" She turned to Niklas.

"No," he replied, his voice still husky from sleep. He finished the ties on his saddle and mounted, turning Maygo toward the water and let out a long breath. It looked like he was trying to soak in the view.

She could not blame him, they would not find another spring like this along the way. The only thing that awaited was snow, ice, and more snow as they went farther north and the season progressed. "But I guess I have to, don't I?"

On wobbly legs Althea mounted Bronte, and clicked her tongue, turning her horse east. She barely waited to see if Niklas followed her. She wanted to make up for the time they had lost.

Chapter Seventeen

—·—

Niklas

It has been one full week since we left home, Niklas thought to himself.

Laying on his back, using his hand as a pillow, he grazed idly at a small piece of toffee and watched as the birds in the trees above him fluttered around, the broken pieces of blue sky he could see beyond the barrier of leaves was deepening.

He had gone through and took stock of the meager amount of food they had left, separating it into two mounds. One for him and one for Althea. It would last them five days if they rationed it and they could always hunt for food. As winter approached, berries and tree nuts would start to become sparse, but wildlife will be out in abundance as they prepare their little animal homes.

He listened to the steady *plunk, plunk, plunk,* of Althea's stone daggers as they hit their mark on a tree trunk. Their evening meal had consisted of an unlucky squirrel that had wandered too close to Althea's target, and a few pieces of bread from his last loaf.

The horses were going to be another problem, the air was steadily becoming colder and sharper the farther they traveled north. It would snow soon, and would cover whatever bits of grass there was left.

"Ugh," Althea groaned. "I cut my hand. I'm going to go wash it off."

Niklas made a noise that was between a 'yeah' and a 'uh–huh', and yawned, bringing his cloak closer to his freshly shaven face.

Althea clicked her tongue, and he could almost hear her shake her head at him. He listened to the sound of her steps as they crunched on dead leaves and faded away, the sound of the stream as it trickled along, the horses blowing air through their lips, and before he knew it, the sounds lulled at him and Niklas closed his eyes.

The rustling of leaves was what woke him. Or maybe it was the feeling of a water droplet on his forehead, though it could have been the itch on his nose. But whatever it was, he was awake now.

He didn't remember falling asleep. He scratched at the itch on his nose and cracked open his eyes. The sky was still dark, and the fire in front of him burned low. He felt something warm pressing against his back through his armor. But he did not dare turn his head, because sitting right in front of him on a log, not even a hand's breadth away from his face, was a frog.

It stared right at him with big, black eyes, its skin a neon green. Its throat moved in and out, in and out. He froze, not daring to blink, not trusting it to leave his sight for a second. It ribbited once and jumped.

"Ahhhh!" Niklas screamed, and scrambled away, rolling over Althea who was laying behind him, clutching at the dirt until he felt a piece of rope and stone, and jumped to his feet, pointing one of Althea's stone daggers at it.

The thing looked up at him and croaked.

"What is it? What happened?" Althea jerked up, gasping. She looked around frantically and picked up her bow from where it rested beside her bedroll.

"That – that THING, tried to attack me." He took a step back, fingers tightening on his weapon. Althea came to stand beside him, her head whipped side to side, up and down, searching for the predator, blowing her sleep mussed hair from her eyes.

"I don't see anything."

"*There on the log*," he whispered, placing Althea in front of him.

Her eyes landed on the frog and she stood there, slack jawed for a moment. Then she let her bow drop to the ground and she laughed. Full belly laughs, doubling over.

"Oh, Niklas," she shook her head at him. She walked to the log and crouched down, holding out her hand. The frog jumped onto her waiting palm.

"What are you doing? It could be poisonous." Niklas took another step back, fighting to keep his hands from shaking.

"It's a tree frog, completely harmless. He's actually kind of cute, don't you think?" She extended her arm towards him.

"Get that thing away from me, or else," he warned.

"Or else what?"

He sputtered, his mouth not able to come up with what he would do, but he knew it would be bad for her. She smiled down at the frog, tucking it close to her chest and went over to the stream.

Sitting on her haunches, she lowered the frog in her cupped hands and set it in the mud next to the water. The frog happily hopped into the stream and over to the other side far away from him, and for that, Niklas was grateful.

Althea rinsed her hands off and stood, turning back to him with a puzzled look on her face. "Wait, I thought you were awake. Weren't you supposed to take first watch, Niklas?"

He swallowed hard, raking a hand through his hair.

"I–" he tried to speak, but Althea didn't give him the chance.

"Are you out of your burning mind? We just saw a *khourge* yesterday, for goodness sake! What if it was following us, Niklas? We could have both been dead before we could even open our eyes!"

"You think I don't know that?" His fear gone, he was now angry at her, thinking him stupid.

"Of course you know it. That is what makes this even more absurd. In case you forgot, we aren't the only ones out here. There are people that would love to do *far* worse things to us than any animal ever could."

"Well you weren't exactly awake either, Little Althea. I fell asleep first, you should have noticed. I didn't get us into this mess, and if I remember correctly, *you* weren't even supposed to be out here in the first place."

"You would have done the same thing, Niklas, if you were in my place," she snarled.

"Let's get one thing straight, Althea," his voice lowered into a growl as he stalked toward her until the toes of their boots touched, forcing her to crane her neck and look into his eyes. "This is not about honor, this is not about code, or oath. We are out here, freezing, starving. This is about surviving *now*. When we reach the Blue, and we find out that this little threat you supposedly heard is fake. I would gladly have been in your shoes, to stay and care for my father before he dies."

She held his gaze with the fierceness he had only seen once before.

When they were still children, Althea had broken her hand after punching a full grown man in the face. He was the town drunk, and had been hitting a woman that accidentally spilled a bucket of mop water onto his boots. Althea had been eight seasons old at the time. Their fathers had sent them on an errand in the market and they'd heard the woman screaming. Althea didn't hesitate, she ran straight into the tavern.

Niklas had never before seen a grown man thrown to the ground like he did that day. She had not cried as they made their way to the infirmary, clutching her fist to her stomach, but the look in her eyes was the same then as it was now.

They stood there, seething at each other, breathing heavily. The air around them steaming with the visible fog of their breath. Althea looked away first, grabbing fistfuls of her braided hair and roared in anger. She turned back, ready to say more, but froze, her eyes went wide.

"No. Oh no no no." She ran over to where their supplies had been shoved between a rock and the base of a tree.

Had been.

Althea knelt in the dirt before it. All that was left was the tattered remains of both their leather satchels. The food that Niklas had carefully separated and wrapped was gone. All of it, not even a remnant of his sweet toffee was left.

The sky brightened, casting a dark blue hue upon the world, and now that he knew something had been here, he could see the tracks that were left behind. Large *khourge* prints.

They looked just like a cat's, but were bigger than Niklas's hand with all of his fingers spread out. He stood frozen to his spot and assessed the rest of the camp, dread settling in his stomach.

Maygo and Bronte, safe. Two bed rolls that were pressed closely together. He must have turned over in his sleep, because he did not remember setting his blanket that close to Althea's. The fire only embers.

The air was cold and wet with the morning dew, and his cloak hung heavy on his shoulders, clinging to his skin, a barrier from the air's icy grip. And with the morning light, he could also see the boot prints.

"Umm, Althea?"

She dropped the empty satchels and made her way to stand next to him, a stricken look on her face. Niklas pointed at the prints that marred the soil beside the fire. "Those aren't mine."

Althea squinted, peering down at the marks, then hovered her foot next to them. They were smaller than hers too, and when Niklas looked closer, he saw that whoever had been here had entered from the south, went past their bed rolls, and turned west, the toes of the prints were pushed in slightly more than the heel. Whoever it was had tried to walk quietly. They had gone right past them. Niklas had been none the wiser in his deep slumber.

"Well this is just great. First the savages, then the *bravs* and the camp, and now this." Niklas rubbed at the crease on his forehead.

"Shhh," Althea pressed a finger to her lips. She faced him but her eyes were looking at something over his right shoulder.

"Don't tell me to be quiet," he snapped, but the retort died on his tongue at the look of overwhelming fear that was plastered on her face. He turned his head and his voice left him at the sight of three *khourges* poised in crouches, observing them. They were much bigger than Niklas thought. Then again he had only seen them from a distance. They are just big, *big*, cats, he tried to tell himself.

Ok, I'd rather deal with the frog.

Niklas felt Althea's hand through the leather on his arm, and without turning or making sudden movements they began to walk backwards, toward their horses. That were – thank God – tacked and ready to flee.

The *khourge* that stood in the center had a leg with more scars than fur. It let out a low yowl and stuck its tongue out, licking at its face before settling onto its stomach, eyes never leaving them. Niklas bit down hard on his lip, fighting the urge to run. The *khourge* to the right, turned its head at a sound, and from the underbrush came a doe, with big eyes that shone bright in the low, morning light. Everything seemed to freeze. Then the doe took off at a sprint and the *khourges* gave chase.

"*Now*," Althea whispered. But Niklas had already turned and raced the last few feet to his bag that was ripped and crumpled on the ground, not caring that its contents were probably unsalvageable, and jumped onto Maygo.

Althea scooped up her bow, and nocked an arrow after she had mounted Bronte. They did not have time to snuff out the glowing embers from their fire, or pick up their bedrolls. He didn't think he would be sleeping anytime soon anyway.

After the last week, everything he thought he knew about the Cerridwen had been greatly disproved.

The rest of the day felt endless. Both of them, scared silent, paid extra close attention to the forest around them. More importantly to who and what might be among the trees.

This land belonged to the kingdom of Valarie, and Niklas was preparing in his head exactly what he was going to tell the queen if he could be given her ear, about what was going on unknowingly in her lands. He would even settle for telling the lowest member of her court.

Wariness surrounded them so densely, that it was a meal in itself.

Every snap of a twig, every chitter of a squirrel, every scream from a fox or coyote had Niklas gripping his reins a little tighter, a hand never far from the hilt of his sword. Out of the corner of his eye, he saw Althea doing the same.

They rode through the day without stopping. And riding throughout the night was only possible for the bright full moon that casted an orange glow over them. It would be harvest time soon.

They didn't answer the call of exhaustion, and pushed past the limits of their hunger. It wasn't until their horses refused to walk any further that they were forced to stop and rest at dawn the next day.

The horses bent their knees and laid down, their ribs beginning to show, exaggerated by their labored breathing. He knew that the horses could no longer continue this journey, they would have no choice but to let them go and fend for themselves.

He sat next to Maygo, letting the horse rest his head on his lap and rubbed his hand down the faithful beast's muzzle, his own stomach cramping with hunger.

Althea was sitting on her feet before her mare Bronte, braiding her mane, whispering quietly to the horse. Bronte's ears were perked up, listening intently to her.

Niklas didn't have a soft spot for animals, but during the last couple of weeks, he discovered that Maygo seemed to have a personality of his own, and they had started to form a sort of bond.

Niklas's father had gifted him the horse when he had passed the entrance test to join the Guard. Oh how he had hated mucking out the horse's stall, and his betting games with Althea had gotten him out of the chore often enough. Now, Niklas wished he hadn't been so stubborn and had spent more time with his horse outside of traveling and training.

It was noon, and they couldn't afford to stay longer. The horses had calmed down and were able to stand and walk steady enough for Niklas and Althea to guide them into a wide meadow that split the forest into halves. Briers tugged at their cloaks cutting into their skin.

An echoed moan came from the forest behind them. He stopped and turned, searching the tree line. Now that he was standing in full sunlight, he could see how deeply shadowed the forest actually was. Niklas could not see farther than a foot into the mass of trees. He honestly didn't know how they were able to see the sky at all while they were in it. He shook his head and continued to march through the meadow.

Althea hadn't stopped when he did and was a good twenty feet ahead of him and he followed in her path, the briers only slightly less viscous against the exposed skin of his hands where the sleeves of his tunic ended. They stopped in the middle at a patch of tall, dry grass. The thorns leaned away as if avoiding it.

"Here. I think we should do it here," Althea whispered.

Niklas looked around, pleased to see that the horses were already nibbling on the grass. Their eyes held a look of understanding. As if they knew what was about to happen and wanted their riders to know they accepted it.

After a long moment, full of silent farewells, they untacked the horses, removing the bits and bridles that had rubbed spots on their backs bald from repeated use, leaving them tucked under the grass. They wouldn't be needing them anymore.

He watched as Althea tied a shiny bronze coin that hung from a leather string to Bronte's mane where she had braided it. A token perhaps, so a piece of Althea would journey with her horse.

He saw what it took for Althea to turn and walk away, tears welled in her eyes, but they did not fall. Niklas did not comment on them. He felt like this was one of the few moments where jesting was not appropriate. And he would be lying to say that he did not have to blink a few times himself.

Niklas's stomach had stopped making its angry protest over an hour ago, a steady hollow ache replaced the growling and the pain had started creeping up into his throat.

Now that they were walking under the full light of the sun after being encased in the dark shade for so many days, the sun beat down on them with fervor. And despite the crisp cold air wafting through the field, they were both dripping with sweat. He constantly wiped at his brow to keep the salt out of his eyes, and he so badly wanted to take the heavy breastplate off his chest, but settled for losing his leather bracers and took the stiff pauldron off his shoulders.

If people were really out here to hurt them, Niklas did not want to chance being exposed. He looked over at Althea then.

She only wore her thick leather sparring jacket that was covered from front to back with deep scars, earned from countless matches in the arena. She was more than capable of taking care of herself, but he still offered the extra gear to her. She refused, of course. He knew she would, so he shrugged and shoved the loose pieces into his roughly stitched bag.

Althea let out a sharp hiss and brought a hand to her cheek. Blood dripped over her fingers, down her neck, and into the collar of her tunic. A tall, dead, rose bush with inch long thorns was to blame.

By the time they reached the other side of the meadow, Niklas and Althea both collapsed from exhaustion. Their faces and hands were covered in stinging cuts and bruises. They had lost all of their bandages and poultices to the *khourges*.

The itch of the cuts grew stronger and was beginning to drive him mad. He needed a distraction.

Althea stared up at him in confusion when he drew his sword, the gray, steel blade shining like fire in the red sunset.

Then he lunged for her.

She only had time to gasp before rolling to the side, missing his blade by an inch. Niklas stopped the sword before it buried itself in a tree, and turned sharply to where Althea now stood, her own sword clutched in a white knuckled grip.

"What is wrong with you?" She croaked, eyes wide in terror... and fury. A strange mix.

He did not answer. He shifted his weight and spun, slashing out with his sword. Althea blocked it easily. He could see behind her eyes as they unfocused, her mind going to that back room, the one their trainers and captains taught them to do. To abandon their humanity.

He smiled wickedly.

It is on.

CHAPTER EIGHTEEN

ALTHEA

What in the burning fireplace is wrong with him?

He had gone crazy, she thought. The look in his scarlet brown eyes was dazed. He was in his fighting calm, and nothing she could say was going to get through to him until the fight was over.

Dread sat heavy in her stomach, as she forced her thoughts away, honing in on the small, almost invisible cues that told her what his next move was going to be, before even *he* knew what it would be. A twitch of the arm here, a thigh tensing there. Putting his weight on the ball of his foot before he made a thrust with his sword. Althea blocked every move with precision, ignoring the burn in her muscles from exhaustion and lack of food.

She ducked to the side as Niklas's blade swung past her shoulder in a downward arc. Their blades sparked in the dimming light and rang with each hit. Althea fought to keep her balance among the roots covering the ground as Niklas pushed her deeper into the cover of the forest.

He landed a glancing blow to Althea's hip, sending a shock wave of pain coursing down her leg. She stumbled as she tried to catch her footing and stay upright, her leg tingling with numbness.

A flash of steel cut across her vision on her left side. Althea arched back, barely missing having her throat cut open like a deer for the slaughter. Her chest was heaving and she couldn't seem to catch her breath. Niklas did not seem to be faring any better than her. Sweat had made his hair stick to the sides of his neck where it curled under his ears. His hands were slick and gripping the hilt of his sword until his knuckles turned white. Althea took a step forward and made a desperate, weak swing at Niklas, catching his sword so close to the hilt that he startled and let go with one hand.

A thick rope vine wrapped around her ankle as she adjusted her stance, and when she took a step back, ready to parry the next strike, the vine went taught. Her ankle sang with pain and she listed, falling back. Her sword fell from her hands, and Althea closed her eyes, bracing herself for the impact.

It didn't come.

She felt a tight squeeze on her right arm and was jerked to a sudden stop. Her eyes flew open to see Niklas standing over her, his hand gripping her forearm.

They stared at each other, their faces a foot apart, lungs wheezing, sending gusts of air onto each other's cheeks, warming them.

Althea didn't know how long they stayed like that, perhaps only for the blink of an eye. Althea, grasping Niklas's elbow, him grasping hers, keeping her suspended in the air.

He blinked, the familiar pomposity returning to his face. He shook his arm free and Althea gasped as she fell. She only fell an inch, onto the soft mound of leaves and lay there, drinking air greedily into her deprived lungs. The blood rushed in her ears, the racing of her heart beginning to dull. She stood up quickly, making herself dizzy, and brushed the soil from her cloak, giving him an exasperated look as she cut her leg free from the tree.

"Do you care to explain what that was about?" She seethed through gritted teeth.

"No." Niklas rolled his shoulders and sat down heavily on a rust colored flagstone, stretching his legs out in front of him.

Althea narrowed her eyes at Niklas. "Well, whatever it was, is it all out of your system now?"

"For now," he smirked.

Althea breathed as the sudden spike of adrenaline that had raced through her was beginning to ebb, leaving her enervated and angry.

She limped over to a light gray, almost white flagstone, across from Niklas, and slowly lowered herself with a groan, wiggling her toes as the feeling in her foot returned. Her side ached where Niklas had struck her and she pulled up the hem of her jacket and tunic, inspecting the skin where a small gash, only an inch wide was red with her blood.

She rolled down the waist of her pants until she could see the wound better, and pulled at the skin on either side to see how deep it went. It wasn't deep enough to need stitches, but they were without bandages, so a small slice of the clean inner lining from her cloak would have to suffice.

Althea took a deep breath and pressed the strip of cloth to her side, holding in the hiss that rose in her throat at the contact. She carefully tucked the cloth underneath her belt and tightened it, effectively holding everything together.

She glanced at Niklas through her lowered eyelashes and let go of her tunic. The fabric fell limp and misshapen, one side hung lower from under her jacket than the other, and she did not need a mirror to tell her what she looked like because she could feel everything. Her muscles felt like a bowl of porridge, thick, jiggly and gross, and her hair was completely unraveled. The brown locks cascaded down her back and over her shoulders. She must have lost the black ribbon long ago that she had used to tie it up.

Niklas was staring at his left hand, rubbing at his palm. She could see discomfort in the lines of his downturned lips. She moved her gaze from his mouth to his hand.

Red.

Without saying anything, Althea cut out two more strips from her already ruined cloak, the width of the whole bottom, and stomped her way to stand in front of him. She waited for him to look up at her, but he just stared at his boots, which were now scuffed and dull, even more than she had thought possible. They hadn't exactly been a sight to behold beforehand.

Before Althea could change her mind, she knelt in front of Niklas and grabbed his wounded hand gently. His gaze lifted slowly, jarringly, like he was fighting back from looking at her.

Althea did not meet his eyes, but she felt the weight of his stare all the same.

She must have cut him when she had hit the hilt of his sword. A jagged gash ran from the top of his wrist across the back of his hand and in between his thumb and forefinger, adding another line to his scars. His hand, calloused and tan from the summer working in the new outside arena, was warm in hers, but it was shaking.

She grabbed her waterskin from where it had been kicked away during the fight and poured the clean water slowly over the cut, blowing on it at the same time to ease the stinging. Niklas did not flinch when she wrapped his hand, looping it around his wrist and over his palm and back again, tying it snuggly.

She looked up at him, his eyes meeting hers, freezing her to the spot. She knelt there for another moment, lips parted with words she wanted to say, but her mouth refused to form.

He looked away first, and Althea stood quickly, wiping his and her own blood from her hands onto a clump of damp moss and meandered her way back to the gray flagstone and sat, bending over to mess with the ties on her boots, giving her hands something to do besides sit idle on her lap.

Her hair fell in the way, blocking her sight. She kept tucking it behind her ears but it refused to stay. She straightened, blowing the hair from her face with a huff, and gathered the strands in her hand to braid them along her head. Her hands would not stop shaking, from hunger, fatigue, and as much as she hated to admit it, fear.

A strand fell out of her hand and was lost among the rest of her hair. She let it all go and tried again. Then the top was too tight and wasn't even remotely centered, so she shook it out and closed her eyes, shaking out her sore arms. She tried again for the third time but her arms burned and her hands shook violently, this time from frustration.

Althea let go of her hair and grabbed her mothers dagger. Whipping it out of its sheath, she grabbed a hearty chunk of her hair and brought the dagger up to it, ready to be done with it when a strong grip wrapped around her wrist, pulling the dagger away from the commitment she was about to make.

"Let me." Niklas pried her fingers from the hilt and slid the blade back into the sheath on her leg, walked around her and collected her hair. Althea noticed that his hands were steady, unlike hers were.

She stayed still and let Niklas's hands twist and bind her hair. It felt like he was doing it right so she had to ask, "Where did you learn how to braid?"

His finger brushed against her ear. "Remember ten seasons ago? When I had hair down to my waist?"

"Hmhm," Althea hummed her response, careful not to nod her head.

"Well," Niklas chuckled. "My father has this mirror from when he lived in Valor, it's huge, and a swirling gold frame and everything. I used to sit in front of it with a candle after he thought I was in bed, and I would practice braiding. I would get myself all excited to go to school the next day with silver rings in my hair, but in the morning after I had slept in it, it all became a mess. I had to cut it when I started training. I look better this way anyway." He ended the memory with a self given complement. He must be feeling better after all. Althea smiled.

"Do you have something to tie the end?" Niklas asked.

He had braided it so fast, Althea was shocked and unprepared. "Umm, yeah, here." Althea patted at her vest and ripped off one of the worn leather straps that were only there for decoration. She handed it back to him and he tied it off.

"Annnd, done," Niklas said with flair.

Althea lifted a hand to gently feel the intricate knots and pattern of her hair.

Niklas had made three braids, one on each side of her head and one on top, weaving the side braids in a S and joined all three of them at the back of her head, before making one braid that cascaded down her back, ending it with the string. It all laid snug and comfortable against her scalp, not one strand pulled at her skin, and not one piece of hair was loose... it was perfect. Althea stared blankly up at Niklas, her mouth hanging open, shocked.

"Thanks, Niklas," he says in a high pitched voice, trying to sound like her. "You're welcome, Althea, it was my pleasure," he answered himself in an exaggeratedly low voice.

Althea laughed, shaking her head. "Thank you, Niklas. For real, I– it's perfect."

He nodded his head, and put his hands on his hips. "Now that we are all cleaned up, I think we should head out. It will be dark soon and I have an idea for a torch."

Althea's heart sank at the thought of traveling through the night.

Even though it saddened her, without having to worry about the horses, they will be able to travel easier in the dark.

She prayed they would be able to find some suitable game to hunt for dinner. Small animals liked to make their presence in the late evening at this time of the season, building up food stores while simultaneously avoiding the hunt of bigger predators. Unlike most felines, *khourges* liked to hunt during the day. They liked to see the life of their kill drain in full light.

Althea and all of the Guard of Taris were taught about what to expect when it came to wild animals. They were the ones that were responsible to respond if there were sightings of various beasts.

One time last season, Althea had crossed paths with a *brav*. She had been on her way to the bathhouse with a couple of her fellow female guards. The two women had screamed and ran back towards the barracks. But Althea had just shaken her head and pulled out her sword, knowing better than to run from the animal. It would make her prey. And she was a predator.

It had taken a swipe at her head, she ducked and made a few ill witted swings at its throat and stomach, standing between the beast's arms as it tried to attack her. The *brav* fell and Althea had stood there breathless, victorious. Then passed out and fell into the pool of the animal's blood.

When she awoke the next morning, clean, and starving, she had been presented with a platter of roasted *brav* meat and a cup of coffee with milk and a caramel square melted in it.

Coffee was an expensive commodity, only the rich had enough money to waste on the bitter drink, but her father had told her that it was a gift from Mayor Florence and his wife, on the behalf of an 'act of honor'.

What Althea had decided not to tell everyone was that she had just been hungry and angry that her dinner would be pushed back because of the beast. But after she tasted the first sip of that caramel sweetened coffee, she accepted the people claiming that she was a hero and told them time and time again that it was by God's hand that she was able to conquer the beast.

And out here, in the forest, potentially lost, and without proper food to give her body strength, Althea was grateful to not be out here alone. Even if her companion was Niklas. She was glad to have him watching her back, and she was glad to have his.

Althea struggled with the small twigs she was using to set up a fire, only as big as her hand, while Niklas scouted around for suitable tree limbs to build the torches. When he was satisfied with the ones he found, Althea handed over one of her stone daggers and he went to work chipping away at tree resin that was frozen against the trunks of the large cedars.

She tried again to start the fire with two chert rocks she had found when they camped beside the hot springs.

It felt like that night was so long ago; the days were beginning to melt into one another. Without any sense of schedule, and without her having her one day off a week, she had no idea what month it even was.

She struck the stones, sending up a skinny wisp of smoke. She struck them together again and again, the pile of dry leaves smoking as the sparks hit them, but as soon as she put her breath to it, it snuffed out. She decided to try a pile of wood shaving instead, brushing away the half-burnt leaves from her workspace.

It worked, the fire roared to life, but it burned too fast and Althea did not have a chance to place the inferno underneath the twigs. She groaned in frustration, hacking at the dead limb again to get more shavings.

Althea snuck a look at Niklas out of the corner of her eye as she whittled.

He had shaved the bark off one end of each of the sticks, and then, taking a dagger, he placed the sharp edge of the stone blade on the end. Taking a small, round rock, he tapped the other side of the blade, making a split in the limb about five inches down. He did the same with the other, and wedged a pine cone in the gaps.

She jerked her eyes back down when he saw her watching him. The pile of shavings she had made was comically large.

She shouted in wordless elation when the fire took, and quickly fed the hungry flame more twigs to keep it burning.

Niklas produced a small tin from his bag and poured the frozen tree resin into it, setting it close to the fire to melt. The melted goo let off a clean crisp scent, and when it began to bubble, Niklas pulled it away with the hem of his cloak.

"Ok, now we have to work fast. Here hold these." Niklas handed her both of the makeshift torches, the ends wrapped in the strips of an extra tunic. He lifted the steaming tin and poured it over the cloth until they were saturated and dipped the ends into the fire. The torches caught and her small fire went out, leaving them with two pillars of light.

The shadows around them deepened even further, and it went without saying that it was time to move.

CHAPTER NINETEEN

—·—

NIKLAS

The moon and stars were absent from the sky, and when Niklas looked up, shielding his eyes from the light of his torch, it was like looking into a void.

He felt like if he stared long enough, it would suck him up and he would be lost to the darkness. So he kept his eyes straight ahead, holding his torch in his injured hand even though it stung as the bandages rubbed against the rough bark, he wanted to be able to use his sword if he had to.

Althea kept looking over her shoulder, over his, up into the trees, and even bent at the knee to look in various berry bushes. Niklas tried and failed to hide his annoyance at her constant flurry. The rustling of leaves and the creeks of leather ate at him until he snapped.

"Will you stop making so much noise?" He whispered forcefully, scaring Althea, who had her back turned to him. She whipped around. "Whatever is out there will only be drawn *toward* your boisterousness," Niklas chided.

She ignored him, scowling, but slowed her pace until she walked beside him, their shoulders brushing against each other, for minutes that turned into an hour, and then another. A sudden gust of wind roared over them, their torches sputtered and flickered.

Niklas sucked in a breath as the temperature dropped by at least twenty degrees and goosebumps littered his skin, prickling against the leather and iron he wore beneath his cloak. He turned his back to the wind, using his body to protect his torch from the brunt of it. Althea's had already died out.

When the wind settled, Niklas used the low flame from his torch to try and reignite hers, but the resin had burned off and the cloth was far too charred to catch.

"Let's just keep going, it will be light soon enough."

If only that were true.

The light of his own torch grew dimmer by the minute, and their progress slowed every time Niklas had to turn his back to the strong wind. Eventually Althea had to hold onto the hem of his cloak, the light of his torch only allowing them to see three feet in each direction. The chill continued with every step they took, until even Niklas's teeth started to chatter.

And then his torch went out.

"Burning fireplace," Niklas hissed.

"*Stifled* fireplace, is what I think you mean," she huffed.

Althea should be glad, he thought to himself, that it was too dark for her to see the murderous fury in his eyes as he scowled in what he thought was her direction. And to make matters worse, the empty void above them began to roar with thunder.

Niklas's chest filled with rage at the earth's insolence. His stomach was burning, his hand throbbing with every beat of his racing heart, and his head ached.

Niklas tilted his head back and screamed out his fury toward the black.

"Niklas!"

He heard Althea shuffle through the dark and felt her hand bump his arm as she tried to find him, her fingers clamping down on his bicep.

He tore his arm away, and his shoulder slammed roughly into a tree. The roar of his blood rushed in his ears, muffling the sounds around him. He felt like he couldn't breathe, he was so angry. The armor encasing his chest felt like it was shrinking, slowly squeezing him until the air couldn't get past his throat. He clawed at his neck in the dark, trying to find the clasps that kept the breastplate in place.

"Niklas, calm down."

All Niklas could do was growl with each labored breath as he fought with the blasted metal clasps. To his cold numbed fingers, the clasps felt like they were forged in place, and that they were never meant to be removed.

Maybe that was what they did, what they wanted. So that the enemy couldn't steal the armor off their fallen bodies for spoil. To take home the fallen soldiers' armor to their wives and children and hang them in their foyers and mount in front of their gates. Decoration, to go with the tales they would tell and the ballads they would sing. How they rose and conquered their enemy, and how their blood fell like rain upon their heads.

"Niklas, where are you? Let me help."

"No," he managed to grind out between his rasping breaths. He had to move, or he might actually begin to suffocate. He moved, bumping into one tree and the next in his hurried, irate escape, the occasional lighting bolt streaking across the sky helped him none.

He heard Althea crash through the brush behind him, or maybe he was hearing his own thrashing, he had no idea.

He had no recollection of time as he walked – crashed – through the forest, breaking small branches that stood in his path.

Another blast of wind, so strong it pushed him back a step and he had to lean into the press of it to stay upright. Leaves lifted from the ground and flew past him, stinging where they hit his skin.

Niklas lifted his hands to his face, pressing his cold fingers against his flushed cheeks, sucking in a long breath. He was shaking. After a few more deep breaths, he began to calm, as did the wind. He fell forward at the release, realizing that it was suddenly too quiet now that his pulse began to slow.

He turned around, and then to the left and right, but he still couldn't see beyond the dark. Niklas did not know where Althea was.

"Althea?" He called softly at first, then louder, "Althea!"

"*Niklas?*" His name drifted to him on a slight breeze.

"Althea!" He cupped his hands around his mouth. No answer. He turned in circles and shouted her name again.

"*Niklas!*" Althea's voice rang from far to his left, he turned and began to walk. Shuffle more like, there were so many rocks in the area he had ended up depositing himself in.

"Don't move. I will come to you!" Niklas shouted.

"*W– I can't – whe–*" Her words were cut off by another gust of wind. It howled and peppered him with sharp leaves and pine needles. If he was having trouble standing upright in this, Althea must be hanging from a tree.

A rock shifted underneath his boot and his foot slipped out from under him. He landed hard on his knee and hissed as a wave of pain shot up into his hip.

A broken whistle reached him.

"*Niklas! K–*" She sounded closer now.

He stood and rubbed his sore knee, limping a few steps as he shook his leg out. The wind was not giving a sign that it would be dying down anytime soon and the dropping temperatures it carried with it burned his lungs as he forced himself to breathe. His already dry lips cracked painfully.

Niklas tucked two fingers under his tongue and whistled back with a mix of two responses in his confusion as he shuffled his way through the dim light.

Wait, light?

In the middle of his panic he had not even noticed that the clouds above him had begun to take on a lighter gray hue. It was finally dawn. But Niklas felt no joy at the prospect of the morning, because he did not receive a response to his whistle. He had signaled a mix of both, *ok?* and *hurt?*

Finally, another broken whistle came at him from his left this time, and he adjusted his footing, but paused when the whistle came again. He only recognized the first and last note, the rest was an echoed jumble. The first was a short, high chirp, and the last was a long, low, trilling tone, but he didn't need the middle notes, he knew it all too well.

'In danger.'

Niklas began to run, his heart racing in time with his feet.

Why did you leave her alone, you half witted imbecile!

"Althea!" Nothing.

"Nova! Althea!" His voice cracked with the strain of his shout. Niklas did not know how many times he called her name, but his voice grew hoarse and his throat burned. He stopped for air, swiping his hair out of his face and rubbing at his eyes as his sight adjusted to the growing light.

"Where are you, Althea?" He whispered.

A scream echoed off the trees.

Niklas took off at a full sprint, pushing against the snagging tree limbs. Squirrels dodged his boots and early birds took flight, a few scraping against him with their talons.

A blur of green and brown suddenly appeared in front of him. A body slammed into his, knocking the air from his lungs. He fell onto his back, Althea landing in a heap on top of him.

"Wha–" he croaked. Althea was already up, grabbed his hand and pulled him straight into a run. He stumbled a few steps before rightening himself. She had a death grip on him, making the cut on his hand reopen and blood oozed through the makeshift bandage.

"Althea, what– what is going on?" Niklas huffed as he fought for breath for the third time in the last hour.

"*Khourge*," was all she said.

Niklas felt his blood drain from his face, he had left her alone, in the pitch dark, out of anger. If something had happened to her... he didn't finish the thought.

Nothing happened, and I will make sure nothing does.

They ran for ten minutes before Niklas tripped on a rock and fell hard on his arm. Althea dug her heels into the rocky floor, falling on her backside with a yelp, scrambling backwards, her feet kicking at open air.

A foot in front of them the earth disappeared, dropping down into a ravine.

Niklas pushed himself up onto his elbows.

A hundred feet below, water flowed around and underneath the formations of layers of ice. He gasped, and Althea fell to her knees beside him. If they had kept going, they would have gone over.

They didn't – couldn't speak for a long time, their lungs begging for air, and the fear of near death hanging over them. The sky was overcast and gray, but at least – even though only faintly – they could now see.

He crawled on his hands and knees to look over the edge of the ravine. It explained the huge gusts of wind that had swept over them.

Directly on the other side, over a hill and past a mile was the base of the Kyran mountains, the only obstacle left for them to tackle, well that, and the ravine, before they could head into the City of Valor.

The mountain pass rested on the other side of the peak closest to them, in between two towering mountain tops. Niklas was not surprised that he had not seen this huge crevice in the earth when he had traveled with the prison wagons.

As soon as Niklas felt like air was getting to his brain, he said, "Little Alth–"

"It's fine." She stared at the space between them on the ground.

"No, its no–"

She lifted her head, eyes full of angry resignation, his next words stopped in his throat.

"Listen, if we can't work things out together out here, we will both die. Do you even get that? I was just trying to help you unclasp your breastplate because your cloak was caught in between the clasp." She squeezed her eyes shut. "I didn't see the *khourge* until I turned when I heard you call my name. I thought I was going to die, Niklas."

"It won't happen again."

Althea did not look completely convinced and Niklas didn't blame her, considering their relationship with each other was not one built on kept promises and camaraderie. He felt a strange urge to make sure he followed through on the promise he made himself at the spring. He didn't want to be alone out here either. Even if it had to be with his rival.

A drop of water fell from the sky, landing on Althea's cheek and Niklas realized that he was staring at her. He turned away and struggled to his feet, brushing away the pebbles that had embedded themselves in the palms of his hands and reached down, offering a hand to Althea.

She looked at his uninjured palm for a moment, and he could see the war playing out behind her eyes, which looked so dark in this light.

She reached up, seeming to have come to a decision and clasped her hand around his forearm, letting him pull her to her feet. Just then the clouds broke. Fat raindrops splattered the stone around them, lifting the scent of the earth. He was still holding her arm when the bush to his right rattled. Her smile dropped and her eyes grew wide. Niklas only had time to tilt his head in question before he felt the weight slam into him. His arm was wrenched from Althea's and he was pushed over the edge of the ravine.

Time slowed, his heart stopped beating. He heard her scream his name. Saw her reach for him, like she could have caught him and not have been pulled down with him. But he found himself reaching back towards her anyway, like he could somehow reverse time, simply climb back up and over the edge.

Niklas fell for an eternity. He felt rather than heard himself screaming her name. Even though he was the one falling.

Maybe he had hit his head on the way down, for he would have never felt that way had he not. If they had not been pushed together that fateful day on the shore of the Norvern river, when she had saved his life, and he had saved hers.

The *khourge* fell with him, flailing its arms and legs. At least he was taking with him one monster that the Cerridwen held within its dark, twisted, foliage.

Niklas hit the water, the ice shattering around him, cutting the skin of his neck and face. The cold felt like a knife of its own, its sharp edge making him suck in a mouthful of water, choking him. The edges of his vision faded black as he fought to find the air that was wrenched from his lungs.

He swam against the current, against the downward pull of his waterlogged armor and broke the surface, coughing violently, vomiting what he had swallowed, but was quickly pulled under again. He could not find his way back up this time, no matter how hard he swam.

His lungs burned for air, the cold stiffened his muscles, his vision fading more, until there was only a pinprick of light that he could see.

He had never been someone who prayed often, but with one last prayer, he prayed for Althea. He asked his God to let her live, even if he could not. And right before he let the water in, he asked God to forgive him... for everything.

CHAPTER TWENTY

ALTHEA

*T*he air was freezing, but the sun was warm on her face as she stared into Niklas's shadowed eyes. A single snowflake drifted down between them, blown away by his huff.

"Why can't you just leave me alone?" Althea complained, crossing her arms over her chest.

"Because, Narie said that we could only come watch the play if I kept an eye on you. Because I am older."

"Keeping an eye on me doesn't mean you have to have me on a leash. And only by one season!"

Niklas lifted his hands in the space between them, palms facing up, making a show of his empty hands. "No leash here," he said exaggeratedly.

"I just wanted to get a better look at Ailith. There are too many big people here. I couldn't see her from where we were sitting." Ailith, the warrioress from the time of King Brioc. She had been the king's highest general and close friend since the time he was only a prince.

It had been said that she often spoke down to royal guests when they let their lips become loose about the Queen of Valarie – King Brioc's mother, *before his reign. They had spoken in loud whispers about how the queen had been too tolerant when it came to the council meetings back before King Brioc made the peace treaty. When all the kings and queens of the four kingdoms had to meet once a year for discussions about the issues of whatever was going on at that time.*

"They are called adults, Little Althea. And you didn't have your eyes on the stage when you tried to make your getaway. Where were you going anyway?"

That nickname again, Little Althea. Like Niklas wasn't almost the same height as her, he was only two inches taller than her. Two.

She rolled her eyes and clapped her hands against her thighs. "Fine, I was going to go to the market and get a strawberry fritter." And with another roll of her eyes she asked, "May I please go and get one?"

He rubbed his chin and looked up in contemplation, tilting his head. An evil grin stretched across his young face, and said, "No, you may not."

Althea's mouth dropped open. "What?"

"I said, no."

Her stomach growled and Althea was not one for pleasantries when she was hungry.

Before he could say more, Althea turned and bolted down the cobblestone aisle, away from the stage, the same path she would one day walk for her ascension ceremony. She earned quite a few glares and angry shushes from the elders. White haired and wrinkle mouthed.

Althea only made it to the gate when Niklas grabbed her arm and whipped her around to face him. They stared at each other, angry little lungs heaving. It began to sprinkle, the water half frozen, not quite snow, and not quite rain, the sun disappearing behind the thick, gray clouds.

Althea and Niklas ignored the rush of people leaving the stage, trying to make it to their warm homes as the slush pelted the audience, putting a hurried end to the play.

He gripped her arm so tight it was painful, but she did not flinch. She squeezed his forearm back, harder. He did not flinch either, but she saw the flicker of pain in his eyes, and she knew that he saw it in hers.

The rain had felt like ice hitting their faces.

The sound of the crowds hurried departure faded away to birdsong, the cobblestones she had felt under her thin boots fell apart, replaced by uneven, loose rock under her thicker Guard boots.

Niklas stayed right where he was in front of her, holding onto her arm, but he was older, and so was she. He stood eight inches taller than her now, his jaw was stronger and so was his grip, his shoulders wider than they had been when he was twelve seasons old.

That moment had marked the very beginning of their rivalry with each other, and she did not know if this moment meant the end of it. She did not know how to feel about that. But, she thought she would have time to ponder on it, that was, until she saw the bush quiver.

One second, Niklas was holding her arm, his hand warm through the leather of her jacket sleeve, and in the next he was gone.

Khourge.

Falling.

Gone.

Althea screamed, the sound tearing painfully from her throat, she barely felt the stones as she fell to her stomach at the edge of the ravine, holding out her hand. Like she could somehow reverse time and simply walk over the edge of the ravine and grab his hand. Guide him back. To hold his arm in the soldier's handclasp. The one that soldiers in the Guard used that meant more than friendship.

She wanted to see the sparkle of new beginnings in his eyes as they held each other's arm for the second time in their lives, after a lifetime of trying to make the other miserable.

He screamed her name. Why was he screaming her name? He was the one falling, not her.

Althea would never forget the sound of the ice shattering when Niklas hit the frozen water below. She continued to scream his name. His head bobbed above the water once before he went below the surface and did not come back up.

She whipped around at the low growl, pushing herself up into a defensive crouch, heels at the edge of the cliff. She pulled her dagger out of its sheath with numb, trembling fingers. Her sight blurred, she could not tell if it was from the rain, or unshed tears.

A second *khourge* prowled out from behind the thick brush, its leg was bare from any fur. It suddenly struck Althea that it was the same *khourge* that had torn through their camp the night before. It had followed them. For *days* it had tracked them. And she had not known. Even with her training she had not sensed that they had been followed.

Anger burned like fire in Althea's chest, her shaking hands steadied on the hilt of her dagger as she slid it back in its sheath and instead drew her sword. The steel was as dirty and dark as the storm above them. The rain washed the filth and rust down the blade and over her hands as she took a step forward, her knuckles a stark white against the bronze hilt.

Everything in Althea wanted to run forward and end this now, but the seasons of training forced her muscles to relax, her mind somehow finding its own way to the back room despite the darkness that blinded its way. She slid her left foot forward, and eased into a fighting stance.

The *khourge* licked its fangs and paced side to side, eyeing Althea from top to bottom, not blinking once. Althea did the same. She took a step forward, angling herself with her right side to the drop instead of her back. The *khourge* stopped, facing her head on, bending on its haunches, prepared to strike.

"Come on, kitty," Althea taunted. The logical side of her mind that would have told her she was being an idiot, was numb. It responded with a low growl, but it just stared at her, tilting its head, confused at her reaction.

"Come on!" She shouted and swung her sword in the open space between them, sending the droplets of water that had collected on her hands into the *khourge's* face. It flinched and crouched lower, baring its fangs.

Then it lunged.

Althea was ready to meet the animal half way, but she was not ready for the other *khourge* that had snuck up behind her. She heard the crunch of a pebble under something big and she twisted out of instinct.

She watched as the *khourge* flew past her, a large claw digging into the flesh of her forearm. With the momentum of her spin, the claw drew all the way from the inside of her elbow down to her wrist.

White hot, searing pain clouded her entire body for a moment, but she shoved it to the side, grunting in pain as the two *khourges* circled around each other once before both faced her.

Her back was to the ravine again, with one *khourge* to her left and the other to her right, leaving too narrow of a gap in front of her to run through. She had no choice but to inch back as they inched forward.

She felt the fear drain from her, dripping out of her like the blood that dripped from her fingertips. There wasn't anything that she feared now. Niklas was gone. She was alone. And to Althea, that was the only thing that she had ever been afraid of.

The heel of her boot sent loose stones scattering down behind her. She risked one quick glance over her shoulder to see her fate. She sighed, letting her shoulders relax, her sword hung useless against her leg, dangling from her weak grip. The *khourges* stopped two feet away from her, waiting. She let her head hang from her shoulders.

The first tear fell, landing on the toe of her boot. The *khourges* took it as if an announcer had called 'fight' to start the match.

They lunged in perfect unison.

But before they could reach where Althea stood, she had already leaned back and let herself fall. The air roared past her, her long, tight braid whipped against her cheek, her cloak wrapped itself around her lithe body. She smiled when the *khourges* flew over the edge after her, at least the world would be safer from the two monsters the Cerridwen held within its darkness.

She fell another ten feet before she grabbed onto a tree limb that jutted out from the steep wall of the ravine. Her shoulders popped and she cried out in pain from the force of the sudden stop. The *khourges* fell past her, bouncing roughly against the wall, dead long before they hit the water below.

Fear suddenly rushed back into her when she realized what she had just done. She grunted and gasped, gritting her teeth. She had not had time to think about what she would do once she got here. Only that she saw an opportunity to live and she took it.

With a roar against the pain in her shoulders and injured arm, she pulled herself up until she sat on the branch, panting hard. The threat of more tears made her throat tight, making it harder to breathe. She couldn't stop a few from falling, but refused to make a sound. She would not mourn, not until her job was done and the queen's life was safe.

Running on fumes, Althea assessed her situation. She already knew before she looked up that climbing back to the top was not an option. Save for the limb she perched on, there were no handholds anywhere on the smooth rock face of the ravine. To her left there was more empty air, erosion having taken out the section of earth and was a straight drop. The sight of the long distance left Althea dizzy and clutching tighter to her branch.

The only possible way to go was to the right, where a solid looking shelf jutted out about a foot from the wall. It was as far away as she was tall, and ten feet below it, the wall was more angled. She could slide down the rest of the distance. It would hurt, no doubt, but she was left with no other options.

The ravine's shore was lined with jagged stones, covered in layers of ice as the light rain turned into sleet, stinging with every frozen drop that landed on her face.

She lifted herself into a crouch, fighting against the ache in her arms and legs as they shook with exhaustion. She wouldn't try to talk herself out of it, she drew in a deep breath and jumped.

She flew through the air, suspended above the earth for only a second that felt like minutes. She thought for sure that she had gauged it wrong, that she would come up short, until she landed on her right knee, and pressed her face against the rock, clinging to the smooth surface. Her right hand clawed for purchase against the unforgiving stone, and her left leg, like a lead column, hung off the side of the shelf. Althea tipped to the side, her momentum had been too much and the shelf too small. She began to tilt.

She gasped, catching herself with her injured wrist pressing into the edge of the shelf, her body hanging by the strength of her fingers. A gush of blood rolled down her arm and over neck, but she held on. Her fingers ached from holding her weight as her feet kicked at the wall, searching blindly for purchase.

Every breath that Althea took grated against her parched throat. She couldn't remember the last time she had a drink. She shook her head. She would worry about that later, whether or not she survived the next few moments.

Her boot latched onto something finally and she used her leg to take some of the weight off her hands. She looked down, past her trembling legs to the rocky earth under her dangling frame.

"*Please*," she whispered, meaning so much more than the one word, squeezed her eyes shut, and let go.

Weightlessness. It was a strange sensation.

Althea twisted midair before her feet met the rising earth. The incline of the wall was great enough that the landing was not as hard as she thought it would be. It was like she was sliding down the slide her father had made when she was a toddler. It now sat in their small yard, rusted after seasons of disuse.

Sharp stones imbed themselves into both of her hands as she grabbed at the earth to slow her descent. The water rushed up to meet her and Althea sucked in a breath, expecting to be met with ice cold, but as soon as she hit the dirt that lined the edge of the water, she slowed, the water lapping at the toes of her boots. She sat, her chest heaving great breaths, and watched the leather darken over her feet. All her senses rushed back into her body at once.

She stood, racing alongside the water, suddenly remembering the glint of bronze she'd seen from where she had stood at the top of the ravine.

There.

Niklas's gentle curls were nearly black from the water, the metal clasp on the shoulder of his breastplate had caught on a dead log, leaving him hanging in the middle of the flowing water to be battered by the current, his face gloriously above the water.

The chances of him being alive were slim to none. But she would not leave him there.

Althea could see from where she stood, knee deep in the water, that getting to him was not going to be easy. The current lapped at her thighs when she took another step, goosebumps flooding her skin, her teeth set to chattering.

She pulled her bow over her head and ripped off her cloak, throwing both over her shoulder to rest on the dry shore behind her and shuffled her feet as she advanced further into the water so the current would not sweep her legs out from under her.

Her head ached, her eyes blurred, her whole body involuntarily convulsed with fatigue, cold and hunger. Althea gritted her teeth against the spasms and kept going, the water now reached up to her chest.

Ten feet.

Niklas's body was perched with an arm thrown over the log, his face tucked against it like he was simply taking a break.

Althea walked on her tiptoes, fighting against the water swirling around her, caressing her chin. A rock rolled out from under her and she was swept under. She drifted a few feet before she managed to catch her footing again and jumped off the floor to break the surface. She swallowed the water that rushed down her throat and sputtered, coughing. She couldn't seem to get her footing again as the water did with her what it wanted, took her where it pleased.

Three feet, that was all that stood between them now, just a little longer than her arm. The current gave a violent lurch. She stretched as much as she dared to try to reach Niklas, a small wave cresting over her face, blinding her.

She screamed into the water, sending bubbles flying around her as she clawed at it desperately. Her body gave a violent hiccup of pain and she was unable to stop herself from taking in a mouthful of water.

She was drowning.

This is it, she thought before a stiff piece of fabric brushed her palm and Althea dug her nails into it, desperately pulling herself to the surface, gasping.

Niklas's cloak. Even in the end, he somehow managed to save her again.

With no hope of finding any footing in the depths, Althea used the cloak to pull herself up the length of Niklas's body. When she was able to, she grabbed onto the log and faced him. Gently, with a numb hand, Althea pushed the hair away from his face. He looked so tired and hungry, even in sleep. Althea ran her palm along his face, from his forehead down to his cheek, his stubble prickled against her skin, and felt along his neck for a pulse. Nothing.

What had she done? She should have sensed those evil creatures from a mile away, she had taught herself the skill from early on. She should have been able to read the signs of the forest around her. The small wildlife had been nearly non-existent since that night at the camp when the *khourges* had stolen their food, leaving them without their blankets and forcing them to return their horses to the wild.

The birds had been noisy, clearly calling out warnings to her. But she had not listened, all she had done was let herself be angry at the one person she actually needed, until she had become blind and deaf in her selfishness.

Sorrow constricted her chest painfully. Her body reacted to it, curling in on itself and coughed up the rest of the water she had swallowed.

A fleeting thought crossed her mind. That she could just stay here forever and forget about her mission. She was tempted to close her eyes and sleep as peacefully as Niklas was. Maybe it wouldn't be so bad. To let it all go silent, to slip away next to him.

No. She had never refused a challenge before, she would not start now.

Althea had only been in the water for one minute, but the water was so cold. Her limbs felt like they were turning into a dead tree, like the one under her frozen hands. She needed to get out and start a fire before the cold sickness could ravage her. But first she had to get Niklas back to solid ground, if only to ease her heart by seeing him to his soul home properly.

Carefully, Althea eased herself around Niklas until the current pushed her chest against his back, where she could see that a slim stick was the only thing holding him in place. A solid kick and he was free. But with the weight of his armor and cloak, he began to sink.

Althea clawed at the clasp of the fabric as she held onto him and was dragged under once more. It was stuck on the stubborn metal of his breastplate, the same problem he had in the darkness of that morning that led to all of this.

She scrambled for the dagger on her thigh, the hilt tangling in the fabric of her waterlogged tunic as they were tossed across the rocky floor. Her lungs burned and the water blocked what little sunlight there was above. She sawed blindly with her dagger to cut him free from his cloak.

With strength that she did not know she possessed, Althea tucked her hands under Niklas's arms and pushed. She swam to the edge of the water and dragged him out. She fell a few times and dropped him heavily on the shore.

"Now remember Althea, just because we don't have very many large bodies of water in Taris, does not mean that someone couldn't slip and drown in a puddle only an inch deep. Over half of the drownings in Llyr last season did not happen in the ocean. So it is very *important to learn how to give someone the breath of life and the beat of the heart. Because you never know when you might need to help someone."*

Althea stood with her father over a pile of hay wrapped in an old pair of clothes and shaped to resemble the body of someone who had been drowning.

She had wondered what her father would use the sheep's stomach from her birthday meal for, the one they shared with Niklas and his father.

Since Niklas and Althea shared the same day of birth, they often celebrated together, as well as their fathers being close, and because money had been tighter in recent days.

Her father bent to fill the stomach with water to resemble drowned lungs. He explained that as she pushed on the person's chest, it would push the water out of their lungs, but it was also vital to give the person new air to flow through their body, since they had none left in them.

"Fold your hands like this." Her father held out his scarred hands over the 'body' and threaded the fingers of his left hand through the fingers of his right stacking them on top of each other, splaying the fingers of the hand on the bottom out. Althea mimicked with her own hands, memorizing the position.

"Good," her father smiled. "Now press your hands in the middle of the chest, and you are going to want to press fast and hard." He demonstrated the process and water flowed out of the 'mouth' of the 'body'.

"Then," her father went on as he poured more water into the stomach. "After ten pushes, you have to open their mouth, make sure to hold the back of their neck up, pinch their nose and push the air from your lungs into theirs. Try for three seconds. And then you do it all over again, however many times it takes for them to wake up and cough the rest out. If it takes longer than three minutes..." He did not finish, even though Althea gave him a curious look.

She performed the methods he showed her perfectly and her father smiled proudly that she grasped the life saving skill so quickly at the age of eight.

Althea smiled back with missing teeth and was overjoyed at having another skill tucked in her belt.

Althea folded her hands together in the way her father had taught her and pushed down hard on Niklas's bare chest. She cursed the breastplate for having taken up precious time until she could pulse his heart. As soon as she pushed on his chest, water spewed from between his blue lips.

After ten pushes, she pulled his neck away from the ground and placed her mouth to his, filling his lungs, and repeated it again.

And again.

And again.

Althea's heart hammered in her chest, and not just from exertion. She couldn't hold it in anymore, her adrenaline had run out and the weight of the day fell on her shoulders like a boulder. She began to yell, her heart wrenching, her soul tearing apart with each push. She pleaded with God. "Please, please."

But she didn't stop, she continued to give everything she could give.

She gave him the air from her lungs, the warmth of her hands, the water from her hair as it dripped onto his closed eyes before rolling down his cheeks and into his hair. It looked like he was crying.

Her right arm buckled under the pressure of pushing on his chest. She had forgotten all about the wound from the *khourge*, and only now saw the blood that mixed with the water over both of their skin. Her arm hung uselessly at her side now, but she continued to push with all of her weight into his chest with her left arm. She quickly became dizzy from breathing for two, and her heart dropped into her stomach when she no longer saw any water flowing from Niklas's mouth. He paled even further.

A strangled scream tore from her throat. "Niklas, please wake up, please. I– I can't do this without you, I nee– I need you!" She roared, curling her hands into fists and slamming them on his unmoving chest.

It wasn't until the words flew unbidden from her mouth that she realized just how much she meant them. That was what she had felt when he had held her hand. She needed him and he was gone. He left her.

Her face burned from unshed tears that she knew if she let fall, it would truly be over. He would truly be gone.

"I need you, Niklas."

Her left arm collapsed on the next push, slipping against the water on his skin and she went sprawling across his chest, almost knocking the wind out of herself. She lay there, unable to move, shoulders shaking. His skin was cold against her blazing cheek where it had landed against his collarbone.

"I never got to call in the last bet I won, you boot stuffer," she sniffled.

If there was a good time to mourn, Althea wouldn't find it, for she still had a duty she needed to fulfill, and she would not let Niklas's sacrifice be for nothing. She would make sure his name was shouted from the rooftops. The banner of his family crest displayed in the streets.

She stayed there, draped half across his unmoving chest, the sound of her heart whooshing in her ear. She closed her eyes.

Suddenly Niklas's whole body jerked under her. Stunned, she jumped back just in time for Niklas to turn over and vomit, coughing violently.

Alive. Alive. *Alive.*

He had been gone for exactly three minutes.

Astonished, Althea remained still as stone while Niklas fought to fill his lungs, his breaths crackling from the water trapped in them. He stared at her, his eyes unfocused and said, voice rasping, "Boot stuffer?"

It was a child's insult that was said about someone who was a guard solely for the status of being one, but didn't pull their weight. All they were good for was quite literally to stuff their feet into their boots and look pretty in uniform, faking that they were accomplishing something great while everyone else worked their fair share.

Althea broke from the spell and pushed away from him, almost sending herself sprawling onto her back, turned and walked a few feet away.

She felt her face crumple, and even though she swore to herself that she would not cry, her body began to weep on its own. She held back as hard as she could, hoping that it just looked like she was shivering from the cold. She held a wet sleeve to her mouth and pressed it against her quivering lips. He was alive.

Her brain did not seem to be able to comprehend these emotions, and it left her senseless. All she could do was stare at the wall of the ravine and think that when she turned back around he would be laying down again. Gone.

"Althea?" It had to be a trick of her mind. She could almost hear the furrow in his brow. He was worried about her, she could tell, and that only made her want to weep harder.

She had been so careful her whole life to never let a single tear fall from her eyes, and until today she had been successful. But it was like the cork that had been holding them back had eroded away, unable to stop the flood that was rising inside her. She sank to the ground, hugging her knees and buried her head in her arms, closing off the outside world and turning into herself.

She cried. For Niklas, for herself, her father. Niklas's father, for she had broken her promise to him to keep his son safe. She cried for her mother that she barely remembered, wishing to have a mother's comfort, and she cried for every time that she ever held her tears back wishing she hadn't.

"Althea, stop." She heard the stones shift under his weight, and felt a hand rest on the toe of her boot. That simple touch drove her the rest of the way mad, and without thinking, she twisted around, lunging for him and wrapped her arms around his neck, tucking her face into his shoulder.

She expected him to resist, to push her away, to say something mean. He hesitated for a second before wrapping his arms around her waist and let her cry.

He let her have the time to grieve for the loss that she had experienced. And Althea thanked her God, over and over and over. She thought to herself that she would never stop thanking God, so long as she held breath in her lungs, she would scream her thanks. She reluctantly pulled herself away, giving Niklas room to catch his breath, and wiped her tears from his skin with her sleeve.

"So you finally admit to thinking that I am a boot stuffer, huh?" Niklas teased her, his words grating in his throat, both of their bodies shaking violently from the cold.

She couldn't stop the smile that split her lips, playfully pushing his shoulder and wiped the back of her hand across her nose.

He lifted himself into a seat and hissed in pain, grabbing his leg. Althea held out her hands like she was trying to approach an injured animal and waited for his nod before prodding his leg, checking for injury.

"It's not broken, just sprained," she told him, letting out a relieved sigh. Sprained, not good, broken, worse.

After a few moments of silence, where they both sat and let their minds reel, Niklas used his chattering teeth to scratch at his bottom lip. "Did you kiss me?"

Blood rushed back to Althea's face, lighting her insides on fire, melting the ice that had been there.

"What!? No!"

"You're blushing, and my lips feel swollen. Did you take advantage of me while I was in my most vulnerable state?" Niklas found his tunic where she had thrown it to the side and covered his bare, quivering chest.

"I was only giving you the breath of life, don't flatter yourself too much. I didn't *want* to."

Steam rolled off of their wet skin as the afternoon sun began to dry them, but the air was still cold, so Althea took to building a fire, larger than any she had since entering the forest, and kept her flushed face turned away.

She retrieved her discarded, dry cloak and let Niklas cover himself while his shirt dried by the flames. His cloak that she had cut from him had gotten snagged between two stones not far from shore. The dark green flowed just under the clear water like long grass blowing in the wind.

She waded barefoot into the water to fetch it. The thick wet wool had to weigh at least as much as Niklas did and she had to fight to drag it back to the fire, where she rolled it into a thin log, walking on it from one end to the other to squeeze out as much water as she could. Even wet, wool would be warmer than having nothing and with Niklas's limping help, they draped it across a shrub to dry.

Althea moved to take a place by the fire, but her legs gave out before she got there, her knees slamming into the sharp rock, jarring her, her breath hissed between her teeth.

"Woah, what happened?" Niklas reached out a hand from inside his bundle, but Althea waved him off pressing her lips in a tight line.

"I'm just– I– I haven't eaten in... I don't know how long, and with everything..." she trailed off, stretching out and putting her bare feet as close to the fire as her skin could stand.

Without saying anything, Niklas scooched a little closer, opened one side of the cloak and draped it over her shoulder, sharing what measly warmth his own body could give. She stiffened at first, unused to being so close to him without the barrier of steel armor, until her skin melted in the shared warmth.

"Thanks, Little Althea. I don't know what I would have done, if it had been the other way," he spoke softly.

"Oh, you probably would have gotten eaten by the other two that came after."

"What? Niklas stared at her open-mouthed. "Two other *khourges*?"

Althea winced, she had not planned on telling him about that. Oh how she wanted to slap herself sometimes. But if they were going to start this new path with each other, and make it out alive, she decided it best to be honest.

"Yeah, um... the *khourge* with the scarred leg. I guess he had his buddies with him again. I don't know how I didn't notice that they had followed us. I'm so foolish. None of this would have happened if I had jus–"

"No, don't do that."

"Do what?"

"Put that on yourself." Niklas shook his head, the thoughts behind his eyes matching the flames as he stared over the fire. "I am a skilled hunter too, and I never thought twice about it. This is different territory than what we are used to. There will be mistakes that are made, and wishing to undo them won't help anything."

Althea looked at her hands, picking the dirt from under her overgrown fingernails, and stayed silent. Because he was right. Fighting to change the past was impossible, all she could do was learn and move on. It was then she noticed the empty scabbard at her side.

Her sword hadn't been a special one, there were others out there. Sharper and engraved with prayers, but she felt the loss of it all the same. Her father had forged it for her.

"So... what happens now? I mean–" Althea waved a hand at the world around them, trying to ask with a signal instead of words that she didn't know how to convey her meaning.

"Between us and our mission?" Niklas asks. Althea nodded and looked up at him, breaking her stare from the water that had almost claimed them both, his expression thoughtful.

"Nothing," he said eventually, shrugging. "I will still be Niklas, and you will still be Althea. Whatever happened, and whatever happens next, it won't change that. But, we will need each other out here, and…" His next words seemed to be as much of a struggle for him to say as it was for Althea to hear. "I'm willing to work with you, as a fellow guard. As a… friend."

"Yeah, I would like to try that," she said softly. Niklas turned his head toward her, leaning back to see her clearly, the wind stirring a strand of her hair that tickled against her cheek.

"To the unknown?" Niklas asks, holding out his hand.

"Together, we shall find," Althea finished the old saying between guards. A promise of sorts. She clasped his arm again. This time on solid ground with everything to look forward to and nothing to forgive.

Chapter Twenty-One

Niklas

The pain in his leg was beyond excruciating. If he didn't know any better he would have thought it was broken. At least he could put weight on it.

He clamped his teeth together and took another step as they made their way towards the white capped Kyran mountains that loomed like a shadow, growing with each step.

The freezing rain had stopped, but it left behind an icy slush under his feet, making it a slippery quest. He hung heavily on Althea's shoulder, her arm wrapped around his waist. An hour into the day, she had spotted a sturdy piece of wood that ended in a point. It came up to his chest and made a suitable walking stick, just big enough to close his fist around its middle.

The sun shone brightly through the trees, casting shadows that danced along the forest floor. It reminded him of the tradition he and his father had of taking lunch under the dogwood trees in the square on the first of every month.

The shadows flickering from the trees in his memory were just like the ones before him now, the wind sweeping through the leaves with the late autumn chill, sending dead leaves falling like red snow.

They passed the time in silence, a heavy blanket that only chilled him further.

"I need to stop for a moment," Niklas ground out, wincing as stabbing pain went through his knee.

"Me too." Althea guided him to a fallen tree and helped lower him to sit on it. She turned and jogged away before he was even settled.

"Wait, where are you going?" Niklas called after her, startled at her sudden movement.

She smirked at him over her shoulder. "To relieve myself. Why, do you want to hold my hand?"

A strangled sound caught in his throat and he coughed to cover it up. They were the same words he had said to her at the spring. But he had to admit that it was a little embarrassing to be on the receiving end of the statement.

"No."

Althea shook her head, laughing as she jogged further into the brush until Niklas could no longer see or hear her. He sighed, stretching out his leg, and tried to breathe through the twinges of pain, massaging a hand down the length of his calf.

His thoughts drifted while he waited, back to the nightmare he had the night before. But the harder he tried to piece it together, the more the dream evaded him. All he remembered was a single dying candle, and the ice filling his veins. He had woken up with a strangled cry. Althea, who had been taking watch, didn't say anything as he panted for breath, and had quickly tucked the hand she had reached out toward him, back under her cloak.

The bushes in front of him rustled, breaking his thoughts.

"Althea?" He asked quietly. A twig snapped and Niklas stood. In one hand he held his walking stick for balance and slipped a dagger into the other. The bush gave a huge shudder, breaking the dead leaves off the stems, landing in a pile amongst the rest.

"Oh, come on Althea, how badly did you have to go?" Niklas flexed the fingers on both of his hands around his weapons and limped back a step. A figure burst through the bush, bellowing.

Niklas screamed at the sudden person that appeared two feet in front of him. It took a few seconds for his brain to register that it was Althea, grinning madly while holding a fat hare in her raised fist.

"Dinner!" She shouted, and laughed at the look of shock on his face. Niklas flattened a palm to his chest, making sure it was still beating, and could not help but laugh with her, sounding half-mad.

"Yeah!" He shouted. "Dinnnnerrrr!" Niklas let the dagger and walking stick fall to the ground and punched his arms into the air. Althea jumped up and down in excitement. He grabbed her by the shoulders and pulled her into a hug. He felt her stiffen for a split second before she threw her arms around him, hopping from foot to foot, unable to control her happiness.

They backed away from each other, feeling awkward at the show of excitement.

Althea picked up the steel dagger that he had dropped – his last one, he tallied – and began to dress the hare while he limped around to collect wood for a fire. His stomach growled, mouth watering in anticipation. The rabbit was big enough to feed both of them for the next two days. Enough time, Niklas hoped, for them to reach the mountain pass and push through until they could reach a market in Valor.

"Annnnd, done," Althea said, carefully pulling a chunk of meat off the sagging spit, her tongue sticking out of the side of her mouth in concentration.

She handed the meat, pierced through with a stick to Niklas and grabbed another for herself, blowing on the steaming food to cool it. Niklas did not have her patience. He bit into the meat, lighting his lips and tongue on fire and huffed with his head back, steam billowing out of his burning mouth like a dragon as he chewed despite the pain.

"Oh my goodness! I have never tasted anything so good." He spoke around another, cooler, mouthful.

"Wow, even without all of your fancy spices?" Althea smiled over at him, the firelight dancing in her eyes and off the grease covering her mouth. He had no doubt that his face was covered in it too. He didn't care.

"I don't think I will ever complain about food again. The only thing that could make this better would be to have toffee for dessert."

"I was thinking something more on the lines of strawberries on top of cream filled bread."

His face scrunched up thoughtfully. "To each their own," he said, lifting one shoulder indifferently and reached for another piece of rabbit. His stomach wasn't grumbling anymore, so he waited until the piece was cool enough to fully enjoy it.

They ate enough to fill their stomachs and were in the process of making jerky with what remained when Althea lifted into a crouch, holding a finger to her lips and pointed to Niklas's right.

He slowed his breathing and tilted his head to listen closely. He detected three sets of footsteps, moving quickly in the crunching leaves beneath what must be fur lined boots. Out of the corner of his eye, he saw Althea grab her bow, nocked an arrow and drew the string back to rest against her cheek, moving to duck behind a bush.

Niklas pulled out his sword, and stood behind a tree with gnarled roots that were sticking out of the ground. He kept his eyes on her, waiting for her signal if there was a threat.

They were here. The sound of their footsteps seized ten feet away, hesitant. Althea lifted three fingers off her bow string, telling him that it was a group of three. They were whispering something Niklas could not understand. He could see the smoldering remains of the fire from where he stood, but the people were out of sight from the low hanging tree limbs. The pile of jerky that they had laid out on a rock to cool still steamed.

"Popuh!" Exclaimed a high pitched, accented voice of a young girl. Niklas saw the figure of a child race toward the fire, cloaked in the white fur of a young wolf.

"*Astelyn*," one of the men gasped, rushing forward, catching the girl around her shoulders and pulled her away.

Niklas shrunk farther behind his tree and he saw Althea do the same. He had not missed the shining glint of the curved scythe in the man's hand. The blade had a section cut out every inch or so and looked like a saw that could cut through trees.

His hands tightened on the cool, metal hilt of his fathers sword, and he closed his eyes, focusing on trying to breathe quietly, assessing the viable outcomes of the situation.

The man seemed scared, and Niklas prayed that he was, that they would move on and decide not to meddle around.

The sound of leaves rustling was what made his eyes open, not the screams and shouts he heard after. He looked with wide eyes to where Althea was... had been.

She stood in the open space between them, an arrow trained on the strangers, shouting and holding their hands above their heads, their weapons cast onto the ground by their feet. They shouted frantically in their language, faces marred with panic, speaking fast, stumbling over each other.

Niklas was surprised that he caught a word or two that he understood. He shook his head at Althea's back, irritated that she had acted without him, and stepped out behind her.

He did not think that the strangers' faces could hold any more fear, but somehow they did. He rummaged through his head for the language that they spoke. It was lilting like that of the south-western parts of Marella, perhaps Pagos. It was a language he knew well, but it sounded off, and he could not put a finger on it.

"Calm yourselves," Niklas spoke on a whim in Pagosie. Instantly the two men and child froze, turning to look at him. At the sword clutched in his fist.

The man on the left spoke first. He was older than Niklas had thought now that he was closer. His back hunched, hair beginning to recede and was losing the fight against the hoar turning his once black hair into a frost of white.

"We heard screams, we came to see if there was someone that was hurt. There have been *brav* attacks lately around here. Forgive us, let us go and we won't tell anyone you were here. Please, at least spare the child." The man's voice was deep, almost as deep as Jekel's.

"We won't hurt you," he assured them. "We are trying to get to the mountain pass and needed a rest, that is all. Please stand, but... leave your weapons on the ground." He turned to Althea and whispered, "Stand down, but be ready." She nodded, not taking her eyes off the kneeling figures. She lowered her bow, keeping the arrow on the string.

Once they all stood, staying on opposite sides of the fire, Niklas asked, "What are your names, and where..."

"Are you from Heriit?" Althea finished, her lips forming to their lilting language so fluidly that Niklas would have thought she had spoken it her whole life. "I've heard of it only once, by an old woman that had stayed with Glady, she had been on her way to Llyr," she said to Niklas in their own tongue without looking at him.

The face of the man with the deep, rumbling voice split into a shocked grin as he glanced between Niklas and Althea. "You speak our language so well. Yes, we are from Heriit, we are a small village, very small, it is not on the map. Our father's fathers built it long ago. I am called Dovas." He gestured with a hand full of crooked with age fingers at the younger man. "This is my son Ronun. And this is my great granddaughter, Astelyn." The girl, no older than ten, waved with a gap filled smile.

"We have a festival around this time of year to celebrate bringing in the crops. To give thanks to God. We were about a mile that way." The man pointed behind him in the direction that they had come from. "Hunting, and we heard shouting. We were afraid someone was hurt. And by the looks of it I think I was right."

The old man's clear blue eyes traveled the length of the two of them, broken, and beaten, covered in weeks worth of muck and scars lining their skin.

"You will need to see a physician for your arm, young one. If you come with us we can help." He pointed at Althea. Niklas looked at her as well, brow furrowed. She had not complained about an injury, but now that he looked at her a bit closer, he could see that her face did seem pale.

"Where?" Niklas asked, confused, having been none the wiser that she had been injured in the process of saving him, and had helped him walk all this time.

Her back stiffened under the weight of his stare. Niklas did not miss the way she tucked her right arm behind her back.

Niklas whipped his hand out, catching her hand and turned her palm over. She had wrapped a piece of her cloak around her forearm, and it was beginning to unravel from the fresh flow of blood wetting the dark fabric even darker.

"It's just a scratch that I got a few days ago, it reopened when I pulled the bow, I'm fine." She covered his hand with her other palm, warm despite the chill in the air. He shook her off and continued to pull at the section of cloth, hissing at the damage he saw. It was deep, not enough to see bone and tendon, but it was mangled and branched off in several directions. It needed stitches. Badly.

He brought the back of his hand up to her forehead, feeling her temperature. She was warm, not feverish yet, but who knew when she would be.

"This place, Heriit, how far away is it?" Niklas asked, dropping Althea's arm gently.

"It is two mil–"

"No," Althea cut off the younger man, Dovas's son, Ronun. "I'm sorry, but we have somewhere to be by the end of the week, we can't waste any time. My arm will be fine, but thank you. May God bless your festival and your village for offering your services." She spoke in their language, but switched back to Valarian when she leaned in close to whisper in Niklas's ear, "We need to go, now."

He leaned back and spoke softly but his words were stern. "You are running warm, and your arm needs stitches. And I don't think I can make it another day on this leg without a proper splint."

Althea closed her eyes and sighed. He could not blame her for being untrusting of the strangers that inhabit the so-called 'uninhabitable' forest they were taught about.

"Just one night, Little Althea. So we can actually defend the *queen* with bodies that will be able to fight. Because right now, neither of us are well." He mouthed the word 'queen' while tilting his head in the other direction, so the villagers would not see who he was talking about. Just in case they happen to speak any Valarian.

One of them approached. It was the girl, Astelyn. She reached out and tugged on Althea's cloak, forcing her to look away from him and at the impossibly small girl.

"Would you please come with us? We have the best willow tea in the whole village, it helps with headaches, and it stops the stinging when you fall and scrape your knees, it even tastes good. And I wouldn't lie about that, because I have tasted a *lot* of nasty medicine, I promise.

"Anyway, I have always wanted to have a friend for the festival. I don't have a sister and mama won't let me come with her, she says that I will mess the evening up, but I know that I won't. Would you please come with us and let us help you?" Astelyn brought a hand to the side of her mouth like she was trying to hide what she was saying from her father and grandfather but still spoke loudly enough for them to hear, and said, "I promise they don't bite. And there is going to be so much music and food!" The girl was out of breath by the time she was done speaking.

Althea looked back at Niklas, biting her lip, distrust and wariness lining her face, searching him for his thoughts.

Before she could say no again, Niklas turned back to the villagers, kicking up leaves and purposefully twirling the tail of his cloak to float around him, feigning regal confidence when in reality he was just as wary of going with them as Althea was. But his heart, body and soul desired proper food and rest. And if he was lucky, a hot bath.

"Lead the way."

CHAPTER TWENTY-TWO

— • —

ALTHEA

Althea walked as far behind the villagers as she dared, not wanting to get lost if they were telling the truth. Dubiety weighed heavily in the hollow of her chest. Shocks ran through her body, sharp shivers that raced across her shoulders and down her back like she was being struck by lightning repeatedly.

Niklas limped right next to the villagers, chatting away as if he were catching up with old friends. His leg seemed less stiff than the day before, which Althea was grateful for. She did not think that she could have handled another day with him hanging on her like a heavy necklace.

The last few days repeatedly replayed in her mind. After the fall and being in the frigid water, her body fighting for warmth each night, and having not eaten nearly enough for days, she was ready to lie down. Althea shook her head against the pull of her eyelids.

"Are you okay?"

She almost leaped out of her skin, hand reaching for her sword only to remember that it was lost in the depths of the ravine. Her heart beat erratically in every part of her sore, stiff body. It was only Ronun. She had not seen or even heard him fall back from those ahead.

He squinted his eyes against the wind. She could see the concern in his gaze as it swept over her face. It seemed genuine – though anyone could feign a face – his eyes seemed so pure. More pure than Althea thought she had ever seen in any man his age. His skin was just beginning to wrinkle, the dreaded switch from careless youth to a wise man.

"Only wondering how there is this 'village'," she twirls a finger in front of her for dramatics. "In the middle of the supposed barren Cerridwen, the mystical forest that swallows up its victims and spits them out with only a half of their minds left. Forgive me if the people I have encountered over the last two weeks have lacked to be desired. Severely."

"I suppose it is a good thing we are not in the Cerridwen then," Ronun said with a shrug, a smile twisting on his lips.

Althea stopped walking and stared openly at the man. "What do you mean we aren't in the Cerridwen?" She fought to get the words out.

"The boundary of the Cerridwen is three miles from where we found you two. Our 'village'," he playfully mocked the hand gesture she had used with a smile. "Rests in the space between the two waterfalls on this side of the Kyran, hidden from sight of even the most renowned anthropologists. It is safe there. I promise on my portion of crops this season."

Althea was stuck on the large word the man used, not knowing the translation and was barely able to hear the rest of what he said.

She did not know how strong an oath on crops was to this man, and even though she wanted to go on her own, she could not leave Niklas alone in the clutches of these strange men... and child. Perhaps she was overreacting and these people were truthfully wanting to help two lost, broken strangers.

"Do you know, perchance, what week of the month we are in?" Althea asked.

"In order to stay hidden we do not leave the village often and don't go very far into Valor unless absolutely necessary. So to answer your question, I have no idea, other than that the crops are ready to harvest, so we celebrate. I really think you two will enjoy the festivities if you let yourself." He looked at her out of the corner of his eyes and they began walking again. "And forgive me if this is too personal a question, but what is your relationship with this young man?" He asked. The question must have been on his mind for some time, for he said the sentence with ease, not stuttering once.

"Uh– well– I," she cleared her throat. "We are fellow guards." He pursed his lips, nodding. They picked their way through a trampled bush and Ronun continued.

"You know, it is not uncommon for young men and women guards to be married so young. It is nothing to be ashamed of. The future is uncertain, and each day holds the ability to be the last. I am not so old yet as to forget what it was like to see my wife for the first time and realized that I belonged to her. Wholly." Ronun's eyes sparkled as he thought back to his youth, his face lit with a joy like that of his niece, who kept running ahead and stopping to wait for the rest of them to catch up, only to run ahead again.

Althea's face burned at his assumption and opened her mouth to correct him, but before she could speak, the forest broke, revealing two, tall waterfalls that branched off the side of the Kyran mountains and fell into a pool of liquid diamonds. The water was so clear that where they were, nearly a mile above, she could see the rocks at the bottom, past the group of women washing clothes.

Others washed their hair and combed through the long strands of black and blonde. Men were entering the village from another part of the forest, carrying fat deer on their shoulders, more were building structures for bonfires.

This small village is a lot bigger than I expected.

It spread out in the shape of an eagle's wings. The wings stretched wide, hugging the curve of the mountain, and where the body of the bird would have been was the massive pool tucked in between the two shorter peaks.

One waterfall on each side flowed into the pool and from there, branched out into four, man-made streams that run behind the rows of fifty squat cobblestone buildings on each side making up the feathers of the wings. The thatched roofs from this angle did nothing to hide the village, but if seen from above on the mountain pass, no one would be able to see anything. Nothing but the tips of trees, and more trees. It was ingenious.

Althea closed her hanging mouth when her throat went dry, realizing that she had fallen further behind in her astonishment. She shivered in the evening air, and gathered enough of her fading strength to catch up to Niklas, and pulled on his arm so they could drop back a few paces. She needed to speak with him privately.

"I don't know about this Niklas, there has to be a reason they are trying so hard to stay hidden. And more so that they have succeeded in it. The mountain pass is only a mile that way." She pointed to the right. Her arm bumped against his chest and she quickly snatched it back, blushing as she remembered what Ronun thought they were to each other. She would not tell Niklas, for he would use it against her and tease her to no end. He looked at her funny, but she ignored it.

"It will only take two – two and a half days – to reach Valor, we should go now and not waste any time." She shivered steadily now from the cold and pulled her cloak tighter around her shoulders.

"And what about when we get there? If we are so exhausted to the point of passing out, who will we be able to protect, Little Althea? Hmm?"

"I don't know, I just…" she trailed off, closed her eyes and rubbed at her sore neck. A cool hand pressed onto her forehead. She opened her eyes to see Niklas leaning over until his eyes were level with hers.

"You are burning hotter than a fireplace in summer, you need help. Now." Althea knew that tone. His lieutenant tone. It meant that no matter how hard she fought, the decision had been made. It did not stop her from trying though. "But–"

"No, Little Althea, not this time. As your Lieutenant, I order you to receive medical attention as soon as we arrive."

"I never ascended, remember? You are not my Lieutenant yet."

"Than as your friend. For me."

Her breath caught in her chest. Maybe it was because he had said the 'F' word, or maybe it was because she was beginning to feel terrible aches in her bones, she did not know, but she relented, giving a hesitant nod and leaned on Niklas's offered arm as they made their way down the steep slope toward the looming unknown in front of them.

The physician's hands were bitterly cold against the warm skin on her stomach as he prodded with the wound on her side, draining the infection from it.

"It is good you got here when you did, the infection is early. As long as you drink the willow draft and get some sleep you should be feeling better by morning." The Physician was at least twenty seasons older than Archibald.

Althea did not know it was possible for someone to still be able to work at his age, but his hands were steady as he stitched her arm, removed the old string from her jaw, and was now working on her side.

"I don't need a draft, and I don't want to be in this sick bed any longer. I'm fine," Althea argued for the second time since the physician had entered the room. Niklas stopped his aimless pacing, the scraping sound that his boots made against the stone floor ceased.

"You are not okay. You collapsed the second our feet touched the first stone inside the village. Or did you forget the whole me having to carry you here, part?"

Althea dropped her head back onto the itchy pillow and forcefully blew air through her lips. The physician gave a sharp tug on the last stitch, producing a yelp from her. She looked at him with wide eyes.

"The boy is right. You need to rest and prioritize your health or all of my work on you would have been for nothing. And I do not take well to people who think their bodies are limitless. Here, drink this and rest." His voice was stern, final, but his face showed care and understanding.

Althea looked at the mug in her hand skeptically before taking a careful sip. She expected to have to fight bitterness and grit. Her eyebrows rose in shock. The drink was sweet and flowed over her tongue like silk, it had been strained from the leaves and tasted like fresh honey, unlike the rough drafts she and her father made at home. The physician smiled knowingly.

"I leave her to you boy, your task is to make sure she does not leave the bed till the sun hits this building on the morrow." He turned his back to her and whispered into Niklas's ear loudly, knowing that she would hear. "Good luck."

Niklas shook the old man's hand, turned and gave her an exasperated look, as the door closed behind the man, locking her in the room with not one, but two headaches.

"I can not believe that man. I am not some delicate little flower that might wilt the second I stand up," Althea huffed and quickly drained the draft, setting the mug on the floor rougher than needed.

"No one ever said you were a delicate flower. Trust me, I know all about the thorns you hide beneath your girlish exterior."

"Girlish?" She sputtered. "I am a woman... of the Guard. And I'm pretty sure I am stronger than half the men in this village." Althea yawned, rubbed her eyes and chided herself for drinking the entire draft. She should have known it probably had something in it to make sure she slept, they knew she didn't want to.

"Now if you don't mind, I'm starving. I'm going to see what this village is all about." Niklas started for the door as soon as Althea's stomach growled.

He stilled with a hand on the door. "I suppose you would like something too?"

He waited for a response and when it didn't come, he looked over his shoulder. Althea's eyes were closed and soft snores were his answer.

Chapter Twenty-Three

Niklas

N iklas strolled between the lively houses, nibbling on a pastry that was given to him by a woman who was trying to corral a barrel full of children into a daytime sitter's house.

Niklas had noticed her struggle and may or may not have used a soldier's stance in his armor to unnerve the kids enough to go inside. Maybe it was the scars that lined his cheeks and forehead. Or the sword he made sure his cloak was tucked behind. It better not have been how he smelt. He would have to ask where a bathhouse was and soon.

As he walked, he watched some of the villagers work. Middle aged men with full beards slammed hammers down on metal; women old and young sat on chairs under the shade of porches, mending clothes and crafting baskets. Children ran around, falling against Niklas's legs, apologizing with low bows.

He was amazed at how welcoming the villagers were, but did not let it show. No matter what path he took, or what shadowed alley he crossed he was greeted with a genuine smile from everyone.

He soon ended up by the waterfalls that fell into the pool that marked the center point of the village. That was where he found what he was looking for.

Gathering his confidence, he forced himself to walk, not run, to the nearest food vender, where massive iron pots were full of a type of stew. Steam rose up from the stand and caught under the canopy before rolling out from it like waves in a storm.

"Hello," the man, wearing a thick leather apron, said. Niklas nodded once, fighting to take his eyes off of the food, afraid it might vanish if he looked away.

"Hello, how much for two bowls?" Niklas hoped he said it right. He would never get used to the swirling language.

"Where are you from bairn? I don't think you have the currency I take here." The man wore a smile but his words were taunting, testing him. So that was how it was going to be.

Niklas ran a tongue across his teeth and smirked his best smirk. He had to admit, it felt good to wear it on his face after so long. It felt like putting on a pair of old leather boots that somehow still fit perfectly.

He used his elbows to push his cloak back, acting like he was just putting his hands on his hips in contemplation, but was really showing off the array of steel and stone daggers on his belt, strapped down his left leg and tucked into his boot.

"Please, pray tell, what currency do you take. I *am* a Lieutenant of the Guard Taris, I can always write a loan script. All you would have to do is bring it to town and it will be filled. To whichever currency you desire." The man's face paled as the sun glinted off the weapons and shined against the stall like glitter. He swallowed audibly and cleared his throat, considering Niklas for a moment.

"Aye, I was just teasing you boy, no need to fear. All are welcome here in Heriit, well, those who happen to stumble upon us that is. Small, small village we are." The man's smile was large and welcoming, his upper lip vanishing underneath his mustache as he laughed nervously.

"I have noticed. Everyone is very friendly."

"Two bowls right? I saw you with your little lady walking into town this morning when I was cutting up the venison, I'm sure she is starving too."

"Yes, two, and I owe you a favor for this."

He waved a hand, dismissing any mention of debt. "No worries, it is payment enough seeing people enjoy my cooking, it's why I'm here everyday."

Niklas hefted the bowls into the crook of his elbows. "Thank you, sir. I will have these bowls returned by tonight." He turned and retraced his steps back through the busy workers, leaving behind one of the stone daggers tucked behind a stack of bowls as a form of payment.

The man was clearly someone who liked unique things by the way the back wall of his shop had been lined with hanging memorabilia of various objects, such as, masks that were carved into haunted expressions, arrows that were far too long to be of any actual use, and curved blades that were carved out of wood, marble, and what looked like stained glass.

He lifted one of the bowls to his lips, having forgotten to ask for a utensil, and nearly boiled his insides. It was probably the best thing he had ever tasted in his life. Or maybe it was the starvation talking, but he didn't care, he wanted to get it to Althea before it went cold.

Niklas juggled the bowls and the cherry filled 'scone' the woman had called it, turning the last corner to the small building that he had locked Althea in.

His steps faltered at the sight of the small crowd gathered outside of the gray building, whispering to one another and pointing. As he came closer one woman turned, picked up the hem of her long skirt and ran to him. She spoke rapidly and Niklas was only able to make out parts of what was said.

"She screamed, no one could get in to see to her."

Niklas's shoulders tensed as he strode forward, the crowd parting for him. Furrowed brows, squinted eyes, and pinched lips were plastered on the worrisome faces of the women.

He handed off the bowls of stew to the person nearest the door and held the scone between his teeth as he pulled his steel dagger from his hip, not bothering with the fancy knot he made in the rope that kept the door closed, and instead sliced through the cord in one clean swipe. The door swung open and he cleared the space from the doorway to the bed in two long strides, leaving the crowd outside to shadow the doorway.

Althea's entire face, neck and arms were slick with large drops of sweat, her breathing uneven, eyes moving back and forth erratically behind her eyelids. He lowered himself to a knee by her head and poked her shoulder with his pointer finger. He knew better than to shake someone awake who was having a nightmare. He had been kicked square in the chest once by his friend Magnus and hadn't been able to train for two days.

He got no response.

A strand of her hair was stuck to the corner of her parted mouth and Niklas brushed it away with the back of his little finger and suddenly Althea had his wrist, twisting it painfully, making him hiss.

She threw herself off the bed, her other hand reaching for his throat, but Niklas recovered in time, leaping back, falling in a heap on the stone, pinned under Althea.

Her eyes, full of fear, widened with recognition and pushed herself away from him, crawling until her back hit the bed and slumped against its rough surface. She wiped the hair and sweat from her eyes, gasping.

Niklas stood, dusting off his clothes that were now more dirt than fabric after their many days without washing and walked over to the door, grabbed the bowls of stew from the frozen woman, now gone cold and closed the door, shutting out the whispers, stares and the glare of the afternoon sun.

He set the stew on top of the single, short stand next to the warm fireplace. The room was only as wide as the small bed and was as long as two men, head to heal, so it only took his two paces to cross the hard floor and grab Althea's hand, helping her up to sit on the bed and lowered himself onto the log-chair next to it.

"What was that all about?" Niklas asked, tilted his head and rubbed at his wrist. Her breathing had slowed down, her face not as pale as it had been the night before.

"I don't really know," she spoke, her voice rasping. "It was so dark. All I could hear was the sound of battle all around me. It was like I was really there, back at the river. I could feel a sword in my hand and the press of my bow against my back." She swallowed, her eyes creasing at the corners turning her expression to one of worry.

"I heard you. You were screaming, with rage like I have never heard before and I felt hot blood spray onto my hair and skin as I was trying to find you and I couldn't see, but... I felt someone grab onto me, trying to hold me back, then flashes of lighting lit the battle and I saw you and–" her words choked off and she coughed, continuing, "Just before someone behind you swung their sword. I reached for you. I screamed to try and tell you to turn around. But the arms were so strong. I woke up and I thought you were the one who I was fighting, I'm sorry."

Despite the quivering in her voice and the threat of her left eye welling up she didn't let a tear fall. Niklas let a minute pass in silence after she finished explaining, then clapped his hands on his knees, sending two plumes of dust floating in the air and stood, pulling Althea to his chest before he convinced himself how weird it would be to hug his childhood enemy.

She gasped and stiffened, but after a long second, she wrapped her arms around the outside of his cloak. He did not miss how badly her arms were shaking as she latched her fingers behind him, resting her cheek on the metal breastplate of his armor. The scent of vanilla wafted off of her hair and filled his nose. *How does her hair still smell so clean?*

"It's called soap you imbecile," Althea chuckled and let go of him, but didn't step back, her eyes flicking over to the bowls of stew he had bought.

A foreign fire raced up Niklas's neck, spread across his cheeks and burned his ears. *I did not just say that out loud.*

The thick door to the building flew open, slamming against the stone wall and in strode Astelyn towing the physician behind her.

The girl's face blushed, eyes darting between them. "Sorry, did we interrupt something?"

Niklas furrowed his brow in confusion as to what the girl was talking about, but then felt Althea shift against him and realized with a start how close they were standing. He all but jumped away from her and rubbed at the back of his neck. "No. I was just helping her up, that's all."

Althea's face was as red as a ripe tomato as the physician did a check on her wounds. "The draft seems to have brought the infection out, although you are still a little warm," he put the back of his hand to her cheek. "But I don't think it is because of a fever," the physician whispered and Niklas did not miss the old man's wink.

"Thank you, sir. I feel as good as new. I am sorry for being a stubborn patient, I just don't usually like asking for help," said Althea.

The man chuckled and dismissed her statement with a wave of his wrinkled hand. "Oh it is no deal, I am just happy that you are feeling well. I give you permission to go and enjoy the festivities tonight, but just try not to dance too hard."

"Yes, sir." Althea stood and saluted with a bright smile, making the man laugh.

"Be at ease, young one."

As soon as the physician left, his place at the bed was taken up by Astelyn, all grin and wind pinkened skin. She grabbed ahold of Althea's hand and clasped it between her own, looking up at her with pitiful doe eyes.

"Are you ok, Miss Althea? I heard that something was wrong and I was so worried that your infection may have gotten worse so I ran and fetched Mr. Iser. He was all the way on the other side of the village. I am so happy that you are feeling better. You are feeling better aren't you?"

It looked like Althea's head was spinning behind her eyes, trying to keep up with Astelyn as the girl raced to say everything in one long breath. She rested her free hand on the girl's shoulder and bent low until they were eye to eye. "I feel better than I have in weeks. Although I *am* famished."

The toll of a bell rang in through the open door and Astelyn jumped up and down with excitement.

"Oooohh, it is four hours until the festival, we must begin preparations. I'll show you the bathing ponds." Turning to Niklas, the girl scrunched up her nose and said, "I will send someone to show you where the men bathe."

She turned back to Althea, making a 'blah' noise and scowled, earning a chuckle from her and she was quickly whisked away in a blur of fabric. Niklas huffed an exasperated chuckle and shook his head.

Making sure no one was looking through the open door he subtly dipped his head to his arm and sniffed.

Chapter Twenty-Four

Althea

The bathing pond was open to the air but tucked behind a small outcropping away from the eyes of the village.

Multiple fires burned around it with large basins of water attached to a spit-like contraption, rolling with steam. Every so often a pair of women would pull on the rope that was tied to both the basin and the nearest tree or rock. The rope would roll on a wheel, tilting the basins and pouring the boiling water into the pond. The basins would be filled black up with the same water and it would be done all over again, making an unnatural hot spring in the left wing of the village and Astelyn told Althea that the men's was all the way on the right wing.

Althea stood behind a bush to undress, even though she would have to walk exposed to the water anyway, and there were plenty of other women already hovering in waist deep water. She felt different from them.

Unlike when she was home around the other women of the Guard, these women were soft, their skin wasn't burnt from the sun or scarred from blades while training. Nor did they have a pattern of itchy red bug bites like she did. She shook her head. The women she had encountered so far had been welcoming. Nothing like the ruffians that hung out in the dark alleys of Taris where people met to do things that were not meant to have light shed on.

Althea crossed her arms over her chest and sank into the hot – not just warm – but blissfully hot water and closed her eyes, breathing in the misty smell of the steam that curled like waves in the gentle, crisp breeze and began to untangle her hair.

She missed her vanilla soap that had been in her bag, but was pleased with the light pink bar that smelt like fresh roses she was offered. She scrubbed her hair with it and used handfuls of the sand from under her feet to scrub the layers of filth that covered her from head to toe until her skin was as pink as the soap.

A pair of hands wound around her hair and Althea turned, coming face to face with a weathered woman whose own was as white as the snow tipped mountains above them, and skin as wrinkled as a piece of paper that had been folded one two many times. She had a full, gentle smile and asked if she could braid her hair for the festival.

Not wanting to be rude, Althea let the women lead her out of the water and sit her on a rock, wrapped in a towel as her clothes had been whisked away by Astelyn to be washed and mended. As the skilled fingers began weaving her hair, she made sure her dagger was where she left it, not too far from her.

Astelyn came running through the bathing area and slid to a stop in front of Althea, her arms full of fabric in all different colors. The girl's mouth dropped open, eyes wide and traveling over her. Althea sat a little straighter and clutched at her towel. "What?" She asked, a blush beginning to bloom across her nose and cheeks.

Astelyn blinked. "You are so beautiful." The woman finished tying off the last piece of her hair. "Are you sure you have trouble seeing, Aunt Mehg?" Mehg replied with a youthful chuckle.

"Oh sweet thing, you don't need to see to know how to use your hands. This was my profession in case you have forgotten."

Astelyn carefully unfolded a clean linen sheet and spread the bundles of fabric she was carrying onto it.

"Hmm, okay." She cupped her chin and tapped her pointer finger against her pursed lips, her other hand rested on the hip she jutted out as she stared down at what Althea could now see were dresses.

Very expensive looking dresses.

"Where did you get all of these?" Althea asked, running her calloused fingers over a smooth, black dress.

"My Momma, Melody. She is a seamstress and these were the ones she didn't like the look of on her, so she gave them to me for when I'm bigger. They should fit you just fine, you are about the same size as Momma."

She picked up an emerald green dress that had a *very* low neckline, and seeing Althea's grimace, cast it aside for another. Jet black and velvet, short, the high neckline that would rest at the base of the neck was beaded with white glass beads.

Astelyn made a similar face to this dress as Althea had made at the last and moved on. A burnt yellow, made of cotton. "Too much like spring."

Then she picked up the last dress and Althea fought to keep her mouth from dropping open. Astelyn grinned wide and without saying anything grabbed her wrist and pulled her to her feet. She pushed the dress into Althea's arms making her fumble to keep her towel on and bounded off, tossing words over shoulder. Something about shoes.

The dress was a deep red, the color of expensive wine, and was a tough cotton fabric.

Taking care to not muse her hair, Althea slipped the dress over her head, letting it glide over her stomach and hips until the hem landed two inches off the ground. It fit perfectly, almost like it had been tailored specifically for her. Her shoulders and back were exposed and the collar was a strip of detailed lace that rested delicately against the base of her neck.

It wasn't anything like the dress her father had forced her into a couple years ago. That one was a dusty blue that had looked far too boxy, emphasizing her shoulders too much instead of her thin waist.

She tied up the strings along her side and a slightly confusing, thin leather belt wrapped around the smallest part of her waist a few times in an X like pattern. The skirt was pleated ever so slightly, flowing with her every move. Two cuts in the front of the dress started up her thighs and exposed her legs from mid thigh down. Despite that, it was modest and allowed her to move freely, to which Althea was grateful.

A joyful squeal broke her admiration of the dress.

"I can't accept this Astelyn, it is too much." Althea tugged at the waist of the dress, her hands giving away how uncomfortable she felt.

"Well, it's too late to change, the festival has already begun. Here put these on." She set a pair of strappy leather sandals on the ground and moved to the left where she bent over and picked up Althea's dagger. "I'll take this to the room we set up for yo-"

"No!" Althea lurched forward and snatched the sheathed blade out of the girl's hands. Not having meant to be so forceful, Althea quickly apologized.

"It's just that... I never go without this. It doesn't leave my side."

She half expected Astelyn to begin crying from her sudden outburst, but she only ran her eyes over Althea's body, popping her lips in thought.

"It doesn't go with the theme I'm working with... but alright, I have an idea. May I?" She reached out a tentative hand and Althea blinked, slowly extending her prized possession.

The girl's slim fingers worked at the leather straps, twisting them into a spiral and wove a vine into it, and when she was done, she knelt down and wrapped the vine and leather cord around her ankle and up her exposed right calf, stopping just below her knee. It looked just like a snake winding its way up her leg.

Althea barely had time to admire the tangle around her leg before Astelyn was pasting a cold lotion on her face and dusting her with powders that she had to fight back sneezing from. She picked up two winter roses, almost the same color as the dress and pinned them in her braided hair. Astelyn scolded her when she tried to lick the berry juice that was used to stain her lips, and with one last rub of rose oil on Althea's collarbone, she stepped back and admired her work.

She let the girl pull her away from the steamy air and through the chilly shadowed streets until they reached the brightly lit square where the festival had just begun. The stars began to wink at Althea as night fell over the earth.

Astelyn ran off to a group of children that must have been her friends, and Althea stood awkwardly near the edge of the courtyard not knowing where to look or who to greet.

At least not until her eyes fell on locks of chestnut and glinting, scarlet brown eyes.

Standing on the opposite side of the square from her, Niklas looked as uncomfortable as she felt. To someone who didn't know him, they probably saw an air of confidence. But after spending nearly a month alone with him, Althea recognized the subtle twitch of his thumb, and the way he blinked twice at a time instead of once.

His eyes met hers and his fiddling stopped. They walked toward each other, meeting in the middle, close to the large bonfire in the center.

Someone had combed his hair, pushing the locks back, but a few stubbornly fell into his eyes. There was a slight sheen to his skin, making his face sparkle ever so slightly when the light of the fire hit it.

He was clothed in a shirt with long sleeves the color of a foggy, moonless dusk, tinged with the slightest hue of blue and pants that were so dark the fabric seemed to absorb any light that came near it. Although he seemed to have managed to convince whoever helped him get ready to keep his dirty hunting boots on.

Her gaze worked its way back up to meet his and she knew that the look on her face matched his. Open mouthed and wide eyed, a blush burned at her skin and she saw the pink on his nose as he breathed in the scent of the winter rose oil she wore.

Althea knew that they must be a sight to behold for the villagers. Two strangers, battered and bruised, covered in stitches and dressed up like they were at the queen's ball itself.

"You look..." Niklas started and Althea finished, "Alright."

Niklas chuckled. "Alright."

"Come on you *vuity*, no need to be shy, it is time to dance." A young woman, wearing a heavy amount of makeup pushed Althea toward Niklas, and spun in circles through the crowd of dancers.

"What does *vuity* mean?" Althea asked.

"I have not the slightest clue, but I think it was an insult." Niklas raised an eyebrow and offered her his hand.

She stared up at him, but didn't think too long before she grasped his warm hand and let him lead her to join the dancers.

She had no idea what the steps of the dance everyone else was doing, but Niklas led her in a twirling foot shuffle that she immediately recognized as a combination of sparring footwork so familiar to her that she would know how to do it in her sleep. Althea couldn't stop the smile that rose on her lips.

Musician sat on a small stage playing the drums and violin. Food stretched out on long tables, and large barrels of wine quickly emptied as the villagers drained them. Astelyn danced in front of the stage with the other children.

They quickly became sweaty as they danced among the warm crush of bodies. She would never in a million seasons have seen herself in a small, hidden village, dancing at a festival instead of spending her free time training for her ascension, helping her Poppa with the garden, or cutting down trees for winter. And she definitely would not have imagined dancing with Niklas. And she was surprised that she was having – dare she think it – fun?

"This is crazy isn't it? I mean, usually the only time we are this close to each other is when we are in the arena. And I clearly remember that it always involved some type of pain," Althea puffed.

"What makes you think that I don't plan on stepping on your foot soon? I don't know why you let them put you in those... slippers?" Niklas looked down.

"Well, I think you underestimated the authority of that little girl. It was almost a battle to convince her to let me keep my dagger." Althea caught a glance of Astelyn on one of their spins. The girl saw her and smiled as she danced with a young boy her age.

"She is definitely a character. She would make a fine nobleman's wife one day. That is, if this village ever manages to be officially recognized." Niklas smiled. "Poor chap."

She laughed as Niklas spun her away, but caught her hand before she went out of his reach and twirled her up the length of his arm, catching her when she lost her footing and held her against his heaving chest. The music swelled and goosebumps erupted over her head and down her arms, something she had never felt before. It left as soon as it came when the music ended in a deep note.

Out of breath and laughing, they fought their way out from among the dancers and sat at the only empty space they could find. Tucked off to the side of the courtyard a two foot tall stone wall separated a small barnyard that held a few goats with long beards from a backyard with laundry strung up to dry.

They sat next to each other on the cold stone, catching their breath and watched the festival in comfortable silence. Althea tilted her head back, looking at the small slip of night sky that found its way to them from between the buildings.

A bright star raced across the gap.

"Look at that star!" She gasped.

It sped across the sky and disappeared behind the looming mountains that separated them from their destination. Another star gave chase to the one that had passed, and soon, hundreds, thousands maybe, lit the sky in bright, brilliant colors. Some were cased in the darkest royal blue, some were vibrant reds and oranges, others green.

The same green as Aezel's eyes, she noticed and she had to swallow a cough as the feeling of missing her friend struck her. She saved the sight in her mind so that if... *when* she saw her friend, she would tell him all about it.

Excited shouting, laughing, and whistling filled the night as the whole village watched the stars rain.

CHAPTER TWENTY-FIVE

NIKLAS

N iklas didn't know that the sky could hold so many colors at once as he watched the reflection of the flying stars in Althea's eyes.

"Do you think they're okay? The others. What is going to happen to them once they get to Caedmon?" She whispered.

Niklas sighed, thinking of what to say. "I have no idea, Little Althea. But one thing is certain, Captain Delmar does not take kindly to unforeseen changes. And he has the best of the best legion of soldiers behind him. Minus one... or two," he finished, blinking a few times, shocked, because he meant it.

Althea tucked her chin to her chest and swung her legs back and forth, her toes barely scraping the dirt from where they sat.

He tended to forget how small she was. The way she holds herself often makes some men look small. But at that moment, when her eyes rose to meet his, she looked her age.

She was just a normal girl, enjoying a celebration. He could see in her eyes her soul refusing to be hardened by everything that had happened in the Cerridwen and all that they still had to face. It made

Niklas forget for a second the pressure of their mission. The weight lifted off of his shoulders, making him feel like he was floating before Astelyn snapped her fingers in between his and Althea's faces, ending the moment. The weight crushed down on him once more, heavier than before.

Astelyn's face broke out in a goofy grin. "Momma said I am only allowed to be out until the moon is fully risen, and I wanted to make sure you know where your rooms are. The festival isn't over yet and you can come back if you want."

Althea hopped off of the wall and stretched her arms above her head, her shoulders popping, and yawned. "I think I have had enough excitement for one day. I feel like hibernating for the rest of the winter."

Astelyn giggled and grabbed onto both of their hands, leading them out from the tucked away alley and through the unending celebrations.

Niklas swiped two huge turkey legs from a table they passed and offered one to Althea. Her stomach roared loudly at the sight of the food in his outstretched hand. Both Astelyn and Niklas grabbed their stomachs, aching from laughing. She shook her head at them but hid her smile behind the leg as she chewed.

"Here we are." Astelyn unbolted the heavy wooden door. It was bright inside, warmed by a freshly lit fireplace in the corner of a kitchen. A tea kettle hovered over the flames, whistling. The girl huffed and carefully removed the kettle, setting it on the thick table in the middle of the small kitchen.

"Sorry, my Momma is a little... unmotivated," Astelyn said.

"Momma," she called out and walked into the dim living space, lit only by a single candle on a side table that was close to running out.

"She must not be back yet. This way is the bathing room."

Niklas stayed behind as Althea quickly changed back into her tunic and pants, leaving her leather jacket and boots by the door. Her face was washed clean of the powders and the healing scratches on her skin were visible once more, at least for a second until Astelyn led her down the opposite hallway to the room she would be staying in.

When he finished washing his face and stepped back into the living room, he almost collided with a woman.

"Sorry miss, I–"

"Who are *you*?" She slurred, clearly having had too many drinks.

"My name is Niklas. Um, Astelyn brought us in?"

The woman snorted and rolled her eyes before walking over to a short couch and fell face first into the dull maroon cushion, knocking over the candle on the table next to it. He hurried to pick it up and blew out the flame before it could do any damage.

The light coming from the kitchen cast shadows around the figure of a large man standing in the doorway. Niklas jumped out of his skin at the sudden appearance, and – thank God – Astelyn came in when she did. She ran down the hallway and jumped into the man's arms.

"Dadda!"

Niklas didn't know if the breath he let out should be relieved or not.

"Dadda, this is Niklas. Momma said that it was okay for him and Althea to stay the night. They are all the way from Taris. And they are going to go through the pass in the morning to see the palace. I want to see the palace someday, can we?"

The man laughed, deep and raspy. "Someday my dear, when you're a little older."

"Hello, Niklas. Sorry for the spook. I am Jerit, Ronun's brother. That is my wife, Melody, and I see you know our little mouse, Astelyn."

Melody hummed a tune from the couch when she heard her name, turned over and went quiet again. Niklas accepted the handshake from Jerit which was surprisingly gentle compared to the size of the man.

"I saw you two young ones on the way in the village, I can't imagine how tired you both must be. Please, my home is yours, have a good rest." Niklas thanked him and let Astelyn pull him away as her father coaxed a groaning Melody off the couch and down the other hallway.

"What does *vuity* mean?" He asked as they approached the open doorway in the hall.

Astelyn stumbled over her feet and giggled. "It's what we call two people who are in love, it means 'two doves'. It is what we usually call people who are married."

A strangled noise escaped Niklas's mouth, and before he could even fully grasp what she said, she was speeding back down the hallway, leaving him to stand in front of an open door.

The room was small, just big enough for a bed and a cluttered desk. A vibrant red rug softened his feet from the rough stone beneath. He figured it must be Astelyn's room by the drawings and half finished projects made from blue yarn that covered the walls and desk.

Niklas took one step into the room and froze. Althea looked up at him startled from where she sat on the bed combing out her hair. The roses that had been braided into it were in a pile next to her and her long, straight hair fell across her shoulders. Niklas sighed and pinched the bridge of his nose, rolling his neck to look up at the low ceiling.

"*Astelyn*," he breathed in annoyance, crossing the room and plopping down into the tiny chair in front of the desk.

"We might have a small problem," he stated, resting his elbows on his knees.

"What do you mean?" Althea asked cautiously.

Niklas looked at the closed door and whispered, "I just learned that *vuity* means…" he cleared his throat. "Lovers. They think we are married, and gave us this room. Together."

Althea stood abruptly, her face burning brighter than the fires that he could see still lit outside the window.

"I'll go correct it. I'll ask for another room, or, I don't know, something." Althea moved for the door but Niklas stopped her.

"They are already down, we shouldn't bother them. Plus it's not like we haven't been sleeping next to each other for a month now."

"This isn't like out there, it's different." Althea crossed her arms.

"I'm not saying we share the bed, Little Althea." He rolled his eyes. "We'll keep the door open. You take the floor." Niklas moved to the bed and rolled onto it, groaning as his lower back was released from the tension from the day's events and brushed the petals onto the floor. A smack on his arm made him open his eyes. Althea stood over him, her arms tense at her sides.

"Shouldn't the lady get the bed?"

"There is a lady? Where? If you tell her to come here, I will gladly give it up." The comment was worth the look on Althea's face.

"Althea, you don't get to have special treatment in Taris when we train, why would you now?" He propped himself up on an elbow and watched her, now sitting on the chair he had just vacated.

"I shouldn't have expected anything less," she whispered.

He placed a hand on his chest, dropping his jaw in mock offense. "You hurt me, Althea. Whatever do you mean?"

"That. That right there." She stood and pointed a finger at him. "I thought we were past this. An entire month, fighting for our lives and for each others. You almost died, and the very second we are out of harm's way, you go back to this– this– façade, that nothing ever bothers you."

Niklas sat up, sobering from his teasing. "I never said it didn't bother me."

She rubbed a hand down her face. "I'm sorry. I'm just having a hard time fathoming all of this. This mission, this village, this…" She gestures between the two of them. He scooted over on the hay filled bed and patted the space next to him. Althea sat down and pulled her legs under her.

"I was born in Valor. I never knew my mother. My father always told me that she wasn't right in her mind. That she was a danger to me. And one day, she lost herself, threatened to kill him. He told me that he couldn't bring himself to hurt her, she cut him up pretty good, and when she backed him into the kitchen with a sword, he made his choice. He took me and ran.

"That's how we ended up in Taris. He's always kept his emotions tucked away, my whole life he has never showed anger or annoyance at my stubbornness. And certainly not fear, never have I ever seen that man afraid. So, I guess I took on that quality. I wouldn't know how to show that I was bothered if I was stabbed by a dagger with the word engraved on it." He chuckled, shaking his head at himself.

"My Poppa is the exact opposite," Althea nodded. "He was very adamant when I was growing up, especially when Momma died, to never let my emotions build up. I never listened though, I always hid them, thought it made me weak if I didn't. I don't know if I was trying to be strong for him or for myself, because when she passed, he changed. He was always the tough guy, but those first few months when it was just the two of us, he lost himself for a while. He cherishes every moment, even the fights we have, and there are quite a few of those." Althea closed her eyes, seeming to try and find the memory.

They stayed up late into the night, curled onto their sides on the bed as they shared whispered stories of their past that they had never told anyone before.

Despite having grown up a few houses from each other, they had led very different lives.

Niklas had traveled with his father, virtually covering the whole of both Valarie and Marella and the southern parts of Palmeria. Whereas Althea, until then, hadn't been farther than Sir Geralt's manor on the outskirts of Count Kopple, the previous Mayor of Taris before Florence was selected to take his place. She knew every inch of Taris like he knew the map of scars covering his palms.

A glance out the window at the moon showed it was around one o'clock, and the noise of the festival finally began to fade. Althea's lids lowered, blinking slower and slower, her chest rose and fell steadily.

"Althea?" Niklas whispered, gently waving a hand in front of her face. She was asleep. He stood, careful not to jostle her and tucked the thin, rough blanket over her.

He waited a moment longer, looking down at her shadowed form in the dark. He could no longer ignore it. Something between them had shifted. A door that opened. One that Niklas didn't even know existed, but she had burst right through it from the other side. Leaving behind pieces of fluttering dust that he could feel tickle in his chest.

He tried to close it, like he did with the door to the kitchen as he stepped outside, but the hinges seemed to be stuck.

Chapter Twenty-Six

Althea

Althea woke with a start at a clatter that came from down the hall, beyond the closed door.

She brought a hand to her forehead, shielding her eyes from the bright sun that shone in through the window, sat up and stretched, careful of the fresh stitches in her side and looked around the room, blinking the blur of sleep from her eyes.

Something was missing. No, someone.

Niklas.

She jumped off the bed and burst into the hall with freezing cold feet. She breathed a heavy, relieved sigh at the sound of his laughter. He was definitely more of a morning person than she was.

A head peaked around the corner from the kitchen.

"Good morning child. Come, have some breakfast." With a soft fluid, voice, Melody guided her to the table.

Seated around the thick oak were Jerit, Dovas, and Ronun. Niklas and the owners of the home, all helping themselves to the food piled in the middle. Astelyn jumped off her chair and then back on at the stern smile her mother gave.

Niklas was talking with Jerit about some type of fencing he should consider to protect his goats. They all gave good-mornings and began to stuff their mouths.

She swallowed at the scent of roasted pork and fresh eggs while Astelyn filled a wooden cup with an orange liquid and set it in front of her. It smelt of fruit, but Althea had never seen one this color before. She took a sip and gasped at the sweetness.

"It is orange juice, we have orange trees and bury some of the fruit to make it last all winter long. Isn't it amazing?" Astelyn cooed.

"It might be the best thing I have ever tasted." Althea drank half the cup in one swallow and savored the rest along with her meal of pork, eggs, and savory flatbread.

Niklas was seated on the opposite of the round table from her. He looked well rested, the circles under his eyes weren't as dark as they were last night.

"Well, Mr. and Mrs. Wiler. Dovas, Ronun, and Astelyn. I cannot begin to thank you for everything. This really was an amazing breakfast and you have been more than…" he picked his brain for the words in their language. "Good. But I am going to head out and see if I can't swindle a couple of horses."

Niklas dipped his head in a bow and met Althea's gaze over the table, his eyes smirking, before turning around and exiting the house.

Althea did not miss the single piece of straw that was tangled in the back of his hair. She coughed in surprise, choking on her orange juice. It answered her burning question of where he had slept last night.

Astelyn jumped out of her seat, her stomach bumping the table and startling everyone. Althea only caught a glimpse of her face before she turned. Tears ran down her cheeks as she darted out the door, taking the warm air from the kitchen with her.

Melody broke the silence first with a sigh. "Forgive her. She gets too easily attached, she is only sad to see you go."

"I'll go talk to her," Althea offered, wiping her hands on her pants, staining the fabric with grease from the food.

"I think she needs that." Jerit nodded.

Althea walked up and down the narrow streets of Heriit for fifteen minutes before she heard the muffled sob coming from a crevice in the rocky wall of the mountain. A trickle of water ran down the side of the opening. She had to suck her stomach in to squeeze through the split, her belt almost getting stuck.

"Astelyn?" Althea gingerly called out into the dark cave.

"Go away," her small voice broke.

Althea's eyes adjusted to the dim light enough to see Astelyn curled into a ball and shaking.

She lowered herself in front of the little girl and sat on her feet, but did not reach out to touch her. To be frank, Althea did not know how to comfort a child. She had been raised and sown for battle. She was trained by grown men and women to be brutal and hard, not to bring comfort. After an awkward minute of silence, Astelyn lifted her eyes just enough to peek over her arms.

"Everyone who leaves never comes back, it's like they forget about me," she whispered.

"I won't forget you, Astelyn. I could never forget you. You have been such a light in the dark for Niklas and I. I don't think we would have survived another day out there if you hadn't found us when you did." Althea cringed at how true that statement turned out to be.

Her yesterday self would have felt otherwise, but she could have fell far worse ill from the infection that had begun in her side. If Astelyn had not been the one to walk across their path that day... It was boggling to think how differently things might have gone.

"What if– if *I* forget you?" Astelyn sniffed, wiping the back of her hand across her nose.

Althea's brow pinched in thought. She reached into the neck of her jacket, tugging on the leather cord until it came free. The bronze coin, warmed from being against her skin, rested in the palm of her sun-tanned, calloused hand. The perfect match to the half that she had tied in Bronte's mane.

She had found the pair buried in the small garden behind her home, long ago. A couple had built the cottage and raised a family there before her Momma and Poppa bought it. When the wife passed away, the husband had buried the pair of necklaces that each other had worn since their engagement. His children forced him to move to their home in Valor so they could better take care of him.

That was all Althea knew of the story when she went searching for the matching pieces.

When she was young she liked to dream up the moments between the beginning of the story and the end. What their life must have looked like, what foods they prepared in the kitchen. The same space her father prepared their meals. She wondered what her father would be doing right now.

Althea forced herself to take Astelyn's hand. Small and cold, and placed the necklace in her palm.

"Whenever you feel scared, or lonely, or even when something exciting happens, look at this and know that I am thinking about you and praying for you. That way you will never forget me." Althea offered what she thought looked like a comforting smile, but felt more like a grimace. She did not know what the world would look like after the next few days. But whatever it was Astelyn saw, seemed to cheer her up as she pulled the leather over her head.

"Thank you, Althea." The girl's language and accent took the 'e' out of her name, and made her name sound like 'Altha'.

"Wait," Astelyn grabbed her hand, "I have something for you too." She reached into a pocket in the rough fabric of her dress and pulled out an iron clasp for a cloak in the shape of a dove in flight.

"Thank you, Astelyn. Where did you get this?" Althea held the ends of her cloak together as the girl pinned them together.

"My Momma's Momma made these before she went to sleep. This is the last one there is. And don't try to give it back, I don't want anyone else having it, not even me."

With that, Althea held Astelyn's hand and they wound their way back through the village to the last building at the edge of the right wing.

Niklas was already there, dressed in his armor, or what was left of it after their trek. His breastplate was dented in multiple places but it had been shined and given new leather ties across both his shoulders. His sword hung against his leg and he held the reins of two black horses in his left hand.

It looked like the entire village was gathered there to see them off.

"Whenever someone leaves the village, everyone comes to say good-bye. We never let anyone leave with a grudge or anger, because Dadda says you never know when the last time you see someone will be," Astelyn looked up at her, still holding tight to Althea's hand as walked to stand beside Niklas. "I will see you again, won't I?"

"I will make sure of it." Althea hoped it was a promise she could keep.

Jerit stepped forward, commanding in his black cloak. "We trust you will keep the knowledge of us away from others?"

"I swear it." Niklas nodded.

"I swear it," Althea echoed.

Astelyn let go of her to hug Niklas, taking him by surprise. He stared at Althea, almost pleading for her to help. She laughed at his expression but the air was squeezed from her lungs when the girl turned on her.

Melody had to pry her daughter's hands from Althea, the girl's eyes becoming twins to the waterfalls of her village, but she did not quiver or make a sound.

Althea accepted the reins from Niklas and pulled herself into the saddle. With one last salute to the villagers, she turned and pressed her heels into the horses sides, setting off at trot.

It began to snow within the first hour, dusting their cloaks and painting the black horses a glittering white. The first of the season.

Althea wiped the flakes from her eyelashes with one hand and held on tightly to the saddle with the other as the horse expertly climbed the steep hill to a hidden entrance that would deposit them a mile into the mountain pass.

The Kyran was the largest mountain in all of Llyr, and she had never believed it more than she did now. It had taken them nearly two hours to just reach the base of it, and another hour of leaning forwards, backwards and twisting in their saddles to avoid low hanging limbs.

The higher they went the colder it became until the air felt like tiny daggers, slicing at their cheeks and cracking the skin of their knuckles until they bled.

Large animal tracks could be seen, crisscrossing over the path. She kept her hand near her dagger at all times and though she did not have any arrows left in her quiver, the weight of her bow was a welcome comfort on her back.

They rode through the sunset and kept going, relying on the light of the moon, stars and the bright blue lines of the night sky, until they were a few miles into the pass, where there were points set for camps. Benefiting weary travelers who sought rest.

Althea's head ached from the few hours of sleep she had gotten after the festival. But at least her stomach was quiet thanks to the bag of food that the villagers had packed for the remainder of their journey. They even gave her a small, clay jug of orange juice.

She was exhausted and cold. Every shiver that rippled through her pulled at the stitches in her side and she nearly fell off of her horse when it came time to stop for the night, her legs shaking from the effort it took to stay in the saddle.

The first marked point of camp was not empty, and Althea had known it wouldn't be. With the blood moon ball looming in the next few days, many people were traveling to join in on the party.

The one thing that the queen wasn't going to do was keep the war from infringing on her plans.

"Over here should be good." Niklas sounded as tired as he looked, lines creased his forehead, the corners of his lips turned down and she had not seen his eyes open more than halfway for the last half hour.

She followed him a little ways away from the cluster of wagons and started to build a fire. Tucked behind a cleft in the rock, they would be able to avoid the prying eyes and questions that might be asked about two lone guards when there was a warfront. People were always too curious for their own good.

Within seconds they both fell into deep slumber, curled around the fire, their backs pressed warmly against each other.

Niklas shook her awake when it was time to leave. It was the hour just before the darkest part of the dawn where the stars disappeared and the moon hung alone in the purple sky. The highest peak of the mountain would soon be aflame from the light of the sun, and would wake the many travelers. Althea knew they needed to get ahead of them.

She felt surprisingly well rested and had an extra spring in her step. Maybe she had become a little too accustomed to life under the open sky instead of the dark wooden ceiling of her loft.

They ate a quick breakfast and kicked some snow onto the fire, the ashes hissing as it melted. The horses were ready to go and trotted happily without hesitation.

The next day was much like the last. They fell back into the rhythm they had developed over the last few weeks. But something felt different, something had shifted between them, but Althea did not know what. She had felt it in Astelyn's small room. That look in his eyes before she fell asleep. When she had seen that piece of hay in his hair.

They spent the day conversing about what the first thing they were going to eat was when they got to a market. What they've always wanted to do in the city of Valor. Anything to keep their thoughts off the night of the ball. At some point they would have to discuss strategy. It could not be avoided, but they could have at least one last day before things changed forever.

There was something palpable as the hours passed. It didn't feel bad. It wasn't a stiffness or unease. It was... nice.

Imagine that, being friends with Niklas turned out to not be such a bad thing after all. They laughed, they sat at midday and ate together sitting on the same stone.

And on that particularly cold night, they shared their cloaks, opting for layering the two and staying warmer. Their backs against each other of course.

They reached the summit on the third afternoon. The sun was bright, hanging over their heads like a ball on a string. Dark clouds rolled behind them.

They doubled their time when the pass widened and began its slope down. The ground turned from rocks to hard packed dirt and the horses cantered on their own, loping side by side. They must have sensed the urgency in their riders.

And there it was, the City of Valor in all its splendor. Sparkling gold and silver and blue.

The palace.

The glittering blue waters that surrounded it looked like sapphires that were on fire. The blue-white marble of the spires disappeared into the low clouds and Althea gasped. She had never seen anything like it before. It was so much more than she could have even imagined. The paintings depicting it did not do it justice.

The anxiousness that Althea had pointedly ignored began to creep up in the back of her mind, hovering and looming around every thought. And it wasn't until she saw the massive palace that she realized the impossibility of what they were trying to do.

God. Direct my feet, lead me and Niklas. Save the queen.

Niklas seemed as confident as ever, it was like they were only on field training and Althea would be lying if she said she wasn't a bit envious of his confidence.

The gates loomed down the last mile and the pass was clogged with brightly colored wagons pulled by oxen, donkeys and horses. Performers' children ran between and underneath the wagons, babies wailed in the rocking arms of mothers, men yelled down the line in a variety of languages that made Althea dizzy as she translated the snippets to herself. She heard one man shouting in Valarian saying, "What's holding everything up?"

Niklas stood in his stirrups, his long legs allowing him to see past the horde. "They're inspecting the wagons. And it looks like they are asking for papers. Invitations." He sat back down with a heavy sigh and looked at Althea, the sparkle of strategizing in his eyes.

There was a reason they promoted him to Lieutenant after all.

"Ok, so you show them your station pendant and we go through," Althea guessed.

"Not exactly." He rubbed the back of his neck. "They didn't have time to make a proper one for me. All I have is a bronze seal instead of the silver one. They won't take my word for it. Not when so many people are here and for an occasion like this." And leaning in to whisper, he said, "Anyone could be the assassin, even the queen's own Guard. We *have* to get through, no matter what. Even if it means..."

Althea did not need clarification, she knew exactly what he meant. Splitting up. And it could be the last time they see each other...

Althea stared at the gates, holding her head high as the line moved forward around a curve in the pass. "No matter what."

Chapter Twenty-Seven

Niklas

I n the distance, past the gates that he now stood under, he heard the first notes of the trumpet call, signaling the queen's appearance at the ball. The sun had just gone down and the blood moon ball had begun.

The guard requiring invitations looked annoyed, his skin was red and speckled with dirt. "Get out of my line."

The guard turned to the people next in line, dismissing him, but Niklas stepped in front of him, using his armor and size to block his path. He looked down at the guard, squaring his shoulders and letting his hands rest at his sides.

"What makes you think that is a good idea, hmm? I am on official business. I am Lieutenant Stallard of the Guard of Taris, and I need you to let me through. I am under oath for the service of the queen and I can have your head if you do not permit me and my partner passage."

The guard tilted his head back, cracking his neck and looked up at Niklas with a brow cocked up toward his shaved head. The name was lost on him.

"I don't care what you and your little... friend call yourselves, but there is no record of your name on my list, so unless you have the queen's pendant seal to prove your identity, you're not getting any farther than the outhouse." The guard scoffed and flicked his wrist to dismiss them.

Althea pushed Niklas out of the line and away from the burly guard before he could do something rash.

"What are you doing, Althea? We have to get through." He tried to walk around her but she grabbed his arm roughly, pulling him back.

"Shh, that is what I am making sure we actually do instead of getting arrested. Ten degrees to your left. A produce wagon with a false bottom." She smacked his arm. "Don't look too closely."

"I'm not." He scowled, rubbing his arm where her knuckles had struck and assessed the wagon she had spoken of out of the corner of his eye. "Too small. Only enough for one and we don't exactly have money to bribe him with."

"Hmm," Althea hummed in thought. "I can sneak in on it, he won't even be able to tell the difference in weight." She bent a knee, pretending to tie the laces on her boot. "Sixty feet down on the right. There is a corner, no patrols by the looks of it. From here it seems to have a couple good handholds, you can climb."

Niklas shook his head, running a hand through his snow dusted hair sending a spray of the white onto his shoulders.

They had sent the horses back before they got in line, using the command the villagers gave and Niklas was beginning to wonder if they had rushed that decision. The villagers had explained to Niklas that the horses knew the alternate route back to the village and would not leave their sides until the command was given.

'Kereh unta gua, lue int oma.'

'May the great One guide you home.'

Even out in the depths of the forest, hidden and excluded from the kingdom and life beyond its borders, his God still managed to fill the hearts of those villagers.

After Althea had scampered away from his side and disappeared into the crowd, he picked his way along the wall sticking to the shadows and used the giant gray columns to his advantage. Hiding behind each on and leaning his back against the cold stone, arms crossed. Lounging and looking around lazily like he was waiting for someone.

He took his chance when a group of guards stopped a wagon full of dancers clothed in sparkling gold. Their faces were covered in shiny, purple clay masks, the eyes and mouths turned down in frowns. All of them had a teardrop shaped sapphire rolling down from the left eye.

The guards had every single performer lift their masks and searched through every pocket of their glittering attire and rummaged through every cubby inside the wagon.

Right before Niklas rounded the corner he caught the lilting voice of one of the guards, a woman with shining blond hair. "Watch the walls, we don't want anyone trying to get around the checkpoints."

"Too late." Niklas chuckled to himself and landed in the shadows inside the City of Valor.

He stood in the shadowed alley beside a perfume shop, painfully holding back a sneeze while he waited, and watched the gates for the wagon that Althea had stowed herself upon to make it through. His last steel dagger clutched in his fist against his thigh.

He kept the hood of his cloak neutral on his head, knowing that if it was pulled too low over his face it would draw suspicion, and the obvious if it was too far back and exposed his rugged appearance which might draw attention from the guards.

His spine stiffened when the wagon was stopped, a muscle in his neck spasmed and his pulse raced until it was pounding in his head. The wagon was stuffed with crates of ruby red apples. It pulled to the side, the guard's gaze roving lazily over the crates and used the tip of his sword to lift the edges of cloth covering, peeking under them and poking a couple piles of hay with his blade.

Niklas's jaw twitched, his knuckles cracking from the grip he had on his dagger. He forced himself to breathe, two short breaths in through the nose and one long out through the mouth.

The guard grunted and waved the wagoner away with a disinterested flick of his wrist. The small horses struggled and pulled with all their might to get the wagon up the slight hill and away from the gate.

He felt his muscles release, almost shaking from relief. That was, until he noticed that Althea was not getting off the wagon; it kept going.

That was the wagon wasn't it? Maybe it wasn't clear and she changed her mind. Did she get on a different one? That's what he tried to tell himself. He knew Althea. She did not often change her mind, but maybe – maybe that once.

He decided after the third wagon had passed, with no sign of Althea, that he would have to honor his vow, and move on without her. Hope that she caught up.

"Are you waiting for someone? Or are you trying to look forlorn on purpose?"

Niklas nearly jumped out of his skin at the whisper breathed in his ear. He whipped around, pinning his forearm into the throat of the mocker. He froze, breath catching in his throat until his eyes focused on the face in front of him.

He removed his arm from her neck, placing his hands on either side of her head, letting the coolness of the wet stone seep into his palms, and calmed himself.

"Little. Althea," he ground out.

"Big. Niklas," Althea coughed, rubbing her throat and smirked. "Were you... worried?"

He pushed himself away and began to walk farther into the alley, where he had earlier seen a path around the back of the shops.

The layout of the City of Valor made no sense to Niklas. It had no rhyme or reason in the placement of the buildings. Houses stand between stores, the buildings staggered. Some hung over the edge of the main street, while others were recessed, making dark, damp pockets where Niklas felt for sure that someone, or something, was watching them from the shadows as they passed. It was like it was built starting in a large circle and moved inwards toward the palace instead of the opposite.

The path curved and led them around to a side street where they could still see the main pass between the buildings, but kept them hidden from the guards and their freshly shined armor.

The farther they went, the thicker the crowds became, all moving in the same direction, ebbing and flowing like a field of grass being pushed by a gentle breeze.

The edge of the blood moon, bright red, like rust, like an old blood stained tunic from a warrior, was steadily rising in the dark ocean of the night sky.

By a quick estimate, Niklas counted four hours until midnight and the palace was still so far away. The main and upper floors were lit with enough lanterns that the sky blue marble of its walls looked as red as the moon and shone like a beacon, blotting out the stars just above the palace with its light. The tallest of its twisting spires split the flowing smoke clouds into two tails, like a swallow-tailed kite. The royal family's crest. How fitting.

"Here. We should change." Niklas guided Althea by her shoulder into an inn that was also a tavern, so crowded that he had to squeeze up against some very unpleasant smelling men.

He'd spent the better part of a month in the middle of the Cerridwen, and even *he* did not smell so atrocious.

He grabbed Althea by the wrist and guided – dragged – her through the crush of the large bellied, scraggly bearded, drunk men and into a dark hallway. He tested the doors to the rooms one by one, hoping that someone had left and forgotten to lock their room behind them in the mess of the busy place.

"Um, this doesn't feel right."

"We don't really have much of a choice now do we, Althea?"

"That's not what I mea–"

The fourth door Niklas tried creaked, the hinges groaning as he pulled it open. He looked back at Althea and smiled. "See?"

That was all he was able to say before he stood face to face with a man as wide as he was tall, and he was taller than Niklas by at least a foot.

"What do you think you lot of thieves are doing coming into my room? I think you picked the wrong one." The man's voice was so deep that Niklas felt the vibrations of it on the rotting wooden floor beneath his booted feet.

CHAPTER TWENTY-EIGHT

ALTHEA

"Uh, no sir, we are n–" Niklas did not get the chance to explain himself.

All Althea saw of the man was his large hand as it crossed the threshold of the room and filled his grip with Niklas's hair.

"Niklas!" Althea yelped, reaching for him as he was dragged into the room. She followed, close on his heels, grabbing for a sword that was no longer in her possession.

The man filled the room, his head of curls brushed the ceiling and Althea's neck cracked with how far back she had to tilt her head to look in his eyes. She felt his laugh rumble deep in her chest.

"Ah, I see. You brought a little mouse with you to pick through the leftovers, have ya? Well, I can think of a few things my group of lads could use ya for. We do like a good maid to clean up after us." His other hand, not currently occupied by a young, squirming boy, reached for her.

"Don't you dare touch me," she growled, pulling out her mothers dagger and one made of stone, palming them with practiced ease.

"Ohhh, we do like some spice."

A primal noise ripped from her chest as she ducked, twisting under the smelly arm as he reached for her and slashed a shallow line along his ribcage. He let out a surprisingly shrill yelp and let go of Niklas.

Big mistake.

Niklas's sword flashed red from the light of the candles as he swung. The hilt landed directly in the man's temple, dropping him like a stone. More like a boulder.

"Sorry about that. Not really." His sword whispered against its scabbard as he replaced it on his hip.

"What do we do now, we can't just leave him like that."

"You are right, Little Althea." Niklas stepped over the man, grabbing the rough, burlap blanket from the bed and tossed it over his unconscious head. "He looked a little cold."

Althea tsked. "Just wait outside." She turned and stepped into the closet sized bathing room and quickly slipped into the dress. It felt all wrong this time. The leather that wrapped around the middle felt too tight, and the snake vine that wrapped around her ankle felt even tighter.

She knew it wasn't the dress, it was the occasion that felt all too terror inducing. They were going to sneak into the most guarded place in all of Laisren, on the biggest, most guarded night of the season.

What if what Niklas said was right? What if this was just a mad dash and she had overheard the rebel's wrong? The doubts she had tried so hard to keep at bay crested over the dam.

No.

She cannot let herself doubt now. If Niklas truly thought that this was a fool's pursuit, he *would* have made it known. And he would not have come this far with her on a wild goose chase.

She stared at her reflection in the grimy, scratched mirror leaning against the water basin, her face dripping from the clean cool water she splashed over her sore, tired eyes. She dusted on the powders she had been sent with, making sure to cover the wound on her arm as well. Taking a deep breath and stealing herself, she turned and walked back into the tiny room.

Niklas had changed into the same neat clothes he had worn during the festival. He sat on the bed, using the corner of the blanket that lay over the man to wipe a scuff mark out of his black leather boots.

Althea didn't feel like she was in control of herself as she moved to stand in front of him. Her hand lifted on its own to his hair, smoothing out the strands that were tousled from being pulled.

Niklas looked up at her, well almost up, there wasn't much more than half a foot difference from where he sat. His eyes reflected the moon from the open window, setting the scarlet aflame, swirling, mixing with the earthy brown as he looked at her.

Her breathing slowed, until she felt like she was holding her breath. She might have thought she was if it wasn't for his smell. Nutty and sweet, with a hint of campfire and... vanilla? The jerk. He had salvaged her soap after all. She thought it had been left far behind them in the Cerridwen.

Her normal reaction would be to kick his shin. But... she didn't. Whoever they were in Taris was not who they are now. The rivalry they had back home was nothing like the friendship – if someone could call it that – they had now.

"If anything happens in there tonight..." Althea had to pause to form the words properly. "I want to say thank you." She squeezed her eyes shut tight against the burn of tears, she had had enough of fear and crying to last a lifetime. She expected Niklas to say something sly, to break the silence as she fought to speak, but he stayed silent, waiting. He absentmindedly held the bottom hem of her dress, rubbing the soft fabric between his fingers, listening. "And I... I don't know if I can do it. What if... what if I mess up? This isn't like training, this – this is real."

Niklas bit his bottom lip in thought and Althea fought to keep her eyes away from them, opting to focus on the space between his brows. There was a line where there had never been one before.

She almost forgot the last month had had its hands on him too. Even though he had acted like every day was a normal hunting trip in the woods behind his house and not a war turned duty to protect his queen from an overthrowing of her kingdom.

When he finally spoke, it was in a soft, low voice. "I trust Captain Delmar. I believe he knows more about the process of war and battle than anyone else, having led many men and women in the battle with Marella himself. I do not think he made a mistake when grading you, and placing you at the top of the class. Well almost the top, I mean." He gestured to himself with the kindest smirk Althea had ever seen him make. She pushed his shoulder and huffed.

"What I'm trying to say is." He grabbed both of her hands, his skin warm against her cold fingers, and let out a breathy chuckle. "*I* do not doubt what my eyes have seen. And I can't believe I am about to say this, but... you are a *good* fighter. No one will be a match for you, Little Althea. Not in their dreams. Annnd... I'm right up there with you. We are going to make it through this. And when that *blasted* moon sets in the morning," he rolled his eyes. "We will meet by, say, the third column by the palace entrance. You know the one?"

"I know the one." Althea lowered her eyes, meeting his in the darkening light. Her lips parted ever so slightly when they came into focus. They were pools of liquid fire, flaming with a fervor. It was not a version of Niklas she had ever seen before. It was probably one that had not existed before now.

A groan broke through their trance. And the movement of the blanket on the floor shocked them back into focus. Smiling, and grabbing each other's hand, they jumped over the man, ran down the stairs and out of the stuffy tavern into the misty night air.

The path was being redirected.

The metal of the guards' armor glinted as they waved their arms, shouting directions in multiple different languages. They blocked off the back road, angling everyone on the path toward the main pass, bustling and practically bursting at the seams with visitors, carriages and wagons overfilled with performers, and food enough to keep the feast within the palace walls from even having a dent.

Deer hung by their feet, skinned and seasoned, ready to be put on a spit over a fire. Apples, oranges, and even bananas from Marella, which were rare.

Althea had never even smelt one before. Like oranges before she was in Heriit. The Queen of Marella must have sent them as a means of apology amidst her absence since she was with her eighth child.

At her side, Althea felt Niklas stiffen and she stumbled when a guard called out to them.

"Hold, you two!" He raised his shiny gauntleted hand, and began to cut through the crowd toward them.

Althea sunk into her training, bringing into focus the surrounding guards who called out random people in the crowd. They were asking people for papers.

"Invitations and passports." She heard a guard on her left demand in the sharp tongue of Palmeria, over the ruckus of the crowd.

Althea grabbed Niklas's arm, tightening her grip on him the closer the guard got. They cannot be stopped, they don't have papers, and she cannot use her being a member of the Guard as an excuse like Niklas could.

A tiny donkey, pulling a small wagon with freshly baked bread wrapped in cloth, crossed between them and the guard, cutting them off from each other's sight.

She took the opportunity of the cover and yanked Niklas with her, ducking beside the wagon. Althea twisted into a notch in a building, and Niklas crushed her into the cold stone just as the wheel of the wagon scraped violently against the wall where they had just been.

Breathing heavily, their chests brushing against one another, they waited one hundred seconds, listening as the shouts of the guard, alarmed, faded deeper into the crowd. She sighed with relief when they were finally able to fall into step with a group of performers that were dressed not dissimilarly from their own festival attire.

One of the performers turned to them, a young boy, no more than eight seasons old with skin as dark as night, and teeth as bright as day. His curly hair that was dusted in a sparkling gold powder made him look like a starry night.

He reached up and set a crown of twisted red roses upon both her and Niklas's brows. Thankfully the thorns had been removed.

"Thank you." Althea bowed her head and spoke in Pother, the language of the city in which people of such smooth, dark skin come from in Marella. The child's eyes lit up from within when the dying language left her lips, Althea smiled at his innocence.

She prayed that he would be spared from whatever might happen in the palace tonight. And she prayed that for everyone's sake, that they would find the queen, safe and happy.

The boy held up one finger, asking them to wait, and took off at a run toward a covered wagon, dodging around the legs of tall men and the full skirts of women.

Althea watched his head of fluffy hair bounce as he jumped into the wagon and out of sight. Niklas turned to her and asked, "I guess this is going to be our way in?"

"I want to say yes, but knowing how things have been happening for us lately I don't think it is going to be that easy."

The boy reappeared out of nowhere and began to walk backwards as the crowd moved, inching toward the Blue, the massive lake surrounding the palace. It spanned at least a mile across, from shore to shore.

In the time of King Brioc, it served as protection. Leaving only four main points of access. Bridges, guarded with soldiers that were armed to the teeth.

For a night like this with the celebration of the blood moon, only one bridge operated at a time, rotating once every hour, announced by the sound of a high, trilling horn.

In Pother, the boy spoke to Niklas first, "Here, let me."

Niklas looked at Althea, with a brow raised and squinted his eyes in question. She shrugged and tilted her head toward the boy. He was confused at the silent conversation between the two, looking back and forth between them. A small container of gold dust was cupped in his palm.

"Oh no, I don't think so– oof." Niklas bent over, coughing and clutching at his ribs where Althea's elbow had struck. She beckoned hurriedly at the boy.

He knew exactly what she meant, and quickly grabbed a handful of the dust, throwing it into the air over their heads. Niklas sputtered, spitting out a mouthful of gold and Althea sneezed. When she looked down at her dress she was slightly unnerved at the sight, but it quickly turned into awe.

The gold sparkled red in the bloody light of the moon on her dress and on the skin of her arms, it made her look like she was clothed in a gown of glittering blood. What better for an occasion, and situation, as such.

Soon, they reached the bridge, just as it was opened for their turn of crossing the Blue. The steel under her sandaled feet was surprisingly warm despite the cold mist that floated up from the water fifty feet below them. Archers held position on the tall supports, eyes darting over every soul that crossed under the archways and onto the bridge made of iron and steel.

The arching supports stood every hundred feet, decorated with red streamers and shining gold ornaments shaped as stars and every one they passed under was more guarded than the last. The thick, black armor of the Queen's Guard made them look like shadowed demons against the railings. They paced, lazily, the length of their section, turning when they got to a certain point and going back.

The closer they got to the palace, a few guards started to become handsy. Licking their greasy lips as they stopped women in tight dance uniforms, pushing children faster than their legs could go, and shoving men roughly against the bridges railing, searching their pockets.

Althea had to clench her fists against the desire to help, but she knew that she needed to stay on track. She had not come all this way to stick her nose where it did not belong. She was sworn to the protection of the queen first, the people second, herself last. That was what being a guard was all about.

A shuddering breath escaped her, her lips quivered against her will. She couldn't believe she was really here, doing this, risking everything. Her honor, her father's faith in her. And it wasn't just about her now, it was about Niklas too. *His* title, *his* honor. His family name could be marred if he was caught leaving post.

Niklas was supposed to be on the front line of Caedmon, and Althea... home, shoveling new latrines probably.

She could feel her resolve begin to shake, her sure feet became numb and it took everything for her to not trip in the crush of bodies as they got closer and closer.

The blue -white marble of the palace walls glistened with the mist, and reflected the light of the bonfires and the moon. It looked like it was ice on fire.

"Hey, we've got this," Niklas bent over her shoulder, whispering so only she could hear, ever the observer.

"You don't have to do this. If you go now, I won't judge you. I don't have anything to lose, you do. It could be your family's name and your honor scarred forever. I don't mean anything to this kingdom, you do."

"That's not true. And no, because we won't get caught. Besides, once the queen finds out that we saved her life, there won't be any question as to what we mean to this kingdom." His breath, warm on her neck, stirred her hair, tickling her. She reached up to scratch it and was roughly pushed from behind.

Her head hit the metal railing, her ears ringing from the hit. Her vision swam, the warm trickle of blood ran down her neck from a cut lost somewhere in her hair. She heard Niklas, shouting something, it echoed before fading away; she didn't catch what he said.

Althea blinked back the darkness at the edge of her sight, and stood shakily, holding onto the railing, slipping on her own blood. As soon as her sight righted itself all she could see was the face of a guard.

He stood so close he was all she could see and hear, he blocked out everything. His words, filled with spit, flecked her skin.

She felt the overwhelming urge to reach a hand up and wipe her eyes, but she knew that any sudden movements would be seen as a threat, and she certainly did not know why this guard attacked her.

Where is Niklas? Is this really only how far I get? Don't let them know. Distract him. Let him get away.

That was what she decided in the millisecond between her being pushed and what she did next.

"Oh, sir, thank you. I got separated from my group and I cannot find where they are, could you help me?"

"Save it. Where are your papers?" He bent closer to see her clearly. "Wait a minute. I know who you are."

Althea's stomach dropped so fast she felt faint, her eyelids fluttered for a half a second before she shoved her body forward. Her already aching head slammed into the face of the guard, his nose breaking, sending more blood into her tangled hair.

The guard dropped like a stone, and Althea was gone before his armor hit the bridge. She expected to be surrounded and pinned, but no guards came for her. No one pointed, shouting that there was an assault, nothing.

A quick, dizzy glance back showed that the guard had pinned her in a blind spot, a dark shadow between one of the arches supports. No one would have known what happened to her. She shuddered, from the cold, or shock she did not know.

"Althea!" A hard body pressed up against her, catching her as her knees wobbled, her head shaking off the hit.

"What happened, are you okay?" Niklas's warm hands held her up and kept her moving. Tucking her under his cloak to hide her as she fought to gain her composure.

"I'm fine. It was the crowd, I got pushed."

"Are you sure? That looks like more than push." He gently brushed her hair away from her face, wiping away the blood with a black handkerchief and straightened the rose crown over her brow.

"I was pushed into the railing. I'm fine, honestly." Niklas cannot find out. She would not let him find out that she was being looked for. "We should split up, it's easier to slip in and out of a crowd that way. I'll go east, you go west. Like you said, third column at daybreak. I will meet you there."

Before Niklas could grab her and stop her from leaving, she rushed forward and hopped over the back of a tiny wagon, with two small, giggling children with red hair being pulled by their father.

She ducked into a shadow and waited until the guard at the far left turned to ask someone for proof of invitation.

A cloud passed under the moon, casting a shadow just long enough for her to slip behind the unsuspecting guard, and at last, into the walls of the Blue.

CHAPTER TWENTY-NINE

NIKLAS

N iklas huffed as Althea vanished into the crowd, the tail of her red dress trailing behind her.

How does she do that? He thought to himself. Now that they were past whatever dispute they had going on between them, Niklas would have to ask her to teach him her tricks. If – *no* – when, they made it home.

It was the performers from Pother's turn to present their invitation at the gates. Niklas bent his knees slightly to match their lesser height, and kept his chin tucked into his chest behind his hood to hide how much paler his skin was than the rest of them.

"How many?" The guard asked unenthused, smacking his jaw on a piece of sugar cane.

The performers all hesitated, unsure of how to say the number in Valarian. They frantically whispered to one another, twisting their heads as they searched for someone among their group.

"I don't have time for this," the guard murmured to himself, rubbing his eyes. "How many!" He grabbed the young boy who had covered him and Althea in the gold dust by his shirt collar, wrinkling the thin gold vest he wore over a white tunic.

Everyone froze while Niklas moved.

He straightened to his full height and took one long stride, wrenching the guard's sweaty hand away from the boy, twisting his arm until his shoulder popped and pushed the boy behind him, all in one fluid motion.

"Ah! What the–"

"Don't lay a hand on them again. Ten," Niklas snarled, letting the guard go, making sure his Lieutenant pendant was visible and prayed that he had not made the wrong decision by making notice of himself.

"Fine, go. Get out of my sight," the guard said, spitting at their feet and scribbled their number on a piece of paper.

Niklas did not waste time and waved the group forward. He waited until they were all past the gate before rushing in after them. He let out a heavy breath, his shoulders slumped over, and wiped away the sweat that had formed on his face and neck.

"What was that? You don't have a translator?" Niklas fumed, speaking to the group as a whole.

One of the men, who looked to be about his age, came forward. "We did, he was with us before we got on the bridge. I don't know when he left us."

Niklas dragged a hand down the side of his face, thinking.

"There is one last checkpoint up there, for the performers." He pointed to the 'checkpoint'. It was more like a rotting wooden table where an old woman, hunched over in her cloak, was stamping peoples hands with the royal family crest.

"Once we get through, we go our separate ways." Niklas could not help sounding gruff and impatient. Niklas was beginning to realize how stupid they were to separate.

He opened his eyes when he felt a small hand grab his. It was the young boy. His fluffy hair had collected the dew from the foggy air, setting off the already sparkling gold into an even brighter shine. His dark brown eyes were wide with fear as he squeezed Niklas's fingers.

"Thank you, sir. I really hope you get to see us perform." Niklas pulled his hand gently from the boy's hold and patted him on the shoulder, envisioning what would come next. One scenario he stood before the queen, getting showered with flower petals, in the next he was kneeling before her, watching her call a guard grabbing his sword.

"I hope so too."

As they neared the last checkpoint a tall man with a round belly, tanned skin and long white hair ran up to them, bent over with his hands on his knees as he tried to catch his breath. He hacked a fierce cough and spit. Straightening himself to his full height, he put his hands on his hips and was immediately met with a thousand questions from the group.

Niklas could only catch a few words here and there, his focus locked onto the newcomer.

"This was our translator." One of the men pointed him out to Niklas and turned, speaking loudly so that the translator could hear. "That we paid *double* his working price for, to make sure that we would not have trouble on the biggest night of the last four years." Niklas stalked over, forcing him back a step. The man held up his hands with his palms down.

"I'm sorry, we got separated. I had to take a break."

"How dare you try and make an excuse like that. You know exactly what happens to foreigners that try to cross the Blue unauthorized. You're lucky I was there, they would have been thrown in *prison*, this *child* would have been thrown in prison, all because you couldn't *keep up*."

"I'm sorry," the man wheezed, taking a breath between each word. "There – was – a commotion. The guards are extra thick tonight, but not only because of the ball."

That peaked Niklas's interest, dulling his anger for the moment. "What do you mean by that?"

The man's pale blue eyes locked onto the pendant showing his rank and widened until Niklas thought they were going to fall out of his head.

I have got *to cover that up.* Niklas adjusted his cloak to cover it.

The man coughed, shaking some sense into himself and spoke, "You haven't heard? There is someone they are trying to find, an ex guard or something, suspected of bailing the draft, I think? Or was it threatening one of the advisors. I didn't quite catch the details because I was running through a crowd as dense as a brick wall to get here. So if you could please excuse my late attendance, I am here now. And as an apology, I will only charge half of my wages."

Niklas stepped back, raising a brow at the group, silently asking them if they accepted the offer. A moment of deliberation and the oldest of them nodded. The translator let out a breath, his belly shaking from nervous laughter.

Niklas decided it best to slip away while the group was distracted. Make it look like he was never really there to begin with. A shadow that watched over them one moment and was gone the next.

248

He crouched behind a wagon just as it made its way through the checkpoint and spilt away from it and into the shadows where the light from the bonfires did not reach, pulling back the hood of his cloak. From there, he could finally see the party, spanning out from within the palace, out into the courtyard and pushing against the shore of the Blue.

He wondered if Althea had made it in yet, if she was easily able to get past the guards that stand against the palace like statues forming a wall, seemingly without a single crack in their defense.

But, Niklas — and Althea as well — knew better than to believe what they saw on the surface. Every wall had its cracks. Every chain had a weak link.

And every soldier had his temptations.

He swiped a bottle of ale from a passing wagon and roughly tousled his hair until it stuck up and out. The end of his cloak tossed over his shoulder and swaying on his feet, he stumbled into people, eyelids open halfway.

He should not be that good at acting drunk, he didn't even know what it felt like, but he hoped he was convincing enough.

"Oh, my bad soildddeer, sir," Niklas slurred, rocking back and forth on his feet, just barely bumping into one of the guards standing in front of a servant's entrance. He took a step back, watching the sentinel's eyes roll and saw his hand rest on the hilt of his sword.

He set the bottle down in the bed of flowers and walked into a bush by a corner of the palace, pretending that he was in awe of the blooming white flowers, but waited with a dagger in his hand.

Out of the corner of his eye, Niklas watched the guard turn his head, left and right, seeing if there was anyone watching before bending down to reach for the discarded bottle of ale.

As soon as the guard lowered his head, Niklas twirled around, darting behind him and into the dark room which turned out to be the kitchen. All without anyone seeing or hearing a thing.

The room was empty but the hearth was red, making the room blissfully warm compared to the icy night behind the door, and the smell of fresh food made his stomach growl. He hadn't eaten anything the whole day, and come to think of it, he didn't remember eating the day before either.

He paused at the open doorway to the hall, turning back and snatching a fresh, herb baked bun and a hunk of venison off of the counter. His steps echoed down the damp, sparsely lit hallway that must lead to some servant space. Once he got past there, he would be in the palace, and then... then he would have to act natural.

He ran a hand through his hair, smoothing down the strands from where he rumpled them, straightened his cloak and counted his daggers realizing he would have to remove his cloak and weapons, or else risk the servants and guards attention.

He slid two of the stone daggers into the side of his leather boot and pulled the leg of his pants over the wheat wrapped hilts, and tucked the steel one into his belt, next to his sword. He wanted to hide his pendant, but thought better of it considering he needed to keep his weapons on him and better to be known as a higher ranking member of the Guard than to be a random, armed fellow.

At the end of the dark hallway there was a thick, wooden door with a dull, iron ring as a handle. Niklas took a deep breath and pulled it open.

He was met with an explosion of color, sounds, and smells. Servants moved quickly this way and that around the space, making his eyes want to cross, but he forced himself to focus as he weaved his way through the servant workspace.

Some only spared him a glance, others stopped and stared with wide eyes. He was technically not supposed to be there. Not because he wasn't allowed, but because of how he was dressed. Clearly not someone of nobility but the clothes were certainly not any old commoners either. It still impressed him how good the villagers were at making the fabrics look so luxurious.

As he neared the curtain separating him from the ball, an old woman, bright eyed despite her deeply wrinkled skin, stepped in front of him. Her face stern and Niklas prepared an excuse that he had gotten turned around while looking for the latrine.

But, to his surprise, she smiled and curtsied. "May I take your cloak, Sir?"

Niklas fumbled for a millisecond, not long enough for anyone to notice, before he shrugged off his cloak and handed it over. The woman folded it neatly into her arms but did not move.

Niklas felt his brows creasing in confusion and tried to step around her. She cleared her throat aggressively, and lowered her eyes to his belt where his sword and dagger were tucked away.

"I am a Lieutenant, ma'am. I have authorization to be armed in the palace," Niklas explained.

The woman wrinkled her nose at the cloak in her hands, the fabric was rough and patched, but at least it was clean.

"It seems you may have been traveling for a while, so I will give you a break. The queen has changed some rules since you've been gone. Every town and province has been notified that all arms are to be left outside of the palace doors. No matter the occasion." Her eyes drop to the pendant dangling from his throat, eyebrow raised. "No matter the rank. Do not fret young man, your weapons will be perfectly safe in the storeroom will all the rest."

That wasn't what Niklas was worried about. Although he did not like to be away from his sword for too long, he was more worried about what was going to happen when – if? – he was met with trouble inside.

He rolled his neck and flexed his hands, deciding it would be best to not cause a scene before even making it into the palace. The leather of his scabbard was clean, having polished it with leftover boiled chicken skin a few nights ago. The metal from his dagger sang when he yanked it from his belt.

His fingers brushed the woman's as he handed over his lifelines, her skin rough and calloused from decades of hard labor, working to please the high and mighty rich, making them comfortable while their people starve and die everyday.

He cringed when the old lady dropped the end of his sword, not expecting it to be as heavy as it was. The steel clanged against the polished marble floor beneath their feet despite being in its sheath.

The woman huffed, snarling up her lip and Niklas was ready with the words he had wished to say since she stepped in front of him, but was cut off by a young servant carrying a red, stiff silk mask, studded with fake red rubies. She pushed the mask into his hands. "What is this for–" He tried to ask, but she was gone before he could finish.

"It is a hidden identity blood moon ball this year, the first of its kind. The queen has been making lots of changes recently, both in preference and in law. Enjoy your evening, sir." The old woman's words were pointed as she turned, dragging the tip of his sword on the ground. The rush of servants around the room closed the space where she was just standing and Niklas rubbed at his eyes, suddenly very agitated.

A masked ball, great. This was going to be a *lot* harder than he expected.

Take the largest, most celebrated night in all of Laisren, turn it into being blindfolded and in a maze, with a clock ticking down. Oh, and include the life of your queen hanging in the balance, and that was what Niklas and Althea were facing tonight.

Niklas could feel the stress in every muscle and in every vein, his jaw hurt from how hard he was clenching his teeth. Angrier than he had been in a week, Niklas roughly tied the mask to his face and punched through the curtain.

Every single person was wearing the same mask. Male, female, servant, and noble.

This was going to be a long night.

CHAPTER THIRTY

ALTHEA

I t was almost too easy to get inside the palace.

The guards had just begun their shift rotations and Althea had been in the right place at the right time and managed to slip into a groove in the wall and climbed through a second story window using the untamed vines that had started to climb up the side of the marble.

She quickly learned that it was a masked ball and walked behind a servant. A tall man wearing full black, shirt and pants, and shiny leather shoes, and swiped a mask that was hanging on the railing next to a group of women who were chatting loudly and oblivious to their surroundings.

Quickly, she tied the mask around her head, rearranging her hair and crown of roses until everything sat comfortably.

She smiled politely, nodding at the guests she passed as she made her way through the crowded balconies. Trying not to catch the eyes of any of the guards, posted like statues next to the actual statues of men and women, muscled bodies posed like athletes, wearing only their bare skin.

Althea blushed and made sure to keep her eyes away from the walls.

As soon as there was an empty space, she grabbed onto the balcony railing, gripping the cold iron and took a deep breath, leaning to watch the crowd below. She wondered if Niklas made it in yet, if he was okay.

It's Niklas, if anyone can stay calm and manage his way into the palace with ease, it would be him.

She trusted Niklas and was going to have to let herself forget about him for now so she could focus fully on the night that was laid out in front of her.

Althea's eyes caught focus on the queen immediately. She was the first thing she saw. No one could miss her.

The queen sat on a raised dais against the back wall in direct sight of every single person attending. Anyone and everyone could see the queen in her dazzlingly bright red dress, sparkling with chunks of rare rubies, small enough that from up on the balcony they looked like glittering pieces of dust instead of rocks sown expertly into the silky fabric.

As a guard, Althea cringed inwardly at the display, but if she were to look at it in a political aspect, it showed power. It showed that the queen would not hide behind a curtain, or behind a wall of soldiers. She would not be cowed, and she wanted the world to know it.

The back of the throne was tall and etched with designs in a dark, almost black wood. A plush cushion in the dark emerald green of Valarie covered the seat. The edges were capped in gold and silver, the arms and legs studded with golden spikes that had been rounded out. It must be terribly uncomfortable.

But the queen didn't seem to think so. She sat sideways, her studded dress lay across her legs that were draped over one of the arms. The light from the chandeliers reflected off the rubies and cast a flare of light on the marble floor every time she moved. In her hand she swirled a glass goblet of wine, watching the crowd enjoy the ball, occasionally taking a sip of the deep, dark red.

"Good evening. Or should I say, happy blood moon," A deep, silky voice came from beside her.

Althea was not taken by surprise, she had heard him walking toward her from the other end of the balcony. His footsteps, though probably seen as light in comparison to the rest of the guests, were even, heel to toe, and the leather of his boots were not cheap by any stretch of the imagination.

She looked up from the strangers shoes, dragging her eyes over the expertly tailored black pants to the deep emerald green fitted shirt, and a black long coat over his broad shoulders, up to the mask over his brow hiding his features. His dirty blonde hair was slicked back from his forehead and curled around his ears.

"Wine?" He asked, holding out a goblet with a sweet smelling mahogany liquid.

"Thank you." Althea curtsied, accepting the goblet. His long, thin fingers were warm against hers where they brushed against each other.

She hoped that the accent she chose was convincing enough. She now knew that she had a warrant over her head and if this man was able to afford what he was wearing, he must be of noble blood. Which meant he must have a guard or two hidden in the crowd around them, watching, waiting.

Althea idly scanned the guests around them, keeping a tiny smile on her lips. To anyone else she would appear as just another girl enjoying the attention of a young man at the biggest ball of the season. But

Althea had already pointed out the guards in question. They weren't even trying to hide themselves.

There were three of them, standing together, facing in her direction, their arms folded across their chests. Every now and then one would say something and the other two would chuckle. She gathered all of that from one, sweeping glance, before turning back to the man in front of her.

She lifted the goblet to her lips, her mouth watering at the scent, but only pretended to take a sip, letting the liquid stain her lips.

His voice was the very definition of Valarian. The sound strong, mouth forming the words he spoke in perfect formality. Definitely noble. Althea just didn't know which family he belonged to. During training it was required that they learned all of the noble families names, crests, and where they resided. As they were the ones that they would be protecting.

"I have not seen you before, although no one can tell who anyone is behind these *ungodly* masks" He made a sound of disgust. "Perhaps it is your first time in the queen's palace?"

Althea squeezed her core and held her breath slightly to force a flush into her face before responding.

"Yes, I've always dreamed of coming, but my father never allowed me too. He always said that what goes on at a ball like this is not for a young girl to see." She ducked her head, a strand of hair falling from behind her ear. "I turn nineteen seasons tomorrow, and he doesn't know I'm here. You wouldn't tell him would you?" Her eyes tilted up toward him, darting all over his face like she had seen other girls do when they were trying to convince a man to do their bidding.

She never thought she had the face for that kind of thing to work. Her skin had always had something on it, a smear of dirt here, a weeping cut there, unlike those women who wore cream to make their skin appear smooth, and crushed berries to dye their lips all of the shades of red you could think of.

But to Althea's surprise, it worked. She saw the exact millisecond he deemed her just another young, silly child who could be played. The man chuckled darkly.

"I must say, your father is a wise man. But do not fret, I wouldn't even know what province to start looking in. Let alone I would not want to get on a bad side with your father, he is right to watch over such a lovely young woman as yourself." He took a commanding step forward, and leaned against the balconies railing next to her.

The mix of thousands of different perfumes wafted up to them and threatened to choke her, but she managed to focus on his scent alone.

Bergamot, vetiver, and perhaps... orange? She remembered the sharp, sweet scent of the fruit and she couldn't help but breathe it in a little deeper. She could feel his eyes on the side of her face, her neck, before turning to the dancers below who had just finished their performance.

The guests moved back onto the floor, picking up handfuls of the golden dust that had been thrown into the air and wiped it onto their skin. The entire ballroom glittered and sparkled. The queen's laughter echoed above the cacophony.

"Would you like to dance with me?"

Althea blinked rapidly, she had forgotten for a second why she was even there, she could feel the expression on her face turn to shock. Her mind raced for a response, mouth opening and closing like the fish Niklas had caught during their time in the Cerridwen.

Niklas. What would he do?

If she knew anything about him at all, he would try and keep up the appearance of just another brainless party goer. It would get her closer to the queen and she would be able to see her better on the floor level rather than in the balconies.

"Miss?" The man dipped and tilted his head, lowering his eyes to her level.

"Yes," she croaked. A fierce blush rose on her face, one that she did not have to try and fake. She could feel the tip of her nose and ears burn like fire.

The man – she would really have to get his name – laughed loudly, deep from within his chest, drawing the stares of the young women crowding the space around them. Most looked at him with wide, fluttering eyes, hoping to catch his attention. And some looked at her with heated, jealous expressions that made Althea squirm. She accepted his arm when he offered it, and let him lead her down the wide marble staircase to the ballroom's floor.

She couldn't help but sweep her eyes over the guests in hopes to catch a sight of Niklas. No such luck, not even a single head of chestnut hair was to be found in the ballroom.

Please, God. Her lips moved with the silent prayer. Althea followed the tug on her hand and let the man lead her into the start of a dance.

A slow dance.

She was equally grateful and discomforted by it. It would be less likely that she would make a fool of herself, but these types of dances tended to draw eyes. She stumbled in the first few steps as she tried to follow the pitch and swell of the orchestra. The low bass filled her chest with an unexplainable feeling and the high trill of the violin rang in her ears. This was nothing like she had ever felt before. Nothing like when she danced with Niklas.

Her face fell, and she was grateful for her mask and that the dance forced her face to be turned away from her partner. No, it did not feel like when she danced with Niklas at all.

This man's hand was pressing too hard on her waist and his palm was too soft in her training roughened hand. He pulled her along more than he was leading her. Like he was dancing for her instead of with her. She sighed in relief when the music dropped off suddenly, the echo of the instruments bouncing around once before everything went silent. The entire palace shook as the crowds erupted with applause and shouts for more.

The next performers cleared out the floor and Althea twisted out of the man's arms, more than ready to be away from him. His hand gripped her arm roughly before she could turn away.

"I never got your name, miss. It would be a shame to go home tonight without knowing who you are. I wouldn't be able to sleep with a mystery eating at my brain." From how close he was pressed to her, Althea could smell the strong liquor on his breath that she hadn't noticed before.

"Sapphira." She stuttered out her mother's name, swallowing audibly. It was not a total lie, it was also her given middle name. She felt deep in her stomach that giving him her true name would not end well, but she didn't know why.

"*Sapphira,*" he ducked low and whispered it in her ear. She fought to not cringe, to not push him away. She hated the feeling. She wanted out. Away. But she leaned in closer, tilting her head.

"I will tell you my name only if you promise to keep it a secret. I'm Xadier."

Althea gasped, pulling back. She recognized him now. The nagging familiarity she had felt when she first saw him. Dark blonde hair, though longer now, ice blue eyes, thin shoulders.

Not Xadier.

Xade.

Her mouth dropped open, eyes widening before she could stop herself.

This man. The man from the rebel camp. Their leader.

Was the queen's brother?

She didn't know how she couldn't have seen it before. They shared the same eyes, the same thick brows, the same dark blonde, thick hair, the same long thin fingers.

"You're–"

"Shh, don't give me away," he chuckled while looking around, catching eyes with his bodyguards. His hand was on her waist. "I'm just trying to enjoy the ball like a normal man for once and not have to play the part of royalty for one night. You understand, right?"

Althea composed herself, closing her mouth and smoothing her face back into something she hoped looks like innocent ignorance. She blanked, whatever she said next could go well, or worse. He was trying to get his sister – *the Queen* of Valarie – killed?

"By the looks of your outfit, I don't think you are accomplishing that very well," she devised.

"Oh, this old thing? It was the least polished out of them all." He picked at his sleeve.

Before he could say anything else, one of his guards came up between them and whispered in the prince's ear, his eyes darkening at what he heard. He nodded once, dismissing the guard and returned his icy stare on her.

"Forgive me, Sapphira. Something has come up that requires my attention." He grabbed her hand and gently kissed her knuckles, lingering for a millisecond too long. "But I wish to thank you for making this night all the more memorable than it already was." The glint in his eyes and the twisted smirk on his lips told her all she needed to know. She had to fight the instinct to reach out and end this altogether. Right now.

Althea took a shuddering breath as soon as he turned his back, wiping her hand on the hem of her skirt. She wished that she could wipe away the feeling of his lips on her skin.

She had to find Niklas.

Now.

CHAPTER THIRTY-ONE

— • —

NIKLAS

Niklas cursed the tight mask on his face as he reached up to adjust it for the tenth time. It kept pinching his nose, the fabric itched on his brow and it was stifling. Not to mention he could barely see out of the blasted thing.

The sequins sewn into all of the masks reflected the light of the chandeliers, creating the illusion of a thousand tiny, dancing red moons all around the ballroom.

He picked a spot twenty feet to the left of the dais, leaning against the wall, listening as the queen laughed and spoke with a few of the higher noble guests.

Niklas accepted food from every passing tray and sipped lazily on a glass of white wine. It was weak, obviously watered down to stretch the reserves to last through the night, and would not muddle his brain.

It did not pass his notice how he was being stared at by a group of young women, pointing and giggling, pushing one another closer to him.

He sighed, wiping the crumbs from his fingers discreetly onto the curtains draped behind him and pushed off the wall. He dodged servants and full bellied men and walked past the noisy group of girls, tilting his head in greeting. He winked at the tallest girl, almost the same height as him, just to do something, and sauntered closer to the dance floor to watch the guests as they spun across the glittering marble.

He felt someone walk up behind him and casually turned his head and was surprised to feel disappointment when he saw that it was the tall girl. Why was he secretly hoping it would have been Althea?

Where is she right now? He wondered, hoping that she was getting more information out of the guests than he had. So far he had spent the last three hours observing every single face, above and below, left and right. Listening for anybody that seemed to even slightly stumble over their words. Nothing. Not even a sneeze seemed to be out of place.

He had even gone back to the kitchen and picked at the spices and herbs, tasted the wine when no one was looking, and was swiftly booted out by the burly chef whose apron strings were too tight around his stomach.

Ruling out the use of poison set his nerves on edge more than they already were. It meant the night could end in red. In more ways than one.

"Hello, sir." Her voice was like a warmed honeycomb, lower than he thought it would have been by the way her lips sat pinched in a kiss. She reminded him of something he would see coming from one of the tapestries on the walls. Some were scenes of a conquering war, another was a woman making a sultry face to deceive a man into making a trade with her.

On the tapestry, she was reaching for a golden bowl clutched in the man's grasp like it was his lifeline, etched with little designs Niklas could not make out from where he stood, in exchange for a hair thin dagger that hung loosely from her long fingers.

While someone else might see a trade between lovers, Niklas saw how the woman's pinky was locked under the hilt. She was aiming at the center of the golden vest over the man's chest, angled left towards his heart.

Niklas would have named it, 'The perfidy of the loyal woman'.

Snapping back into reality, he didn't hear what the girl said next. Instead of asking her to repeat herself and admit that he hadn't been listening, he nodded his head in what he thought was nonchalance.

His hair spilled onto his forehead and he raised a hand to brush it back, but was stopped short when the girl grabbed him and pulled him toward the dancers.

His eyelashes caught on the inside of his mask as they widened in surprise. He was about to pull away but the guests closed in behind him, cutting off his path of retreat.

"Why me?" He groaned under his breath, the music swallowing his words.

"What was that?" The girl asked, snaking an arm around his shoulder and began to lead him into the steps of the dance.

"I asked, what is your name?" He responded a little too quickly in his fight for composure. He was not a dancer. Many people would say sparring was like a dance, but the arena was as close to a dance floor as anyone would catch him.

"Zariah. It's after my grandmother. What is yours?"

He twisted her into a spin, copying the moves of those around him and thought hard for a name that was not his own.

"Larod," he spilled out, cringing, suddenly grateful for the mask. Out of all the names on the face of the planet, he had to pick that one?

"You dance well, Larod."

He caught a flash of deep red out of the corner of his eye. Was that Althea? He whipped his head around. But there wasn't a color even remotely similar to that of her dress among the swirling bodies.

Many of the guests wore deep purples and greens, but most wore black to represent the darkness that would swallow the land when the moon sets, the hour before the sun rises. It was usually tailed to be a cleansing before the dawn.

Besides, Althea hated dancing, almost more so than himself. She wouldn't be caught dead in a dance, not when tonight needed no distraction.

She danced with me. He held back a smirk. *But that was much different.*

"You didn't look too excited to be here when you were with your group," he changed the topic back to her. He really needed to put away the tone that he had developed from spending so many nights with Althea. Just thinking her name made him feel like he was betraying her by being pulled into the dance.

He pictured her in his head, hands on her hips, namely the one closest to her sword, shaking her head at him with narrowed eyes, asking him if he had lost his mind.

Zariah rolled her dark brown eyes behind her mask, tossing her long, black hair over her bare shoulder and huffed.

"Those are my sisters. My father wasn't able to make it tonight because of council meetings. He is making me watch over them. They wouldn't stop begging him to allow them to attend tonight, so here I am. By the way, do you know anything about the *big* thing that is supposed to happen tonight? I overheard a noble say that at three bells something big was planned."

That caught his attention.

"No. What big thing?" He asked, having to raise his voice over the sudden crescendo of music, then it stopped. His ears rang from the sudden hush that fell over the crowd before it was quickly swallowed by the roar of applause.

"What big thing?" Niklas asked again almost aggressively, his heart rate increasing, the beat pounding in time with the crowd. He did not get an answer. Her sisters rushed forward, surrounding her and carried her away, squealing like pigs.

"Ugh," he growled out, rushing from the dance floor. What a waste of his time.

He needed to find Althea.

Now.

CHAPTER THIRTY-TWO

—·—

ALTHEA

A lthea bumped into a servant in her rush, almost knocking the tray that he carried out of his hands.

"I am so sorry." Was all the time she gave herself to say before hurrying away, dodging more and more people the closer she got to the dais.

For what seemed like the first time in her life, she didn't know what to do. Didn't know the best path or steps to take. It made her feel blind. She had always had a brain for strategy and was always one step ahead. Captain Delmar said she was the highest ranking tracker he had seen in his time. But none of that prepared her for this. She couldn't believe that her mind was stalling. Who was she, if she did not have her skill.

Make it to one of the queen's advisers. Start there. Give a warning.

A large group of young women rushed in front of her, sweeping her away in a current. She was pulled in by the force of the group, and to avoid being trampled she had no other choice but to follow them and was pushed up the stairs and onto the balconies again.

God. Please. I don't know what to do.

Althea finally spun away from the group as soon as she was on the balcony. Her foot caught on the fabric of her dress, tripping her and her stomach rammed into the base of one of the statues.

A guard posted next to it reached out a hand to steady her. "Are you alright, miss?"

She coughed from the force of the blow, sending another jolt of pain through her bruised ribs.

"I am fine, thank you."

The guard tilted his head and Althea gasped. She had forgotten to use her cover accent. She recognized him, he had been near her when she had spoken to the prince.

"Wait, I thought you were from Llyr. Why do you now sound like you're from Taris?" His grip on her arm tightened ever so slightly and she could hear the pieces click together in his head.

Without thinking she freaked out, striking the exposed space of his inner elbow, yanking her arm from his loosened grip and ran. The guard shouted after her. She was so done for.

Whipping around a corner, Althea found the first unlocked room that she could find and slammed the door shut behind her, praying that the music and the talking crowds was enough to hide the sound.

She quickly accessed the dark, floral wallpapered room, the plush carpet denting under her steps to the wardrobe against the far wall. Inside were dresses that ranged from night to day and everything in between.

They were all far too noticeable for her liking, but she needed something different from what she wore. She pulled down the first piece she could grab onto and ran into the adjoining bathing room, careful to fluff the carpet from her prints and closed the door behind her just as she heard the one to the room open. She leaned her back against the cold door, clutching a hand over her mouth, trying to keep her shuddering breaths quiet as her heart raced.

She heard two booted steps walk into the room. "All clear, check the others, she was wearing red." The door clicked shut and the heavy steps faded down the hall. She let out a stuttering breath, shaking her head, she needed to get it together. She looked down at the fabric that was wrinkling in her tight fists and sighed.

It was an inky midnight blue that flared red when moved in the light. It just so happened to be the perfect size too. It flowed all the way to the floor, tight around her knees.

Althea used her dagger to make a knee high slit on the left side that made it easier to move in, and tucked the dagger into its sheath on her right thigh, to keep it hidden, wrapping the vine from her calf around a fake plant in the corner.

She readjusted her mask and slathered on a dark red lip stain that was discarded on the dark mahogany cabinet under the mirror. She definitely looked different. She looked like a night sky full of stars with the way the gold dust still clung to her skin, shining against the dark, silky fabric.

She peered down at her red dress, rubbing a thumb over the fabric. She didn't know what to do with it so she hung it up in the empty space in the wardrobe. A dress for a dress.

Althea held a hand against the pain in her stomach as she slid around a corner and down into an empty hallway. No guards, no guests, just door after door of locked rooms.

She had only glimpsed the bruise beginning form on her abdomen when she changed, but she knew that it was going to grow larger and more painful as time went on. It already hurt to breathe.

A door at the end of the hall of doors stood open, a dark hallway beyond its frame. It looked like a portal to hell.

She inched forward until she stood a foot from it and could see that it curved off to the right. In her head, Althea laid out the spaces in the palace that she had already been to, in relation to the windows from the outside, and created a mental map of sorts. She smiled a little to herself, comforted that her brain seemed to be working like it was supposed to again.

She looked over her shoulder to make sure no one saw her before lightly stepping under the dark doorway. In the faint light of the torches behind her, she could see large boot prints in the swirled dust under her sandaled feet. The passage had clearly not been used in a very long time. Until then.

She felt the breath on her neck a second before a hand clamped over her mouth.

CHAPTER THIRTY-THREE

NIKLAS

"*Althea? Althea!*" Niklas hissed into an empty hallway. His eyes must have been playing a trick on him.

The woman he saw hadn't even been wearing a red dress. But what he thought he saw was the long, brown hair cascading down her back and assumed at a quick glance that it had been her, before a literal wave of women crossed in front of him, blinding him with their perfume.

He was about to turn down the next set of quarters when something caught his eye at the end of the long hall. His steps faltered when he got closer. It was a crown of roses.

Feet shuffled behind him and his neck cracked as he whipped around, heart jumping in his chest. It was just a young servant girl.

"Are you lost, sir? This section of guest's quarters isn't being used. I can help you find where you need to go if you would like." Her voice was soft and innocent.

"Actually, I was looking for someone. About your height, brown hair, red dress?" He snapped his fingers, remembering something that would stand out in a crowd. "Gold dust. Yeah, gold on her face and shoulders."

The girl looked up at him with ice blue eyes, her lips perched in thought. "I do remember seeing someone like that not too long ago. She was walking with a gentleman but her dress looked darker."

"Which way did they go?" He asked, tone clipped and urgent.

She recognized his fear, her face becoming serious, ready to help. "I saw them walking somewhere around here, but..." She scrunched her brow. "There is nothing down here, all the rooms are locked."

He did not feel like he was moving fast enough as he pulled on the door handles, slamming a fist onto each one. He reached the door at the end of the hall, and shoved against it with his shoulder. It opened. He caught himself from falling and stared at the footprints in the dust.

At the base of the door was a swirled mess, with one or two distinct, small foot prints and a couple sets of large ones further in. Whoever they belonged to must be very heavy and injured. One foot planted evenly, and the other dragged by the toe, indicating a limp.

"Where does this lead?" He twirled around, kicking up the dust into the air.

The servant shrugged, her mouth hanging open, her eyes wide with fear.

"The third balcony!" She gasped, eyes alight as she remembered. "This hallway isn't used anymore. The third floor used to be where the king lived with the queen before he passed, but it usually sits vacant. I had not heard of the queen having deemed it for use tonight, but I am usually the last to hear of those things. It's supposed to always be locked."

Niklas was through the door and racing down the dark hallway before she could finish. He cursed the darkness for forcing his steps to slow. He wished his heart would stop beating so loud. A breath echoed behind him.

He pulled out a dagger, pushing the person against the wall. It was the girl. She had followed him. She sucked in a startled breath, her eyes locked onto the point of the knife and flattened herself against the wall, trying to get as far away from it as she could.

He instantly lowered the weapon. "I'm sorry." He stepped back instantly. "The girl I was telling you about, she might be in danger. I need to find her and help her." He took a deep breath, closing his eyes and letting it out, forcing his heart to calm.

When he opened them, the girl stared over his shoulder, eyes as wide as saucers. A hand covering her mouth, she pointed at something behind him.

It was then that he realized that it was not the sound of his heart beating against his skull at all. It was the sound of a fight.

Chapter Thirty-Four

Althea

The grip the man had on her upper arm was only going to add to the colorful bruises forming across her body. Her right knee twinged with every step she took.

As soon as she had felt that hand on her skin, her instincts had taken over. She had grabbed onto the large forearm of her attacker and dropped to her knees, her bones cracking on the floor, tucked and rolled, bringing the man over her shoulder.

She didn't wait to hear the thud of his body on the uneven stone before she turned, ready to run back to the crowds she only seconds ago wished she could leave behind.

Her toes had barely crossed the threshold of the door when someone blocked her escape. His lithe body was nothing but a dark silhouette against the torches shining behind him. She lurched back a step, only for her exposed spine to bump into the leather clad chest of her first attacker. Rough hands grabbed her shoulders.

The man in front of her leaned his shoulder against the frame of the door, hands shoved into his pockets. With a sigh, and a shake of his head, he spoke, "I really hoped that you wouldn't have been here for the reason that I thought you were. But I guess I should have suspected such a thing from the likes of this kingdom."

Her blood turned to ice. Xadier.

"I bet you're wondering how I know who you are... Althea." He stepped forward, his face coming into view, blue eyes sparkling with evil, a smirk twisting his seemingly handsome face into something out of a nightmare.

"Althea," he hummed. "Or would you prefer deserter? I like that better. Imagine this." He splayed his hands in the air in front of him like he was a painter presenting his art to people behind him. "Ex-guard, Althea Nova, charged for treason against the throne of our *glorious* Queen Azora during this rapidly growing rebellion." He laughed darkly, waving at the guard holding her to follow him as he walked past her.

She couldn't help but cringe away from the tendrils of darkness that seemed to flow off of him like smoke. She felt it, as real as she felt the calloused hands on her bare skin.

She hissed in pain at the tight ropes that tied her hands together, her wrists raw and bleeding. One last twist of her skilled fingers and she had the rope untied, but made sure to act like it was still tight. It was not time yet for her to fight back.

She was outnumbered, four to one.

One guarded the door from the outside. The other three sat at a small table — or maybe the table was a normal size and they were just giants. Every time they shifted their weight the wooden chairs would groan beneath them and Althea wished one would just shatter already, so she could grab a wooden spike and then she could get out of here and find Niklas. Tell him there had been a change of plans. She knew who was behind the threat now and she was itching to finish this. Itched more than her rope burned wrists.

The only good part of the detour was that it helped her discover more of the palace's layout, and she updated the map in her head. The large set of double doors on the far wall should lead out onto the third level of balconies she had seen from below.

The men talked in low voices. From where she sat on the floor, it all sounded like grunts and growls. Every inch of her was on fire for more reasons than one. Embarrassment, anger, the dust that coated her from the dank passageway she had been forcefully carried through. And worst of all, fear, to name a few. At least they took the pinching mask off of her.

She leaned her back against the huge four poster bed, the cool silk bedding the only comfort against her burning skin.

If they knew about her, then they must know about Niklas.

God, even if you don't help me. Help him.

"What is she going on about over there?" Xadier, the prince, scoffed, pausing his aggravated pacing, his arms crossed over his chest as he stared at her from across the room. She hadn't realized she had been praying out loud. First mistake while being held captive, she drew attention to herself. She winced.

One of the hulking men, covered in furs despite the blisteringly humid air in the room, walked over and picked her up off the carpet effortlessly, like she was a small pup and not a grown woman and tossed her onto the tall bed like a dirty, discarded shirt so she would be in their line of sight. Probably so she wouldn't try anything.

Too late. She held onto the rope covering her hands, holding it in place tight against her red skin and sat up unceremoniously, fighting to set herself upright without the use of her hands.

She sat cross legged like she would at a picnic, kept her hands in her lap and glowered at the prince in front of her through her dark hair. Even though she knew she should feign innocence, she wouldn't let them think she was afraid.

She blew the loose strands of hair out of her face with a huff. That was why she always wore it in a braid. She could not stand the feeling of her hair when it was down. Why did she let Niklas stop her from cutting it when she had the chance?

Xadier lowered his face over her, forcing her to lean away from him and the smell of liquor that rolled off his tongue. "I underestimated you, Althea. You escaped many grasps on your little adventure here. As the Head of the Guard, I know everything when it comes to everyone. Who should be where they are supposed to be and when they are not. You are not an exception, no matter how insignificant you might be. You didn't think I didn't know you found my camp did you? I could smell you from up in that tree."

He started to pace again, moving his hands while he talked. "You see, I got a little letter from a very angry mayor, that one of his pets was missing. Oh, and just so you know, he doesn't want it back. Perfect timing by the way. Seeing that my dear trusting sister gave full command of the Guard over to me, I turned your, what should I call it, escapade into the perfect diversion.

"You should have seen it. 'Some of the highest ranking guards in the country joined a band of rebels that kidnapped a certain nobleman's son of Palmeria; they have demands for his safe return.' Blah, blah, blah. I mean honestly, Cerdic? Did anyone honestly think that they were going to help anyone but themselves? They are the real traitors up there. They were the first to join my cause. Jumping for someone like me to show up and fix things around here."

He spoke like he was in a trance, his eyes taking on a faraway look, unfocusing for a moment to play on whatever evil his mind devised.

"So the war, none of it was real?" She was disgusted by the man in front of her.

"Oh no, it is very real. The Guard of Valarie just won't be meeting the enemy they think they are."

Despite Althea's attempt at seeming not to care, she sucked in a sharp breath as the meaning of his words began to take shape. Aezel, Captain Delmar, all of the people she grew up with, trained with. They won't know that Cerdic had sided with the rebellion until their numbers were already among their ranks, fighting.

Her heart raced, her stomach soured and churned, her mouth tasted of bile. She felt the strength in her muscles tremble and turn to gel.

The prince, having succeeded in making her show fear, grinned. He cleared his throat and made for the door. "I have *things* to attend to. Keep her in your sights. She's stronger than she looks." And then he was gone, the door closing almost too softly, on well oiled hinges.

The other two men continued on in their game of dice, grunting when one lost, laughing when one won. Occasionally, they remembered she was still there and threw dark glares at her over their shoulders.

What they didn't see was the dagger in her freed hands. She fought the urge to scratch at her skin and kept her head low. Trying to look defeated. But she felt strengthened by the second instead.

The prince got one thing right after all.

She was stronger than she looked.

A loud thump came from behind the door that the prince left through just minutes ago. Everyone, including Althea, jumped at the unexpected noise.

"I'll watch the girl, you go see what that was," the one in the furs said.

"No, you go. I'll watch her," the smaller of the two retorted.

Furs huffed, rolling his eyes, and shrugged off his coat, taking a long drink out of a bottle of what could only be liquor for its honey-amber color.

He shouldered the door open and disappeared into the dark, dimly lit hallway. Something caught Althea's eye before the door shut, and she leaned forward to look around the closing door.

It was a large portrait, of who could only be King Marcus, or who he was before he passed when Althea was too young to know why her kingdom had mourned.

It might have been a trick of the light the flickering torch cast on the oils of the painting, but she could have sworn it looked like Niklas.

She must have been so worried about him that she was seeing his face in every shadow, hearing him in every voice that echoed up to her from the double doors to the balcony, and heard his familiar footsteps in every creak of the floorboards.

She saw him clearly when she squeezed her eyes shut as if he was standing right before her. His hands on his hips, eyes blinking slowly like a cat who was judging her for getting herself into the position she was in.

"What is taking that buff so long?" The small guard groaned from where he stood at the table. He looked between her and the door, and back to her, then back to the door again, contemplating.

"It's not exactly like I can go anywhere," Althea stated, deadpan, what the obvious would look like to him.

"Shut up, little girl." He walked over to her and reached for her wrist to check that the bindings were still tight.

They were not.

He shouted in surprise when she leaped off the bed, threw the rope at his face, slashed at his reaching palm with her dagger and ran for the double doors.

A hand grabbed a fistful of her hair, sharp nails digging into her scalp. She twisted and kicked blindly behind her, satisfied at the grunt she heard and the hand fell away.

She burst through the door and slid to a stop, teetering on the edge of the balcony where pieces of the iron railing had been taken apart. The ballroom was in the shape of a large oval, not unlike the arena where she trained every day, but had multiple levels. She was on the third floor. That would have been a long fall.

The prince's guard caught up to her when she reached the narrowest curve of the oval, directly above the queen's dais where she was standing, swaying her hips to the loud music that blared this close to the ceiling. It pounded in her chest and it took every inch of her training to keep her mind in the back room as she dodged his fists.

He was as fast as she expected him to be with his thin frame, his fists raining down on her like lightning. Good thing she was faster. Her forearms screamed with every block and her knuckles ached with every punch she landed. She became winded far quicker than she was used to after the month she spent in the forest, eating nothing but berries and what little creatures they could catch that weren't stowed away for the winter yet. But even in the worst of states, she always had to be stronger, faster and smarter than her larger opponents in order to prove her worth, to keep the spot in the Guard she had earned.

He jumped in the air, spinning, kicking and slashing in a way that Althea had never seen anyone fight before. He landed a hard jab into her stomach, right on the bruise from where she had fallen on the statue. Her entire body rang like a bell as her balance teetered. She tilted back, used her momentum to somersault backwards, and paused on her knees, trying to get her lungs to unfreeze.

"Why are you doing this? What cause do you have according to the law?" Althea wheezed past the pain.

"You're just a kid, you don't know anything," he spit. "And if you can't see the evil that the queen has let fall over this kingdom, then you are just as blind as everyone else," he growled, stalking closer, slowly. Predator and prey.

Althea pushed herself to her feet and shuffled back, keeping five feet between them. She was getting close to another section of railing that was missing. He saw it too, his eyes moved back to her, glinting, licking his incisors like an animal.

Her muscles tensed as he reminded her of the *khourges* she'd faced. Alone, scared, and cowed with her back facing the open air.

"Niklas," she involuntarily whispered. She was frozen, again. That same feeling of helplessness flooded her veins. She had sworn that she would never feel like that again.

"Oh. Niklas. Is that your little lover? Well, I sure hope he has someone else to hold, because you sure won't be making it home tonight." A small gust of wind blew in from an open window behind her. The torches flickered around the palace. A door to her right creaked ever so slightly.

She stole herself and ran for the door. But in her panicked state, she had wrongly gauged the distance between herself and her attacker.

He rushed forward at the same time she did and slammed his body into hers, throwing them both down and sliding, close to the balcony's edge. He had her right hand pinned to the ground by her head, but couldn't catch her left hand fast enough. She clawed at his face, undoing his mask in the process. Her heart lurched when she saw who it was.

Barty.

He was one of them? Memories sprang to the front of her mind. Barty missing practices, seeing him talking to rumored conspiracists. He could never pass the ascension test.

Her eyes widened until she felt like they would fall out of her skull.

Words swelled in her mouth, stronger than the nausea that flooded her stomach. She never got the chance to open her mouth. Barty leaned out of her reach and dug his long fingers into the wound on her forearm that never fully healed.

She could feel the stitches as they were ripped out of her flesh.

She screamed.

The warmth of the blood running up her arm threatened to make her lose the contents of her stomach. She saw stars and her body refused to move under her command.

A sob raked through her, and then things started to get dark.

Chapter Thirty-Five

Niklas

"Okay, okay, calm down you guys." Niklas held each of the drunken men by their suit collars as they thrashed, still trying to hit each other though they could barely stand up straight on their own.

"Take it back!" One slurred.

"I won't, it was not a lie. Your wife really does look like one!" The other shot back.

With a roar, the first one who spoke lurched at the other, his hands splayed like claws as he reached for the man's throat.

Niklas rolled his eyes and sighed, releasing the grip he had on him and pulled the other man back a step. The first man tripped as he flew past, grabbing onto thin air and landed on his stomach. He didn't get back up, but continued to writhe and groan, splayed on the ground like a star.

Niklas adjusted his mask yet again and pushed the last man standing toward the passage back to the ballroom. He turned to the servant girl, whose hands were still shaking, and asked, "Why was that door unlocked if this whole floor is supposed to be vacant?"

Her mouth opened and closed, unable to say why and eventually shrugged.

"No matter, let's just make sure no one else is up here." She nodded and followed after him, her steps were as quiet as his, he couldn't hear her breathing and barely felt her presence behind him. She had potential, Niklas thought, and made a mental note to ask for her name later. She would make an excellent guard.

Hurried footsteps crunched on the dusty carpet in the darkness in front of them. Niklas quickly grabbed the girl, tucking them in the darkest notch he could find. Behind the only open door in the long hallway.

"I have to do *everything* myself. A bunch of imbeciles are what they are, all of them," the man, speaking to himself, came into view. He stopped beside them and took a deep breath, straightening the lapels of his coat.

It was dark. The man was nothing but a silhouette, but Niklas could see as the outline tilted its head, listening. He laid a hand on the girl's shoulder, quietly angling himself in front of her, keeping his hand near his dagger, holding his breath.

The man shook his head, mumbling unintelligibly under his breath and continued on, disappearing around the corner they had just come from.

Niklas leaned away from the door, letting his breath out in a heavy sigh, listening extra carefully now that he knew the halls weren't vacant. He paused when he realized the girl wasn't following him anymore. She was facing the way the man had gone.

"Hey, it's okay. I can take you back if you want. But it might be safer if we keep going." She didn't turn around, her dark form stood still, frozen.

"Miss?"

She startled, and walked backwards toward him, shaking her head.

"Tha– that was– I–"

"What is it?" Niklas asked.

"That was the prince." She turned, taking a startled step back when she bumped into his chest.

"The prince?" Niklas pressed.

"Sir Xadier. The queen's brother. I know I am not supposed to say anything, but he wasn't supposed to be here tonight. The queen had given him orders to lead the armies in Caedmon. He shouldn't be here." She grabbed his hand tightly and looked up into his eyes. "Do you think something went wrong? Did we lose?" Her voice quivered on that last word.

"Miss– what is your name?"

"Farah," she gulped.

"Farah, I need you to listen to me very carefully. My name is Niklas, I am a Lieutenant of the Guard of Taris. I will do everything I can to protect you, but you have to do exactly as I say." She nodded, eyes wide and attentive.

"The girl I'm looking for, she is also a guard of Taris. She was scouting ahead after our march had been ambushed by a band of rebels and we were separated from them. We stumbled upon a camp. A rebel camp. There was a command tent, and my friend... she heard them say that the war was the perfect distraction to make an attempt for the throne."

"I don't understand, why would someone want to hurt Her Majesty?"

"I don't know yet. But if the prince is here when he is supposed to be five hundred miles away, then I have a pretty good idea."

There was one guard standing at a thick, wooden door. He seemed disinterested, picking at his nails while leaning against the wall. A low, flickering torch tried its best to give the hallway its light, but the shadows must have been stronger, they pressed in with a palpable weight.

Niklas had roughly taught Farah a few warning signals that might not be suspicious in the dull, thick air. A series of taps against the window they'd pried open.

"Okay, I'm going to scout ahead, do you remember the code?" He had asked. She pressed her lips into a thin, determined line, and nodded. It reminded him so much of Althea, and his heart beat a little faster. If she was hurt...

Niklas cupped his hand around his mouth and clicked his tongue, throwing the sound down the hall past the guard. His head flew up and he looked around frantically. The guard drew a long dagger from his belt and carefully walked down the hall away from Niklas. Now was his chance.

He was one step away from the guard when he turned. Niklas wrapped his arm around the guard's throat faster than the man could react. With his other hand, Niklas fought to keep the guard's dagger away from his face.

Once the guard knew that the fight for his weapon was fruitless, he reached behind his head and tried to pull at Niklas's hair, but was already too weak.

In the last second before the guard passed out, he threw a kick, not at Niklas but at the wall. A resounding bang reverberated in the hall. And then he went limp in his arms.

A spike of fear shot up his throat. He could hear muffled, confused voices from behind the wall, but couldn't make out what they were saying. He quickly dragged the guard to a shadowed corner, but didn't have time to hide himself before the door opened. He froze, holding his breath. All he could do was wait.

A hulking man entered the hall and stood with his hands on his hips, looked both ways and spoke to himself, "That weasel, always taking off. I need a drink."

Niklas started to stand, hand outstretched when the man turned. He was heading straight for Farah. But if Niklas followed now, he would reveal himself. An impossible choice. He waited.

Nothing happened. Footsteps retreated into the darkness, followed by silence. All he could hear was his blood whooshing in his ears, all thoughts escaped him. Until a shadow grew closer to him. He held his dagger in a death grip, the blade pointed down and against his forearm.

"It's all clear, Niklas." Farah shuffled closer, a smile spread across her face and gave him a thumbs up.

Niklas fought a cough against the dust that got stuck in his throat and met her halfway until they stood together before the door.

"Are you okay? Are you certain you weren't seen?" He roved his eyes over her face but couldn't make out anything in this light.

"Yes, sir, I'm fine. When I saw him coming I hid behind the bust in the corner. He didn't have a clue."

He couldn't stop the smile on his face despite the situation. Her excitement was contagious.

It reminded him of when he went on his first assignment as a Red Jewel. Albeit, that was only trapping a squirrel that kept getting into a bakery and was eating holes through the bread. He had been ten seasons, but it was a triumph all the same. His father had cooked the squirrel and they celebrated his victory over the dinner.

A shout broke through the quiet, followed by two sets of feet running. He heard a door slam open from inside the room and the music blared in, chasing every inch of quiet from the hall with the highs and lows of the orchestra.

Without thinking, Niklas wrenched the door open and took in every detail of the space in seconds as he ran across the plush carpet to the gaping double doors.

A game of cards on the table with three hands dealt. The purple sheets were wrinkled and hanging off the bed. A red mask, and a rope. A splatter of blood across the pillow. Niklas swallowed in fear.

A scream, shrieking in time with the high trill of a violin.

His vision turned red and he ran faster than ever before.

There she was. A dark shadow writhing on the floor, her head so close to the edge of the balcony. She was pinned down by a man in a black suit, his hands covered in her blood, one on her arm the other around her throat.

Niklas roared. He felt a piece of his soul crack with the sound.

He tackled the man, shoving him off Althea, grabbed him by his collar and lifted his head off the ground. He hit, and hit, and hit. He didn't stop until a hand caught him by the elbow.

He whipped around, breathing heavily, growling through his teeth barred in rage.

It was Farah, she didn't look afraid. She should be afraid of him. He failed. He didn't keep his secret promise to Althea.

Instead, she pulled him away from the body that was still breathing, shallowly. The man's eyes were open, blue irises peeking around the purple bruises forming.

He smiled, spitting blood. "You're too late. Just like your girl-friend."

Niklas did not – could not – recognize him by his features, but when he spoke, Niklas instantly knew. The face, now mottled and swollen, belonged to Barty.

"Traitor," Niklas spit the word, ready to lunge for him again, save for the steady hand on his arm, an anchor pulling his soul back into his body.

"Niklas, she needs you."

His heart stopped its race and began to beat erratically. He would deal with Barty later, he would not be getting up soon, not without help anyway.

Niklas limped over to his friend, not having realized that he had re-injured his twisted ankle in the fight, and dropped to his knees by Althea.

She coughed, red spraying from between her lips. She tried to push herself up onto her elbows, but he stopped her with a hand on her shoulder.

"Always so stubborn," he whispered.

He wrapped one arm behind her back and one under her knees groaning as he picked her up, putting the extra weight on his good leg.

"Show me somewhere safe." He followed Farah through hidden servant passageways, some so narrow that he had to walk sideways to fit through with Althea in his arms. The crack inside him deepened as he kept telling her to stay awake when her head lolled against his chest.

The wound on her arm that had been neatly stitched by the doctor in Heriit was open and flowing, soaking through her dress, causing the fabric to stick to her skin.

"I know, Althea. Just a bit longer, please. Please, God."

"Here, this is my room, put her on the bed. No one will be in these quarters until sunrise. I will fetch the doctor I trust. He will keep this quiet." Farah turned to go.

"Wait," Niklas called after her.

She turned, hand still on the doorknob, ready to help.

"Thank you, Farah."

"The night is not over yet, Sir Niklas." And then she was gone, the door clicking shut behind her.

Althea was sleeping, her chest rose and fell shallowly, her face covered in a thin sheen of sweat.

The doctor told him that there was not any internal bleeding, but that she had bitten the inside of her cheek, which was the cause of her spitting up blood.

When the doctor cut the fabric to look at a wound on her side Niklas had to turn away, clenching his shaking hands into fists at the bruises he saw on her stomach, the ones forming on her throat, and arms.

How could he let this happen?

The only thing that kept him from fully blaming himself was Farah. She helped the doctor tend to Althea, all the while repeating to him that this was not his doing. He could not have known what was happening. That he got there in time and that was what mattered in the end.

If only he believed her.

He left Farah with specific instructions for when Althea woke up. He knew she would be scared, and he knew that her body would react on instinct before her mind could process where she was and what had happened.

He made her recite the words three times before he left.

"Sir Niklas, it will all be okay, go. And be careful."

Now he stalked among the milling guests, the blood moon glowing brighter as it passed its apex. He no longer tried to act like he was just here to enjoy the night.

He grabbed people's shoulders, looking into their faces. Mumbling apologies, saying that they looked like someone he knew. He worked his way around the room, closing in on the dais.

It wasn't until a servant passed in front of him, blocking his view, that he realized the queen's guards were no longer standing at the foot of the dais.

He quickened his pace, shoving people out of the way now. They shouted after him, but no one tried to stop him. They were all too drunk to do anything anyway.

The queen sat alone on her throne, a fresh glass of wine in her pale hands, her nails painted the color of fresh blood.

Another figure pushing through the crowd opposite him caught his eye. A man wearing all black, including the mask that covered his brow. Sleeves that ended at his shoulders, showing the corded muscles in his arms, leading all the way to the needle-thin dagger in his hand, concealed against the inside of his forearm. Just like the one he saw the woman holding in the tapestry.

The man was closer to the dais than Niklas. And the harder he fought to get through the crowd it seemed like it closed in tighter around him, choking the oxygen from the air in the room.

One foot raised onto the steps of the dais, then the other.

Then Niklas broke free.

His steps ate up the distance and the crowd began to part, letting him race through. The assassin, cloaked in the shadows of the dying torches, paused, turning his head to look behind him at the sudden shift in the air.

Niklas jumped, tackling him to the cold, hard marble of the dais. The dagger flew from his hand, sliding until it came to rest at the toe of the queen's jeweled, heeled shoes.

She turned to look at what happened, her eyes widening as they roamed the sight of the two men wrestling behind her throne. The crowd started to realize that something was wrong, even the air sensed the shift.

Her eyes lowered to her feet.

To the dagger.

And she screamed.

The crowd rushed away from the dais. People ran, some fell and were trampled. Screams filled the air as the torches began to snuff out, one by one, casting shadows that might as well have had faces and claws for how they stretched and swallowed the guests in their darkness.

The assassin underneath Niklas tried to kick and twist himself free. But Niklas had unlocked a new level of strength fueled by anger, fear, and... love. These people hurt the ones he loved. And he would not rest until they were all thrown in the darkest of dungeons he could find.

"What is the meaning of this nonsense?"

Niklas looked up... and into the face of the prince.

He stood next to the queen, a protective arm around his sister's shoulder, and angled her behind him, putting on a farce of bravery for the eyes of the few left in the vacating ballroom.

"He is an assassin with the rebellion. He was trying to kill you, Your Majesty!" Niklas spoke to the queen directly, lowering his eyes in respect, ignoring the prince altogether.

"By the looks of it, *you* are the one who is a danger. You are strangling that man!" Xadier responded before she could.

Niklas looked down. His forearm was pressed against the throat of the assassin, his lips beginning to turn blue. He was still making feeble attempts to break Niklas's hold.

"Guards!" Xadier shouted, and began to pull his sister away.

"No, wait!" Niklas leapt off the man, leaving him to sputter and cough on the floor.

Everything froze, the guards stopped their advance, looking between Niklas, the queen and the assassin, not knowing what to do. The queen had not given an order yet, and these few in armor did not seem to answer to Xadier. They were loyal to the throne.

Niklas held out his hands to show he held no weapon, and with his foot, he nudged the dagger out of his boot and kicked it to the side, it disappeared under the throne.

"Your Majesty, I am Lieutenant Stallard from the Guard of Taris. I am loyal to the throne. Exactly one month ago we received the news of your command to march with Caedmon. But while my army was traveling through the Cerridwen we were ambushed at the Norvern river and I had been separated with one of my fellow guards. While we tried to find a way around to reconvene with our men, we found a rebel war camp, only four days walk from our city. We overheard Xadier and the commanders say that they were using the war to disguise their attempt on your life.

"Please, believe me, Your Majesty. Your brother is behind all of this."

"How *dare* you accuse your prince! Guards, take him!" Xadier shouted, his eyes betraying his fear despite the anger in his voice, but Niklas was the only one close enough to see it. He began to shuffle backward an inch at a time, pulling the queen with him.

Tears fell down the queen's face in fear, her lips quivered, the hem of her dress was soaked in split wine.

The guards didn't move, but one knelt, a fist on his heart and said, "Your Majesty, we await your command."

"Do you forget that the queen gave full command of the Guard to me? I control you. *Take. Him.*"

The queen looked at the guard and shakily shook her head. In unison, the guards took their first steps forward, and Niklas was about to protest, dropping his weight into his back leg, ready to go down with a fight. But they walked past him.

"We are not under oath to you, Sir Xadier. We serve the throne of Valarie. Hand over our queen." It was a woman's voice.

Niklas turned, his stomach twisting.

Althea.

She was back to wearing the red dress she had worn into the palace. Her skin, pale and sickly, was washed clean from her blood, her arm wrapped in a clean bandage.

Xadier backed away faster now, reaching up to throw his mask off the side of the dais. His boot connected with the thin dagger and he picked it up quickly, holding it against the queen's throat.

She cried out, grabbing his wrist and tried to push his hand away.

"Xadier, what are you doing? Why?" Her voice strained as she leaned as far away from the blade as she could.

"Oh, dear sister, the fact that you have to ask is reason enough." He kept backing away.

The guards pulled out their swords and surround the pair in a semi circle, forcing Xadier's back to the wall.

Niklas joined in their formation with nothing but the stone dagger that he had kept hidden in his pocket. He never allowed himself to be weaponless, even in front of the queen.

"The throne was always supposed to be mine after father died, but then you had to go and marry that Taris *garbage*. You never earned the throne, it was yours by tradition only."

Xadier started to shake, the dagger in his hand pressed into the soft hollow of the queen's throat, his movements becoming jerky as he looked at the guards closing in around him, to the servants that stood against the walls like sentries, witnessing his betrayal. His throat bobbed up and down. The prince's time was running out, and he knew it.

Niklas saw the exact moment in the prince's eyes when he made his decision. He pulled his arm back, a torch's light sparkling against the steel in his hand, and brought the dagger down.

But not before Niklas threw his.

The stone soared through the air, catching the sleeve of the prince's coat, pinning his arm to the wall. Niklas launched himself forward before the dagger's hilt stopped vibrating.

The prince was faster than he expected, but clearly untrained. He tugged on the dagger, pulling with all his might and yanked it free just as Niklas got within reach of him.

Althea moved at the same time he did, grabbing the queen's arm, running towards the servants area where Farah's room was. The other servants raced after them, desperate to help protect their queen.

Niklas grabbed the prince's wrist, slamming it against the wall, once, twice, until he let go of the dagger. They were the same height, but Niklas had fifty pounds on him at least.

The prince swung wildly with his other arm, catching Niklas across the face, a ruby studded cufflink sunk into his cheek.

Blood flowed down his face and dripped onto the white marble between their feet. The stone cutting the strap to his mask and it fell away.

The prince's eyes widened and his fight stuttered.

Gritting his teeth, Niklas yanked the prince away from the wall, twisting his arms behind his back, almost dislocating his shoulder. Xadier cried out as it popped and Niklas looked to the guards. They all stood there, mouths open in shock, swords still raised. Niklas turned to the guard that looked to be of the highest rank.

"Show me to the dungeon," he snarled.

CHAPTER THIRTY-SIX

ALTHEA

Althea's entire body ached, and parts of her soul felt bruised as well.

Her dress was soaking wet, though she didn't remember swimming. She thought she was at the ball with Niklas. Where was he now? Where was *she*?

That was until she had woken up in an unfamiliar room, with a young girl standing over her.

Althea sat straight up, or tried to. The muscles in her abdomen spasmed, feeling like glass that shattered with every move, every breath. She whimpered.

"Hold on Miss. Nikl–" The young girl reached for her. Althea didn't know who she was, where she was. Her body moved of its own accord.

She tried to leap out of the bed, groping for the dagger she always kept on her thigh but it wasn't there. The girl jumped back, pressing against the wall as far away from her as she could in the small room. Althea only managed to land in a heap on the floor.

"Who are you," she coughed, another glass muscle shattered. "How do you know about Niklas?"

The girl stood in the corner, shaking, her eyes wide. She took a deep breath and her hands stilled, determination sharpening her features.

"I helped Niklas when he was looking for you. He said that you wouldn't trust me at first, but if I told you something only the two of you would know, you would," she paused, looking up at the ceiling, trying to remember.

"It went something like, 'With the jaws of lions... yeah right, more like with the lips of a frog,' and I quote, 'Blech'. Does that sound about right?" She spoke the words flatly, and it sounded so much like Niklas that Althea couldn't help but laugh.

And immediately regretted it. Her body shuddered.

"Ow."

"Oh Miss, let me help you. My name is Farah."

"Althea. Miss makes it sound like I'm an old lady, though I feel like one right about now."

"I meant no offense, Mi– Althea." A small smile lifted her lips.

"None taken."

Sitting on the edge of the bed, Althea took a few steadying breaths and tested some of her muscles, stretching them, trying to ease the pain as much as possible. She twisted her neck to the side and caught sight of a dagger on the nightstand. Her dagger.

She grabbed it quickly, inspecting it for damage and held it to her chest, heart racing. She hadn't realized until she held it, the small void that the absence of the familiar weight had caused.

"That means a lot to you, doesn't it? The doctor had taken it from you in order to safely access your injuries. You kept trying to swing it at him with your eyes closed." She tried to hide her giggle behind a hand, and Althea smiled.

Her smile fell away as quick as it came.

"Wait... if Niklas isn't here, then where is he?"

Farah's smile fell away as well.

"He went to save the queen."

Farah trailed behind Althea as she walked as fast as she could. Her head was light and her breathing was heavy, her skin pale. The fabric of her red dress stuck uncomfortably to her sweaty skin.

She had taken one look at the black dress she wore, ripped and soaked in blood and asked Farah if she knew the rooms on the second floor well. She asked her to find the dress she left in the wardrobe.

Althea had waited impatiently, and tried hard not to run out of the room to go get it herself. Farah was only gone for three minutes exactly, far faster than Althea would have been in her state but it had felt like an eternity.

As they neared the ballroom, shouts and screams echoed down the empty hallway. And then like a flood, people ran.

Althea and Farah were almost crushed against the wall, but at the last second Farah pulled her behind the statue that stood under the archway connecting the hall to the ballroom. The ground shook underneath her sandaled feet. The heat and fear and crush of thousands of bodies racing for the exits threatened to choke her.

This was exactly what she was afraid would happen. Chaos always went hand in hand with casualties. Althea could already see a few bodies lying motionless on the cold floor, dressed feet stomping onto their backs and hands. Althea prayed that they knew God, that they went somewhere without pain.

She could not wait any longer. If Niklas was out there, he must already be involved in what caused this chaos. She saw a break in the crowd and took it. Farah shouted behind her.

"Just wait there, Farah. Stay safe!" She did not know if her words reached the girl, but she didn't stop to see if she followed.

She pushed and shoved weakly against the opposite current of the crowd, toward the madness. She took a second when she finally broke into the ballroom to lean against the cold wall to catch her breath, to assess.

Over the heads of the running stragglers, Althea could see the queen's guards standing on the dais. Xadier had an arm around the queen's shoulders, almost like he was trying to protect her. His mouth was moving, but Althea was too far away to hear.

As she moved closer, sticking to the shadows, his words started to form.

"-ontrol you. *Take. Him.*"

The guards parted as they took a step forward, revealing Niklas. To anyone else, he stood normally, but to Althea, who had fought with him since they were able to walk, knew that he was not going to be taken without a fight.

She rounded the dais, walking up a step, her balance not quite right. "We are not under oath to you, Sir Xadier. We serve the throne of Valarie. Hand over our queen." Her voice sounded stronger than she felt as she stepped out of the shadows.

Niklas whirled around, meeting Althea's eyes. She could see his thoughts, even behind the mask he wore. His reprimands would have to wait.

Xadier backed away, pulling the queen with him.

She saw his mouth open, moving as he spoke, but she couldn't hear anything. A loud buzzing filled her head, sweeping in with a wave of nausea. She forced it down and fought through the dizziness, standing just behind the guards formation. Sweat trickled down her exposed back despite the chill that overtook the room.

Althea closed her eyes for a second, focusing on the feeling of the stone under her sandals, trying not to fall over. When she opened her eyes a half second later, everything had moved. Niklas pinned the prince to the wall, wrestling a dagger out of his hand.

When did he get over there? Her consciousness edged closer to darkness.

Althea lurched forward and scrabbled for the queen's arm. The queen grabbed Althea's instead and they took off at a sprint. She had kicked off her heeled shoes and ran surprisingly fast in the full skirt of her dress.

A small burst of energy roared in Althea's veins, sharpening her focus as she guided the queen toward the servants hall. She didn't know where else to go that might be safe, but there had to be an exit that way.

She blinked, and when she opened her eyes, Farah was pulling her towards a servants staircase tucked into the wall.

When did Farah get here?

"Your Majesty!" A gravelly shout came from down the hall. A tall soldier, wearing the dark armor of the Queen's Guard ran toward them, a sword in his hand.

Althea moved to stand in front of the queen, but she wasn't by her side anymore. She was running toward the guard.

"Lueren!" She gasped, throwing her arms around the man, holding tight.

"Are you okay? Are you hurt?" He put his sword in its sheath and grabbed the queen's face in both of his hands, turning her head this way and that, looking to see if she was injured. Fear was plastered plainly on his face. "I came as quickly as I could when I saw the guests running."

"Oh, Lueren. I always knew he was jealous that I was heir. I just thought if I gave him the Guard to attend to it would help him overcome his hunger for power."

"Let's not worry about the why just yet. He is in our custody now, as well as those he hired. You need to see a doctor, just in case."

Farah pulled on Althea's arm again, trying to pull her up the stairs. But her feet felt numb, she couldn't get them to move.

More men in armor clanked down the hallway and the queen turned back the way they had come.

Farah pulled on her harder, her feet slipped up the first few steps until a guard grabbed her other wrist.

Her vision went completely black and she faintly heard the guard say, "Althea Nova, you need to come with us."

Chapter Thirty-Seven

Niklas

He had been pulled into the Command of Guard's headquarters, by someone named Lueren, and questioned intensively about where he had come from, how he had come to find out about the rebellion's intention to assassinate the queen, and if he knew anything more than what he already said. He was then escorted to a room in the palace to wait for more orders.

He paced, looking at everything, opening every drawer, door and cabinet in the room until boredom started to set in and he began to worry about Althea. He hadn't seen her since she got the queen to safety.

The sun was fully risen now. The light that shone through the large window chased away the last of the shadows. He had already tried the door hours ago. Locked. Same with the window. The small circle window in the bathing room was far too small to even think about crawling out that way.

Even if he found a way out, he definitely wouldn't be getting back in if Althea was still here.

He was supposed to meet her by the third column an hour ago. That was what they had planned. When day broke, they would have met there. But things never went as they were planned. Niklas should have known that by now. What if she was already there waiting for him? He wished he could tell her to leave, to go without him and get word to Delmar about the war being a farce.

But she was supposed to be home, safe in Taris, so who would believe her anyway?

Nobody.

By the time he heard the keys jingle against the door, a small path had been worn through the plush carpeting underneath his boots, and a painful blister had formed on his heel.

A butler took a step into the room. "The queen has requested your presence at once. Then you are to be made... presentable."

Two guards stood on either side of the butler, and the man tried to hide the scrunch of his nose when Niklas walked past.

He kept his shoulders back and chin up, not caring to respond. He would like to see the thin man survive a month in Laisren's most dangerous forest.

The palace had been completely cleaned from floor to ceiling in the few hours he had been locked away. Niklas thought it would have taken weeks to clean the chaos that the blood moon ball was. But the halls looked like nothing had ever happened.

He glanced into the ballroom when they passed the open doors. The floors were shining and freshly waxed, not a scuff to be seen, or a crooked tapestry. Not even a single flake of ash was below the sconces.

Niklas fidgeted, suddenly becoming aware of the dirt under his nails, the scratches on his face that were beginning to scab and his unkempt hair. The scars lining his hands and forearms from years of being a guard and the time he spent in the Cerridwen. All hidden under the fading powder Althea had put on him before they left the inn.

This felt wrong. Althea should be here with him. He never would have been able to do what he did without her. Did she already meet the queen separately? Was this some game they were playing, trying to see if their stories matched up?

"How long is this going to take?" Niklas whispered, leaning closer to the butler as they walked for what felt like miles, full of twists and turns.

The man looked at him from the side of his eye, raising a single black brow in judgment. "Do you have more pressing matters to attend to than meeting your queen?"

Niklas scoffed, opening his mouth to say something he might regret, but was cut off when the doors opened. He set his shoulders back again and straightened his rumpled shirt.

The first thing that caught Niklas's eyes was the ceiling. It was made of the same marble that the flooring was, a light tan with gold throughout, but that wasn't what he saw first. It was the large circle in the center that was made entirely of glass, the edges stained a deep red making it look like fire crackled in the corners of the room where the sun shimmered through.

It was a strange contrast considering the palace was namely called 'The Blue'.

Then his eyes fell on the queen. She had not yet looked up from the paper she held in her hands, engrossed with whatever it was that was scripted on it. She sat poised on her throne and lazily grazed on a green apple, leaving behind a smudge of her dark red lip stain on its peel. Being out of its season it must have been a very, very expensive apple.

All the members of the queen's high court stood around her throne, each one staring at him as he entered the room and waited for his signal to approach.

The queen gestured at the adviser closest to her, turning the paper in her hands to read the other side, and he beaconed Niklas forward.

The room was dead silent, there wasn't any sound besides the paper rustling in the queen's hand, her teeth on the apple, and Niklas's boots echoing with each step. He hoped he wasn't leaving behind a trail of mud.

He dropped to one knee and gave a proper soldier's salute, head bowed with his right fist on his heart, waiting for the okay to rise.

And he waited.

One of the advisers, which one Niklas could not tell with his eyes lowered, whispered to the queen, "Your Majesty."

"Hmm?"

"The man you requested to see is here."

"Oh. Rise."

Niklas stood, and raised his head, taking a single step forward.

"I have met with Lueren and my advisers this morning, and they have explained everything to me concerning what has all happened. You will be rewarded for your bravery and measures to secure the throne of Valarie. I would like to invite you to dinner in the private dining room tonight at eight o'clock sharp," she spoke the words with disinterest. Like she had rehearsed them, or whatever she was reading on the paper in her hand demanded her attention more.

It all seemed to happen in slow motion, the queen set aside her paper and lifted her blue eyes to meet his. Then they widened, and her mouth hung open. The apple fell from her fingers and rolled down the two steps until it came to a stop at Niklas's dirty boots. His eyes followed it the entire way.

He raised his head back up to meet the stare of open shock on the queen's face, the sun shining brightly through the red glass into his eyes.

"Marcus?" The queen cried out.

Was she shaking?

"You are mistaken, Your Majesty," Niklas bowed again. "My name is Niklas Stallard, I come from the city of Taris." When he straightened, the queen's brow was furrowed and she sat back, holding a hand to her forehead like she was faint, breathing heavily through her nose.

"No mind. You are dismissed." She blinked at him, whispering furiously with an adviser.

He bowed once more and was led away by the strong hands of two guards. He tensed under their hands, fighting back the urge to push them away. It was completely unnecessary for them to handle him like a criminal. It wasn't until the butler met up with them around a corner that the guards removed themselves.

Niklas rubbed his sore arms, giving the guards angry sideways glances that spoke much louder than his words.

He opened his mouth to speak, but the butler, without turning, said, "You care for your friend deeply, no?" He was stunned and didn't know what to say in response to the butler's assumption. How did he know he was going to ask about Althea? "If you do, it would be in both of your best interests to lay low, and don't ask questions."

He stopped in front of a room with the door wide open. Inside were casts of torsos and fabrics that filled every inch of the space in an organized chaos. The tailor, a short man, flitted around his desk, turning only when the butler cleared his throat.

No words were exchanged. He must already know what his orders were. He pulled a string around Niklas's chest and hips, murmuring to himself at the measurements and twirled back to his desk when he had all the information he needed.

Niklas was led back through the hall, the only sound was their four sets of boots. Well, three, and the butler's pair of shiny dress shoes.

The scent of fresh, hot water drifted to him from around a corner and they entered what could only be described as a mini heaven on earth.

The entire floor was tiled with clear-blue glass, leading down a soft slope and disappearing into steaming water. A heavy mist clung to the air but it was not unpleasant. A skylight in the roof acted as a vent to keep the heat from overwhelming the space. Through it, the sound of birds chirping, and wind rustling the trees mingled with the soft lapping of the water against the bathing pool's edge.

"There are towels and a clean change of clothes on the bench over there. If you need anything, please ring the bell by the door." The butler held his hands together in front of him and bowed deeply, his thick black hair staying perfectly in place.

"Thanks?" Niklas said.

"Enjoy your stay, sir." The butler turned with a flair of his coat tails and the guards followed, leaving Niklas to himself, his thoughts, and the water that was calling his name.

He walked over to the wooden bench that had been sanded and polished and ran a hand over it, coming away without a single splinter.

"Hmm," he hummed in approval, and picked up the towel. It was a brilliant, bright white and soft, softer than any towel back in Taris. Or maybe it was just because his hands had gotten used to the rough leather and other harsh material he had handled over the years and wasn't used to the feeling of luxury.

He lifted it to his nose and breathed in the light scent of vanilla. It reminded him of that bar of soap he had taken from Althea's tattered bag not even a week ago. It felt like it happened to someone else in another lifetime, not him.

So much had happened in the last month Niklas didn't even know where to start to try and put every event in order in his brain. He was just happy that last night was over with. That he and Althea managed to pull off what they did with just the two of them, and was ready to move on.

He didn't know where their paths would go after this. He knew his would most likely lead to the battlefield in Caedmon. As Lieutenant, he would be expected to be present with the Guard. If there was a Guard to go back to, that is.

Althea, seeing that she had not ascended yet, would get to go home and be with her father and continue training for the next ascension tests. He felt a little jealous at that thought.

Even if nothing had changed between them in the forest, he knew that she would look after his father as her own. Rivalry or not, she was not evil. He only wished he could go home and sleep, *really* sleep. In his own bed, in his own house and with the sound of his father tinkering about outside his room.

Niklas stripped off the layers of clothing from Heriit and left them in the basket next to the bench, taking his first step into the water. Blissful heat radiated over his foot and up his ankle, and he couldn't help but fall the rest of the way in, groaning as his muscles melted, becoming one with the water.

An array of soaps sat on a tray on the ledge of the pool in the shapes of flowers. He picked one up and sniffed, impressed at how each one smelt like the flower it was carved to represent.

I knew the queen was rich, but I had no idea she was this rich.

Finally, he settled on the rose. It didn't smell like the sharp, thick rose oil like the women back home wore, it had more of a musk to it that Niklas couldn't explain. If he had to describe it, he would say it was like they had harvested the oil from a black rose. He tried to tell himself that it was because it was the best smelling out of the bunch, and not because it reminded him of who had worn rose perfume the night of the festival.

He was so lost in his thoughts that he hadn't heard the servant walk up to the edge of the pool, presenting a platter of food. Niklas jumped out of his skin, almost knocking the servant into the water, fully clothed, food and all. "I'm sorry. You caught me off guard," Niklas apologized, wiping water out of his eyes.

"No, sir, do not be sorry. I should have waited after I called in to be summoned. The fault is mine. Please do not tell the queen." He couldn't have been more than fourteen seasons old. His hands were shaking, rattling the crackers on the tray close to its edge.

"I am the last person you should be afraid of for that. What is your name?" Niklas perched his elbows on the glass tiles, cool against his warmed skin.

"Tiernan, sir." He set the platter on the floor, pushing the crackers back to their rightful place and gestured to the array of meats and cheeses, grapes, and a glass of coffee.

"Tiernan, what is all this for?"

"My Mo– Her Majesty the Queen wanted you to have a light breakfast so you would not be too full for the feast tonight."

Niklas fought to keep the groan in his head at the mention of another night, staying up late until who knew when. But at least was cowed enough by his imagination and pride at what other foods he would get to try. He could enjoy one night being treated like a prince couldn't he? Tiernan turned to leave, almost scurrying.

"Wait a second." The boy hurried back, his eyes wide and eager. "Why don't you sit with me and eat? This is too much for just one person."

His eyes couldn't have widened more if it were possible. "Really?"

"Really," Niklas chuckled.

The boy did not hesitate, kicking off his shoes and rolled the legs of his pants up to his thighs, plopping his feet into the water. He grabbed a handful of the food and made little sandwiches with the crackers. He offered Niklas one and he took it, smiling.

"I could get used to this," he sighed. "Hey, that girl I came here with, have you seen her? She was wearing a red dress. I haven't seen her since last night. We were supposed to meet this morning but I haven't exactly been allowed to leave," Niklas asked after swallowing a mouthful of the bitter coffee.

Tiernan shook his head. "I wasn't allowed to attend the ball last night." He looked away almost shamefully. "I may have snuck out of my room for a minute or two and there *was* a girl who I passed by when I was heading back. Did she have a crown of roses on?"

"Yeah, that's her." Niklas felt hope swell in his chest, that his mind had just made up silly scenarios and that she was fine.

Tiernan tilted his head, flipping through his memory of last night and nodded, his cheeks pinking. "Then I *did* see her, she was really pretty."

"Yeah," Niklas whispered before shaking his head. "No, that's not what I meant. Do you know where she is? Have you seen her recently, or heard about where she might be?"

The boy brushed a few crumbs off of his lap. Niklas hadn't realized until then, the expensive looking fabric of his pants. There wasn't a single loose strand and looked like they were tailored to fit him perfectly. Odd for a mere servant.

Niklas looked at him, slowly becoming suspicious. He was not just any servant child.

Tiernan, without missing a beat, or even blinking for that matter, shook his head. "No, sir. I am not allowed to say or even to know where our guests are unless I am serving. I only saw her in passing when she had walked through the hall."

Something he said pricked Niklas's attention.

"*Our* guests? What do you mean?"

"Oh." His face became stricken. "Stupid Tiernan, you always have to open your big mouth. Mom's gonna be so mad." The boy quickly lifted his feet out of the water, not stopping to dry his feet before he shoved them back into his boots.

"Wait, don't go, I'm sorry. I'm not going to tell anyone. You won't get in trouble." Niklas scrambled out of the water, his fingers and toes pruned from the bath and quickly wrapped a towel around his waist.

Tiernan made for the door, slipping on the wet tile. Niklas was used to keeping his balance in any circumstance, and easily caught up to him with sure feet. He grabbed the boy's shoulder, turning him back around to face him.

"On my honor, I promise no one will know what is said between us. What did you mean by 'our guests'? Whose house do you belong to?" The boy had to be from a noble family, maybe the youngest son who had no stakes in any inheritance.

Tiernan's face scrunched up, his shoulders almost touching his ears. He fumbled with his hands and refused to meet Niklas's eyes.

Niklas lowered himself, leaning his hands on his knees, coming face to face with the boy. "You can trust me."

He looked up at him then, with ice blue eyes and dirty blond hair falling over his forehead. Niklas saw it the moment before he said, "I am the son of Queen Azora, and the late King Marcus. I am *Prince* Tiernan."

"I shouldn't have told you. If someone would have overheard me I would be in so much trouble."

"Why would your mother– I mean, the queen, make you serve men that are beneath you in title?" Niklas stood in front of a full-length mirror and adjusted the uncomfortable collar of the white, buttoned shirt that felt like it was strangling him. Did the tailor even look at his measurements when he sewed the outfit?

He looked back at Tiernan, who lay sprawled out on the four poster bed, his fingers playing with the black mesh curtains that were tied up around the posts in great swoops.

"I never asked. I was just happy to be a part of something for once I guess. Whenever there would be court with the other kingdoms or if we were hosting someone I was always sent to my room for the duration of their stay. But one day, half of the servants had become ill, and they needed someone to host a nobleman from Marella. So my mother sent a butler to my room with an apron. I've been helping serve ever since."

"None of the noblemen were curious why the country's only heir wasn't attending any of the council meetings?"

"I snuck in a couple of times using the rafters. One time she said I was feeling ill, and the next that I was visiting my cousin in Caedmon. I don't even have cousin's there. I got caught once in the hallway outside of the council room when I was leaving, and I was locked in my room for a week. They only sent me one meal that whole time.

"I learned quickly that if I questioned, complained or even thought about sneaking around again, that there would be consequences. My mother was always like this, but it got worse after Papa died."

"Wait." Niklas tuned, abandoning his tie for the moment. "You knew the king– I mean your father? I thought he passed away before you were born." Niklas sat on the bed next to him, and Tiernan pushed himself up.

"If it isn't out of my place to ask, how old are you? I remember when the queen announced you as heir after the king... You must be of age to start making appearances in royal functions."

"I am fourteen seasons old. Mother hid my birth for two years. I asked my teacher why on my birthday one time when I was seven. She quoted Mom, saying that letting the kingdom know too early of another heir was bad luck and would result in the same curse that took her first son."

"But that was what the country needed, hope. Knowing that there was a successor to the throne could have prevented the start of the rebellion entirely." Niklas crossed his arms. "Was she always this irrational?"

"As long as I have memory of her, yes."

"That... actually explains a lot. Do you... um... know about what happened last night?"

Tiernan tilted his head, a confused look splayed across his young face. "I couldn't sleep because of the noise and that's why I snuck out, but then I heard a lot of screaming and when I tried to get back into my room, the door was locked. I had to climb through the window and over the balcony. I was waiting for my teacher to come get me for my morning torture – I mean 'lesson', but she never came. I haven't seen her at all today, which is weird.

"Butler Gerald found me when I was on my way to the kitchen for breakfast, and that was when he told me to come serve you." He moved to the edge of the bed. "Why? Did something bad happen?"

Niklas felt the need to tell the young prince the truth rather than keep him in the dark like it seemed everyone was already doing to him. He was far old enough, and smart enough to understand the implication of what last night meant for this kingdom and his own life as heir to a throne that was beginning to crack.

He carefully explained the happenings of last night, how he and Althea found out about the assassination attempt, how his uncle had been arrested for his crimes, and what it might mean for his future.

Tiernan sat still, not breaking eye contact, and nodded along when Niklas paused to see if he was understanding what he was saying.

"The throne is at its weakest right now. Even though Xadier will answer for what he has done, we cannot deny the seeds of doubt he has sown. It will strengthen the voice of the rebellion." Xadier had his claws in the kingdom for far longer than anyone would have thought, even before the queen took the crown. Niklas had overheard the guards outside the room he had been locked in earlier talking about the things they had seen over the last few years that made perfect sense to them now. Things about certain visitors the prince would have and about late night trips he would take.

"Hey, can I show you something?" The boy stood.

Niklas looked at the huge grandfather clock, and seeing that he still had two more hours to kill until dinner, shrugged. "Sure, why not?"

"Woah, *this* is your room?" Niklas stepped onto the thick, dark blue carpet and looked around the spacious room.

Every available space was covered with paper that held sketches of people, animals and star patterns. Some were just black lines, carefully etched to form realistic scenes, others held bursts of vibrant colors. It felt like if he were to look at them for too long he might be able to walk right through the paper and into the world beyond.

"You drew all of these? They are amazing." Niklas closed his gaping mouth.

Tiernan looked at his feet, shying away from the compliment, the toe of his boot twisting on the carpet.

"No one knows about these, except for Butler Gerald. He helps me hide them whenever my mother comes to my room. I'm not supposed to have them out like this." He went into action, piling the paper into his arms and placed them gently in the bottom drawer of his wardrobe, dusting his hands off when he was finished.

"But that's not what I wanted to show you. Over here." He waved Niklas over to a set of glass doors. Beyond the foggy window panes was the palace gardens. The balcony faced the Kyran mountains, shadows already beginning to creep over the walls surrounding the palace as night beckoned.

"It's amazing." Niklas opened the door and let the cool, crisp air wash over him. The sun shined the last of its warmth on a thin layer of snow that covered most of the green shrubs and rose bushes below, creating a million twinkling lights. He hadn't even realized it had snowed.

Although winter was here, dark, rolling clouds loomed ominously in the not so far distance, the last of the fall not ready to give up its time in the world yet. Lighting flickered in them but didn't strike or make a sound.

The smell of the gardens mixing with the scent of incoming rain was intoxicating in a way, and Niklas wished he could have his dinner out here on the balcony instead of some dark, closed up room surrounded by strangers.

But his father didn't teach him proper etiquette for nothing. Having worked in the palace before Niklas was born, he was expected to teach the young nobles and future heirs all about court rulings and how to properly hold a spoon.

God forbid you had your pinky in the wrong spot.

That was until the queen's first born didn't make it. And Niklas's mother had left his father after he was born. He had wanted a fresh start. But that didn't mean Niklas got away without learning the art of dinner affairs by the time he was five.

"I come out here to draw and paint when I'm not allowed out of my room, even to help serve. I know I was probably too young to remember right, but there was one moment that I remember vividly. I was sitting on my father's lap, right here." He pointed to a large wicker chair that looked like something ancient. Out of place with all of the finery of the rest of the place. "And he was drawing the sunrise over the mountains. I don't remember the sight of it much, but more the smell. The flowers. The rain that had just gone through the night before, and the paint. Mostly I remember the oils he would wear. Amber and Vetiver? I think that is how you say it.

"Last season, I snuck out to talk to the head gardener and asked if he could plant those beneath my window, and he *did*, it is the nicest thing anyone has ever done for me."

Now that he said it, Niklas could smell the sweet musk and spice of the amber, and the soft wood of the vetiver. It was comforting and by the good things he had always heard about the king, it did match the man.

Niklas felt a pang that he would never get to meet the man that had been beneath the crown.

The story went that King Marcus had grown up in Taris, and though poor, had never wished for anything.

Two elderly ladies that he had known in Taris, knew the man far before he became king. When they retold stories after he passed, they always quoted him, saying, 'God has given me everything I need right here, I shall not want,' and they would point to their hearts. Their eyes would become misty and they couldn't carry on unless they wanted to fall into tears in the middle of the market.

The royal family was on a tour to all the kingdoms, and one day they stopped in Taris. When Marcus had heard that there would be a feast for them, he had left home on his only horse and hunted for two days. When he came back he was dragging two of the largest stags anyone had ever seen before.

The feast had already started by then, but hunting had been scarce and there hadn't been enough meat for anyone but the royals. He showed up to the feast at the mayor's house, covered in dirt and leaves sticking to him, dragging the food behind him. The king laughed and laughed with joy at the sight and made him sit at the table with them, and couldn't stop talking about how he had never seen anything like it, and the town ate like never before.

The next season he was invited to the blood moon ball and the king asked for Marcus's hand to marry his daughter and become the next king of Valarie. It was something that was rarely done. The son, no matter the birth order, was next in line for the crown, unless — a rule made during King Brioc's reign — the eldest child married first.

The queen was ecstatic, not because of the throne, but because she had been loved by Marcus. During their vows, he had mentioned that during that feast, when he had laid eyes on her for the first time, he hadn't been able to sleep for days. He had holed himself into his small home, thinking she was gone from his life forever, not only because of the distance between them but their difference in status. Until that letter came and for the first time in his life, he had wanted something.

Whenever Niklas heard the stories, he felt like he should have been able to know the man. Like a piece of his life was missing. But, with any good storyteller, they say the words just right to pull on your heart, to make you feel like you were in a dream the whole time. Like you were the one they were telling the story about.

"Father grew ill before he died, but he always smiled. Except for portraits, mom got mad at him when he did. I copied one from the great room, but I added a smile to it." Tiernan went back to his wardrobe and pulled out a couple of his paintings. The pages had been folded many times and the paint had creased, but the man on the paper was unmistakable.

King Marcus looked to be about thirty-five seasons in the picture. He had chestnut brown hair that curled over his ears, a full matching beard, except for a small patch on his cheek where a dimple showed through when he smiled. His teeth were straight and white, and his brown eyes looked like they held a forge in them.

"Wow, you are really good, Tiernan. I couldn't dream of doing anything like this." Tiernan looked between him and the picture in his hands, his brow pinched. Niklas handed the paper back to him, and patted his pockets.

"Ah, there it is. Maybe you could fill this picture in sometime."

He handed Tiernan the picture he had carried with him from the start of his journey. It stayed with him through the Cerridwen. Through all of the battles and near deaths, and outfit changes. The picture of his father holding him as a baby, wrapped in a bundle in his arms.

Tiernan's face lit up. "Can I?"

"Just make sure I get it back before I leave. It's the only thing I have from home."

"I'll be super careful with it sir, I promise."

"Niklas. Call me Niklas."

Chapter Thirty-Eight

Niklas

The dining room was huge even though it was in the private living sector of the palace.

The walls were a dark, sparkling gold, the floors a rich, red stained wood that matched the table which was also huge. It could seat thirty people at least, with chairs covered in emerald velvet and high backs that no one's heads could reach.

The majority of the noble houses had fled last night. Some were found guilty of being joined with the rebels and were arrested. Others were afraid for lack of security, and wished to go back to the safety of their own homes. Five of the houses stayed when the queen invited them to dinner for an apology, after she had already given them each a heavy chest of what Niklas could only imagine to be filled with gold and jewels. Earned allies much.

"Attention, houses of Marella, Llyr, Valor, Reerdan and Pother." The queen stood, wearing a royal blue evening gown, her heeled shoes adding at least five inches to her already tall height, and raised her crystal glass of white wine. "It is my utmost pleasure to have you in my home this evening. And you have my sincerest apologies for the interruption of our festivities last night. But please be reassured to know that I have the best of the best men and women of my own Guard scouring all of the corners of this country as we speak to quell the flame of this rebellion before it has a chance to spark."

She took a sip from her glass and Niklas fumbled for his when he realized everyone else had taken a drink in agreement. The words sounded nice, but her face looked like she had eaten something bitter, though her voice didn't betray it.

"Here, here," the few noblemen agreed and lifted their glasses in the air.

The dark clouds that he had seen from Tiernan's room had found their way to the Blue, matching his mood. The storm raged outside, but the walls and windows were so thick that no sound came through. Just the slightest rumble from the thunder and flashes of purple when the lighting struck the mountains.

Niklas hated it. He felt trapped without the feeling of the water on his skin and his heart wouldn't rest from its racing. The more he ate the emptier he felt.

Althea wasn't there. She had looked so tired and weak when he had last seen her. He trusted Farah, but could he trust anybody else here?

He was starting to become agitated. Whenever the door opened, he was expecting it to be her. But it was just another servant bringing in who knew what course they were on.

The world outside the windows had gone dark hours ago, and the storm was not showing any sign of stopping. A single bolt of lightning struck one of the spires and Niklas felt the thunder rumble from under his boots all the way up his spine.

"Your Majesty, how is the young prince, if I may ask?" The dark skinned man from Pother asked dabbing the corners of his mouth with a blood red napkin. "We were so worried for him last night."

"He is in his study right now, for his safety, until further notice. No need to worry. I have sent my own Guard that I trust with my life to watch over him."

Niklas started to roll his eyes, but played off the motion quickly as if he was merely studying the portraits of past kings and queens that hung around the room. His eyes landed on the one of King Marcus.

He did look familiar, but then again, he was from Taris and had most of the characteristics that were common there. It was no wonder the queen thought she recognized Niklas.

"Sir Stallard, we cannot even begin to thank you for your actions during the ball. If it were not for your quick thinking and love for our queen that spurred you to make that difficult journey we would not be sitting here now and enjoying our stay as we are," the wife of the nobleman of Reerdan praised him in her thick, northern accent.

"Yes," agreed the wife of the nobleman of Pother. "Last night was terrifying indeed. While everyone else ran away, only you and a few of the queen's guards ran towards the danger. Very brave indeed."

Niklas felt nauseous.

"It wasn't just me. My fellow guard Althea Nova is the one who you should be thanking. Speaking of, she was injured while subduing the rebels." Niklas knew that he was told to not ask questions, but he felt that he had every right to ask at least this one. He looked over at the queen, keeping his face blank despite his impatience to see Althea. "Have you gotten word about her condition, Your Majesty?"

The queen speared a piece of her steak a little too fast, and answered without looking at him. "She is resting." Her tone itself dismissed him even before her look of warning. He hardly spoke again for the rest of the dinner.

The night could not have been over soon enough. His ears were still ringing from the nauseating small talk that he had to partake in. But he did relish the dessert they had, something called a brownie. He ran his tongue over his teeth, trying to find the last bits of the flavor.

The butler led him to the room he had dressed in earlier and bid him a good night. As soon as the door closed and the butler's shoes clicked away, Niklas had it open again, and was fighting not to run down the dim hallway.

He had noted the patterns of the turns he had been led through and quickly found his way down into the servants area. There were no torches lit in this section of the palace but his eyes adjusted quickly to the darkness. The only thing he had forgotten was which room was Farah's.

He shuffled lightly on his toes, the leather soles of his boots squeaking lightly on the polished marble. Even the servants lived in a small form of luxury compared to Taris where everything was made from the trees that their families fell themselves. But it was at the expense of their freedom.

If Niklas was king, he would pay these servants their fair wage and no one would be forced to live separate from their families.

But, he was not a king, and he would have to swallow the bitter taste in his mouth along with a lot of other things he wished he could change.

"*Farah*," he hissed.

"*Farah.*" He risked opening a few doors as he went. One ended up just being a broom closet and the other a small bedroom with a sleeping woman in a rocking chair. He eased the door shut, turning the knob as he closed it so it would not click.

Maybe he had gone down the wrong hallway. There were four branches that led down each corner of the palace; he was sure that the hall in the front right, the archway opening into the ballroom, was the right one.

Just as he placed a booted foot onto the polished, ballroom floor, he heard a muffled sob. He froze, titling his head to the left, focusing his hearing. It was echoing from the hall he was just in and... to the left.

Niklas turned around, walking back into the dark hallway. The sobbing grew louder, though it was still muffled, like someone was crying into their hand or a pillow.

He stopped at the second to last door on the left. This was it, he recognized it instantly by the light pink scarf hanging from the sconce on the wall. A soft, flickering strip of light shone through the gap at the bottom of the door.

Niklas was about to reach for the handle, but thought better of charging in unannounced. He raised his hand and rapped quietly on the door and waited. She must not have heard him. He was about to knock again, but the door cracked open and Niklas froze, hand hovering in the air between them. Wide blue eyes that were rimmed in red looked up.

And at the sight of him, Farah lost all composure.

She threw the door open, openly sobbing now. She fought to speak through her tears.

"I tried, Niklas. I tried, I tried, I tried. Can you ever forgive me?" She cradled her left arm close to her chest.

"Wait, slow down. You're not making any sense. What happened?" Niklas looked left and right down the hall to make sure no one had woken and entered Farah's room, closing the door behind him and guided the young girl to sit on the edge of the bed.

He waited for her to compose herself, whispering softly, telling her to take a deep breath. He took a few himself. His hands were shaking from anger as his fingers prodded at her arm.

It was broken.

By the time Niklas had torn a pillow cover into thin stripes and bandaged her arm to stabilize it, Farah had calmed just enough to speak around her sobbing hiccups.

"I fought, Niklas, please believe me. They were too s-s-strong. There were three of them. T-they *took* her, Niklas. I tried."

"Where," he growled. It was not a question.

"T-they took her t-to the dungeon."

Chapter Thirty-Nine

Althea

It was cold.

She felt numb.

There was a sound like chittering mice.

It annoyed her.

She was tired, so she went back to sleep.

CHAPTER FORTY

— · —

NIKLAS

N iklas had walked with Farah to the doctor in the hallway opposite her own.

Really he was just an old servant who had been a medic in a war when he was young and Niklas made sure Farah would be taken care of properly.

He was sure she would be after he threatened the man's fingers, leaving behind a shaking man and woman, both with eyes wide from fear. Each for a different reason.

He no longer tried to be furtive as he stormed through the hallways, waking servants who stuck their heads out to see what was haunting their halls.

He entered the dark, damp stairwell that led to the dungeon. Water ran down the length of the slippery stone from the storm that continued to rage outside. Lightning flashed, casting his shadow against the wall and filled the cold place with its roar.

Niklas was the storm.

When he reached the first level of the dungeons he was met by two guards in leather armor. They heard his approach and moved in front of him, blocking his way.

"Oh would you look at this," the shorter one said to the taller. "What little rat did he bring for us this time? The queen send her little pup to save the day again?"

"Looks like they were playing dress up to me," the tall one laughed.

That was until Niklas stepped out from the shadow of the stairwell and into the light of the torch.

Their words died in their throats, and whatever they must have seen in his eyes made them step aside, letting him pass.

He felt them following him at a safe distance as he passed cell after cell of prisoners. Some were new since he had brought Xadier, others he could tell have been in here for years. Skin sagging over their bones, faces but a shell of the human they used to be. None were her.

They had just been given a meal and the sounds of fingers scraping on bowls filled the tense silence The stench grew the further he went.

Niklas stopped at the descent to the second level.

"Where is Althea?" He asked, facing the darkness in front of him.

"W-who?"

Niklas started to turn.

"Oh!" Exclaimed the tall one before Niklas could face them. "The girl! She isn't here."

Niklas leaned forward, waiting for him to continue. If looks could kill, these two would not be standing on their feet.

The short one elbowed his friend in the ribs, earning a wince and a confused look. Short spoke for both of them, "What he meant to say was that they had taken her out about an hour or two ago? They didn't say why, they just took her."

"*Who. Took. Her.*"

"The Head of the Guard, Lueren."

Niklas didn't remember when he had exited the dungeon, his eyes refocusing on a painting he had stopped in front of. It was the family portrait of the king and queen with their first born son in their arms. The child had obviously been painted from memory.

Niklas didn't know why he couldn't move. His eyes refused to blink as he stared at the newborn. The babes eyes were the same fiery brown as the fathers. Niklas patted his pocket for the picture he always carried with him and almost had a heart attack when he couldn't find it until he remembered he had lent it to Tiernan to paint.

A ray of sunlight tilted through a window, splaying across the queen's face, breaking the spell he was under. He shook his head, dazed.

The distinct sound of people gathering began to fill the courtyard and Niklas finally found the door he needed. He didn't knock and pushed the door open.

Chapter Forty-One

Althea

Her body ached worse than it had ever ached before. Even her lungs hurt as she breathed in the cold morning air. Her eyes hurt when she tried to blink away their dryness. Did she get sand in them? But her heart ached worst of all.

She only remembered snippets of what happened after they took her away from the queen and Farah.

The guards had had to carry her. Where they took her, she did not know. She had lost her sight hours ago. All she saw were shapes and colors, the blurriness taking over. Blood trickled down her cheek from where her head had hit on the stone when the guards threw her in a dark room.

They had laughed as one pulled her over his shoulder when she was too weak to walk.

They'd passed a hall lined with pictures from floor to ceiling of kings and queens. There was one that Althea's blurry eyes had landed on. It looked like the picture of Niklas when he was a baby, she chuckled against the guards armored back. She hadn't remembered hitting her head *that* hard.

She let herself sleep when the pain became too much, not really knowing what was happening. It felt like it had only been mere minutes of relief before she was grabbed roughly by the arm and lifted off the floor, which was now cleaner than before as the grime now stuck to her skin and clothes.

The sun had risen above the mountain line and took away the last of the shade, calling to wake up the world. But all it did was send a spike of pain through her head.

She knew they were approaching the gardens by the smell of the flowers. Each section she was dragged through had its distinct scent. Roses, Snowdrops, Violets and Pansies. All plants that bloomed at the start of the winter season.

Althea couldn't believe it was already winter. Yesterday she and Niklas had left home in the middle of the rainy fall. Today her bare feet crunched on the frost. She heard people talking, chairs scraping across stone, hammers banging on wood.

What is happening? Her breath quickened in her chest, the desire to plant her feet and pull against the strong arms of the guards overwhelmed her. But she could barely manage to walk on her own.

As they drew closer to the garden square where people had begun to gather, her sight began to sharpen. Noble men and women sat in a structured circle that was four layers deep. The seats staggered to where every set of eyes could see the four foot tall wooden post that was being hammered into a hole in the stone, directly centered in the circle. Ropes were wrapped around the middle of it and Althea knew instantly what was going to happen.

Her muscles tensed, all thoughts of the aching she felt flew out of her mind, a surge of strength rushed through her as her mind awoke and began to understand what the guards were leading her towards.

Instinct took over and she dropped all of her weight down into a crouch, throwing the guard on her right off balance and managed to yank her arm away. With her free hand she grabbed the other guard's thumb, pulling his hand away from her wrist.

But she was not strong enough, the damage that had been done to her body was too much and her vigor left as quickly as it had come. No one in the garden saw what had happened, no one was coming to help.

The guard on her right kicked her in the side of her stomach while she was down. Her heart cried out to God, and to Niklas when her lips were no longer able to move in any other form than a pained moan.

Niklas isn't coming, is he?

A miniscule part of her didn't want him to. Didn't want him to see her like this, weak and at the mercy of man. But the bigger, more selfish part of her yearned for him. All she wanted, all she needed, was to look in his eyes and for him to tell her that she was going to be okay.

She was marched into the circle and the chatter ceased immediately, even the birds that had been chirping happily before went silent.

The guards, each with a hand on her shoulders, forced her – lowered – her to her knees. Her eyes stayed locked onto the blood stained wood in front of her as her hands were raised and tied above her head using the thick rope. It burned like fire as it pulled tight against her already rope burned wrists.

Althea did not blink at the pain, nor did she let her breath catch. She didn't do anything wrong, why was she here, tied to this post like a lamb for the slaughter?

One of the guards, Althea refused to see which one, grabbed the back of the tan shirt she didn't remember changing into and tore the fabric from her body.

She gasped at the pressure it put against her bruised throat and fought to keep the tears of humiliation from escaping as the shirt fell away. Thankfully her chest had been bound, although it was too tight, she was thankful for the small ounce of dignity it provided.

The crowd gasped and murmured at the sight of her broken body and from what Althea could see of her front she could only imagine what her back must look like. The bruises on her stomach started from above the binding and continued down, past the waistband of a pair of black pants.

She was more blue and black than she was her light tan skin, her color faded now that summer was over.

The muscles in her thighs began to cramp as she was neither fully on her knees or standing. They had measured the height of the pole perfectly to make this all the more uncomfortable for her.

Another hush fell over the onlookers, but this time it felt different. The rustling of clothing seemed to roar as everyone stood.

Althea glanced out of the side of her eye, watching as the queen entered the circle and marched over to a small throne directly in front of her. It sat a few feet further into the center of the circle than the rest of the chairs.

It was simple and plain. White wrought iron, twisted with the shapes of roses around the legs. The apex was sharpened into three spikes, the one in the middle was larger and taller than the outer two. A plush, red cushion rested on the seat.

The queen's shoes clacked loudly with each step she took until she stood before her garden throne. Every single step felt like a knife being driven into Althea's ears.

The queen looked regal in her black dress, the sleeves a shimmery black lace that turned to a point half way down her hand. The dress itself looks like a soft, warm cotton. It was loosely fitted and trailed all the way to the ground like a waterfall, pooling at her feet. It was a stark contrast to her blonde hair and blue eyes.

Althea didn't see Queen Azora when she looked at the woman, all she saw was Xadier in those eyes. Her countenance was a fierce sternness, not fury, but certainly not friendly either.

Althea looked away, wrapping her fingers around the rope and squeezing until it cut into her palms. What's another mark? She welcomed the pain, it distracted her from the anger and hurt that was making her heart beat even faster than it already had been.

The queen cleared her throat. "Ladies and gentlemen. As you all know and have heard, Prince Xadier, son of King Egaled, my brother, has joined with the rebellion of the west who seek to take over this country and our kingdom." She paused, allowing the crowd to have a moment to murmur to one another.

Curses flew from the mouths of the nobles. It didn't explain why she was tied to a post under their seething eyes. She was not a part of that wretched rebellion.

"Now, now," the queen cooed, a devilish smirk marring her red lips. "Everything is under control. As we stand here now, all over the country the rebels are being burned to the ground. Their hideouts are being discovered and arrests are being made. This rebellion will *not* continue for as long as I live, and for the many generations that will inherit the throne after me. This kingdom belongs to the Plerette name and it will continue to be so.

"My dear son." A young man, with matching hair and eyes, walked over to the queen's side, his face and eyes red with the tears he was withholding. "Tiernan Plerette has been very busy learning the ways of this kingdom, and as a result, has not been able to attend many of the discussions we have had. Nor is he old enough to fully understand the reality of these hard decisions we must make daily. But I felt this particular matter to be rather important for him to witness. So when it comes time for him to occupy my seat, he knows what happens to people who do not follow our law."

The boy hiccupped quietly when he met Althea's eyes and jerked his head back down. He quickly wiped away a rebellious tear.

"This woman you see before you. Althea Nova, daughter to Quint and Sapphira Nova. Member of the Guard of Taris, second rank." The queen took a breath. "Has been found guilty of treason against the throne."

Gasps erupted around her. Her own joined with the cacophony.

"N-no, no, I didn't, I wouldn't." Althea panted, but she wasn't loud enough, she wasn't even sure if her mouth moved at all.

"But," the queen spoke softly but was heard over the noise. "My life was spared. The conspiracies of my ability to rule *will* be quelled." She clasped her hands behind her back and lifted her chin. "And this will serve as a reminder. For the reason of abandoning her assigned post during the time of this terrible war and rebellion, she will receive forty stripes, one for each day she has failed to fulfill her duties."

She clapped her manicured hands once. "Guards."

A sob bubbled out of the boy's mouth, quickly shushed by his mother, tears falling freely down his face now. Althea's breath quickened until blackness threatened the edges of her sight.

"No, no, please. Give me a chance to explai–" She wasn't allowed to finish. She heard the crack of the leather whip as it cut through the air before it sank into her skin. Her words turned into a scream. Her back arched and the second one fell upon her. She didn't think she could grip the rope any tighter. But right then she did, until the bones in her hand cracked.

She lost count after ten. Red flooded her vision as her blood misted around her. The next strike of the whip curled over her shoulder, cutting a gash across her chest.

She couldn't scream even if she wanted to, her lungs refused to work. Burning tears poured over her burning skin, soaking her chest binding. And as the tears left her eyes, so did a piece of her.

Over the sound of the whip meeting her flesh, the prince crying, and the cheers of the onlookers, she heard boots stomping on the stone.

What, clapping your hands isn't enough? You have to stomp your feet too? She thought to herself.

But then it grew louder. It wasn't stomping, someone was running. Running towards her.

Blackness closed in until it was like looking through a pipe. But she saw a pair of dirty, leather boots.

A sudden warmth covered her. She hadn't realized how cold she had been, and she welcomed it, called for it, and her soul ran toward it.

The pain was gone.

It's over.

Chapter Forty-Two

—:—

Niklas

The first strike took his breath away.

He felt blood seep through his shirt and down his back. He tucked his face into Althea's neck, covering her body with his own, holding onto her like his life depended on it.

Through the dirt and grime and the iron of blood that covered her, she still smelt like home. How was that possible?

The entire garden, even the wind, froze, not daring to disturb the moment. Niklas gasped for air, he had run from the palace as soon as he saw Althea tied to the post. He had been so far away, it had taken him too long. He hadn't reached her in time to stop them.

Her blood soaked the front of his shirt.

Twenty strikes. That was how many Althea had taken before he took the twenty-first. He had counted every single one as he ran, flinching with each hit.

Niklas looked up at the queen. Burning, bubbling rage filled his veins. A tiny piece of satisfaction filled a space in him when the queen retreated a step, eyes wide. But she quickly recovered, smoothing a hand over her dress.

"What is the meaning of this, Sir Stallard? She has committed a crime and is being rightfully punished," she said, acting exasperated for the crowd.

"Crime? Rightfully punished!?" Niklas roared. "She left her home and her family behind to fight *for* you, not against you." He turned to the people that gathered to see such a heinous thing. Enjoyed it nonetheless. "What she did was *honorable,* and something clearly none of you would ever do yourselves. And I am just as guilty of leaving my post.

"The queen would not be standing here today if it had not been for this woman. *She* was the one who discovered the prince's plans. *She* was the one who convinced me to step away from my march to go on a race for the queen's life.

"I tried to talk her out of it *every single day* when we were traveling. I told her it was nonsense that someone would want the queen dead." Turning his fury back towards the queen he said, "I didn't believe her until the moment I saw the dagger in his hands."

After a moment of stunned silence, the queen leaned forward and spoke only loud enough for him to hear. "Fine. I already gave you your reward, but if you insist on playing the hero yet again, you will receive the other half of *her* punishment, plus ten."

"Guards!" She screamed and threw herself down onto her throne, crossing her legs, wrists hanging off the arms of the wrought iron.

Niklas didn't even get a chance to blink before the lashes came. One after another, harder as they went. Soon his shirt hung in tatters, pieces of the once soft cloth embedded into his wounds.

He clung to Althea's limp form, wrapping himself around her to make sure the whip couldn't touch her again.

The sound of a sob pierced through the deafening pain and Niklas raised his head when the whip paused. His eyes fell on Tiernan, who was pulling against the arm of the guard holding the whip.

Tears ran down his face like two small waterfalls, meeting at the point of his sharp chin before dripping into the grass. Butler Gerlad ran forward and lifted the boy off his feet, pulling him away to stand back at the queen's side.

The whip descended, cracking across his face. He couldn't hold in the scream any longer. His left eye went blind from the strike and blood mixed with his tears of anger and pain.

"Mom! Mom, stop this please! He's my friend! Don't hurt him anymore!" Tiernan's voice echoed through the fog that had overcome him, but no one moved, no one scolded him for crying out. The queen didn't even care that her son had claimed to know one of her guests though she had forbidden him to interact with them.

The very last strike nearly ended him. The sound of his panting echoed through the sudden quiet. No one spoke, letting the image of the two, bloody guards strung up before them sink in.

The queen was the first to break the silence. "You may have saved my life, which means that I cannot take yours without just reason. But let this punishment serve as a lesson to all who *dare* to undermine me and the law I uphold." She paused to dare anyone to correct her. "I hereby declare, Althea Nova, and Niklas Stallard to have paid justly for their due crimes. Guards, fetch the physician."

The tighter Niklas tried to hold onto Althea the more his arms loosened, until he felt himself tip back. The guards were not pulling him away, he realized. He was falling, his strength failing him. He landed on his knees as he fought against the pull of the blackness.

His shoulder hit the stone and the last thing he saw before his sight went black was the guards cutting the rope away from Althea's hands and tossed her to the ground beside him.

Niklas woke up with a start in an unfamiliar room. The scent of tinctures, fire and mint assaulted him, making him cough in the cold air.

He was lying facedown on his stomach. His body tried to sit up on its own accord, but the second he moved, fire rained down his back, leaving him gasping like a fish out of water. A blurry face appeared next to him.

"Hold on Niklas, let me help." He recognized the sweet cooing voice of the servant girl, her name... Why couldn't he remember her name?

Fea?

Farah. That was it.

She helped him sit up with one arm, the other freshly bandaged and in a sling tied around the back of her neck. She put a pillow in his lap for him to lean forward on.

The room was lit by a crackling fireplace and he greedily drank the cup of water she offered to him, and then another. She had to pry the cup from his hands before he finished the third.

He sucked down the cold air coming from the open window. Outside, snow fell in a dusty flurry, and Niklas welcomed the cold on his fever warmed skin.

The sound of sheets rustling brought his mind back. Another person was in the room with them. Sitting on the bed next to the one he occupied was Althea.

Niklas openly stared at her. She stared back, the skin around her eyes were as purple as the bruises covering her arms. But they were sparkling and bright, her countenance had changed from where it had been when he had last seen her.

If Niklas was in this much pain, he could only imagine what she was feeling, but she didn't show it. The corners of her lips lifted into a soft smile. Niklas instantly felt suspicion curl in his veins. She never smiled at him.

"What?" He asked incredulously.

Althea shook her head, looking down at her hands to hide a chuckle. They were heavily bandaged to the point that she could barely move them.

"Oh nothing, just... you think what I did was honorable?"

Niklas scoffed, rolling his eyes, and sucked in a gasp when pain shot through his left eye. He could still see out of it, but it was blurry and the shapes of the furniture in the room were distorted. He prayed it healed, it was his strong eye.

"As if," he jested. "The only reason I was out there was because I had started eating my dessert before the queen took the first bite of hers, that's all. She nearly had me flogged right at the table next to the roasted pig, but at least had enough decency to wait."

"Oh, okay, I see. How terrible that must have been for you. At least I was able to eat my moldy bread in unmannered peace with the mice while I laid in the dungeon." Blonde hair swished back and forward.

Farah's eyes darted between the two as they bantered, perched on the edge of Althea's bed, her eyebrows crinkled with worry.

"Thank you for your concern, Little Althea, but I think we both know our own limits when it comes to our weaknesses." Althea's laugh filled the room until it turned into a coughing fit. She held her stomach until she could breathe again.

"Farah, please don't look so scared, we are only joking with one another." Althea used a bandaged hand to brush a lock of the girl's hair behind her shoulder.

"Oh, alright. You two have a very strange relationship. I thought I was going to have to separate you." Farah put her hands on her hips and gave them a playful, stern look.

Tell me about it, Niklas thought. Memories of his childhood came up in his mind of the things he and Althea used to fight over. All three laughed easily as they retold some of the more ridiculous moments.

Farah grabbed a small tin of a fragrant salve and gently applied it to the smaller cuts on Althea's face and arms while she listened and turned to do the same for Niklas.

"I bet you two are starving. The physician said to have you eat as soon as you awoke since the medicine could make you a bit nauseous. I will be back quickly."

A few minutes passed where their breathing and the crackling of the fire were the only sounds that filled the room, in what Niklas could now see was a small infirmary. Four empty beds were lined up against the opposite wall and two more were to the left of him. A large basin filled with clean water sat next to a table in the far corner that had needle and thread laid across it.

Althea was the first to break the silence. "What happens now?" Her voice rasped from dryness, or from the screaming he still heard echoing in his head. His heart dropped in his chest.

Niklas stayed silent for a moment longer before he responded, quietly, "I don't know. We won't be of any help in Caedmon in our condition. If I had to guess, I'd think we would be sent home, and then after that... only God knows."

"They didn't tell you, did they? About Caedmon." She looked out the window.

"Tell me what?"

She told him. Everything. How could they do this? Turn on their own kingdom, like a wolf turning on its own pack, all for this sham of a rebellion.

"I can't go back, Niklas. Not while they are still out there. While *Aezel* is still out there..." She trailed off, her eyes unfocusing.

"Attilio, Magnus," Niklas added. "Many that I never took the time to learn their names. We can beat ourselves up all we want, Althea. Regret wasting our time to save a queen who wouldn't even blink at our deaths. But I can't make myself hate the time in the Cerridwen. I've tried to, believe me," Niklas chuckled and earned a small smile from Althea. "We weren't exactly best buddies when I left Taris."

"No, we weren't," she agreed.

He didn't know exactly who she was to him now, but whatever it was, he wanted to take the time to study it. To learn it and to teach it to her so she knew it as well.

"Look at us." Niklas shook his head, staring at his hands. The thick scars on his left hand from the last time he earned a whip. The red, freshly healed scar from when he 'sparred' with Althea in the clearing.

CHAPTER FORTY-THREE

ALTHEA

With fresh bandages and a thick, slimy salve covering her back, she walked slowly with Niklas to the stable, both refusing to lean on each other in the sight of the guards who openly stared at them behind the helms they wore.

The stable stood outside the palace at least a half mile walk from its doors. The closer they got, the more familiar the smells became. Hay, dirt and camp fires.

The sun glinted off of the pale blue water that surrounded the palace and a cold breeze brought the scent of fresh, cold water their way, purifying the air they breathed.

Sweat tickled her as it dripped down her face and neck despite the cold, soaking her freshly cleaned shirt and leather tunic. Farah knew a servant that was going into Valor to buy a special wax for the floors of the palace and asked him if he could stop by the inn where they had stashed their armor. Thankfully it had been put in a lost and found bucket and he was able to swoop it up.

Althea promised to pay him fairly for his services when she got home, but he repeatedly refused. He had said that the good you do to others always comes back around in unexpected ways.

She had smiled at his humbleness, but a piece of her still felt guilty for all the people that have helped her this last month and a half, while she had only taken from them.

Farah had tended to her and Niklas for three more painful days after they woke in the infirmary and then it came time for them to leave. They had to go back home.

She didn't want to, but the order was given by the Head of the Guard. She felt unfulfilled. She thought back to the day when she rode Bronte through the gates of Taris, racing over the footprints of the guards that went before her.

And for what?

The queen was as harsh as everyone said she was. Althea had not expected to be rewarded, but a simple thank you from the red lips of the queen would have sufficed. Instead, her words left a different kind of mark, a visible one in the scars that would soon form across her back and chest.

What was it all for? Was it worth it?

She forced those thoughts away. They would produce nothing but bitterness and hatred. Both emotions she fought with well enough on their own, and pushed forward, past her itchy, healing skin and kept her head up, ignoring the stares that followed them.

She refused to think about what would happen when her father saw her. Would he tell her that he was right? That she really was a fool all along? He didn't have to tell her, she already felt it.

The stable was massive. It had been built out of a dark stained oak and didn't smell like an ounce of manure. The horses inside were kept clean and groomed, their coats shined, and their manes and tales were neatly cut short. Plumes of fog rolled out from their nostrils as they whinnied and grunted, clearly excited for it to be feeding time.

A stableman rolled a cart down the walkway, filled with hay and barley, stopping to toss an armful into each stall. When he saw the two guards in uniform standing in the open bay door he straightened and dusted his hands onto his already dusty pants.

"Stallard? Nova?" He asked.

"Yes, sir." Althea nodded. When the stableman turned, gesturing for them to follow, she whispered to Niklas, "Why did he say your name first?"

"Probably because I'm wearing *actual* armor? You know, the kind you get when you ascend?"

Althea forced her smile down into what she hoped was a good frown, but she saw the glint in his eyes that said she failed. She desperately wanted to elbow him in the ribs, but she had had enough of her stitches ripping open to last a lifetime.

The stableman led them through another bay door and turned to an outdoor arena that sat behind the stable. Guards were sparring in the circle, swords clanging and laughter peeled out of the breathless men and women.

A few servants had stopped to watch, baskets in the girls arms full of forgotten vegetables as they blushed at the men training and men cheered for the women as they tossed each other around, kicking up snow and dirt.

Althea felt a pull in her chest at the sight. The sounds and smells hit her like a brick. She hadn't realized how much she missed being in the arena until she saw the familiarity of it.

Niklas nudged the back of her hand with his and she swallowed past the dryness in her throat, shaking her head slightly as she looked up at him. He knew her better than he let on, but she was grateful he didn't pry.

"Over here are your mounts." Two, large black horses stood to the right. Their coats, steaming in the cool air. "They have been warmed up and there are provisions for two days in the satchels. You must have the horses returned before the sun sets on the winter solstice, not an hour late. I think you both know what the punishment for theft is, do you not?" The stableman gave them a stern, knowing look from beneath his brows.

Niklas stared, deadpan. Althea giggled, earning a raised eyebrow from him.

"Good, then I shouldn't have to worry about you being late then?"

"No, you do not." Niklas started for the horses and Althea shuffled after him.

She grabbed the saddle's stirrup and grimaced. This horse was taller than any she had ever ridden before, its back at least five inches above her head and the stirrup only reached her waist. She looked around. The stableman was already walking away and Niklas had just barely got into the saddle himself.

With a sigh, Althea rested her forehead on the horse's warm side. *This is going to hurt.*

Stealing herself, she took a deep breath, held it and stretched her leg up. Her sight sparkled as pain radiated across her spine. She pulled up, up, and then suddenly she was being lifted.

She yelped in surprise, clinging onto the saddle before she fell over the other side. The beast had the nerve to huff in annoyance.

She forced herself to sit up despite the ache and looked down. Two men around her age were standing at her side. They smiled politely and Althea thanked them for helping her.

"Why?" She asked, stopping them from turning away. Many of the guards they had passed on their way here looked disgusted at the sight of them. But these two looked up in awe, and she suddenly realized that the entire arena had gone quiet. Men and women of the Guard, servants and gardeners, stopped to watch them. Smiles on their faces, ones not from scorn either.

"We heard what you both did. About Prince Xadier," one said, his hair was curly and as dark as night, he had a perfect smile with straight teeth. His eyes squinted against the sun as he looked up at the both of them.

The other, thin but made out of nothing but muscle, with short blonde hair and green eyes, nodded his head. He looked like he could have been Aezel's cousin.

"We were all drunk and clueless about assassins being in the palace. If it weren't for you both..." His voice dropped to a whisper. "We all think the queen was too harsh. After you guys saved her life, everyone thought you would be put on a pedestal and rewarded beyond imagination. At least have your name cleared for leaving post. Not tortured in public. Word spreads fast around here and I cannot think of anyone among us who would have done what you both did. So thank you."

"For what?" Niklas asked, angling his horse to the bridge.

"For showing what a true guard should look like. And reminding us to not let fear block our path when we are fighting for what we believe in," black hair answered.

"What are your names?" Althea asked, taking up her reins.

"Deatris." The one with the black, curly hair dropped to a knee and saluted with his fist on his heart. Althea's mouth went dry when the thin one did the same.

"Yendar."

The sound of swords being sheathed and leather armor creaking floated through the still winter air as at least a hundred guards and guards in training, knelt. Saluting their two, broken, fellow guards whose jaws were hanging open.

CHAPTER FORTY-FOUR

NIKLAS

M en, women, and a few small children followed them to the bridge. The expanse of the Blue laid out before them and the gate leading to Valor swung open.

Niklas looked back once more at the sparkling faces that surrounded them and raised his right fist to his right shoulder, punching it to the sky with a shout in the salute of Taris, "For God and Kingdom!"

"For God and Kingdom!"

"For God and Kingdom!"

"For God and Kingdom!"

The shouts rang out and echoed across the water as they took their first steps to the long journey back home. He wondered what it would feel like. Would he be able to go back to normal? *What even is normal anymore?*

They made it ten feet before the shout came.

"Stop!" Niklas and Althea froze, looking at each other. "Stop in the name of the queen!"

He pulled on his horse's reins and turned back to the crowd as it parted, making way for a queen's guard. And then the queen herself.

Her face was as red as the lip stain she wore, her eyes as dark as the navy blue dress that she fought to walk in with its full skirts.

Niklas couldn't even dismount before the queen was at his side, her breathing labored from running and shoved a piece of paper in his face. "Where did you get this?"

Niklas swallowed.

"Where!?" She screeched, her entire body shaking.

"It is only a picture of me and my father," Niklas answered slowly, how could he have forgotten about it? Tiernan had painted it like he had asked, and it made the picture look like it had come to life. But why was the queen so worked up over it?

"This man," she pointed aggressively to his father on the paper. "He was the king's closest adviser and friend. He disappeared after the king died, so tell me. How. Did. You. Get. This."

"Your majesty. I have no idea what is going on. My father was only a teacher in the palace before I was born. He never said anything about knowing the king, you must be mistaken."

"Are you saying I'm crazy? I would know this man's face anywhere. My husband spent more time with him than he did with me! This man was the one who took my son to prepare him for burial! So I will ask you one more time, how do you have a picture of this man holding a baby that looks exactly like my son." Her voice lowered into a growl.

His mouth dropped open and he looked to Althea for help. A hand covered her mouth, eyes wide with shock as she took in the picture.

"Althea? What's wrong?" He asked, his chest suddenly feeling tight. He didn't know what was going on.

Her gray-green eyes met his and she opened her mouth to speak. "You–" But she was cut off by another guard running full speed toward them. His armor clanking, his boots thudding on the steel of the bridge.

The guard that had come with the queen pulled her behind him. Niklas had seen a clear sense of distrust among the soldiers since the ball. No one trusted each other anymore. Anyone could have betrayed the queen and turned to the rebellion.

The guard slid to a stop in front of them, doubled over, hands on his knees and wheezing. He dropped to a knee and saluted with a fist over his heart. "Your– Majesty!" He coughed in between the words.

"What is it, can't you see I was talking? Guards, don't let them leave."

A pair of armed guards stepped out of the crowd, brows furrowed in confusion and shared with them a look of apology as they grabbed onto the reins and helped them dismount.

"Your– Majesty." The guard swallowed and grunted as he fought for air. "The prin– Xadi– he."

"Spit it out you fool, what is it!" Niklas didn't think the queen's face could become any redder, but she proved him wrong.

"Xadier, he escaped."

"WHAT!" The queen stomped over to the guard and pulled him to his feet by the pauldron he wore. "You let him escape!?"

"No, your majesty. Ivan– one of the guards was poisoned, and the door to the prince's cell was open and he was gone. I only found out just now when I was bringing food in for the prisoners."

The queen let out an angry cry and pushed the guard away. He slipped on a puddle and landed hard. Turning to the one that had escorted her, she commanded, "I want every guard that we can spare to search for Xadier NOW! I don't want to see any of your faces again unless you are holding his head!" Both of the guards saluted and ran back toward the palace to spread the command.

"As for you two—" A loud rumbling cut her off. It sounded like thunder rolling through the valley that the Blue rested in, sweeping over the Kyran mountains and shaking the earth.

The horses tossed their heads uneasily, the whites of their eyes showing, but they stood dutifully still. "What is that?" The queen held onto the bridge's railing for support as the metal beneath their feet hummed.

"Horses," Niklas and Althea whispered at the same time, their eyes locked onto the plume of steam and snow that billowed up in a dense cloud that quickly grew as the seconds ticked by.

"Everyone inside, defend the palace. Protect your queen!" A high ranking guard shouted, Niklas recognized Lueren, breaking the shock of the moment. And like a wave, the guards and guards in training began to pull the heavy gates closed, taking up arms.

Althea didn't move, and Niklas set a hand on her shoulder, pulling her back into the safety of the Blue. She stared at the mountain pass, squinting against the sun.

"Althea," he demanded.

The first horses raced around the curve of the mountain. A few seconds later more followed in a hoard. The two fastest riders were wearing full black. The skin of their jet black horses frothed from exertion.

Niklas heard the twang of a bowstring, then another. The riders dodged the arrows that were shot from the arches. Swords sang as they were pulled from their sheaths, armor clattering as men and women took position, ready to defend.

One horse was pushed faster than Niklas thought possible. The man standing in the stirrups waved his hands over his head. Althea pulled away from his grip and ran further up the bridge waving her arms the same way. "HEY!" She shouted.

"What are you *doing*? Are you insane, get inside the gates, NOW!" A senior Lieutenant shouted down, pulling another arrow from his quiver.

"Althea!" Niklas grabbed her wrist, pulling her back behind the line of guards.

"It's them. Niklas it's *them*!" She turned and grabbed onto the front of his cloak, wrinkling the fabric in her fists.

He looked back up, over her head and wide eyes, to the approaching army. Niklas instantly saw who it was. "Stop!" He shouted, running further onto the bridge, his back facing the new arrivals. "Stop shooting!"

"I won't tell you again, get inside or we'll drag you in!" The guard dropped his bow and began to descend the ladder from the point of the arch where archers were shooting arrow after arrow.

"It's the army of Taris, they are loyal to the throne! Look, your Admiral Erling is in the front!" Niklas had to cup his hands around his mouth to shout over the thunder of the hoofbeats.

The guard stopped on a rung of the ladder, shading his eyes from the sun. His mouth dropped open at what he saw and raced back up the ladder screaming. "Stand down. Friendlies. STAND DOWN!"

The last arrow stuck in the ground a mere two inches from the stead.

The bridge rocked and swayed under the Admiral's horse. Erling all but jumped off of his horse when he got close. Jekel and Keetie raced in after him. Erling met the guard who called the stand down, clasping a hand onto each other's forearms.

"The queen?" Erling's gravely voice asks.

"Alive, safe in the palace." Erling's head drooped slightly, taking a deep breath. "There is something you should know." The guard spoke lowly, pulling Erling off to the side. Erling's response wasn't as quiet.

"Xadier!?"

There were more low words spoken that Niklas could not hear, and then with one last clasp of their hands they pulled apart.

Erling turned and then froze, his eyes locked onto Niklas. "You." He pointed at him. "Come." He did not wait to see if Niklas followed. It was a command from a queen's guard, there was no refusal.

Althea grabbed his wrist. "I'm coming with you."

Niklas nodded, allowing her to hold onto his shirt sleeve as they wove through the crowd of the army of Taris and the push of curious servants, noblemen and guards that had parted for Erling's authoritative presence.

They entered the palace and walked through the maze of halls, leading him to the throne room for the second time in a week.

Erling didn't knock. He pushed the large doors open and took a step inside. "Wait here," he said without turning. The large wooden doors closed with a loud bang that echoed down the empty hall.

They didn't speak, they didn't look at each other, they barely breathed.

The voices inside carried, but the door muffled the words. A few shouts, and something was thrown against a wall. Niklas choked when the door swung open.

Erling grabbed the front of his shirt and pulled him into the room by force. "Nova, stay outside." He closed the door in her shocked face and pulled him before the queen, sitting on her throne.

Niklas dropped to a knee and was about to salute when the queen told him to stand. He had never felt more confused in his life than he had in the last hour.

"Look at me," the queen commanded, her voice shaking.

Slowly, he lifted his eyes, feeling like a petulant child that did something wrong and was about to be scolded. But the look on the queen's face was not one he had expected.

She had been crying, he realized. Red surrounded her blue irises and her chin quivered as she stood, taking a step down from her small dais. She still held his picture in her fist.

"I found this in my son's room, next to a portrait of my first son that I had ordered to be painted before his burial. You know I never got to hold him?" The queen chuckled pitifully. "They took him from the room before I could hold him. I only saw him as they wrapped him in a towel and left me to soak in my own blood. His eyes were open, unblinking." She looked up from the wrinkled picture to meet his eyes.

"He had his father's eyes." She took another step closer until she was within arms reach of him. "Brown." She reached up caressing his cheek with one finger, the bite of her sharp nail threatening to nick his skin. Niklas didn't dare to breathe. "Swirled with scarlet."

Niklas took a shaky step back. "What are you trying to say, Your Majesty?"

"Erling spoke with Raphael while he was in Taris. An old friend who had a favor to call in. He told Erling to protect you with his life. Why, pray tell?"

"To protect the bloodline." Erling's voice grated more than usual.

"What are you guys talking about? I'm a nobody from Taris. I'm not some– some nobleman. I'm sorry, Your Majesty, but might I request to leave? There are things that I need to attend to before I can leave for Taris." He didn't have anything that needed his attention, he just made up something to try and leave this room with these people who must have knocked their heads together. "And may I have the picture of my father back?" He added.

"Don't you get it?" The queen's palm slid to rest on his shoulder.

"Get what?" Niklas completely forgot to check his tone, he was getting angry, and all he wanted was to go home.

"You..."

"Me?"

"You are my *son*."

GLOSSARY

Brav - (Bur-av) A large grizzly bear, often the size of two horses.

Ketabome - (Ket-uh-bome) A highly poisonous fruit that looks identical to blueberries, but has blue innards rather than purple. If eaten, will make your stomach swell severely and in cases, make your intestines explode.

Khourge - (Corg) A large cougar that hunts during the day and is strategic in cornering its prey.

Seasons - A complete rotation of all four seasons. A single year.

ACKNOWLEDGEMENTS

Thank you, God!

For the encouragement from my friends and family and YOU readers, this would not have been possible without you. Special thanks to Mark and Paul for letting me create worlds when work was slow. And thank you to my grandmothers, who gave me the motivation to continue when the going got tough.

Thanks to my hard headed mom and dad, who yelled at me when I wouldn't stop talking about my book during movie nights, for not throwing me out on my head. Love you!

Thanks to my sister, who put up with me, (and for letting me steal her printer).

And most importantly, if it wasn't for my one, all power God, I wouldn't be here today, writing my heart on these pages.

UP NEXT

Don't miss
Bleeding Red
Book 2 in the history of Reach The Blue.
Coming soon!

ABOUT THE AUTHOR

Gabrielle — on TikTok as gabbyrose956 —and her feisty chi-huahua, Sparky live in Florida but thrive in the cold. She is a part time fantasy author and a full time daydreamer, always writing snippets here and there until one dream stuck out from the rest and wouldn't let her go.